Other Books by George Seaton

The Death of Elias Ives
Big Diehl: The Road Home
Big Diehl: Comes a Peace
Finding Skylar Hand
The Palisade
Finding Deaglan
Whispers of Old Winds
Shane Thorpe Knew Jesus and Rode Bulls
The White Buck and other stories

Listening to the Dead

George Seaton

For old cops who gave a damn.

Published in 2020 by George Seaton

Pine, Colorado

Author's Website: https://www.gmseatonauthor.com/

Cover Art: Adobe Stock

ISBN: 978-1-7344732-3-0

Notes:

This is a reissue of the work first published by LETHE PRESS in 2017, with substantial edits and revisions.

Listening to the Dead

This is what I believe

After I understood what Stanton was doing and learned to do it myself, I sat across the table from a man named Bob who'd yet to admit to what he'd done. I saw in his eyes the emptiness that belied his claimed innocence. I asked him about that. He told me eyes don't kill, and neither did he. I then asked him the questions that had been asked of me when I touched his victim, and Bob's left eye twitched with each question, then he bowed his head and sobbed. When he raised his head, I saw in his eyes the same emptiness as before, but he did tell me the story of how and why he'd stuck an ice pick into the man's neck just below the Adam's apple. Then, as he pulled the sleeve of his shirt across his eyes, Bob told me he'd slipped the ice pick out of that man's neck, stuck it in that man's left eye and then his right eye, and then the left ear, and then the right. I thanked him for his story, told him I'd write up his confession, he could sign it, and the courts would take it from there. He looked at my shirt pocket, smiled, and asked for a cigarette. I gave him one, lit it for him, and I stood up and walked toward the interrogation room door because I didn't want to breathe the exhale from the depth of him. I then turned and asked him why he'd done what he had. Bob said the man had looked at him as if in judgment, and he would not be judged. By anyone.

He was judged and given a life sentence to be served at Old Max in Canon City, Colorado. I believe he is still alive today as he was only nineteen when he committed that murder. I do not care to know if he has found Jesus in all those years behind bars, or if he has excelled in the trade of making license plates, or has read Plato, or has lost his hair and grown a paunch. He is lost to me, but his victim is not.

The dead remain. Most of the dead spoke to me, and I found their killers precisely because they had spoken. They remain in my memory as comforted souls. Those dead who were silent and for whom I did not find their killers remain as troubled spirits lost in the indefiniteness of place and time.

I will tell you that a cop who develops a passion for solving murders soon becomes less of a cop and more of a magician, or, in the purest sense of what I believe, he becomes a necromancer. This is what I believe. This is what Stanton taught me.

Jack Dolan

The Finding

He found the two bodies sprawled anywise, like ragdolls absently tossed to the ground by a careless child, bloodied and still as the place of their final repose itself. It was a lonely place, or a place some thought lonely because it seldom saw visitors. Those that did hike or ride a horse up that way tended to keep moving past it, most sensing a palpable unease that crept from the place like a presence with noiseless feet, foul breath, and evil intent. A place to die, he supposed some thought.

His bay gelding, a quarter horse he'd named Shy, had first sensed the deaths from the smell and not the sight of them. He'd snorted and jerked his head, reared a bit at the prospect of entering the dark clearing off to the side of the rutted trail.

He tightened the reins, calmed Shy down, stroked his neck, and whispered, "Whoa, Shy-boy. Easy now." And Shy had eased his tenseness, positioned himself sideways to the awful thing, and turned his head away from it. He dismounted, tied Shy off, and stepped into the gloom of what the horse had perceived. And there he saw the bodies: young men was his conclusion, blood-bathed and naked.

Thirty years as a Denver cop, twenty-five of them spent dealing with the whys and wherefores of death from violence, had taught him that for now all he could do was walk a circle around the bodies from several feet away, careful not to disturb what appeared to be the killing ground itself. That would come later once he'd called the Eagle County sheriff and told him what he'd found. Though now retired, he would lead the sheriff and his men back to the spot; the sooner, the better. Wouldn't be long before the critters got to the bodies and returned them to dust.

ONE

Many years ago, Jack was still in his wrinkled and once-white workaday shirt, the top button undone, his tie loosened with the knot hanging to his third button, and a Lucky Strike dangling from the side of his mouth dripping ashes. He stood before the two-burner gas stove frying two eggs, sizzling in bacon grease in an iron skillet. He watched the eggs for the desired moment and flipped them over with the intent their yolks would diffuse and harden.

Irish from his father, Italian from his mother, then in his twenty-ninth year, he was beholding to his father for his nose, shoulders, temper, and blue eyes. From his mother had come his black hair and things not seen but felt. From his three years as a Marine, he'd brought back from the war images, sounds, and odors he seldom talked about. When he did, he left the telling of them to the fact he'd served in Vietnam, which was usually enough to shut up for a while whoever had asked. He didn't talk about his two Purple Hearts or Bronze Star. Wounded at Keh Sanh in June of '68, he'd come back to Denver, healed, worked about five years in construction, and then sought work with the Denver Police Department. By June of '76, he wore a holster turned backward on his left hip, with a snub-nosed

Colt .38-caliber Detective Special nestled within.

Jack slid the spatula underneath the eggs, lifted them onto the plate to his right, turned off the gas, and carried the meal to a small table fronting the single window in his studio apartment. He returned to the kitchen area that was separated from the rest of the apartment by only the four steps it took to get there. Opened the chest-high refrigerator and pulled out a Coors, popped the tab, and returned to his eggs.

He'd worked late at headquarters downtown, well into the evening, and well after his partner had gone home. Tried to piece together the disparate facts and gut hunches he'd detailed on a yellow legal pad regarding the homicide of a middle-aged woman left on a downslope that bottomed out at the lazy meander of the South Platte River, just past the confluence of Cherry Creek and the Platte itself. His partner had let him take this case on as his own. As he cut the eggs with a fork, and, for about the sixth time in the last ten hours, he reread the notes of the event as they'd been related to him by the uniforms that had found the body. Scribbled off to the side of the pages, most of his personal observations ended with question marks: *Why was the jewelry still on her? Why was there still money in her purse? Why no rape? No I.D.? Who was this woman? Who murdered her?*

Six months before, his first assignment as a homicide detective saw him paired with a grizzled cop by the name of Marshall Stanton. Stanton had been a Denver cop since '46 and was referred to by other coppers as *Old Grim* because he was old, and because he'd spent the last fifteen years working homicides, solving most as if the Grim Reaper were his confidant. At first, the seeming callousness Stanton displayed toward the dead repulsed Jack. Stanton treated the bodies as if they were gunnysacks filled with offal, turning them, flipping them, and treating them with disrespect. Jack soon noticed something else, though. After the physical examination was complete; after all that was needed for forensics was gathered; after the uniforms had left and the coroner was standing by; after Stanton had moved the bodies and reexamined them to his liking, he would step beside the dead, squat or kneel down, and place his hand on the head, chest, or back of the deceased. Stanton's lips would move as he gently stroked the corpse. Most of the time, he would even nod or shake his head as if acknowledging something unsaid. Well, that's what Jack didn't understand at first. *What the hell is he doing?* After the third homicide he'd worked with Stanton, he finally asked him, "Why do you…talk to them? Why do you touch them?"

Stanton stared at him, took the time to allow his face to form something akin to a smile, and said, "They ask me to."

It took some time for him to understand Stanton's response. Still, in the meantime, Jack studied *Old Grim* with the interest of a small boy observing a magician. *What's the secret?* The difference he would discover between Stanton and a magician was that there wasn't any sleight of hand going on, there were no mirrors, no tricks. When a homicide wasn't quickly solved, and Stanton's *magic* hadn't worked, Stanton and Jack would eat greasy cheeseburgers at the Rockybilt at North Speer and Federal, or step into Gaetano's at 38th and Tejon for a nip or two, where the conversation over lunch or booze was always about the lack of a reasonable next step and the fact they'd hit a dead end. Literally. Stanton would shake his head, sigh, and say something was missing, something they hadn't seen. Then he'd go back to square one, providing a recitation of things they knew and didn't know about the case from the first minute they'd taken it on.

It was after two or three seemingly unsolvable homicides when Jack asked the question: "The other ones? The ones we did solve? What was different?"

They had stopped at Gaetano's on 38th, an Italian restaurant that had been in the Smaldone family—Denver's version of the Italian mob—for decades. It was a place where, for them and most Denver cops, drinks were usually free, and meals came at a discount. A cop never had to display a badge for verification at Gaetano's, the proprietors just *knew...* They slid into the booth, both of them ordered a whiskey, and they placed their notes on the table.

Stanton paused a moment before answering Jack, relaxed into the overstuffed booth, and placed his hands palm down on the table. "Something about cops, Jack, is that there are two kinds: The first kind is the guy who goes on the job because he's got some idea that he wants to enforce the law. That's okay." He said, lightly slapping the tabletop. "That's fine as far as it goes," he continued. "Thing is, though, that guy just wanted a job, too. You know, to advance through the ranks, pin on the stripes and bars and stars, see his badge turn from silver to gold. You understand?"

"Sure," Jack said, not knowing how this was going to provide an answer to his question but happy that Stanton, a man usually of few words, was opening up.

"Okay," Stanton said, pulling a four-inch cigar from his inside coat pocket. "The other kind of cop is the one who's got something else going on—a calling, say kind of like a vocation calls a Catholic boy to the priesthood or Baptist boy to the pulpit." He licked the cigar, end to end, put it in his mouth, and lit it with a stick match scraped against his thumbnail. "Take, for instance, the auto-theft guys," he continued, sucking the cigar, and huffing a cloud over Jack's head. "Most of those guys never want to rise above the rank of detective because they know if they do, they won't be working auto theft anymore. Same with most of the guys working vice or, yeah, homicide, just like us." He stopped to take a sip of his drink, another puff, and then went on, occasionally glancing at Jack, but mostly looking off to the side or down at his notes. "These guys don't think about law enforcement that much. Hell, the auto-theft guys take it as a personal affront when some sonofabitch destroys or files down a VIN on a primo stolen car. They look at that car stripped down for parts, and they get physically sick. They love cars. Loved them all their lives. They're passionate about cars and what they can do—horsepower, torque, mileage, injectors. All that crap. And they don't do their job because they've got some serious interest in enforcing the law. No, they do their jobs because there's something in them that just can't tolerate the vileness of somebody messing with the object of their passions. That make any sense at all?"

Jack wasn't sure if what Stanton had just described was the way things actually were or not. He'd seen cops transfer out of auto theft, some even promoting out. "Well, Jimmy McIntyre just left auto theft—"

"Yeah, I know. It's not true for all of them, but it is for most. Take my word for it. You asked a minute ago why some homicides are quickly solved, and others aren't. You asked what the difference is between them?" Stanton placed his hand on his notes, his cigar between his fingers with the business end pointing up. "Let me give you the best, maybe the only answer I've got. Like those cops in auto theft, the ones who've found their passion there? Well, it's the same thing that's kept me in homicide all these years. Yeah, I have my own passion. But it's more than that." He again stopped, sipped his drink, and tapped his cigar on the brim of the glass ashtray between them. "I told you once that the bodies, the dead, ask me to speak to them. Bet you thought that was strange?" He looked at Jack and waited for an answer.

"Well, yeah. I mean, you've got to admit that's getting into some weird territory."

Stanton nodded and stared into Jack's eyes. "Yeah, it is. But it's true. Most of the time, when I touch a body, I know immediately I've got to ask more questions, right then and there, before whatever is left of what used to be a living, breathing person is gone forever. It's as if they ask me to talk to them, like I told you, but also a hunch, something in my gut tells me they've got something to say to me about what was done to them and why."

Jack stared back at Stanton's eyes, red and watery with smoke and age, eyes that hadn't moved from his for the time it had taken Stanton to reveal what he'd just said. "I…," Jack tried to think of something to say. "I guess, then, with these cases we're not solving…" Jack placed his hands on his own notes. "For those, the bodies didn't, um, speak to you?"

Stanton downed his drink and winked at Jack. "No," he said, "they didn't. That's why we're up shit creek right now. That's why I'm heading up to Steamboat Springs this weekend without the wife to see if I can recharge the batteries. You ought to try it sometime. I've been going up there for years." Stanton stood up, stuck the cigar between his teeth, gathered up his notes, and began walking down the aisle to the front door.

They would eventually solve the particular homicide that had urged Jack to ask Stanton *the* question over drinks at Gaetano's. But it wasn't until the killer was arrested for committing a burglary and had, during the interrogation for the lesser crime, spilled his guts about accidentally slicing his second cousin's neck open with a fishing knife.

Jack finished his eggs, wished he'd made toast. Shoved the plate to the side of the table. Flipping through to the last page of notes he'd written, he looked at the words again that he'd heard or sensed when he'd touched her forehead: *Till death do us part.*

Yes, Jack had touched the woman, just as Stanton had done with all the others. He had asked the questions of her that puzzled him, and the answers had come from somewhere. As Jack finished his beer and stared out the window that looked out upon Sherman Street— the trees bare of leaves, just skeletons of themselves, a car's exhaust visible, a lone woman huffing steam in a puffed parka—he knew that all his notes, all his worry, all the time he'd spent on the case came down to what the woman had told him there, at the slope to the river.

The next day, Jack spent some time with Charlie, one of the two detectives assigned to missing persons, and scanned reports of husbands who'd reported their wives had gone missing.

TWO

Jack never rose above the rank of detective in his thirty years with the Denver Police Department. He never wanted to. During his entire career as a murder cop, he never thought he was enforcing the law. He'd understood Stanton's passion and had taken it as his own, and thought, too, that he gave some closure to the families of those who had died from violence. With his marriage long ago irretrievably broken by passions focused more on the dead than his living wife, no children, and a constant but mostly unfulfilled flirtation with a deeply buried desire for the touch of another man, he retired to seven acres and a six-room cabin fifteen miles north of Vail. He'd purchased it cheap two years before he retired, the seller a man thankful Jack had closed the file on the death of his daughter.

After moving into the cabin, Jack purchased a five-year-old quarter horse stallion, bay in color with the pastern of his left rear leg dappled white with black spots—the only hint the horse had been sired by an Appaloosa. He named the horse Shy upon first seeing it because it seemed to be a loner, not frantically busy protecting a harem of mares as had the other stallions. Shy was green as could be and had lived with a herd kept on a hillside in the Yampa Valley, near the town of Oak Creek, a two-minute burg eighty miles north from his cabin.

He'd been told the herd was owned by an Indian woman of seventy-two who collected horses as some do cats. He knew nothing about horses except that he'd wanted one since childhood, and now had the land and the time to devote to it. When it finally dawned on Jack that his ignorance about caring for Shy, not to mention the prospect of riding him, was absolute, he approached the horse concession wrangler at the Pinecone Lodge, two miles east of his cabin. "Can you help me with this horse?" The wrangler, a handsome young man named Tyler Bray, had agreed, but only if Jack would have the horse gelded first thing, and Jack shortly arranged for that ugly business to be done.

**

Jack had heard about the old Indian selling horses from another retired cop who'd taken up hunting for sport and had leased a couple horses from the woman to enhance the wilderness experience he'd sought. He'd told Jack that the woman was selling them for *pennies on the dollar* because the State of Colorado was after her to thin out the herd and repair and upgrade the environment for those horses that would be allowed to stay. He'd given Jack her number, and Jack called twice. Both times the call was lost in the ether above the hills where she lived, her voice cracking to dead air. She called him back once she came down from the hills, and sitting on a barstool in the Depot Café in Oak Creek, she'd said, "C'mon up. You got my number. Call when you're fifteen minutes from town."

19

As the old woman had instructed, Jack found the Depot Café on Oak Creek's Main Street. He stepped in and saw bare pine walls, chandeliers of elk and deer racks, deer and elk heads stared with cold eyes from high up on the walls, red cushioned booths, a seven-foot-high fireplace, a bar at the far end of the large room. Waylon was singing about a world gone crazy. He walked toward the bar and saw four people with their butts firmly planted on red-topped stools. They turned their heads in unison toward him, and then all but one, an old woman with gray braids hanging along her cheeks to the top of her shoulders, turned back.

"You Dolan?"

Jack smiled, walked to her, and held out his hand. "Jack Dolan."

The old woman smiled slightly, her faced lined as a road map. She wiped her hand on the chest of her blue overalls and grabbed Jack's hand. "Tess Shinab," she said. "So, you're looking to buy a horse?"

"Yes, I am."

"Okay, then. Sit down here, and we can have a beer." She tapped the stool next to her. "Maybe talk about horses."

"Sure." He pulled the stool out and sat down. "Are they far?"

"No," she said with a little giggle, "they're up there." She raised her right arm and motioned toward the north, "On the hill. You're in a hurry to see the horses, I think. They'll still be there after we have a beer."

"No, I guess I'm not in a hurry," he said, feeling a little patronized as he noticed the smiles on the faces of the other three loafers sitting at the bar, as well as the female bartender who placed a napkin on the bar top in front of him.

"Tess's horses don't generally go anywhere unless she means for them to," she said, brushing errant strands of blonde hair from her

20

eyes. "What'll it be?"

Jack ordered a beer and another for Tess, and he waited for Tess to say something. When she didn't, he asked, "So, Roy Tanner said you leased him a horse a while back?"

"Yeah, he comes to kill the antelope. I lease him two horses: one to ride and one to carry his provisions and his kills. One that won't spook with the smell of blood on its back. You a cop, too?"

"Used to be. Roy and I are both retired."

"He's a big man with a lot of big talk. Tells me about the wilderness. Tells me he wants to experience the wild as the old-timers did. I told him, 'Mister Tanner, old-timers didn't have sleeping bags and butane.' And he kind of snorted. Don't think he liked what I said."

"Well, I don't want to hunt anything. I just want to get a horse I can ride."

"You a horse rider?"

"No. Well, as a kid, I did. At summer camp. I haven't ridden for a very long time."

Tess nodded, smiled. "What kind of cop were you?"

"I was in homicide for most of my whole career."

She was just about to sip her beer, then set it back on the bar and turned to him. "The dead?" she asked, too seriously.

Jack didn't know what to say. *Of course, "the dead."*

She nodded again without a smile. "Okay," she said, turning away.

Jack didn't know what *that* had meant. He felt some intimacy had passed between them but didn't understand the significance of it.

"Drink your beer," Tess said. "Let's go look at the horses."

Tess climbed into Jack's SUV and told him to follow Colorado 131 out of town.

After about a mile, when they came within sight of a turnoff on the other side of the road that went steeply down, she said, "Slow up. That's where you want to go." She pointed to the turnoff.

Jack turned off the highway, started the descent on a dirt road, and saw an enormity of litter in the river valley below, obviously the detritus of a collector of junk metals: shells of vehicles, axles stacked upon one another, three horse trailers without tires, piles of twisted fence sections. Situated among the junk were red and green metal corrals and some makeshift pens constructed of chicken wire and wooden posts. A few with mares and newborn foals were in the makeshift affairs. Other mares with older foals were corralled together in larger enclosures, and a few fully-grown horses had a pen to themselves. Mud was everywhere. It was early June, and there were still pockets of snow melting into small pools, making more mud.

"Just pull up here," Tess said, pointing to a space in front of an ancient semi-tractor with a trailer attached.

When they got out of the vehicle, Tess walked directly to a small pen of chicken wire covered on three sides with a blue tarp. Within the enclosure, layered with straw, a filthy mare nosed a foal, its long spindly legs pulled underneath itself.

"That's the newest," Tess said, peering into the pen. "Sunshine is the mare, Beamer is the colt. Born two days ago. The sire, Big Boy, is up on the hill." She absently motioned with her right arm toward the rise behind them.

"He's beautiful," Jack said, standing beside Tess. "Beamer? After the car?"

Tess gave him a sideways glance. "No, not after the car. After sunshine." She then walked to the largest corral, where four older paint-colored foals stood, mud covering their legs and stomachs.

"This mud ever go away?"

"This place is seven months of snow, three months of mud, and two months of the devil's frying pan," Tess said. "We're into the second month of mud. These paints are for sale." She leaned her arms on the pen's horizontal post.

Jack watched as the sole fully-grown horse amongst the foals—a mare, he assumed without looking that closely—lazily squished through the mud and approached them, stopping when it was able to touch Tess's hand. Tess stroked the horse's nose.

"You know," Jack said, hoping he didn't sound too maudlin in saying it, "Ever since I was a boy, I always had the desire to have a bay-colored horse."

Tess spoke without looking at him. "You see some bay-colored horses on TV? Cowboys and Indians?"

"Yeah." Jack nodded, knowing Tess had honed in on the sentimentality of it. "On TV."

"Never wanted a white stallion to say 'Hi-Yo Silver' to?"

Jack shook his head. "No, never did." He wondered if she was playing with him a bit.

"Got some bays up on the hill," Tess said. "Never wanted a white stallion, either." She turned around and looked at the hills rising from the other side of the highway. "You think your car can get up there?" She nodded toward the highway and the hills beyond.

Jack turned and looked. "Sure."

The road up the hill was not so much a road, but ruts gouged into the incline from a front loader that Tess said her son, Saw, used to take grass hay to the herd she kept up there. Jack immediately switched to four-wheel drive when he saw the mud-soaked and water-pooled path that at first appeared to have no end. But it did end, topping out at a glen where black goats were running around, and a huge palomino-colored horse with a white mane pranced amongst other less magnificent horses.

"That's Good Day," Tess said. "He's keeping his harem in line. Keeping the other stallions away, too. You can stop here."

They climbed out of the SUV, and Tess began walking west, climbing the rise to the top of the hill. "The others are up here," she said.

Jack followed, and once they'd topped the hill, he saw ten more horses, not corralled, all with bowed heads digging into a spread of grass hay on the ground.

"Those two bays are for sale. Both stallions," Tess said, pointing at the assemblage. "They're green and won't come to you. They're good horses. That one with the dappled foot was sired by an Appy."

"Appaloosa?"

"Yup." Tess smiled.

"What's his name?"

"Haven't named him. Don't know why. I just call him Buddy."

Jack stepped a little closer to the bay. The bay stepped back, still munching.

"He's not been handled much," Tess said. "He's not afraid, just…"

"Wary?" Jack said when Tess didn't finish her thought.

"That is a good word for it."

"Or maybe he's just shy," Jack said, trying again to get closer to

24

the horse.

"Maybe that, too," Tess said as the horse again stepped away from Jack's approach.

Jack knew immediately he'd just named the horse he would buy. "I don't know much about horses," he said. "Matter of fact, I don't know anything at all. But he's about what I was looking for."

Tess stepped back a ways from Jack and the bay. "He's a good one. You don't think an Indian would sell you a bad horse, do you?"

Jack turned and saw she was smiling. "No, I don't. How much are you asking for him?" He stepped nearer to Tess and then turned to look back at the bay.

"State is on me to sell some of my horses. They don't think I can care for them all anymore. I guess I can let you have him for a hundred dollars per year. He's five, so I guess five hundred would do it."

Jack had assumed he'd be paying somewhere near a thousand, maybe two thousand dollars. "Well, that sounds reasonable. Actually, more than reasonable."

"Okay, then," Tess said. "Believe we need another beer. We'll drink on it."

Jack's bladder was about to burst from the beer he'd earlier downed at the Depot and was just about to excuse himself and step behind a tree. "Sounds good," he said, relieved that a restroom was in his near future.

They got back in the SUV and headed down the hill.

Tess ushered Jack into a booth, away from the bar. After he used the restroom and the waitress brought their beers, Tess stared at him to the point it became uncomfortable. "You said you were a homicide cop?" Tess finally asked, still staring.

"Yes, I did. I was."

"You ever," Tess said, and then she paused, broke her stare, and looked down at her hands folded on the table. "You ever alone with the bodies?"

"Yes," he said, remembering their earlier conversation.

"You ever… touch the dead? Talk to them?"

The images of the times Jack had done what Tess had just said flashed through his mind. *Old Grim* appeared, too. He nodded. "Yes, I did."

Tess sipped her beer, looked again into Jack's eyes. "They tell you stories?"

He noticed Tess was squeezing her hands together. "You know something about this, don't you, Tess?"

Tess caressed her beer between her palms, nodded, "Yeah, a little," she said. "My last name means Wolf in the Ute language—Shin-ab. My family, the Yamparika Utes, lived here—" She raised her arms and gestured a circle "—since the time of the Creator, Senawahv. Senawahv gave us the name Ute and decided we would be a very brave people just like Bear." She attempted a smile and continued, "Hah! Got to be brave to deal with the State of Colorado, huh? Telling me what to do with my horses and my land, just like the Mormons did to my ancestors."

"I'll bet that's a pain in the ass."

"Pains my heart," Tess said. "But that's another thing. Not what I want to talk about. My family long ago took the name of Wolf, maybe because at the beginning of our time we were like Wolf or we learned things from Wolf." She stopped and placed her hand atop

Jack's. "You think I'm crazy yet?"

"No." Jack shook his head. *Do the dead speak to you, too?*

"Okay, then," Tess said, moving her hand away from his. "All my life, I've known what was taught to my ancestors about Wolf. And my ancestors believed it, and I believe it because I knew it was true. I have seen it myself. I have done it."

When Tess didn't go on and relaxed back in the booth, Jack asked, "And what have you seen?"

"The dead. They speak to me. Like Wolf, who speaks to the dead and the dead speak back... Like my ancestors, like Wolf, I do too. Sometimes, too, just like Wolf, I can speak to the spirits of the dead, long after they've been put under the ground or taken from where they died. And the spirits speak to me. They come back to where their bodies fell."

Jack relaxed back into the booth. After Stanton had first mentioned the messages the dead provided, they'd never spoken about it again, except to share what a victim had told them. And in all Jack's years working homicides, he'd never revealed their secret to anyone, not even the rookies he'd trained, though he probably would have if any of them had asked. Except for Mike Day. He'd been the only one. But that had been different. Mike was the man Jack had once loved. Maybe he still did. Now, this Indian, this old woman named Wolf, had detailed his and Stanton's, oh, mysticism, he thought was the right word, albeit she'd put her own Native take on it. Like wolves, Jack thought. *Wolves.*

"Tess," Jack began, then shook his head and tried to smile. "I guess what you wanted to tell me is that the dead speak and that both of us know that."

Tess nodded. "Yes, that is it. I wanted to know if a person like you who dealt with the dead knows what I know. I can't talk about this with people who are not my family. Most Yamparika are afraid of the dead. They believe in ghosts. They wouldn't understand. But when you said you worked with the dead... I had to know."

Jack leaned across the table. "I always thought it was weird, kind of crazy that I did what I did. Touching the bodies, speaking to them. But it always led to something positive, you know, finding the killer or, at least, determining a cause of death if it wasn't immediately apparent. To know that you, well... I guess knowing I wasn't totally nuts doing what I did is a comfort. I... I'm thinking now that the circumstances of me coming up here to buy a horse were more than... coincidental."

"Yeah, maybe... Maybe you were called up here. I remember, a long time ago, my mother told me about meeting a marshal from Denver whose car broke down on the highway near our hill where the horses are. He was going to Steamboat Springs, and his car shut down on him. My mother and her brother helped this man get his car going, and while they did it, they talked about him being a marshal, and he told them he worked on murders in Denver. My mother told him about speaking to the dead. That's what got in my mind when I heard you were a homicide cop. I just had to ask you... I always wondered if that was something that marshal took back to Denver with him."

"That word, Tess. Marshal? Could it have been the cop's name— Marshall?"

Tess shook her head. "No, he was a marshal is all my mother told me. Don't know what his name was. I'll get a bill of sale for the horse," she said, slipping out of the booth. "They keep some behind the bar for me."

Jack watched her walk toward the bar. *You never told me, Old Grim. You sly old sonofabitch, you never told me.*

THREE

Through late spring and the first summer Shy had taken up residence on Jack's seven acres, Tyler, the Pinecone Lodge horse wrangler, showed up at about four p.m. three days a week. During the first few visits, he made sure the geld had healed, and then he began to deal with the horse's temperament, which wasn't good. Tyler had already schooled Jack on feeding and basic care and had helped him construct a round pen for training purposes. He'd cautioned Jack that the horse wasn't a puppy dog and shouldn't be treated like one.

"He's fearful, is all," Tyler had said after the first time he'd managed to get a rope halter on Shy and dealt with nervous squeals, stomps, rearing, and tugging on the lead rope. Tyler dug his heels into the ground while calmly saying, "Whoa now. Whoa…"

Jack watched Tyler patiently and without a word raised in anger, deal with Shy's left and right side fears and anxiousness to the point, by the dog days of August, Shy was walking, trotting, cantering on cue, and coming to Tyler when he pursed his lips and kissed.

"You got to work both sides of him separately," Tyler said, the first time he brought Jack into the round pen with him and Shy. "Horse brain works that way. They kinda won't put two and two together 'til they see it from both sides."

As the summer passed into fall, as the aspens shivered their leaves to reds, oranges, and golds, and as the land whispered of the freeze to come, Shy's coat began to thicken. When the first snowfall arrived, he appeared shaggy and stout. Tyler had yet to allow Jack to sit the horse, saying that would come in the spring.

"Get through the winter, exercise him in the round pen, and walk him on the trails when you can. You'll be on him by July."

And by July, Jack was atop him, just walks at first in the round pen, and then walks along the flat trail that led to Piney Lake. By mid-July, Tyler had Jack trot Shy for the first time with Jack on his back. He was able to stay on, and Shy seemed comfortable with him. Thereafter, Shy and Jack would leave early in the morning and pass the nearby campgrounds spotted here and there with campers in tents who had yet to rouse themselves from the previous night's campfire nightmare stories and drinking binges. They'd ride past Piney Lake and along the trails headed east toward the slopes of the Gore Range that peaked with Mount Powell, jagged as a saw's edge.

Heading home one day at not yet nine in the morning, they came down the trail from a meager summit where Jack halted Shy to look at the scenery below. Piney Lake shone as a blue-green jewel surrounded by the upsweep of purely green pine intertwined with the brown decay of beetle destruction. As they passed a small clearing to their left, half-hidden by the overlap of pine boughs, Shy sidestepped off the trail, then stopped and stood dead still, raised his head, curled his lip, and tasted the air about him. Jack tried to rein him back onto the path, but Shy was determined to keep his distance from the shrouded entrance to the clearing and had turned his head away from it.

Jack had come to respect Shy's judgment when it came to going one way or the other on trails they'd never explored. A horse's sense of things in the natural world seemed to Jack to be a reflection of what God had given to the horse: a discernment of sorts that Jack possessed only when laying his hands upon the dead. Shy had saved them from stepping into waist-deep muck within the valley, unstable rocks on the hillsides, and the presences of critters not likely to look kindly upon their passing.

Now, as Jack swung his leg off Shy and tied the reins to the limb of a felled tree, he knew caution was what Shy had shared with him. He stepped to the clearing and looked in. The sun shined directly overhead and lit the interior of the place as though a spotlight beamed a circle upon it. Jack thought he saw something not human, perhaps rag-stuffed dummies both facedown—the legs bent wrong, and the arms unnaturally splayed. The blood, though, spoke its own truth, as it lathered the bodies' backs and buttocks, the arms, legs, and heads. The blackness of the ground near one's head and the other's chest bore witness the bodies had bled mostly from those places. But there wasn't enough blood to determine if this had actually been the killing ground. The shapes of the bodies, the small hips, the broad shoulders, even the blood-encrusted hair, told Jack these were young men, maybe even teenagers.

Jack stepped into the clearing, taking care to keep to the periphery of the five-foot circle he'd mentally drawn beyond the immediate area where the bodies lay. The urge to touch them was nearly overwhelming, but he knew he could not disturb the scene. He would touch them later. He would speak to them and hope they spoke back. But for now, he kept to the edge of the circle he'd established and slowly stepped around it, a full three-sixty, his eyes focused on anything that might prove helpful in answering the questions he, and he was sure the Eagle County sheriff's crew as well, would have when he later led them up here. Jack could see signs of blunt force and skin-piercing trauma. But it was the way the limbs spread anywise that he knew this would be an image like no other he would forever hold on to.

Jack sat on his haunches at the end of his three-sixty, looked up at the circle of sky and sun above, then looked back down at the bodies. "We'll figure this out," he whispered. "Bless you, boys. I'll be coming back." He then stood up, stretched out the kink in his back, and stepped from the place. He knew there would be a search of the hillside, maybe even a search of the valley as well. A one hundred yard search in all directions was critical, but his call to the sheriff was more important, and that is what he had to do.

FOUR

Brian Hill and Mark Harris were both twenty-two. As they danced upon a floor bathed in the colors of the rainbow, the other revelers moved about them while the music boomed with heavy bass and wild treble, the diva's voice pleading for a never-ending love to come their way. For Brian and Mark, it had, or so they thought. The strobes flashed, and both boys watched the other's robotic movements with wonderment and smiles. It had been Friday night, and the entire world had become this moment, this place of fantasy.

They had met almost a year before. Both Midwest flatland emigrants, they hoped the mile-high promise of Denver and the call of the mountains to the west would be fulfilling. They knew their degrees from obscure schools were as marketable as water in a deluge. They moved into a Colfax Avenue two-room walkup where the bed folded down from the wall, and the bathroom was the second room. They waited tables at an upscale Denver Lodo eatery where they wore white shirts, black vests and pants, and red bowties. In mid-autumn, they packed their 2000 Mazda and headed west to Vail, where their credentials saw them placed in an even more exclusive restaurant that specialized in red-runny steaks, crispy shrimp, fine wines, and luscious desserts served on crystal plates. Their mornings free until eleven, they skied the slopes of Vail, and their late nights were often spent among other gay boys and girls in the few bars and bistros that welcomed them. They had moved into a single-wide trailer in Avon, only fifteen minutes from Vail. After experiencing their first taste of the mountains, their decision was easy. They would stay there and not return to Denver or anywhere else when the ski season was over. They had what they wanted at this time in their lives—an uncomplicated existence that was more or less a fantasy come true.

One Friday night in late spring, Brian and Mark sat at a table in a bar in Vail, sipped beer, and watched two other boys do the same at a table across the room. They were obviously real cowboys or something akin to that, and Brian and Mark were intrigued. The other boys were watching them, too. Pretty soon, they were all sitting at the same table, getting to know one another and trading tidbits of their histories. The other boys worked about an hour and a half north of Vail, one at the Pinecone Lodge as a horse wrangler, the other as a fishing and hunting guide. They explained they both lived at the Whisper River Ranch a few miles west of the lodge. One thing led to another that night, and all the boys ended up at the single-wide where they got to know each other even better. Intimately, in fact.

By July, after three more encounters with the wrangler and the guide in Vail, Brian and Mark decided they'd drive up to the lodge on their day off and ride horses. The wrangler had offered them that, and they were excited to live the experience. As they were leaving the lodge's compound after their ride, the wrangler took them aside and discussed a proposition he had for them. It would be worth two hundred and fifty dollars each if they'd do it. "Just kind of a hide and seek thing," the wrangler said, and he mentioned he'd be there to make sure nothing got out of hand.

"We're not really into that," Mark said.

"Don't worry," the wrangler said. "The guys who want to do it have promised nothing heavy will go down. We'll get you set up at a campsite and, other than the hour or two you'll be…playin' the game, you can just take it easy—camping, hiking, anything you want to do."

Brian and Mark thought about that and decided it might be fun. They'd have to take a couple days off work, but that was no problem. Besides, they'd be making money while having fun.

"Okay, we'll do it," Brian said after discussing it with Mark.

"Good. You'll enjoy it," the wrangler said. He told them he'd pick them up and take them back so they wouldn't have to worry about driving.

***

The evening, a Sunday, of Brian's and Mark's excellent adventure, was spent in a gray domed tent with the wrangler, Tyler, and the guide, Ben. They drank some, fooled around some, and then shortly after midnight, Tyler and Ben took Brian and Mark to where the game would commence. Tyler told the boys to be aware of where the trail was at all times, and Ben gave them flashlights so they could see where they were going.

"But the idea is not to be seen," Tyler told them. And they all agreed Brian and Mark would not turn on their flashlights unless they absolutely needed to, making sure nobody was around at the time.

"You're sure you'll be out there somewhere if we need you?" Brian asked.

"A course," Tyler said. "Just give us a shout, and we'll come running. When those guys find you, all they'll do is tape a red star on your back. All those guys will do is just tape a red star on your back, and send you back down the trail."

Tyler and Ben stood at the foot of the trail and watched the boys disappear up the hill on a half-moon night.

FIVE

"You'd think there'd be signs of claw marks," the uniformed sheriff's deputy said, who also kept to Jack's established five-foot distance from the bodies. Six other deputies were combing the hillside above and to the sides of the place for evidence. They would eventually work their way down to the valley. "I mean… There are bears up here, especially this far into the summer. But, I don't see… Ah, hell…" He turned to Jack. "Whaddaya think? You've been through this before."

"Don't believe it was a bear," Jack said. "Soon as the CBI gets up here and works the scene, we can get a little closer to the bodies."

"They're on their way as we speak," the deputy said. "The lodge has four ATVs waiting for them. Can you tell me how you found the bodies?" He pulled a notepad from his shirt pocket. "Got the paperwork to do."

Jack recounted in detail what had happened, ending his story where he'd stopped at the Pinecone Lodge to call the sheriff's office. He'd known the Colorado Bureau of Investigation would probably be called in as the sheriff's department most likely lacked the expertise to conduct a thorough forensics investigation, but did have the manpower to search the area for anything that might help. Even if they did have the forensics expertise, the presence of the CBI would enhance and validate the investigation once a case was taken to court.

"The horse smelled it?" the deputy asked his expression one of incredulity.

"What I said."

The deputy nodded. "Okay, that's what I'll put in the report. I'm not a horse person myself, so…"

The unmistakable and irritating clatter of ATVs nearby signaled the CBI team had arrived. When Jack heard shuffling outside the clearing and the voices of new arrivals, he turned toward the entrance and saw a face he hadn't seen in years but had never forgotten, and he smiled.

"Mike," he said, shoving the pine boughs aside. He saw the surprised expression on the face of the man he'd loved at one time and probably still did.

"Jack Dolan in the flesh," Mike said as he stopped and looked at Jack. Jack stared back and remembered the last time Mike and he had shared an intimacy. Jack had told him it just wouldn't work, that they'd be better off apart.

Jack shook his hand. "I see they sent their best," he said, backing up a bit.

Mike drew his hand through his gray-brown hair, nodded, and said, "None better than you, Jack."

They stared at one another as the other three new arrivals, two men and one woman, two of them carrying metal suitcases, stood behind Mike. They leaned one way or the other to get a look at whom their lead agent was talking to.

"Jack," Mike said, turning, "this is Abe Gomez, Kate Snow, Al Sutton, and Carl Dunfree. They're forensics. And this, gentlemen," he held his arm out to Jack, "is Jack Dolan, DPD homicide, retired."

"Nice to meet you," Jack said. He looked at Mike. "This is a bad one. We've kept the immediate perimeter clean, except for the critters that we couldn't do anything about. Sheriff's deputies are spread out up the hill."

"That's not your horse, is it?" Mike asked, turning to look at Shy.

"Yup, he's mine. Helluva horse."

"Never knew you rode horses."

"I didn't when we…used to know each other."

"A thousand years ago, huh?"

"Yeah, seems like."

"Well…" Mike again drew his fingers through his hair. "We better get started here. You found them, I guess?"

"Yeah, this morning," Jack said, remembering Mike had always belied his calm demeanor by putting his hand to his hair.

"Let me get a look at it," Mike said, stepping just under the pine-framed opening to the place.

Jack stayed where he was and watched Mike step into the clearing. After a few minutes, he came back out, his expression pained and hard. "Like you said, it's a bad one. Listen up and gather round." He raised his voice. "Jack is going to take us through the sequence from when he first found the scene up to now. We don't have a lot of time." He paused and looked at his watch. "It's already three. That okay with you, Jack?"

"Of course," Jack said. Once the small crowd had closed in a bit, he again recited the events of his morning up to the point that he'd led the sheriff's deputies up the trail three hours ago. "And, yeah," he added, "we're already losing some of the light. The scene will get pretty dark long before sunset."

"Okay, gentlemen and lady," Mike said, "get on it. Is the coroner on his way?"

"Yessir," the uniformed deputy said. "He should be here shortly."

Mike and Jack stepped off to the side of the trail and watched the forensics team enter the clearing. Jack glanced at Shy and saw he was craning his neck to get at grasses, barely within his reach.

"You want to sit down over here?" Jack said, motioning toward a felled tree about ten yards off the trail.

"Sure." Mike followed him up the hill's incline. "So," he said, sitting on the grayed trunk, "I guess you noticed I was a little surprised to see you up here. I mean, of all places…"

"Yeah," Jack said, untying Shy and moving him to where he could easily chomp on the grasses. Jack retied him, then straddled the tree trunk and sat, facing Mike. "Small world about sums that up."

"Gets smaller every day." Mike removed his lined jacket and laid it to his side. "Are you going to… touch them, Jack?"

"You know me. Yeah, that's the plan. As soon as your boys get done in there, I'd like to have just a few minutes alone."

Mike shook his head. "You still believe in that stuff, huh?"

"It'd be remiss of me not to do it. You know that."

"I do know." Mike nodded and looked into Jack's eyes. Jack thought Mike's expression held a plea as if searching for something unsaid between them. "How have you been?" Mike continued. "All these years since I left the department, since we… We lost touch with one another. What have you been up to, Jack Dolan?"

41

"Bought a nice place up here before I left the force. When I retired, I moved up here and haven't looked back for a moment. Bought a horse, as you've noticed, and am thinking about a good dog to take on. Life's good, Mike. No regrets. How about you? You getting ready to retire?"

"Oh," Mike said, shaking his head and looking up at the blue sky, beginning to become spotted with puffs of clouds, "I'm thinking about it. The CBI has been good to me, but it's not the DPD." He cocked his head a bit toward Jack. "You know what I mean?"

"Sure," Jack said, smiling. "Unlike CBI… You call yourselves agents. Right?" Jack paused and returned Mike's smile. "Unlike agents, not every copper on the DPD had an advanced degree in one goddamned thing or another."

"Yeah," Mike said, "we were cops then, in the truest sense of the word. That and, oh, I guess I miss the real characters we used to have on the force. Guys like Stanton, God bless him, couldn't have made it at the CBI. There is definitely no room for hard-drinking, hard-hitting curmudgeons like Stanton at the CBI. Hell, maybe even the DPD wouldn't have room for him nowadays either."

"Don't believe they would," Jack agreed. "Do you remember the time—you were just a rookie, I think—when Stanton and I were working a homicide where somebody had stabbed to death a homeless guy on Larimer Street?"

"Like it was yesterday. Stanton had you buy a fifth of whiskey, and he put it in the dead guy's hand. Then you two hid across the street and waited for somebody to come along and steal the whiskey. You had to do it about four or five times until you caught the right guy, the killer who still had the bloody knife in his pocket."

"Hah! Now that was brilliant police work," Jack laughed. "Stanton had touched the body, and all he got from it was an image of another homeless person. I didn't even have enough sense to fudge a bit on the report about how we nabbed the guy. I got reprimanded for it by that fat-ass captain, Orville Neeley, who hadn't worked the streets in twenty years. Said I hadn't followed procedure. Said I'd not respected the dead. You remember? It was a time when the department was trying to become, oh, more professional or some shit like that."

"I remember," Mike said, nodding. "That's when I met you. They put you back in a uniform for about a month."

"Until Stanton raised so much hell, they let me go back to homicide. They didn't dare reprimand him. Hell, he was a legend…"

"You'd yet to become legendary," Mike said. "I was thinking about you last night in the context of… Well, I guess the only context was just remembering things."

"I do it too, Mike. Good memories."

"Yes, they—"

"Can you come in here for a minute, Mike," the man whom Mike had introduced as Abe Gomez said as he stepped out of the clearing and waved at him.

"Sure," Mike said. "We'll talk some more later, Jack." He stood up and walked to Gomez, who ushered him into the clearing.

Jack stood up, walked to Shy, and patted his neck. "How ya doin', bud?" Shy jerked the reins tied to the stump and flicked his tail. "Yeah, I know. We'll be heading out of here in a while. I've—" Jack stopped himself, realizing that since he'd brought Shy into his life, he'd shared more deeply felt thoughts and emotions with his horse than he'd ever done with people. Except Mike, who'd been a good listener once upon a time. He had even left his wife out of the loop when it came to his sensibilities. "I've got to touch them," Jack finished his thought and then unbuckled the latigo, unfurled the leather from the D ring, pulled the saddle and pad off, propped the saddle against the felled stump, and put the pad on top. He then untied the lead rope, walked Shy about ten feet to an aspen tree, and tied him off with the lead rope where the grasses were even richer and taller. "Won't be long now," he told Shy. He walked back to the gray stump, sat, and, for some reason, he remembered Elizabeth.

***

Jack had taken on the mortgage of the three-bedroom ranch-style in southwest Denver because that's what Elizabeth had wanted and because the area was where a goodly number of Denver cops lived. They'd married when he was thirty-two. She was a year older with a degree in education, and she taught home economics in high school.

They'd known each other before Jack had gone to 'Nam. They first met when they were both lifeguards at a municipal swimming pool in North Denver where old Italian families used to live and where Latinos now lived but wanted to be called Chicanos. Elizabeth had been good with the younger kids at the swimming pool, less so with the teenagers who believed machismo was their birthright and interpreted that right in terms of petty violence and disrespect for authority, lifeguards included. Jack had dealt with the teenagers in the only way he knew how and what he knew was tit for tat. He soon became, if not feared, respected.

After Jack returned from 'Nam, where the horror of Keh Sanh saw him twice suffer the searing stab of shrapnel firstly into his thigh, then a half-hour later his ass. He'd struggled to pull three grievously wounded Marines from an outer bulwark to the interior of the camp.

After all the muck, blood, death, and terror of that evil place, he returned to Denver, slept twice with Elizabeth, and then gave her a ring. He didn't know if he loved her then but knew he needed something to assuage the demons of the nighttime, and she had been there upon his return. He'd not had the courage to seek the comfort of another man and considered that an impossible dream.

Jack knew it wouldn't work almost before it had begun. She was a good woman who didn't want children because she taught children every day. That was enough for her to know that parenting was something akin to a perpetual classroom in which she surely didn't want to be stuck. He didn't want children either. Period. And that part of their marriage was fine. But the compatibility part was not fine when he promoted into homicide, and soon knew solving murders was where his calling was. It was if he'd been born to do it.

He knew too that that calling might just have something to do with those Marines who'd died in 'Nam for vague reasons he'd yet to understand. And when he finally partnered with Stanton, when he began to believe the unsettled dead and their living families could be given peace by the touch of his hands, whispered words, and good police work, it was then he understood his marriage was done. Elizabeth's soufflés were delicious, and her sewing skills unmatched. But her acceptance of Jack's outward-turned passions were ruinous to her sense of what she believed marriage should be. He rarely touched her anymore after the first year of their marriage. He never told her about touching the dead, or the words that were spoken; she would never have understood such a thing. He accepted the divorce, the cause of which was termed irreconcilable differences, and he blamed himself for it all. It hadn't helped either that throughout their short marriage, he had often wondered what it would be like to act on his seemingly lifelong urge to love another man, as intimately as most men love women—the impossible dream. But after the divorce, he set that aside. His life became his job; his job became his life.

Then Mike Day appeared, and that had made all the difference. All the difference, of course, because Mike was a cop too. Jack had learned cops were quirky as hell, and there was no worth in trying to understand those vagaries but just to accept them. Even though Mike's father had been a Denver cop for almost forty years, Mike had struggled within the department because he dared show his intellect rather than the he-man personae cops saw as the first principle of good police work.

Mike was also smaller than most cops and had a face not so much handsome as pretty. From the moment he'd graduated from the academy, supervisory and command officers had taken one look at Mike and assigned him tasks more suited to clerks and near-retirees. He was put in the property bureau where evidence and stolen property were cataloged and stored, and then on to the jail where he ushered prisoners here and there. It wasn't police work at all. Mike had wanted more, and he gently but persistently insinuated himself to the point where he was eventually assigned to uniform street duties. He proved himself to be a partner anyone would want by their side. He was a tough cop with a bright mind who had gotten more than a couple older cops out of bad situations.

Mike soon advanced through the ranks, though not as quickly as he'd wanted, and soon he put in a request to be assigned to homicide. Once there, he watched Stanton and Jack solve more cases than they didn't. He'd been paired with a fleshy cop who sat behind a desk more than he hit the streets and seemed to value Mike only to the extent that Mike was good at anticipating when a new batch of coffee needed making. Still, Mike watched Stanton and Jack and wondered how they did it.

"So… How are you doing with Teague?" Jack had asked Mike one evening before they'd yet to share a bed. They'd both worked late and had decided that a burrito and a drink at the Satire Lounge on East Colfax would be the thing to do. They hadn't revealed any intimacies about their lives, other than their work.

"Ah," Mike had said, stirring his scotch and water. He watched two men who were obviously a couple step through the front door. They stopped for a second to adjust their eyes to the darkness, then sat in a booth near the door. "You know Teague. He's about as interested in actually working a scene as he is in trying to keep the front of his shirt from pulling out of his pants. I think he's just biding his time until he can retire."

"Yeah," Jack had said, lighting a Lucky Strike from the candle flame flickering on the tabletop. "I think he's only about a month away." Jack raised his head and exhaled the smoke toward the ceiling.

Mike had continued to stir his drink and stared at it as he said, "I've always wanted to know… You and Stanton…" He paused then, looked at Jack, and asked, "How did you two do it? Well, you still do. But how…"

"How did we solve them so quickly?"

"Yes, how?"

Jack had sipped his beer, told him, and Mike had shaken his head and smiled. Mike had then said to Jack that he didn't believe him and asked Jack if he was just toying with him.

Jack hadn't smiled with his response. "Sure, if you think so." Jack had then dug into the smothered burrito the waiter placed before him.

Mike had done the same and appeared to consider Jack's comment as he took his first bite, and then he put his fork on the rim of his plate and looked at Jack again and asked, "You're not playing with me?"

"No, I'm not."

Jack had invited Mike to his apartment that night just to talk about homicide, about the job that had captured their souls.

Jack knew Mike was single. He also knew that there was just something about Mike he couldn't put his finger on. He had watched him since his first day in homicide and had felt the long ago buried longings for another man's touch arise. It wasn't just that Mike was as handsome as any man could hope to be. Something in Mike's eyes spoke of a possible intimacy when he looked at Jack.

Jack told Mike to have a seat at his dining table as he upended two glasses from the drainboard and began to pour bourbon in one. He stopped himself. "Ah, forgot you're a scotch man," Jack said.

"'S'ok," Mike said. "Bourbon'll do."

They talked more about themselves than the job. Mike explained he'd been too young for 'Nam and had entered college the year before the fall of Saigon. He told Jack he'd never married and, now, knowing what working homicides took from a man, figured any long-term emotional commitment to anybody was probably not in the cards. At least not until he finished his career.

"Yeah, that's the story of my marriage," Jack told him, tipping the bottle over the glasses once again.

As the first hint of daylight eased into the room, Mike attempted to stand up and immediately sat back down. "Whoa," he said. "That ain't gonna work."

Jack helped him up, and they both crossed the room to a single bed, the only furniture in the apartment besides the small dining set and an end table by the bed. "It's small, but it'll do, huh?"

"Sure," Mike said as he and Jack sat down on the bed. Mike kicked off his shoes, and Jack did the same.

Mike and Jack would often share the bed, in the third story of that studio apartment on Sherman Street, in a building named after a poet who'd once considered the purpose of fences.

***

Jack noticed the six sheriff's deputies, who'd been up above the scene, were now down below it, spreading out into the valley. One by one, the CBI forensics team emerged from the recess off the trail, lugging the metal suitcases to the waiting ATVs. It'd been almost two hours since they'd arrived. Jack stood from the stump, looked up, and saw the inevitability of rain, then watched Mike come out of the clearing. Mike walked to Jack across the sloped hill.

"They done?" Jack asked.

"Yeah, they got everything they could. Wasn't much to get, though. Those boys were beaten to hell, Jack."

"Can I go in?"

"Sure. I'll stay here."

The bodies had been moved and now lay with their faces looking up, their eyes closed. Jack looked at their faces, their heads, and knew no bone had survived intact from the violence done to them. He stepped closer, knelt down, and placed his hand on the ruined forehead of the one closest to him.

"I am here," he whispered. A puff of cloud passed over, and the clearing became dark and close. "What happened here?" Jack closed his eyes and bowed his head. He nodded and waited, and then nodded again. "All right." He stood up, stepped around the body, and knelt near the head of the other. "What happened here?" he again asked after he placed his hand on the other boy's misshapen forehead. He looked up when he felt the mist-like sensation of moisture on the back of his hand. As the cloud passed, he saw the delicate shards of the late-day shower seemingly suspended overhead, then another cloud gave darkness again. He looked down at the ruined face and did not nod but lifted his hand from the forehead and stood up. He backed away a few steps and looked over the area once again. "Okay," he said and stepped out of the opening.

"All done?" Mike asked.

"All done. The coroner here?"

"Just showed up. My guys are going to help with the getting the bodies down the hill. Did they... say anything?"

"One did," Jack said. "But you don't believe in that stuff?"

Mike smiled. "I guess I don't, Jack. Here." He reached into his coat pocket and pulled out a soft package of wipes. "You ought to wash off. Wish I had a cigarette about now."

Jack grabbed wipes from the package, and, as he wiped his hands, looked at Mike, who was staring off across the valley. "You're still smoking?"

"When I need to," he said, turning his head and smiling at Jack.

"You thinking about me last night?"

"Yes."

"If you've got time, I'll show you my place. We can have some supper or drive into Vail to eat and have a drink. How's that sound?"

"Sounds good," Mike said. "But I've got to fly out with the team. How about I drive up here on Friday?"

"That's a plan. I'll meet you at the turnoff from I-70 and lead you back up here."

Mike reached out a notebook and pen to Jack, and Jack wrote down his phone number. "That's my landline. Cell signals are always iffy. Just call me when you leave Denver, and I'll be waiting for you. Will you be able to stay over?"

Mike smiled. "Maybe. Don't know if we... We'll see, Jack." He pulled a contact card from his pocket and handed it to Jack.

"Understood." Jack took the card, put it in his shirt pocket, and grabbed Mike's hand. "Goddamned good to see you again."

Mike squeezed Jack's hand and glanced at the team coming up the hill with two stretchers, the sheriff's deputies all gathered around the ATVs. "A nice surprise for me, too, Jack. I'll see you early Friday." He then stepped back to the clearing's entrance and walked into it.

Jack headed down the hillside and stopped at the base of the trail, where he met the deputy who'd taken notes on what he'd told him. "Your men find anything?"

"Nothing," the deputy said. "No blood, no clothes, nothing. Forgot to get your number."

Jack gave him his number, thanked him, and watched all the deputies walk down the main trail that would open up at the lodge.

Jack walked back up the hillside, stepped back to the stump, hefted the saddle from it, and carried it to where he'd tied off Shy. He rested the weight of the saddle on his knee, then placed the blanket on Shy's back and heaved the saddle there too.

After pulling the latigo tight, he buckled it, untied the reins from the aspen tree, and led Shy down the hill to the trail where he mounted. "Whoa," he said when Shy danced around a bit with an eagerness to just get moving again.

As they passed the lodge, he saw two uniformed deputies talking to people outside the main building. Farther along the road, he saw another pair of deputies talking to campers who'd pitched their tents about forty yards from the road. He considered the likelihood that any campers had heard or seen anything that had to do with the murders and concluded that was a fat chance. If anyone had heard anything and they were not involved in it, they would have come forward long before now.

SIX

Once the sleek chartered jet had landed at DIA after the short hop from Vail, Mike and half the forensics crew rode back to the CBI headquarters in downtown Denver in a state-owned black Chevrolet Suburban. It was past nine, and everyone had put in a long, hard day. When the option of a late dinner together had come up, Mike, like everyone else except the tech who'd brought it up, had said no. He just wanted to go home and veg out for a while. Once they reached the CBI parking garage, Mike said good night to all, and maneuvered his Lincoln MKS out of the garage and drove the few miles to his apartment overlooking Cheesman Park.

He eased his legs up to the comfortable embrace of his couch and snuggled into what was the usual salve that dulled the day's hectic edge. Holding the book of Hemingway short stories open with his right hand, he reached for the Chardonnay on the table to his left, where a Tiffany reproduction bathed the proximate area in a soft glow. As he drank the fine dry wine from a jelly jar, he pondered his mind's image of Ernest Hemingway, cramming the business end of a shotgun into his mouth and pulling the trigger. An act that probably vacated his brain from his skull in a New York minute. Like toi-let-paper spit wads, he thought. He supposed the old man's brain had mucked up the walls and ceiling of that bedroom in Idaho with the most god-awful mess one would ever want to see. Imagining it was bad enough. But seeing it?

"But, then, one would never want to see something like that, would one?" he said as he looked over the top of the book and smiled at Gertrude. His precocious calico suffered a red ribbon tied around her neck. She lolled on the coffee table in front of him, ignoring his banter as she always did. He thought a moment about what he'd just said and smiled. He didn't have enough fingers and toes to count the times he'd seen the ugly results of suicides and murders by gunfire.

Lowering the book to his lap, he considered the absurd notion that death was Hemingway's final frontier, something he quite deliber-ately intended to conquer before it conquered him. One could nev-er really conquer death, he thought. One simply slipped into it by accident, violence, deliberately, regretfully, or furiously, depend-ing upon bad luck, health, or psyche. No, he thought, Hemingway hadn't conquered death. He was just dead. Period. No great, final symbolic statement to the world there, Ernest, he concluded. Just dead.

He then pictured Jack in Vail, living his new life and probably not wanting the death of innocents or the not-so-innocent to ever again rob him of his peace of mind, or intrude upon his every waking mo-ment as it had for so many years. Now, though, death from violence had once again touched him. Ah, Jack, he thought, feeling comfort-ed by Jack's renewed presence in his life. He'd have someone to talk to, someone to share with.

He smiled again. "What would Papa Hemingway have told you,

Jack?" He imagined Jack kneeling at the side of Hemingway's ruined head, placing his hand into the muck and asking the question:
Why?

Gertrude rose to her feet, shook her head, and sat down. Obsessed
with the proper contortion of neck and head, she flailed her front
paws in an attempt to grab hold of and rid herself of the red ribbon that projected heavenward at the base of her skull. Her guttur-
al moan confirmed another failed attempt. These frantic episodes
to unhitch the fabric had resulted in the destruction of three crystal
goblets. So far. The jelly jar had thus come out.

"Hah!" Mike said. "I finally figured out how to tie it, didn't I?"

Gertrude arched her back with a hiss, leaped from the coffee table,
and pranced with her tail held high into the kitchen, an open-ended
adjunct to Mike's living room, separated only by a granite-topped
island. Gertrude's food and water sat on the floor at the base of a
cupboard.

Mike then placed the collection of Hemingway short stories on the
coffee table and began to reach for the wine when his cell beeped.

He looked at the readout. Abe Gomez. "Abe," he said, "you got
something already?"

"Hey, Mike," Abe Gomez, his lead forensics guy, said. "Not much
at all. We do know they used tape on the eyes, mouths, wrists, and
ankles. Duct tape, I'd guess. Don't know why they took it off."

"Thought as much when I noticed the fine layer of dirt clinging to
their ankles."

"Yeah, no surprise," Abe said. "You were kinda quiet on the way
back."

"Oh," he said, reaching for the Chardonnay, "it's always tough.
You know that. Maybe I'm getting a little, oh, I don't know... wea-

ry of it all. And, seeing Jack up there, retired and happy, riding a horse for Christ's sake... You guys were great, though, Abe. I hope you're home."

"Carl and I just got off the phone with the Eagle County coroner. Prelims just confirm those boys were beaten to death. Time of death was probably within a seventy-two-hour window. I'm heading home right now."

"Good. Get some sleep. Thanks for calling."

He stared at the cell for a moment, half expecting it to ring again. But who would be calling? Jack? He shook his head, laid the cell on the coffee table, sipped from the jelly jar, and smiled. What possessed him to expect Jack would call? Hell, he was half expecting he'd win the lottery, too.

He looked at the Hemingway on the coffee table. "Death be not proud, huh, Ernest?" he said, reaching for his pack of Camel Lights next to where he'd placed the cell. He lit up and exhaled a long stream of gray-white into the living room. He settled back on the couch, put his bare feet up on the coffee table, and gazed past the black metal cone-shaped freestanding fireplace centered on the strip of ceramic tile that fronted the sliding glass doors to his balcony.

The view from fourteen floors above the street spread south toward the elegant high-rises that graced the northwestern edge of Cheesman Park. The view of the park itself, late July, was as green as it would get this year and was already showing patches of brown. The ancient oak, maple, pine, and spruce trees that dotted the perimeter were, as always, stoic, watchful, waiting for the frigid slink of another Colorado winter not far ahead. Able to see little of the park as twilight slip-slid to black, he wondered what those within the lambent blush of windows two blocks away were doing. Probably just hanging out, he thought. Dinner. TV. Conversation.

He inhaled deeply of the cigarette. As he watched the smoke carried on his exhale rise, dissipate, and disappear, he knew his nightly routine of dulling the edge wouldn't ease the bitch of what the day had become. No, the day would not be easily paled by thoughts of Hemingway, Chardonnay, a stale cigarette, or even Gertrude's charming, at times, hilarious prance and pomp about his apartment. The impact of what he'd seen in the mountains today hadn't for a moment slipped from his consciousness, his soul. And seeing Jack again after he'd been on his mind for a while? Coincidence? No, he thought, it was more like kismet, one of those things just meant to be. But he wasn't getting any younger. That fact in itself had been working on him for the past year. Seeing Jack again had crystallized so much of what he had lately been feeling, thinking, perhaps yearning for. And he didn't know why it all was working on him as something hard, something impossible to reconcile or correct.

"Sorry, Old Pop," he whispered, remembering his father's admonition that no problem should be worried about, just slept on after a little booze had eased the weight of the damned thing. By morning, the problem would become a solution. "Maybe in your day it worked, Old Pop," he raised his voice slightly. "But, now… Well, the older I get, it ain't all that accommodating. Sleep ain't gonna solve this sonofabitch," he said to his mind's image of his father, an old cop who, like the old soldier of song, had just faded away two years before.

Mike Day knew cops. And he knew most cops' families couldn't avoid living that cop's life pretty much as intimately as the cop himself did. Hell, he'd lived under the same roof with one, his father, for eighteen of his now sixty-one years, the last forty of which he himself had been one. Even Jack's wife had pulled the plug on their marriage for her own sanity. Mike remembered the men he'd loved throughout his life, none of whom he'd been brave enough to actually live with. Even Jack had realized the dangerous territory they'd once traversed, their secret working on them both to the point Jack had told him it wouldn't work. The fear of being found out by their peers was a chance they'd not been willing to take. Now that he thought about it, though, maybe that fear was more a Jack's than his.

Old Pop, he'd called him. A bear of a man who'd pinned on the badge ten years before Mike's birth. Old Pop had followed the old school of law enforcement at a time when old-school was pretty much all a cop had to work with. His father's perception of the difference between right and wrong constituted the sum total of his view of the world. Shared with his son—his wife, Mike's mother, dead from ovarian cancer when Mike was two—Old Pop's stories varied little in their content, and were told over the dinner table from as far back as Mike could remember.

The evening meal ended with bourbon and ice within his father's reach, and his cigar lit. The stories were, at times, raw, crude, not fit for the delicacy of Mike's youth. Old Pop saw it as just a telling of the world's hard knocks, lessons taught to his only child. After all, Mike would conclude years later, what else did Old Pop have? What else did he have to give to him?

"Vile and crude" were the words that Old Pop had begun those tough lessons with, a puff on the cigar, raising his head, the smoke seeping from his lips.

Old Pop would continue. "Human beings are capable of inflicting vileness upon each other." He'd raise the bourbon and sip. "Human beings, cut, sliced, stabbed, beat, or shot. Stone-dead still, lying in their own blood, able only to silently swear that another human being was responsible for their death.

"Children." He'd point the business end of the cigar at Mike and repeat it, "Children abused, black and blue, from the slaps, the fists of their parents." He'd raise his voice, "Parents, for Christ's sake, who can't deal with themselves much less their children, much less the cruel, complex world they believe has picked them, and only them, to defeat, to put down, to destroy. Lice-infested drunks and derelicts lying in gutters with matted hair and urine-soaked clothes, vomit-stained shirts, and no shoes. The hookers and pimps workin' one corner, with boys and girls—children for Christ's sake!—on the other, selling their bodies for the price of a meal."

Old Pop would pause every time after the telling of the children. Then he'd close his eyes for a moment, suck on the big cigar, and sip more whiskey. "Automobiles wrecked beyond manufacturer recognition," he'd continue, "with four or five or six dead young bodies inside who only wanted to have good time at a hundred and ten miles an hour. Dopers and pushers, and good outstanding pillars of the community, high as kites after snorting or shooting or popping or drinking their particular ticket to nirvana. Nirvana... a kind of heaven," he'd explain to Mike more than once. "The homeless and sick wandering the streets, babbling to themselves and cursing the unseen demons that haunt their souls. Ah, hell, ten thousand filthy, disgustingly sad, sad pictures, images I'm supposed to deal with. Hell, every cop is supposed to deal with them. We're *expected* to deal with them. That's our job. Again and again, society delegates the responsibility of dealing with its failures to one class of people, the cop.

"Your homework done?" Old Pop's stories would end abruptly, a smile shining from his face, bourbon downed, the big cigar tamped dead.

A lesson learned from Old Pop: There are good cops, and there are bad cops. There are cops who give a damn, and there are cops who don't. Old Pop gave a damn. What was churning in Mike's gut was beginning to affirm that he'd lost Old Pop's passion. Yes, he still gave a damn, but not much of one anymore.

SEVEN

Jack thought about the day he'd had as he brushed out Shy, spread two flakes of grass and alfalfa hay in the feed bin, and filled the water trough. He stepped into the cabin and did not eat but poured himself a bourbon and soda and wished he had a cigarette—the habit long ago dropped, but the desire remained. Built a fire in the five-foot-high and six-foot-long fireplace made of river rock and mortar against the chill that came nightly and persisted until midday. Sitting on the sofa facing the fireplace, he bent over the coffee table and wrote detailed notes about his gruesome find and the ensuing events of the day, including his moment alone with the bodies. *Just a game, at first*, he wrote. *Thought we were friends*. He studied the last words he'd written, the words spoken to him from the boy who was able to speak. He reread them, spoke them, leaned his head back, and was soon asleep.

At ten a.m. the next morning, Jack saddled Shy and rode toward the lodge's stable. He wanted to find Tyler so he could pin down exactly when the wrangler would be able to give Shy and him another lesson. Both of them had progressed well with the learning but only to the point where the finer points of western riding were still ahead of him. He knew if Tyler was asked whether the horse or the rider was doing better than the other, the answer would undoubtedly be the horse. Just like dogs, Jack figured it was difficult to teach an old man new tricks. But he was determined to make the best of it.

"They get that mess taken care of?" Tyler asked when Shy, and Jack approached him. "They take down all that plastic tape?"

"Well," Jack said from atop Shy, "they did what they had to do. And, yeah, they probably took the tape down. Don't think they've made any conclusions, though."

Tyler had four horses tied off to the hitching post, brushing them down and picking their hooves before hefting saddles on their backs. "Conclusions about *who* did it?"

"Yeah," Jack said. "Exactly." He thought Tyler looked tired, moving slower than he usually did.

"The deputies asked me some questions. Didn't have any answers that could help 'em, though. Funny how nobody, ah… heard anything. If they were anywhere near here, if any screamin' or hollerin' was goin' on, the valley would have carried that sound to somebody, some camper or somebody here at the lodge."

"Sure it would have," Jack said. He, too, had thought about the screams that such a fierce beating would evoke. *Maybe they couldn't scream?* "Lots of unanswered questions," he added.

"Were you lookin' for a lesson today?" Tyler said, as he pulled a roan mare's foreleg up and looked at its foot.

"If you've got the time."

"Well." Tyler sighed as he pulled a pick from his back pocket and dug into the buildup of crud within the folds of the horse's frog. "I might have time nearer to five or five-thirty than four. Got some yahoos from Chicago comin' up from Vail about three-thirty for a horsey ride."

"That'll work. My place or here?"

"I'll ride up to your place after I get the stock all settled and close up shop."

"Okay." Jack reined Shy and clicked once to get him moving. "We'll be there."

Jack decided he needed to stay away from the place where he'd found the boys. Just for a while. He thought if he just let it all simmer for a time, things might become more evident. After talking to Tyler, instead of heading up the trail toward the Gore Range and the murder scene, he reined Shy back down the road that would eventually take them to the turnoff leading to his property. On both sides of the road, public campsites spotted the terrain, rarely vacant from late spring until early autumn. The truth of it was the whole area was overused by campers. The forest service was barely able to cordon off the most severely trampled to death areas in need of a season or two of natural regrowth. Of course, those areas cordoned off with signs that read: KEEP OUT – CAMPSITE CLOSED were usually the first spots taken by campers who'd pull the posted signs out of the ground and hide them somewhere, believing the forest service wouldn't remember where they'd put them. As thin as the ranks of the forest service had become, there wasn't much chance anyone would be caught, fined, or told to pack up and move on.

Jack reined Shy to the left, off the road and onto a trail that led to several campsites. He'd done this before and was often greeted by city folks with kids who'd come up to Piney Lake just for two or three days to build campfires, hike, rent the canoes, eat meals of hamburger, hotdogs, and potato salad, and surely fit at least one horse ride into the mix. These folks always greeted Shy and Jack with smiles and wonderment, wanting to pet Shy and talk about horses and ask questions about where the best trails were and where they could see wild animals. Jack would tell them where to go and how to get there.

"If you get up early enough and stay quiet, you can see mule deer off the other side of the road if you walk a ways toward the lake. There's an old fox, too, who hangs around here and eats scraps of food. He's not dangerous. Never saw a bear, though I'm told there are occasional sightings." And invariably, the folks would want to know just exactly where the bears had been seen. Jack would sweep his hand toward the southern and northern ridges and say, "Well, if you take a horse ride, just ask the wrangler. He'll tell you." Soon Shy and he would move on, stopping at another campsite or not, or just turn back toward home.

Jack stopped Shy at a gray domed tent set back off the trail about twenty feet with the entrance flap open. Leaning down a bit, he looked into the tent and saw the dishevelment of sleeping bags, clothes, and some other items within. Straightening up, he scanned the area and settled his attention on the fire pit that appeared long-unused as he saw only black ash that seemed to be wet. There were no cars about. There was one aluminum-and-fiberglass lawn chair lying on its side.

"Good morning," a voice came from behind him. He turned and saw a young man in shorts, hiking boots, and a sleeveless down vest walking toward him from the road.

Jack turned Shy and nodded. "Good morning."

The young man stopped several feet away from them and smiled. "Not too fond of horses. Sorry."

"That's okay," Jack said. "He won't bite. Well," he considered what he'd just said, "actually he will, but he hasn't lately. This your campsite?"

"I thought maybe it was yours." The young man stepped a little closer. "I'm Stephen." He stretched his hand out and up but kept his distance from Shy.

Jack dismounted. He turned to the young man and shook his hand. "I'm Jack. And this is Shy. And, no, this isn't our campsite."

"The reason I'm asking," Stephen said, bending his head to peer into the tent and looking back at Jack, "is that this is kind of a primo spot if you know what I mean. My buddies and I come up here every summer. We really wanted to get this spot, but somebody was already here. But we've yet to see them. In three days, we haven't seen any signs of life over here."

"Three days?"

"Yeah. And we've only got another two days up here and…"

"The sheriff's deputies talk to you yesterday?"

"No. Damn. What'd we do wrong?"

"So, you weren't at your campsite yesterday?"

Stephen stuck his hands in the pockets of his vest. "Are you a cop? You kind of sound like a cop."

Jack smiled. "No, I'm not a cop. But the deputies were up here yesterday talking to campers about an incident that happened up in the nearby hills a couple days ago. Guess you and your buddies weren't around when the deputies came by?"

"No, we weren't. We were hiking the back trails and ridges. We actually stayed overnight up there and just got back a little while ago. What happened?"

"Two young men were murdered up above the valley."

"Christ! Wow…"

"Yeah," Jack said. "'Wow.' I don't know what to tell you about this here." He looked at the tent and the fire pit. "Nobody's been here lately. I'll probably call the sheriff and see if they want to come back up and take a look if they didn't yesterday."

"Well, I guess we'll just stay where we are. Wow," he said again, "somebody got murdered."

"Helluva thing," Jack said, holding his hand out. "Nice to have met you, Stephen."

The young man shook Jack's hand. "Same here."

"Where are you boys camped?"

"We're up the road," he said, pointing east, "and about fifty yards in. We've got a red-and-blue tent and a green one. If the sheriff wants to talk to us, we'll be around this evening, probably in the morning, too."

"They might," Jack said as he grabbed the saddle horn and stuck his boot in the stirrup. He hefted himself up and watched Stephen back away as Shy flicked his head up and snorted. Nudging Shy into a walk, Jack continued down the trail to the next campsite. After only about thirty yards, he stopped Shy, glanced back at the domed tent, and knew what he had to do. After turning Shy around, he retraced their route, dismounted, tied Shy off, and stepped around to the front of the tent. Sitting on his haunches, he peered in. Once again, he saw the dishevelment inside. Extending himself to his hands and knees, he crawled through the opening.

He raised his head up and saw the two sleeping bags unzipped, appearing as though they'd been used for their intended purpose and left just as they were when whoever had used them had crawled out. The two blow-up mattresses had deflated. Scanning the interior of the tent, he saw at least two changes of clothes at the foot of the sleeping bags, and two pairs of Nikes. There was a battery-powered lantern, a knapsack, a bag of potato chips and another of trail mix, a quarter-full bottle of vodka, four bottles of water, two empty Gatorade bottles, and a half-open canvas bag that appeared to contain toiletries. He was careful not to touch anything, knowing he'd probably call the Eagle County sheriffs back up to take a look if they hadn't already.

Emerging from the tent, Jack stood and turned full circle. He looked at the immediate area around the tent—the cold fire pit, the toppled aluminum chair. Stepping behind the tent, he saw nothing unusual. He glanced at Shy, who'd cocked his left leg and was probably napping. He then walked to the rutted road where the campers would have turned their vehicle if they'd had one, to unload its contents. Tire tracks were visible but muddy from the daily afternoon showers.

"Shy-boy," Jack said softly, not wanting to spook him out of his nap. He gently placed his hand on Shy's hip. Taking one last look around, he then untied the reins and led Shy from the trees and mounted him in the clearing in front of the tent. He stroked Shy's neck, turned him, and rode back to the main road, where he reined Shy to the left and headed back to his cabin.

***

"How's he been?" Tyler asked across the top fence post as he dismounted from the black horse he'd named Bear, turned his head, and spat a wad of brown onto the ground.

Jack had been working Shy for a half-hour in the round pen, slapping a rolled lasso against his thigh. He walked to where Tyler was looking over the fence, his black cowboy hat typically set deep on his head. His Wranglers appeared new, his shirt a red-and-black block pattern. "He's doing great," Jack said, hanging the lasso on the fence post. "We rode some trails this morning, and he took it all in stride. Didn't spook at all, and we had a nice trot all the way down the road home."

"His turns are comin' along, too?"

"Yes." Jack nodded. "He's pretty much aced those. Even when I screw up, he seems to know it and does what I intended anyway."

"Well, good deal," Tyler said. He stuck his finger in his mouth, pulled out the wet glob he'd had in his cheek, and tossed it to the ground. He wiped his hand on his pants, tied off Bear on the fence post, and slipped between two strands of fence wire and into the pasture.

"That's nasty stuff," Jack said.

"What? The tobacco?"

"Yeah. Just because you're not smoking it..."

"Save me the lecture, Jack. Know all about the dangers."

Shy snorted and ambled over to where they stood. Tyler fished in his jeans pocket, pulled out a piece of horse candy, and let Shy lip it from his open palm.

"Any more news on the murders?"

"No, not that I've heard of." Jack wondered if he should tell him about the abandoned tent he'd examined earlier but thought better of it. He'd already called the Eagle County Sheriff's Office shortly after he'd turned Shy out into the pasture and was waiting for a call-back. Besides, it probably wasn't related to the murders at all.

"They may never figure out what happened up there," Tyler said as he stepped around Shy and looked at his conformation. "Still can't get over the fact you paid only five hundred for this boy. He's a good lookin' horse, Jack."

"Yeah, he is. Nothing like Bear, but he'll do."

"Yes, I believe he will," Tyler said. "Why don't you tack him up, and we'll get started workin' on some turns. Like to see you post a trot, too."

Tyler spent two hours with Shy and Jack, and just past seven-thirty as the day began to slip from them, Tyler mounted Bear and rode back toward the lodge. For some reason, Jack knew with certainty, he envisioned Tyler slowing near the trail off the side of the road that led to the domed tent. He concluded the nylon shelter would remain there until Tyler or someone other than those who'd put it up took it down. Jack didn't know why this had crossed his mind. Just a hunch that'd probably go nowhere.

EIGHT

One hundred and sixty miles northwest of Michael Day's Cheesman Park condo and eighty miles north of Jack's cabin, the town of Oak Creek was just beginning to stir with the new day. Within the Flat Top Diner, two tables by the window fronted Oak Creek's Main Street. One of them was occupied by a heavyset woman wearing a red-and-yellow bandana on her head sitting with a skinny man who poured sugar into his coffee. Harley sat down at the other table, looked out the window, and hoped not to see the boys that had been shooting the shit with Denman when he'd fired the suppressed Walther P22 at him. He had aimed for Denman's neck and had hit it square from forty yards, the jugular surely pierced. He'd seen the first two squirts of blood rise almost three feet into the air. When Denman collapsed to the ground, Harley had turned and walked down the alley as Denman's friends scattered. Knowing the suppressor wouldn't be that hot after firing only one shot, he'd unscrewed it from the barrel as he walked. Put it in his inside coat pocket, and stuck the weapon itself under his belt at his side.

"Hi, Harley."

Harley turned and saw Marlene staring down at him, holding a pot of coffee. He gave her a smile. "How are you today, Marlene?"

"Just as fine as can be. How you doin'?"

"Believe I'll be okay if I can get some coffee, two eggs, bacon, and a couple pieces of toast."

"Your usual then, I guess."

"That's it."

Marlene reached for the downturned cup on the table, turned it right side up, and poured coffee into it. "Be right back."

Harley watched the movement of Marlene's butt and thighs bulge through the blue denim of her jeans. Happy she'd not worn her stretch pants today, something that usually ruined his appetite, he pried open a plastic container of cream and dumped it into his coffee. He picked up his spoon, stirred, and looked out the window as Oak Creek's only police cruiser, with Dale Chase inside, accelerated down the street, its light bar and siren popping on simultaneously. Set his spoon down and sipped his coffee.

***

Not long after eating his breakfast, Harley opened the door to Otis Schrock, Esq.'s office, heard the bell above the door ding, and saw Schrock's secretary was not at her desk. He saw, too, that the door to Schrock's office was ajar. He set down the two duffel bags he'd brought with him, stepped across the gray carpet, peeked in, and found Schrock leaning back in his red leather chair holding a sandwich to his mouth. Harley opened the door another foot and tilted his head in.

"Eatin' at your desk, huh," he said, grinning at the lawyer.

Schrock looked at Harley and motioned with the sandwich for him to come in. "Sit down," he said, grabbing a napkin and wiping mayonnaise from his lips.

Harley sat, taking the leather wingback chair in front of Schrock's desk. He watched the lawyer put his sandwich on the desktop, grab a can of Mountain Dew, tip it to his lips, and wipe himself again with his napkin. Schrock leaned his chair back and folded his hands in his lap.

"So, Doris ain't here today?" Harley asked.

"No, hell," Schrock said, "she took a couple days off to go to Denver for some damned thing. You know women, huh? Anyway, I heard the siren, Harley."

"I was eatin' my breakfast at the café when I saw Dale turn on his lights and head down the street. Whatever coulda happened, I wonder?"

"Yessiree, I'll bet you're just beside yourself wondering what the hell was going on."

Harley nodded and smiled.

"You see him fall?"

"A course I did. Saw the blood squirt as he went down."

"No chance he's going to stand back up again?"

"He might."

Schrock tensed and scratched his head. "I hope you're kidding."

"He may stand before the Lord when he's judged."

"He going to be judged before suppertime?"

"Expect so. Didn't hear the Life Flight copter landin' in the park. So, I believe the authorities have deemed him a goner already."

Schrock leaned forward and opened the drawer to his right. He took out an envelope and tossed it across his desktop. "That'll get you a nice new truck or at least a down payment."

Harley stood up, grabbed the envelope, and opened it. He spent a moment doing a quick count of the bills inside, and stuck the envelope in his inside coat pocket, pulled out the suppressor, and grabbed the Walther out of his belt.

"What're you doing there, Harley?"

Harley screwed the suppressor on the end of the weapon, aimed it at Schrock's head, and saw the old lawyer's eyes grow wide with panic. "Miguel thought I ought to get rid of the loose ends, Sam." He barely put pressure on the trigger, and the weapon spat a hole into the middle of Schrock's forehead just above where his eyebrows faintly met. Schrock's head rocked back, then slumped forward. Harley unscrewed the suppressor, put it back in his pocket, and slipped the weapon back where it'd been. He then emptied all the desk drawers into a pile in the middle of the room and did the same with the file cabinets. He cleared out the credenza behind the desk as well, grabbed the duffel bags he'd left in the outer office, and stuffed the pile of paperwork, notebooks, folders, and other items into the bags.

He hefted both bags with his left hand, turned, and walked from the office. Pulled out his hanky, wiped the doorframe where he'd touched it, and walked out onto Main Street. He looked up the street and down it, then across it. Of the few folks visible, none of them were looking his way. He turned and wiped off both ends of the street-side doorknob. After walking a block east, he turned and walked the half block to where he'd parked his truck. He nodded at the young man sitting behind the wheel of a Dodge Charger, his gesture indicating it was okay to go into the office and cleanse it of anything he had missed. He opened the door, threw the bags onto the floor, got in, started the engine, and made a U-turn. As he headed west on Main, he remembered he'd wanted to pick up some of Lila Worthington's cinnamon rolls at Lila's Sweets but decided he'd forgo that for now. Best he just get up to his cabin, pack what he needed, head for Vail where he'd spend Friday and Saturday nights having some fun, and head for the Whisper River Ranch on Sunday or Monday as Miguel had instructed him to do. He'd destroy what he'd taken from Schrock's office later.

***

Harley Sweet was born and raised in Craig, Colorado, a town that seemed never to quit spreading in senseless directions over the high plains of northwestern Colorado. Strip malls had overcome the place by the time he was eighteen, and by nineteen, he'd hired on at the Peabody Coal operation forty miles to the southeast. It was there he learned to love the sunshine and hate time clocks more than he'd ever realized. That didn't last but five months, when he hooked up with a man who saw promise in Harley's attitude. Over a cold one in a dark bar just off Colorado Highway 13 in Craig, Harley told the man he'd do just about anything except work coal or cows, and the man said, "Okay, you come work for me."

And he did go to work for the man, Miguel Rosario. Rosario had spent his own childhood tending sheep in the hills of Moffat and Routt Counties and, as a teenager, had found himself looking for something different as well. What Miguel did was steal a .38 Colt from his uncle, commence to sticking up gas stations and conve-

nience stores. He soon found himself dishing slop to his fellow in-
mates at the Colorado Division of Youth Corrections in a dismal
place called Grand Junction in far-western Colorado. From there,
Miguel headed back to Craig, his thumb raised to passing traffic.
Once there, his intent was to acquire a Glock 9 and use it only for
the business he'd learned in the correctional facility. He would li-
aise with the contacts he'd made in Grand Junction who, once they
got back on their feet, would supply him with the black tar heroin
he would sell to the burgeoning market in Craig and nearby burgs.
He'd live happily ever after.

And that had gone fine for a while, but Miguel had wanted more.
He had gotten more by recruiting other disaffected boys to help him
out, not only with his H enterprise but cocaine and marijuana as
well. As things will in this business, new entrepreneurs occasionally popped up. And, if Miguel couldn't convince them of the wisdom
in becoming a part of his operation, firstly, a little blood would flow
by nonlethal means. Secondly, said entrepreneur would find his final
rest in some remote spot where Miguel had whiled too many days of
his youth tending to his daddy's sheep. Third strikes were never af-
forded to anyone.

From somewhere, Miguel had learned the efficacy of diversifica-
tion. He soon began to buy businesses that would provide for his
long-term plans to get out of the drug business and into other ne-
fariousness behind the respectability of legitimate enterprises. By
the time Harley ran into Miguel in that homey bar in Craig, Miguel
had owned a Dairy Queen, two McDonald's franchises, three bars—
two in Craig, and one in Oak Creek—three condos in Steamboat
Springs, two upscale restaurants in Steamboat, five thousand acres
of ranchland outside of Vail, eight hundred acres in the Yampa Valley, and a lawyer in Oak Creek by the name of Otis Schrock. In fact,

over 50 percent of Schrock's practice was devoted to Rambouillet Enterprises, LLC, named after a particularly robust breed of sheep that Miguel had known well as a child.

While Miguel split his time between a house in Craig and one of the condos in Steamboat Springs, he also owned some land in the scrubby hills above Oak Creek. It was there he'd built a spacious cabin in which his most favored business partners lived free of charge.

Three years ago, when Miguel saw the young face sitting in his bar sipping on a beer he probably shouldn't have been served, he'd approached the kid and asked him for his ID. When the kid mumbled something like, "Oh, that's okay. I'll just leave," Miguel had grabbed the kid's arm, looked into his big brown eyes, and asked him what his name was.

"I'm Harley."

"Harley, what?"

"Harley Sweet."

"Uh-huh," Miguel had said, thinking, yeah, you are. "You just passing through?"

"No, I live here."

"You work?"

"Used to."

"Where?"

"Peabody Coal."

Miguel had nodded, thought he saw in the boy's eyes what he'd learned to read a long time ago. "You a punk? A wannabe tough guy?"

Harley had squirmed in his chair, looked off into space for a minute. "No, I ain't. Don't think that's any of your business."

"Might be." Miguel had smiled.

"Well…" Harley had said, still squirming. "You own the place or somethin'?"

"Yes. I do."

"Well…"

"Let me buy you another beer. We'll talk."

"I guess I won't pass on that."

And, so, they had their first beer together. Talked about life and the torment of the world, and after a third beer, Harley had said maybe he did have some ideas about living his life outside of the law. "I ain't a punk, and I can take care of myself. Not afraid to do what I gotta do to get by."

At thirty-eight, Miguel was a handsome man with a rough edge. Harley was nineteen and cute as a koala. An unlikely pair, they walked out of that bar together, climbed into Miguel's Lexus, and fifty minutes later were drinking white wine in Miguel's condo in Steamboat Springs. A month later, Harley was living in the cabin above Oak Creek and had not suffered the angst he'd thought he would with his first kill, a man in Craig who'd stiffed Miguel one too many times. In fact, after he did it, he began to believe that maybe ridding the world of those who deserved it had been his calling all along.

***

Harley had never met Denman, the man he'd shot in the neck, but knew him by reputation. He had never seen any worth in befriending him even though he was one of Miguel's boys who lived in Oak Creek. Denman was black leather, motorcycles, and good times. He had worked for Miguel for several years by the time Miguel was easing himself out of the drug business. So too, Harley knew Denman often went to Denver, Chicago, and New York, where he fulfilled his desire to hurt men in sexual situations. The men actually wanted to be hurt, but not to the extent Denman usually ended up providing. He was a sadist.

Harley didn't understand that and thought the allure of heavy BDSM a sickness, much like the sickness his father had savored for all the years Harley could remember. He didn't understand either why Miguel would keep Denman on the cash-only payroll. It was Miguel's practice to stay more than an arm's length from such troubled men now that he was a legitimate businessman. Well, legitimate only to the extent that he took great pains to keep his other enterprises hidden from the decent folks who bought his burgers and ice cream, four-course dinners, fine wines, and viewed his real estate with lustful desire. Even Harley didn't know about everything Miguel was involved in. And that didn't bother Harley at all. He had his own job to do, and he did it well, knowing too that his job was one of those things Miguel would disavow if pressed.

The one man who knew nearly everything about Miguel Rosario and his enterprises was the old lawyer in Oak Creek, Otis Schrock. Or, better said, Otis Schrock *used* to know everything. He didn't anymore. Harley had taken care of that loose end. Harley had liked the old guy and had gotten to know him well. Harley lived in the hills above Oak Creek, away from the prying eyes of the town's residents. He'd become the link between Schrock and Miguel whenever paperwork or packages or verbal messages needed to go from one to the other.

When Miguel learned of the incident with Denman near his Whisper River Ranch—two boys killed for no damned reason that had piqued the interest of the Eagle County Sheriff's Office and the Colorado Bureau of Investigation—and that Denman had made a quick visit to Otis Schrock to talk about it, both men had immediately become expendable. Ironically, Otis himself had told Miguel what had happened after Denman had paid the old man a little visit.

Otis had called Harley and told him he needed to speak with Miguel. Once Miguel had talked to Otis, he still didn't know what to do about Calvin Semple, the manager of the Whisper River Ranch, where the whole sordid mess had been planned and later executed in the hills above Piney Lake. Calvin was a tough sonofabitch who Miguel trusted implicitly. Still, he'd shown poor judgment in actually organizing the thing that had gotten so out of hand so quickly. He'd told Harley what needed to be done with Schrock and Denman. After talking to Calvin and learning two others at the ranch had been involved, he ordered Harley to head up there in a few days and let him know what the situation was. Calvin and those two others would have to be dealt with one way or another. They all had a story to tell that would eventually lead right back to him. Yes, there were still decisions to be made. And after his last phone conversation with Calvin, Miguel knew this thing was far from over.

NINE

"I'll be there," Jack said, holding the receiver to his ear and glancing at the clock on the mantel. "It's eight now, so I'll be there about nine-thirty. I've got a red Explorer. ...Okay. I'll see you then."

Jack hung up and smiled with the image of Mike in his Cheesman Park fourteenth-floor condo in Denver, where he was probably filling up his cat's food and water bowls. He was also probably walking through each room of his home one last time before he left to assure himself he hadn't forgotten anything. Jack had never known a cop who didn't take one last look at something to make sure they'd not missed even the smallest detail that might be significant or later prove to be significant to an investigation. It seemed to be inborn with cops.

Jack finished his coffee, rinsed the cup, and stepped out of the cabin. Looking south to the fenced pasture where he kept Shy, he saw that the horse had heard the door close and was slowly walking toward the northern edge of the pasture where Jack daily spread hay in an aluminum tub.

"Shy-boy," Jack said. Shy flicked his head, nickered, and then lowered his head over the fence wire. Jack opened up the feed shed and tack room, pulled some flakes from the bale, and tossed them into the tub. Shy raised his head, pursed his lips, and then stepped back and lowered his head into the tub and partook of his breakfast. As Shy raised his head and gnawed on a mouthful of alfalfa hay, Jack turned on the spigot and filled the water tank.

Jack smiled as he always did when he thought about the antics of this animal who'd stolen his heart and fulfilled his boyhood dream. Jack considered Shy the best friend he had at this time in his life and wondered, too, why people had become so ancillary for him. He believed he knew why. Critters were just so much easier to come to terms with than people were. Even the dead imposed on him as mysteries requiring his attention to the point of distraction. He'd moved up here in an attempt to avoid that. But, he shook his head and sighed with the thought, those boys on the side of that hill deserved his attention as distracting as that might be or become.

Jack went back into the cabin, grabbed his car keys, and wallet off the side table next to the door, then stopped and looked toward the bedroom. He seldom wore his holstered .38 snub-nosed Colt anymore but now thought about grabbing it from the top shelf in the closet. He decided he would. He unsnapped his belt buckle and threaded the belt through the holster's loop, then refastened the belt.

Before closing and locking the front door, Jack looked back and surveyed the living room and the kitchen beyond, just as he'd imagined Mike had done before leaving his apartment in Denver, and for the same reason. Seeing nothing out of place, he closed the door and locked it, then climbed into his SUV parked on the pebbled path that led from the cabin to the main road. Giving one last glance at Shy, who was still eating, he slowly eased the SUV from his drive. He headed west and then south on the less than well-maintained dirt and gravel road that would take him to the outskirts of Vail and the turnoff from I-70 where he'd meet Mike.

***

Jack saw the charcoal-gray Lincoln MKS parked on the apron of the paved access road at the base of the hill unappealingly adorned with condos seemingly mounted one atop another. He didn't know if this was Mike's car, but as he pulled onto the apron on the other side of the road, he saw Mike smiling from behind the wheel. Mike then opened his door and stepped out.

Jack got out as well. "Howdy."

"Hey, Jack," Mike said. He brushed a hand across the lap of his denim jeans.

Jack walked across the road, and they both moved behind the Lincoln, where Jack crossed his arms and asked, "How was the drive?"

"Just fine, once I got out of Denver." Mike pulled a hard pack of cigarettes from his beige leather coat and tapped one out. "Sorry, Jack, but I've lately rediscovered the worth of cigarettes." He held the pack out to Jack, and Jack shook his head. Mike lit up.

"That bad, huh?"

"Yeah, I believe it is. Promised myself I wouldn't smoke in the car, so if we can just hang here for a minute…"

"Sure. No problem. Any news on the boys?"

Mike exhaled as if the simple act itself encompassed nirvana. "Just prelim stuff. The lab says there's adhesive residue on the wrists, ankles, and mouths."

"Duct tape," Jack said, and it wasn't a question.

"Yup. As if we've never come across that before," Mike said, sighing. "Death was in the neighborhood of seventy-two hours before you found them."

Jack nodded. "I'm assuming this rediscovery of nicotine is more about things in general than the murders?"

"You assume correctly," Mike said. He inhaled once more and dropped the cigarette onto the ground. When he didn't smash the still-burning ember with his foot, Jack did. "Sorry," Mike said.

"Yeah, folks worry about wildfires up here. You ready to head up to my place, or you want to go to Vail and have some lunch?"

"I'd just as soon go up the mountain. Vail has become so… Oh, I don't know. So many people, so much… noise."

Jack smiled. "Know exactly what you mean. I'll turn around, and you can follow me." Jack stepped to the other side of the road and turned back. "Take it easy after we get off the asphalt. You'll high center if you're not careful. Got about fifteen miles to go."

"Got it," Mike said.

As Jack pulled the SUV next to the Lincoln, he saw that Mike had opened his window and was blowing smoke out of it. Obviously, Mike had broken his own promise to himself not to smoke in his car. Not a good sign, Jack thought, as he checked his rearview. Mike was right behind him. Jack turned right and started up the hill he'd just come down. Wondered what would come of this.

***

"He's a good horse, smart as can be," Jack said after they parked their cars, and Mike had walked to the fence where Shy was standing, nodding his head at them.

"Is he saying hello, or just wanting some attention?"

"Oh, he does that when he wants a cookie." Jack stroked Shy's cheek. "We'll get some, and you can give them to him."

"Oh, I don't know…" Mike watched from a safe distance. "I've never been around horses."

"Well, you're going to be around at least one of them for… How long are you going to stay?"

"At least through tomorrow, if that's okay. If you'll have me that long." He shook his head. "I didn't mean that in the… literal sense, Jack."

"I know what you meant. You can stay as long as you want. C'mon, let me show you the cabin."

"You wear your peashooter everywhere you go?"

Jack placed his hand on the butt of the weapon. "Old habits, I guess."

"Why'd you never go with a Glock?"

"Like I said, 'Old habits.'"

"Well, I've got mine." Mike smiled and followed Jack into the cabin.

"Two bedrooms," Jack said. "And look, I even have an indoor bathroom."

Mike peered into each room as Jack led him through the cabin. Returning to the parlor, they sat on the sofa across from the fireplace.

"You hungry?" Jack asked. He stood in the middle of the room and noticed he'd left the notes he'd written about the boys on the coffee table.

"To tell you the truth, I'd like a drink."

"You got it." Jack leaned down and gathered up his notes. Stepping into the kitchen, he laid the notes on the counter and stopped before grabbing glasses from the cupboard. "What's your pleasure?"

"You still drinking bourbon?"

"Yes, and I'm surprised you remembered."

"White wine is usually my drink these days. If you don't have that, then, yeah, I'll have scotch if you've got it," Mike said. He reached into his pocket and pulled out his cigarettes.

"No wine. But, I always keep a little scotch on hand for… whatever." Jack grabbed two tall glasses from the cupboard, mixed the drinks, and carried them the few steps to the sofa. He noticed Mike had a cigarette in one hand and a lighter in the other.

"Can we sit outside? Gotta feed my renewed addiction."

"Sure. You can smoke in here, though. Might have one myself."

Mike grabbed his pack, stood up, and opened the screen door for Jack. "Leave it to me to corrupt the innocent. And, no, I don't want the odor of my addiction staying here longer than I do."

"Hah!" Jack laughed as he walked out. He placed the two glasses on the pine table just to the left of the door. "I don't think innocent is the best word to describe me at this time in my life. Maybe retired would work better."

"And happy." Mike sat in one of the two pine chairs at the table.

"Happier than I've ever been, Mike."

Mike tapped another cigarette out of the pack and held it out to Jack.

"Thank you," Jack said, as Mike lit his cigarette and then his own.

"This is a wonderful place, Jack. Kind of place that just begs contentment, peace."

"Yeah, it is that. Good stuff." Jack raised his head and blew out the smoke. "I still dream about sucking on one of these."

Mike sampled his drink. "Well, don't get too enamored of it. Addictions and all that."

"Yeah, I know. So, tell me—" Jack paused to sip his drink. "What got you thinking about me? We kind of lost touch when you went to the CBI."

Mike didn't answer for a moment as he, too, exhaled smoke. "You remember my father, don't you?"

"Of course. Old Pop. He retired the same year I joined the force."

"You came to the funeral."

"Hell, every cop in Denver came to the funeral. He was… I guess respected is the right word. A cop, honest to the core."

Mike flicked the ash from his cigarette. "Yup, that he was. He talked a lot about honesty, cops giving a damn. He'd come across a lot of dishonest cops in his day."

Jack coughed with his second drag. "So did we." He smashed the cigarette out in the ashtray.

Mike nodded. "Yeah, we did. But both of us shared, oh, an integrity of sorts. We were always honest at work and with each other. Except, well, we kept our secret, ours." He paused, smiled at Jack. "You're the last person on earth I thought I'd be sharing this with, but I don't have anybody else, Jack. Friends I can confide in? Nah, not a one. Hell, I've built such a shell around me, that…"

"We shared some things that we couldn't tell anybody else in the old days. Hah! Listen to me, 'the old days.'"

"Well, that's what they were, good old days." Mike took another sip. "I've been thinking about you, Jack, because I need to tell somebody who understands that I'm tired of it all—the routine, the victims, the death, the killers. All of it. You can't be an honest cop unless you're honest with yourself, and I've got to tell somebody else what I'm feeling. I'm tired of being a cop, and I've got to tell somebody about that." He raised his glass as if in a toast. "And, congratulations, you're that somebody."

"No big deal, Mike. I've been there." Jack extended his arm and swept it from right to left, "This is the world I've made for myself, away from all that… crap."

"Except for those boys you found," Mike said, smashing his cigarette out.

"Yeah, except for that." Jack stood up when the landline inside the cabin began to ring. "Excuse me."

Jack stood at the window as he spoke to the Eagle County sheriff's deputy. He looked at Mike watching Shy ease himself to the ground and roll onto his back, then thrust himself to his right side and then to his left. Shy then stood up, shook himself from head to tail, and dust rained about him. Shy began to strut about the pasture, shaking his head up and down and side to side. He saw Mike smile at Shy's antics.

"I'm sorry." Jack returned to the porch and sat down. "That was the Eagle County Sheriff's Office. I called them yesterday about what appears to be an abandoned tent not far up the road. I thought they might want to come and take a look."

"You think it was theirs? The boys'?"

"Don't know. The deputy just now said he thought they'd seen it when they were up here, but he'd leave a note for the lead investigator who might want to check it out on Monday."

"It could be gone by Monday."

"Read my mind." Jack tapped his hand on the tabletop. "Mike, I'm sorry you're going through burnout. As I said, I've been there, and it's no fun until you decide to do something about it. You can surely retire? Hell, you'll have two pensions to live on."

"I know Jack. But pulling the plug… In the back of my mind, I keep thinking that, if I do retire, I'll probably just end up lying in bed all day with a gallon of wine by my side and… It's tough to envision a reality where I'm not doing what I've been doing for so long."

Jack continued to tap the table, anxious about what he knew had to be done. "Either you leave while you're still able to enjoy life away from the routine, or you stick with it and die with your boots on."

Mike looked at Jack, watched him tap the table. "You're antsy, and I know why. C'mon, let's go look at that tent. Die with my boots on?"

Jack stopped the SUV ten feet into the turnout that led to several camping spots in the area. The abandoned domed tent was the nearest to the road, and Jack pointed to it: "That's it. I talked to a kid yesterday who said nobody's been there in three, well, it's four days now. The kid and his buddies wanted that spot—he called it a 'primo spot'—but somebody had already taken it when they got here."

"Did you check it out?" Mike asked.

"Yeah. I rode Shy through here yesterday. I even crawled into the tent. Didn't find anything unusual. Wanna do the cop thing?" Jack smiled at Mike as he turned off the engine.

"Sure." Mike opened his door and stepped out of the SUV.

Jack followed Mike as he walked to the perimeter of the campsite. They both stopped and looked at the scene before stepping into it.

"Nothing odd here," Mike said, "except if the absence of a vehicle is unusual."

"Look at the fire pit." Jack took three steps into the area and stood over the depression in the ground that had been lined and encircled with large river rocks. "There hasn't been a fire here for a while."

Mike stepped beside Jack and looked down. "Yup. It looks wet, too."

"Not much in the tent," Jack said, taking the few steps to the tent's flap. He lifted it up and knelt down. "Some shoes, bottles, other stuff."

"You go in there?" Mike knelt down beside him.

"Yeah, I did. You want to?"

Mike looked at the road, then further down at the other visible campsites. "You sure nobody's going to… Besides you, folks do carry weapons up here. Right?"

"Some do. But, I've got a hunch nobody's going to mind you poking around in there."

"Okay," Mike said. He knelt down and stepped inside. He then got on his hands and knees and surveyed the interior as Jack stayed outside watching. "I really think if we're going to do this right, we need to pull all this stuff out."

"That's what I wanted to do yesterday. If the sheriff wants to check it out, we'd better leave it alone. They'll want pictures and an inventory."

Mike crawled farther into the tent. "Damn," he said, raising his knee and sitting down.

"What's wrong?"

"Ah, I just jabbed my knee on something under the sleeping bag."

Jack bent down and entered the tent. "Where?"

"Right here." Mike felt the area with his hand.

Jack pulled up the edge of the sleeping bag and exposed what was beneath it.

"Skoal," Mike said. "Crisp Blend, Long Cut," he read the label aloud.

"In the green can," Jack said. "I didn't bring any bags with me."

"You think it's evidence?"

"Could be. Probably ought to treat it as such. Hate to leave it here, though."

Mike stood up and again studied what had been left in the tent. "All of this would be considered a crime scene if something actually happened here. But then, if the sheriff decides to check the campsite out…"

Jack nodded and stepped out of the tent. Mike followed and then looked at Jack's face. "What are you thinking?"

"Oh, you know me. Just considering the possibilities. Don't know if something actually happened here, or if the tent belonged to those boys at all. But it's worth thinking about… "

"From seven different angles."

"Maybe eight," Jack said. "I guess we can leave it here. Then again, I guess we could come back here tomorrow and bag a few things."

"Sounds like a plan."

"Okay, then." Jack took one last look at the campsite and walked to the SUV.

Mike did his own last-minute inventory and climbed into the vehicle.

"Now that I think about it," Jack said as he backed the SUV onto the main road, "maybe we ought to get some sacks from the cab-in and come back here and bag some things. At least get the Skoal bagged today."

"Got nothing else better to do," Mike said.

TEN

Tyler Bray had this morning already led a string of five Denver lawyers across the hillside trails north and west of the Pinecone Lodge's stables. Now he helped them dismount from the gentle horses he'd sat them upon an hour earlier. The lawyers were experiencing what they called a team-building retreat at the lodge. Tyler had thought that was fine as long as the team stayed behind him, didn't attempt to crowd the horse in front of them, and resisted any temptation to speed up their slow traipse.

As they'd come off a trail to the west, he'd noticed Jack Dolan's SUV pulling off the road from where the domed tent still stood, unused for good reason. He'd seen someone sitting in the passenger seat beside Jack and thought he'd like to know who Jack had brought there and if they'd, in fact, taken a look at that tent and what was inside. He'd understood the necessity to remove the tent and everything inside and outside of it but had not had the opportunity to do it. He had goddamned the fact the tent was so visible from the road.

Once Tyler had supervised the lawyers' dismounts, removed the tack from their horses, and put the horses into the fenced pasture, he told one of the junior wranglers, Dakota Tate, a blond, well-pack-aged girl of seventeen, to take care of the preparation for his next scheduled ride—three of the lawyers' wives and probably one girl-friend. He told her he'd be back in time to lead them up the trail. He then drove off in his Ford 250, headed west, with his destination and purpose settled. When he saw Jack Dolan's SUV again, but this time headed back toward the domed tent, he waved as he passed them, and noticed the man sitting next to Jack.

"Fuck me," Tyler said, as he watched Jack pull off the main road and stop just beyond the abandoned campsite. He shook his head and slapped his steering wheel hard. Kept heading west, crossed a log bridge over a skinny ditch, and passed under the wooden mar-quee, with the words WHISPER WIND RANCH etched with the letters torched black, that led to the main house and outbuildings of the ranch itself. This was where he and Ben and the other lodge em-ployees lived. He again shook his head, spit out the window, and knew, *just knew* he should have done what he'd wanted to Monday morning.

***

"That's Tyler, the lodge's horse wrangler," Jack said as he re-turned Tyler's wave. "He also taught me pretty much everything I know about horses and has been training both Shy and me since last spring."

"He wasn't smiling," Mike said.

"No, he wasn't." Jack turned off the road toward the domed tent. "He lives on the ranch west of here. Prob'ly where he's going now. He's got a... I was going to say dark side, but I guess he's just got his serious moments. Don't know if anybody but a cop would have found his sour expression remarkable."

"Reading faces has kept us both out of harm's way lots of times. A tool of the trade..."

Jack braked the SUV and turned off the engine. "Having a helluva time letting go of all those tools, Mike."

"You'll never let them go entirely, Jack. You know that."

"Yeah, I suppose I do."

Mike stood outside the tent's flap as Jack kneeled down inside, grabbed the Skoal container they'd found earlier—his hand inside a plastic baggie—and put it into a paper sack. Long ago, they'd learned that storing containers like this in a plastic bag might be conducive to cross-contamination or the growth of microbes that would screw up DNA testing.

"There's other stuff that ought to be looked at," Jack said, as he eased himself out of the tent and stood up. "But, I think we ought to wait and see if the deputies are going to head up here again." He handed the sack to Mike.

"And if they don't?"

"I guess we'll be coming back. And you're sure you can get the lab to take a look at that when you get back to Denver?"

"Yes. Of course." Mike opened the SUV's door and put the sack on the seat. "I'll get it to them Monday morning."

"Good." Jack walked around the SUV and got behind the wheel as Mike climbed in and closed his door. "If whoever did that to those boys are ever caught," Jack said, resting his arms on the steering wheel and staring straight ahead, "and if this is, in fact, the boys' tent, I'm now wondering if a court would believe the chain of evidence had been preserved, or if we just fucked up by taking that can out of there?"

"Too many ifs, Jack. Who knows? And while we're on the subject, how come you think the Skoal can is evidence? Something you're not telling me?"

Jack put the key in the ignition and started the engine, glanced at Mike, and smiled. "Yeah, there's something I didn't tell you, and it's probably a long shot and might not mean anything."

Mike turned toward him, rested his back against the door, and waited for Jack to continue. When he didn't, he asked, "Well, you going to tell me, or you keeping secrets?"

"Nah, not a secret." Jack backed the SUV onto the main road and then headed it once again toward the cabin. "That fellow we passed in the pickup, the wrangler…"

"Yeah."

"He enjoys sucking on tobacco that comes in a green can."

Mike nodded and turned back forward in the seat. "Okay, then."

***

After rushing to the Whisper River Ranch, Tyler Bray stopped his pickup just outside the front door to the common area, a two-story pine building where, on the first floor just inside the entrance, couches and padded chairs spotted the space. Farther back sat a twenty-place dining table just before the hallway to the kitchen. The place had once been a dude ranch. Now it was the seasonal home to the employees of the Pinecone Lodge. Hunters and fishermen rented one- or two-room cabins spread on the ranch's property. The second story of the common area housed the manager's rooms and some guest rooms.

The ranch's manager, Calvin Semple, sat at the small desk in what he called his office. His desk was littered with paperwork piled high, a PC fed by satellite, and an ashtray formed from what he told visitors was the thigh bone of a Ute warrior killed at Milk Creek during the Meeker Massacre. One wall held the skulls of a brown bear, a buffalo, and a puma, all their glass eyes staring into the center of the room with menace. Calvin sat behind the desk smoking a stubby cigar, the smoke swirling about his head, his four-day growth of beard grayer than his gray-black hair. He barely raised his eyes from the document on his desk when he heard the knock on the door.

"Enter," he said.

Tyler walked in, closed the door behind him, and stood in front of the desk. "Cal, we got a problem."

Calvin slowly eased back in his swivel chair and motioned with his hand that Tyler should sit.

Tyler sat down in one of the two horsehair chairs and shook his head. "Ol' Jack is nosin' around the tent we put up for those boys. I knew I shoulda tore it down but didn't."

"So, take it down," Calvin said.

"Well… Sure, I gotta take it down. But since he's watchin' it and all, and I don't have a good reason to do it… Hell, I don't know what to do. If he or somebody else asks me why I'm over there, what am I supposed to say?"

"The sheriff hasn't already checked it out?"

"Not that I know of."

Calvin leaned in and tapped his cigar on the rim of the ashtray. "There's a plastic bag in the cellar. Here." He opened his desk drawer, grabbed a key, and tossed it to Tyler. "There's a lock on the door. You get that sack, relock the door, and bring the key back to me. You take that sack, and you and Ben go over there where the tent is tonight. Late tonight. Take it down and then bury everything in the canyon up the road about ten miles. Put it down in that canyon. Way down. You know where I mean?"

"Yes." Tyler nodded and rubbed his hands together. "I don't know why... It's not really my responsibility, but I've worried about it ever since..."

"Ever since you, Ben, Denman, and those others nuts had a heyday with those boys, and what happened later." Calvin stood up, turned, and looked out his window. "I'm not your priest, Tyler. I can't absolve you of this. And I frankly don't want to deal with it." He turned back around. "If you want to protect yourself and Ben, then do what you wanted to do in the first place. Get rid of the tent and everything in it. Seems simple to me."

Tyler felt the stares from the dead presences on the wall as well as Calvin's. "It was Denman and those other scumbags he brought with him. It wasn't me and Ben. We liked those boys. But, yeah, I guess that's all I can do. Have to do." He bowed his head slightly, shook it, and then stood up. He began to turn toward the door and then stopped. "What's my story, though, if somebody wants to know what I'm doing?"

Calvin sat down and resumed studying the document on his desk. "You'll think of something, I'm sure."

After driving the quarter-mile to the two-room cabin where he and

Ben Harmon lived from about the middle of May to mid-October, Tyler climbed out of his truck and saw a note stuck on the nail in the door. Ben, a twenty-year-old roamer from Missoula, had first met Tyler in a Leather/Levi bar in Denver during the National Western Stock Show a year ago. He made a meager living by guiding hunters into the White River National Forest. If he happened to get a job when Tyler wasn't there, or if Tyler was going into Vail for some reason, they'd both leave a note on the door for the other. "Back tonight. Just a day trip," the note read, signed with a B.

Tyler stuck the note in his pocket, opened the door, and walked the few steps to his cot. He knelt down and rummaged beneath it, pulling out the Colt .44 snub-nosed revolver he kept in a white tube sock. Untied the top of the sock and stuck the weapon into his waist. He fished Ben's note out of his pocket, stepped to the card table in the middle of the room, and wrote, "Don't go anywhere. I need to see you tonight. If I'm not here, wait for me." He then went outside, put the note back on the nail, climbed into this truck, and shoved the weapon between the seat and the console. The wives and girlfriends of the lawyers—the *team builders* he'd earlier taken on a horseback ride—were, as he glanced at his watch, probably already awaiting his services. He drove the way he'd come in and, again, passing the boy's tent, shook his head and damned to hell the necessity to do what he should have done days ago. He glanced down at the weapon's butt at his waist, pulled it out, and stuck it under the seat. He wondered why he'd brought the gun and concluded only that his gut had made that decision.

ELEVEN

Mike and Jack went back to the cabin where Jack grilled hamburgers and heated some barbecued beans. The potato salad was store-bought and tasted like it. They sat on the porch and talked shop, the usual habits of two old cops whose stories spanned almost three decades. Hell, even rookies of a few months, couldn't seem to find their way around a sentence unless it was peppered with war stories from the mean streets. Jack supposed if an onlooker had been present, they'd have turned away from the subject matter—the details of the killings both of them had seen. They drank a little, smoked a little, and, as the sun began to slide farther west, Jack asked Mike about his personal life.

"I go home at the end of the day," he said, "feed Gertrude—that's my cat—get comfortable on the sofa, drink a little white wine, and usually bury my nose in a book. That's pretty much the extent of my personal life, Jack."

Jack had looked him over that day when he and his crew first came up to the clearing. He'd thought Mike still seemed as tight as he always was, his smooth movements, his chest, and arms still pressing against his shirt as if he'd just curled two-hundred pounds about ten times. Now, telling him about his after-work routine, Jack was having a hard time envisioning Mike relaxing on a sofa and reading a book. And a cat?

"You still workout? Still run like you used to?"

"Not so much anymore. I don't run as far or lift as much as I used to, but I still get out there. If I don't stop smoking, though…"

"You ever… see anybody for longer than a quick minute?" Jack wondered if their short relationship had spoiled Mike for good. Or had been what he believed it was—just an impossible thing to pursue, considering their circumstances.

Mike lit another cigarette and waited a moment before answering. He shook his head. "No, other than a couple… encounters—I drive all the way to Boulder for them—I've never actually become, oh, attached, I guess is the right word, to anybody. You?"

"No, hell. It never worked out. Lived pretty much like a goddamned priest for a lot of years. Well—" Jack caught himself, knowing the stigma lately attached to priests was something he abhorred. "Well, no, not like a priest. You know what I mean? Celibate? Always finding something else to do, when the want of some desire for closeness in the night crept up on me? Hated hanging around in those dark bars, watching a bunch of old farts singing show tunes around a baby grand."

"I don't even know any show tunes," Mike said, a slight grin on his face.

They both turned and watched as Shy got a bug up his ass and began to gallop short sprints from one end of the pasture to the other and back again. Jack hadn't ridden him that day and felt a little neglectful about it. Shy was still his best friend, and he owed him the comfort of what had become their daily routine, or at least some hands-on attention.

"Let's go work Shy a bit," he said, standing up and stretching. When Mike looked at him and didn't say anything, Jack asked, "You wanna?"

Mike stood up, smashed his cigarette out in the ashtray. "Like I told you, I've never been around horses. Just be warned."

"You'll be okay." Jack put his hand on Mike's back, and they walked toward the pasture. Jack left his hand there for probably longer than he should have. Felt good to touch another human being, especially one that he'd once loved.

After they worked Shy on his turns and lunged him to a walk, trot, and canter—Jack showed Mike how to do it, and he did well—they picked up the leavings of their dinner from the table and brought everything back into the cabin. Jack cleaned up the dishes, put things away, and as the night turned cool and quiet, he built a fire. Mike and he settled on the sofa with a drink.

"I think those boys weren't killed where I found them," Jack said, breaking the silence as they both stared at the fire.

"I don't think they were either. Not enough blood on the ground. Not enough disruption of the area. You going to tell me what they told you?"

"So, you're a believer now?"

"No. But I'd like to hear it."

Jack stood up, grabbed his notes from the kitchen counter, and placed them on the coffee table. "One of the boys didn't tell me anything. The other said—" Jack pointed to what he'd written, and Mike bent down to look at the words as Jack spoke them. "—Just a game, at first. We thought they were friends."

"So, they knew their killers?"

"Thought you didn't believe in this nonsense?"

Mike looked at Jack and nodded. "I believe in your hunches, Jack."

Jack couldn't help but smile. "Okay. If that's how you want to look at it. But, yeah, as with about 90 percent of the homicides I've worked, the victims knew their killers. The boys got involved with some goddamned game that got out of hand and went too far."

"But who with?"

"Yeah. That'd be the question," Jack said, drinking the last of the bourbon in his glass. He stood up and stretched. "I put clean sheets on your bed. Put some extra blankets on the chair in there. Gets cold up here at night." He stepped around the coffee table and took his glass into the kitchen. "I'm bushed."

Mike followed him to the kitchen, stood there a moment, and smiled at Jack. "Good to see you again, Jack," he said, giving Jack a hug.

As they held each other, Jack ran his hand over Mike's back and then patted his arm. "Been too long, Mike." Jack stepped back and rinsed his glass out in the sink. "If you're going to stay up a bit, I'd appreciate it if you'd make sure that firescreen is pulled tight against the firebox before you go to bed."

Mike nodded, started to turn back to the parlor, then faced Jack once again. "I really mean it, Jack. It is good to see you again."

"I know." Jack nodded. "We'll take this slow, Mike. It's been a long time since... Well, it's just been a long time. See you in the morning." He then walked down the hallway to his bedroom.

***

"Jesus, Ty, we don't have to do this. It was Denman, not us," Ben said after Tyler told him what the deal was. "Goddamn, I wish we'd stayed closer to those boys on Sunday. And when they didn't come back to the tent… Nobody woulda seen us. Nobody up and around on a Sunday night."

Tyler had come back to the small cabin at about five-thirty and fretted his wait until Ben had walked in the door shortly after nine.

"What's done is done, Ben. What if we woulda found those boys dead up there? We'd be in the same damned mess we're in right now. Maybe worse. And, yes we do have to do this," Tyler reached for the Wild Turkey on the card table and poured himself another couple of fingers. "You want some?"

"Sure. Yeah." Ben sat down on one of the two aluminum-and-frizzed-fiberglass chairs at the table. "We get caught takin' that tent down, and there are all kinds of questions. It's not our problem."

"Yes, it is," Tyler said, handing Ben his drink.

"Christ." Ben sighed and downed the whiskey. "Just our luck, an old cop lives in the fuckin' neighborhood."

"I don't think there's anything in the tent that can come back on us, but we gotta get that stuff outta there. Cal said to bury it in the canyon."

"What canyon?"

"Along the access road, a couple miles in from I-70."

"How the hell we gonna get down that canyon in the night?"

"Don't know, but we gotta do it."

"This sucks. What's in that tent, anyway? You leave somethin' in there?"

"Maybe my fuckin' DNA, Ben. Yours, too." Tyler raised his voice.

"Okay. Get your point." Ben gulped his drink and grabbed the bottle. "Let's go do it." As he turned to walk out the door, Tyler stopped him.

"Let's wait a couple hours. We gotta grab a sack from the cellar under the main building, too. That's gotta go in with everything from the campsite. No sense doin' it 'til folks settle in for the night."

"What the hell is in the sack?"

"I don't know, and I don't want to know, Ben."

Ben shook his head, sat back down in the chair, and placed the bottle back on the table. "Guess I won't go take a shower if I'm gonna be rollin' down the canyon later."

"Guess you won't," Tyler said as he sat in the other chair, laid the key Calvin had given to him on the table and stared at it.

TWELVE

Jack woke that night after seeing in his dream the old Indian standing in the middle of the place where he'd found those boys. She'd turned around and around, her arms outstretched, her eyes closed, chanting something he could not understand. She'd stopped turning and looked up at a black sky between the tops of the trees. Kneeling down, she'd put her hands together and scooped up dirt from where he'd found the boys, letting the earth sift through her fingers.

Jack glanced at the clock and saw that it was half-past three, and then he listened a moment for a sound from where Mike slept across the hall. He heard nothing. Pulling off his bedclothes, he slid to the side of the bed and put his feet on the floor. He grabbed his robe from the foot of the bed, stood up, quietly opened the door, and walked into the parlor. Sitting down on the couch, he replayed his dream, and his mind wandered to a case Stanton, and he had worked a long time ago.

They'd been working a double homicide in the living room of a Capitol Hill Victorian built in 1879 by a silver miner who'd struck it rich near Leadville. The two men had probably died immediately because they'd suffered head wounds, the weapon held not more than two inches from their skulls. They'd theorized the sequence of the killings as one of the victim's arms lay over the other, his hand upon the other's shoulder. The scene appeared to be their last attempt at intimacy or maybe a farewell gesture from one to the other. Stanton touched each of the men as Jack stood back, looking over the richly colored room, the red velvet drapes, the antique chairs, and tables. Jack held the coroner's people back while Stanton kneeled over the bodies. When Stanton stood up, he nodded at Jack, and Jack let the attendants bag the bodies.

"One is sorry, the other regrets his kindness," Stanton said as they moved farther back in the room.

"Okay," Jack said. By that time, Jack had accepted and practiced for more than a year what Stanton had taught him, and he wondered what the two old guys had meant. About a month later, a vagrant was arrested for stealing cigarettes from a corner grocery in Capitol Hill and fought the uniformed officer who'd apprehended him. When they got him to jail, they had him dump out what was in his pockets—a set of six solid silver demitasse spoons, two gold rings set with three and four-carat diamonds, a .38-caliber pistol, and a credit card belonging to one of the victims Stanton and Jack had found in the Victorian a month ago.

Stanton and Jack sat down with the vagrant and asked him where he'd gotten the items. When he said he'd found them in an alley, Stanton asked him if the two old queers had been kind to him. The vagrant thought about that for a moment and bowed his head.

"Yes, they were," he said, and then he told the whole story as he wiped his eyes and snot flowed freely from his nose. Eventually, they learned that the old men were indeed a couple—Stanton had already figured that out. One of them was the great-grandson of the old miner who'd built the house. They'd fed the vagrant after finding him rifling through their garbage, let him sleep a night in one of their bedrooms. The next day the vagrant began to shake from withdrawals and had, as he told it, "…just lost it, man," when the old guys' largesse did not include cash money.

Jack later asked Stanton why he'd asked that question when he had. "How did you know that was the question that'd break him?"

"I didn't," Stanton said. "But *he* did."

Still later, Stanton told Jack he'd come to believe that murderers are psychically connected to their victims until they, the murderers, died, and maybe beyond even that. "They may not know it," he told Jack. "But even if they have no remorse, they will, maybe upon the moment of their own deaths, recall the final thoughts of their victims, the things you and I hear when we touch the bodies."

Why that particular remembrance arose as Jack sat alone in the dark on the sofa, with Mike sleeping just down the hall, mystified him, as did Stanton's answer and explanation. Well, he thought, he wasn't perplexed by the notion that confession is good for the soul. Anyone's soul. Still, he wondered why Stanton had chosen that moment to ask that question. He wondered too if the boys' killers would admit their deed after hearing the words they surely carried with them: *We thought they were friends.*

***

As Jack waited for the coffee to finish brewing the next morning, his landline rang. It was the Eagle County sheriff's investigator assigned to the boys' case. He told Jack he'd gotten his message, and, no, they'd not searched any unoccupied tents that he knew of. Still, he'd check with the uniforms' supervisor and let Jack know later in the day. Jack thanked him and told Mike what he'd said.

"If they didn't, they should have," Mike said as he stoked the fire Jack had started an hour earlier.

Jack carried two cups and the coffeepot into the parlor and set them on the table. "I'd like to head back over there again this morning," he said, returning to the kitchen for cream and sugar. They both sat on the sofa, and Jack poured the coffee.

"Sure," Mike said as he poured a little cream into his cup. "We can look around some more. No harm in that. Tell me about your horse, Jack."

"My horse? Well…" Jack raised his cup and watched Mike absently grab his cigarettes from the coffee table. "You want to light one up, go ahead."

"Sorry." He put the pack in his shirt pocket. "I can wait."

"Nah, hell…" Jack stood up, walked into his bedroom, and pulled two light jackets from the closet. "Here." He held one out to Mike. "Let's go out on the porch. I'll have one, too."

Once they were settled on the porch, they watched Shy lumber from the far end of the pasture and lean his head over the fence. He nodded at them a few times and snorted a bit. They both lit up.

"He hungry?" Mike asked.

"Yeah. He's always hungry."

"So, where'd you get him?"

"Got a lead on an Indian woman in Oak Creek, up in the Yampa Valley about eighty miles from here. You remember Roy Tanner?"

"Yeah. Worked vice mostly. Retired a while back."

"Right. He told me about Tess—that's the Indian's name—who he leases horses from when he goes up there to hunt. She's got a large herd she has trouble taking care of. Anyway, I've always wanted a horse and thought I'd go see her. I did, and that—" Jack gestured toward the pasture. "—is what I brought home. Tyler, the kid that passed us on the road yesterday, has taught me pretty much everything I know about horses and riding."

Mike smiled and took a sip of his coffee. "So, you said."

"Had a dream about that Indian last night," Jack said, wondering if he should tell Mike about Tess.

When all Mike said was, "Yeah," Jack decided to tell him about Stanton's trips to Steamboat Springs to *recharge his batteries.*

"And you think that's where Stanton got it? From Tess's mother?"

"Yes, I do. He never mentioned the incident, but it's too coincidental."

"What'd you dream about?"

"Oh, she was up there where I found the boys, doing some dance and chanting. She kneeled down and sifted some dirt through her fingers."

Mike smashed his cigarette out. "Does that mean anything to you?"

"Dreams always mean something, Mike. I suppose I'm subconsciously putting her in the picture. The fact she told me she can speak to the spirits of the dead long after they've been buried, or been taken from where they died, has been working on me. Right now, it occurs to me that maybe I ought to see if I can get her to come up here and take a look around."

Mike smiled again and shook his head. "Jack," he said, and he left it at that as he stood up. "You got anything to eat in there?"

"I'm sorry." Jack stood up and opened the screen door. "I was going to get something going as soon as you got up. You want eggs? Bacon?"

"That'll be fine," Mike said as he followed Jack back into the cabin.

As Jack laid the slabs of bacon in the pan, he said, "You ever think a murderer subconsciously or consciously carries the last thought of his victim with him? Something that can trigger a confession?"

Mike leaned against the counter. "Oh, Jack... You're getting way out there for me. You mean if A kills B, and B's last thought is A did it, that A will somehow respond to that little voice in his head and just confess?"

"Something like that."

"No, I don't think I believe that. Do you?"

"Yes, I believe that I do. Let me tell you what came to mind after I got up from that dream about Tess."

And, as Jack watched over the bacon and cracked eggs, he told Mike about the two old lovers who'd done a guy a favor.

***

After Jack fed Shy, Mike and he drove back to the campsite. The tent had been so visible from the road, they could see the tent wasn't there anymore before they got there. Jack pulled the SUV up to where the campsite used to be, and they both got out.

"Guess we should have helped ourselves yesterday," Mike said as he walked around the campsite where the tent used to be, his eyes focused on the ground.

Jack stood in front of the SUV, surveying the scene, looking for anything peculiar, besides the absence of everything they'd seen yesterday. "Shouldn't have driven in here," he said, knowing that if any fresh tire tracks had been in the barely damp soil, he'd just destroyed that evidence. If it proved to be evidence at all. Hell, he didn't even know if this was where the boys had camped, or if they'd camped at all before doing whatever it was that had got them murdered.

"Yeah," Mike said, glancing at where Jack had parked. He then knelt down and lightly brushed the surface of the ground with his palm. He stayed on his haunches for a minute and looked from side to side.

"It's really clean, Jack."

Jack walked the circumference of the site. Looked again at the fire pit, as he'd done the prior times they'd been here, and Mike stood and stepped next to him.

"You want to walk up the trail a bit. See if anybody heard or saw anything?" Mike asked.

Jack looked up the trail, remembering the boy, Stephen, who'd spoken to him about the *primo* campsite. He and his buddies had wanted the site, but it had already been taken by phantom campers.

"No, the nearest site was just up a way, and those boys are gone." He looked around and saw the closest tents were now about a hundred or more yards away. "My gut tells me something isn't right about this, but I've also got the feeling that we'd be wasting our time."

"All I got is time," Mike said. "And besides, I'll bet sound travels in the night around here. Somebody might have heard or even seen something."

Jack looked at Mike. "Okay," he said, nodding. "You got your badge with you?"

Mike pulled his leather badge case out of his jacket pocket and flipped it open. "Never leave home without it."

"Well, let's go," Jack said. "We'll walk, but let me move the rig off the trail." Mike waited for him to back the SUV into some scrub just off the road.

"This is a nice area, Jack," Mike said as they walked north on the road to the next turnoff where they saw a parked truck with a camper shell on the bed, and a nylon awning spread from the side of it.

"Yeah, it is. I used to think I wanted to retire to a coast, probably east, but once I came up here, I knew I wouldn't find anything I liked better. I'd come up years ago, after the divorce because I'd heard about it from a guy I'd met in one bar or another. Came up periodically after that. Stayed a few times at the lodge. When I was ready to think about retirement... Well, I just knew where I'd have to settle. Got a deal on this place, and jumped on it."

"The first time you came up, after your divorce, had we met by then?"

"No, we hadn't. But I was still coming up here after we did meet. Thought a time or two about asking if you'd want to come up with me."

"Why didn't you?"

They stepped off the road and started to walk up the trail to the camper. "I guess there're a lot of things I didn't do back then that I should have. To ask you to come with me then would have, oh, complicated things, if you know what I mean."

Mike nodded but didn't say anything.

As they stopped at the back of the camper, an older man opened the door, and a golden retriever leaped out. The dog scampered over to them, his entire body shaking with his greeting.

"Jigs, cut that out," the man said, stepping off the truck with a smile. "Sorry, fellas, but he does get excited."

Jack noticed the man was dressed for a hike—boots, cargo shorts, a water bottle strapped on his belt. He looked to be on the far side of forty, maybe even early fifties. "Morning," Jack said. "I'm Jack, and this is Mike."

They shook hands, the man said his name was Fred, and Mike ran with it. "I'm with the Colorado Bureau of Investigation," he said, showing Fred his badge. "We're just asking folks if they heard or saw anything from the campsite just west of here during the last several days and nights."

"What kind of things?"

"There was an abandoned campsite," Jack said, "just down the way. A gray domed tent that was taken down sometime yesterday night or early this morning."

Fred looked back toward where Jack had indicated, then shook his head. "No. Other than the usual stuff you hear at night. You know, just the fireside laughter and people having a good time."

"You don't remember the tent that was there?" Mike asked.

"No, I don't. I've been up here since Thursday. Jigs and me. We've been hiking the trails in the other direction."

"Okay then," Jack said. "Thank you."

They shook hands again, and Mike and Jack walked about seventy-five yards to the next campsite. In all, they spoke to six or seven folks, none of whom had seen or heard anything having to do with the gray tent. They headed back to the SUV and then went back to the cabin.

The landline was ringing when Jack opened the door. It was Tim Harrison, the lead investigator for the Eagle County Sheriff's Office. He told Jack he'd looked over the reports from the uniforms assigned to fan out and get statements from campers and the folks at the lodge. He couldn't tell me one way or the other if they'd come upon an abandoned campsite. He asked if Jack thought there was a need for him to send the men back up here, and Jack told him no. The need had vanished overnight. Jack thanked him and stepped out onto the porch, where Mike had sat down and was smoking a cigarette.

"That was the investigator," Jack said as he sat. "He can't tell from the reports if they checked that tent or not. Told him it doesn't matter now."

"You want to revisit the scene?"

"Where I found the boys?"

"Yeah."

Jack thought about that for a minute. He had intentionally stayed away since the day he'd found the boys. Had hoped the next time he visited the place, he'd have some sense of what might have happened up there, besides the obvious. But nothing he'd done to this point, even with Mike's help, had revealed anything that would further his understanding of it all. But, he thought, what the hell...

"Sure, we can head up there. Need to get Shy moving anyway. Let's tack him up. You can drive up to the lodge, and Shy and I will meet you there."

"Good," Mike said. He took one last puff on his cigarette, smashed it out, and stood.

"Unless you want to ride Shy," Jack said.

"Oh, no," Mike said, shaking his head. "That would not turn out well at all."

Jack laughed, and they both walked over to the pasture, where Jack saddled Shy, and Mike watched from a safe distance. Jack walked Shy out of the pasture, then had Mike hold the reins while he gathered his keys from the kitchen counter. He gave Mike the keys, and Mike climbed into the SUV, headed for the lodge. Jack mounted Shy, who danced around a bit, anxious with the prospect of moving.

As Shy and Jack passed the lodge's horse concession, Jack looked for Tyler but didn't see him. The place was busy. Saturday was the day when all the weekenders showed up to get in a few hours of whatever adventure they could talk about at the office or the schoolyard on Monday morning—hiking, canoeing, fishing, horseback riding.

Mike was waiting in the parking lot, and Jack told him to follow him up the trail.

Shy once again veered off the trail once they got a few yards from the scene. Jack tied him off where he could grab some grasses and saw Mike waiting for him on the trail right at the opening to the small clearing.

"You want to go first?" Mike asked.

Jack shook his head. "No. No reason to, I guess." He pulled the pine boughs back. "Go ahead."

Mike kept to the perimeter, looking at the ground in the middle of the place as he walked the circle. Jack stood just past the opening, gazing up at the sky framed by the trees, and then to where the boys had lain that day.

"Kind of creepy, Jack," Mike said, as he stopped walking and dropped to his haunches.

"Yeah, it is. Suppose it forever will be." Jack stepped into the middle of the clearing, and like Mike, he squatted, and then, like his vision of Tess, he grabbed a handful of dirt and let it sift through his fingers. He felt nothing but thought again about what Tess might see or feel if she were here. He looked at Mike. "That Indian I told you about? I think I'll get in touch with her and see if she'll come up. Nothing else seems to be panning out."

Mike stood up, stepped closer to Jack, and nodded. "Wouldn't hurt," he said. "Hell, I've heard of stranger things solving cases." They stepped out of the clearing.

They both stood off to the side of the trail as two hikers approached them. The hikers veered off the trail as they passed. One of them glanced into the recess where Jack had found the boys and frowned as she crossed her arms over her chest as if suddenly cold.

THIRTEEN

The morning was nonstop for Tyler Bray, as it seemed everyone who'd never ridden a horse had come up to the lodge to do just that. He'd not slept but a couple of hours and had left his and Ben's cabin about six that morning, with Ben still snoring contentedly on one of the cots.

Shortly after midnight, Tyler and Ben had unlocked the main building's cellar door and grabbed the black plastic sack just inside the doorframe. They then headed for the campsite, where they pulled everything from the tent as quietly as they could and put it all in trash bags except for the sleeping bags. Then they'd taken the tent down. After loading everything into Tyler's truck, they'd brushed the area down with pine boughs, and drove almost ten miles down the access road to where the western side of the landscape opened up into a deep, sandstone canyon. Tyler had pulled off to the side of the road as far as he could. They both got out and stood for a moment looking down into the chasm, its depths blacker than the night surrounding them. Tyler grabbed a shovel and two trash bags while Ben had held the flashlight along with the remaining two trash bags.

"This is fuckin' nuts," Ben said, shining the flashlight's beam on the steep slope before them.

"Just take it slow," Tyler said.

"Oh, as if I wasn't gonna do that. Why don't we just throw it down there?"

"'Cause Calvin said to bury it. Just go," Tyler said, his frustration tightening his voice.

Ben started the descent and immediately fell to his ass and began to slide down. "Jesusfuckingchrist!" He dug his heels into the loose soil and managed to stop his slide, turning the flashlight on Tyler. "You really think we're gonna get down there without killing ourselves?"

"Gimme the fuckin' flashlight," Tyler said, bracing himself and leaning down to grab the light. He fanned the beam across the downslope and saw a rock outcropping about twenty yards below. "Right there," he said. "Just ease down to that point. And no, we aren't going to try to get to the bottom."

Once Ben was reasonably secure with his footing, Tyler eased the trash bags, tent, and sleeping bags down to him. Tyler climbed down and held the flashlight as Ben dug into the slope behind them, trying to carve out a recess large enough for everything. "We won't tell Calvin we didn't get all the way to the bottom," he huffed as he dug. "Did you and Calvin ever talk any more about what happened?"

"In a roundabout way." Tyler drew his arm across his brow. "He gets pissed if I bring it up."

"Calvin always knows more than we do."

"Yeah, he does. Get the feeling sometimes even he's got a boss, and maybe that boss is somehow involved, too. See if you can shove the tent and sleeping bags in there first, then the trash bags." Tyler stepped to the side of the hole. "I try not to talk to Calvin any more than I have to."

"Know what you mean," Ben said as he dropped to his knees and packed the hole with the items. "I think we got it, partner." He stood up, and Tyler handed him the flashlight.

Tyler grabbed the shovel and started shoveling dirt back into the hole. "Get some a them rocks off to the side. We need to pack it in good."

When they'd finished their task, they climbed up the hillside again and drove back to the ranch, discussing as they had in the past their lousy luck with Calvin. Calvin had caught them together in their cabin, Tyler on top, Ben on the bottom. Ever after that, Calvin had demanded a lot from them, his silence in exchange for their absolute fealty. They'd both decided this would be their last summer at the Whisper River Ranch.

Both exhausted, they had collapsed on their cots. Tyler had woken as he always did when the first slip of sunrise entered their cabin.

***

By noon, Tyler felt as tired as he'd ever felt. With the lunchtime lull, he walked down to the lodge's small restaurant, sat down at one of only two small tables set off in the corner of the room, and ordered a burger and a beer. He watched the happy crowd sitting at the picnic-style tables and nodded at two hefty women who entered the room. He'd taken them up the trail earlier. They saw him and waved.

He felt the alcohol go straight to his head and wondered if he'd actually get through the rest of the day without telling some sonofabitch weekender to go straight to hell. *If you knew you were gonna ride a damned horse, why'd you wear tennis shoes and shorts? No sir, we don't trot the horses 'cause you'd prob'ly break your fuckin' neck!*

When he got back to the horse concession, he looked at the schedule and saw he had at least two and maybe three more trail rides to lead before he could finally go back to the cabin and get some sleep. He'd have only a half-day of work tomorrow and envisioned himself just drinking through the afternoon and collapsing when he could no longer keep his eyes open.

***

Calvin Semple walked down the stairs and into the great room where he saw Ben sitting at the far end of the common dining table eating lunch. He walked over to him and placed his hands on the top of a chair as Ben swallowed his last bite.

"You and Ty get that job done?"

Ben nodded, grabbed his beer, and took a sip. "Yessir, we did."

"All the way down in the canyon?"

Ben hesitated for a moment, then again nodded. "All the way down."

"And you got that sack of stuff from the cellar?"

"Yessir."

"Good. I want to talk to you and Ty together. Soon as he comes in tonight, you two come up and see me, or find me if I'm not in the office."

"Yessir."

Calvin gently slapped his hands on the top of the chair. "I got some more guys coming up next week. Same deal."

"Oh," Ben shook his head, "I don't know, Calvin. I—"

"It won't get outta hand this time. We'll keep it on ranch property. You just make sure you and Ty find me tonight."

"Yessir, we will."

Calvin turned and walked across the great room to the front door. He stepped out onto the porch, pulled a cigar from his shirt pocket, lit up, and then walked to his F350, sitting just beyond the porch. He climbed into the truck, started it, and drove east.

***

When they got back to the cabin, Jack asked Mike if he wanted to ride Shy. Mike said, "No, but thank you." Jack laughed as he walked Shy into the pasture, tied him off, and removed his tack.

"Here," Jack said as he came out of the shed, "you can at least help brush him down."

Mike opened the gate, came into the pasture, and took the brush Jack held out to him. "Just all over, or any specific areas?"

"Yeah, all over. You get his back, and I'll work on his neck. Don't cross his backend too close, though."

"Don't tell me he'll kick me."

"Okay, I won't. But he might. Just give him a wide berth if you step behind him."

"I could really get used to this."

"Brushing out a horse?"

"Sure. That and everything else you've got going on up here, Jack. I see the allure."

"The allure is being able to do what you want when you want to do it. It's called retirement."

"Yeah. That's the first step for sure. Don't know if I'd know how to act if I didn't have someplace to go every day and something to do that I'm good at."

Jack started brushing Shy's mane and looked at Mike, whose eyes focused on the task at hand. "You get some vacation time, come on up here for a week or two, and I'll bet you're never at a loss for something to do. And I guarantee you'll become an expert at something. Hell, you might excel at just sitting on the porch all day."

"That's what I'm afraid of." Mike studied his brush and picked out the loose hairs that had accumulated on it.

"Get his hip area," Jack said. They both saw the big pickup pull into the drive. "That's Calvin. He operates the ranch a little west of here."

Jack walked to the fence line and greeted Calvin as he stepped out of his truck.

"Hi, Jack," Calvin said as he walked toward Jack. "See you got some help."

"Yeah, that's Mike Day. Another old cop." Jack glanced at Mike and motioned for him to come to the fence. "Mike, this is Calvin Semple. He runs the ranch northwest of here."

"Nice to meet you," Mike said as they shook hands.

"Actually," Calvin said, "it's not much of a ranch anymore. I rent out rooms and cabins to the lodge's employees, and I get a lot of hunters and fishermen, too. It's a living, I guess. So, you retired like Jack here?"

Mike shook his head. "No, still working. I'm with the CBI right now."

"Uh-huh." Calvin nodded. "That was terrible about the murders. You working on that?"

"Yeah, I'm the supervisor on the case," Mike said.

Calvin smiled. "Lucky you had Jack up here to help out."

"Oh." Mike smiled too. "Jack's the best when it comes to homicides."

"So…" Calvin paused a moment. "Any new leads on what might have happened?"

Mike gave the standard answer. "It's an active case, and I can't really say."

"Understand," Calvin said, nodding. "Just thought I'd stop and say hello. Nice to meet you, Mike."

Calvin and Mike once again shook hands, and Mike and Jack watched Calvin get back into his big-ass truck and head down the road toward the lodge.

"He's an odd character," Jack said. "I always get an uneasy feeling when I'm around him."

"How so?"

"Well—" Jack took Mike's brush as they walked back to where he'd tied off Shy. "He's got the Whisper River Ranch a mile or so west of here. I've been there a couple times. Besides the lodge's employees, he rents out cabins—about eight or nine one-room affairs— to some hunters and fishermen." He put the brushes in the shed and grabbed the hoof pick. "I heard they were having a 4th of July party up there last summer and…" He lifted Shy's foreleg and picked out his hoof. "I sort of invited myself to the party. I didn't stay long. Lots of biker types. You know, the ones that you can tell are hardcore, dangerous men who were probably smoking something besides marijuana and cigarettes, though I didn't see it." Jack let loose of Shy's foreleg and raised the other one. "Seemed as though Calvin was well respected by those guys. Kind of like a Boy Scout den leader or something. He saw me standing around, taking it all in, and he ushered me away from where most of the activity was going on. I left after that. Anyway, I got the feeling that day…" He moved to Shy's rear legs and pulled one up. "Hell, you know about those *feelings* we get."

Mike didn't say anything for a minute, and then he lit a smoke. "You don't think—"

"Yeah, I've thought about it," Jack said, anticipating what Mike was going to say. "Thought about asking Tyler about Calvin and his… guests since he lives up there and all. But, hell…"

"Tyler's the kid we saw yesterday. Right? Your horse trainer?"

"Yeah, the same." Jack let Shy's hoof hit the ground and looked at Mike. "Might be Tyler's can of chew we found, too."

"So, if you talk to Tyler, Tyler talks to Calvin and… I see the problem."

"Yup." Jack put the pick back in the shed, untied Shy, and slapped him on the ass. Shy made a dash for the other end of the pasture. "And suddenly nobody knows anything. But I do have that feeling, Mike."

FOURTEEN

"What does he want to talk about?" Tyler said as he sat on his cot and pulled off his boots. He'd made it back to the cabin by six p.m. and wanted only to get some sleep.

"He said he's got some more guys coming up." Ben sat in the aluminum lawn chair, his arm resting on the card table, his hands cradling a shot glass of whiskey.

"You gotta be shittin' me." Tyler bowed his head, raised his hands to the top of his head, and held on to it as if holding something in that wanted to get out. "After everything that's happened…"

"What he said." Ben downed his whiskey.

"Pour me some a that," Tyler said, still caressing his head.

Ben filled two shot glasses nearly to the rim and handed one to Tyler. "He said it wouldn't get outta hand this time, and he'd keep it on the ranch."

Tyler grabbed the shot glass. "How's he gonna make sure a that?" He sipped the whiskey.

"Don't know." Ben gulped his shot. "But we ought to go see him. We get back here, and maybe we'll… Been feelin' horny all day, Ty.

We ain't... done it for a while."

"I don't feel like doin' anything except sleepin'. What's got you so horny?"

"Been here all day, and that goddamned prick tease Jason has been runnin' around in his joggin' shorts and no shirt. He musta had the day off. Goddamn, that is one fine specimen."

"Christ, Ben!" Tyler shook his head. "Him and Dakota, that new girl we got workin' horses is goin' at it every night. Jason gets his canoes parked at night, and they head off into the woods."

"I know it." Ben stood up and scratched his crotch. "But he is nice to look at, and what I could do to that fine ass..."

Tyler downed his whiskey, sat the shot glass on the floor, and pulled on his boots. "Well, all you're gettin' tonight is a date with your hand." He stood up and stepped to the door. "C'mon, let's go see Calvin."

***

Tyler and Ben sat in front of Calvin's desk as Calvin leaned back in his chair and huffed smoke from his mouth. They'd been sitting there for over a minute without a word said between them.

"What I told you today, Ben, about some more guys coming up for a little romp in the woods?" Calving finally broke the silence.

"Yessir," Ben said.

"Well, that's off. I went over to see Jack Dolan after I talked to you, and he's got a CBI supervisor staying with him, and..." Calvin sat forward and leaned himself halfway across the desk. "I hope you two did exactly what I told you to do because those old sonsabitches will probably figure this thing out. You did do it? Exactly like I told you to? Right?"

Ben glanced at Tyler, and Tyler stared at Calvin.

"Yes, we did," Tyler said. "Exactly what you told me to do."

"Where's the key I gave you?"

Tyler pulled the key from his pants pocket and placed it on the desk.

Calvin put the key back in the desk drawer and continued to study both of their faces before he eased himself back into his chair. "Cops are one thing. Old cops who've been around for a long time can smell a lie before you tell it. Has Jack talked to you, Ty? About the murders?"

"No. Well, yeah," Tyler said, "we've talked about it, but just, you know... We're friends. I've trained him and his horse, and we talk about a lot of things."

"But nothing to indicate he's, oh, interrogating you?"

"Hell, no."

"Has he talked to you, Ben?"

"I don't even know him," Ben said, rubbing his palms against his thighs.

Calvin turned slightly to the side and propped his feet on the desk. "I told the guys we'd maybe think about another session in a couple of months. I hate to turn away all that money, but... You know what the real kicker is to this?" Calvin put his hands behind his head. When Tyler or Ben didn't say anything, Calvin laughed. "I guess you don't. The real kicker is that the guys tried to convince me to have you two fill in as the chased if we didn't want to get anybody else up here."

"Oh, man," Tyler again shook his head. "No way is that gonna happen."

"I told them you knew the area too well, and it'd probably not be that much of a hunt. But I'm also thinking—" Calvin pulled his feet down and again leaned over the desk toward Tyler and Ben. "If you didn't do what I told you to do, or if I ever hear that you're talking to Jack or anybody else about this, well... The hunted doesn't always know when it's being hunted. You get my point?"

Both Tyler and Ben were silent and stared at Calvin for a moment, and then they both nodded in unison. "Yeah, I get your point, Calvin," Tyler said as he stood up. "Is that all?"

"Yup. That's about it. For now."

"C'mon, Ben," Tyler said, grabbing the shoulder of Ben's jean jacket.

"Nighty-night," Calvin said as Tyler and Ben walked out of his office.

**

Saturday night, Jack cooked supper again for Mike, and afterward, they sat on the porch and shot the shit. Mike brought up an old case Jack hadn't forgotten but also hadn't thought about in years.

Stanton and Jack had worked together for about three years when Stanton got a call from the Idaho Springs Chief of Police. Idaho Springs was a little mountain town about forty miles from Denver. They had about three cops at that time, the chief and two patrol officers. They also had a homicide they couldn't make heads or tails of. The chief didn't want to call the CBI in. He had some notion that if he called in the state, it would somehow reflect poorly on him and his little department. He'd heard of Stanton's uncanny ability to solve homicides, so one day he called Stanton and asked if he'd come up the next weekend and just take a look at what they had.

They went up there one Saturday, and Chief Harris laid out all the evidence for them as they drank coffee in one of the four rooms of the small department. The story was that a hiker had found the body of a young man about ten miles from the town. It was early spring, and the nights were still cold, usually below freezing, and the body was pretty well preserved. Death was from an arrow that had pierced the heart. The tip and about an inch of the shaft were found at autopsy, but the rest had been broken off. The body had other small punctures in it, all from arrows. The body had been identified as a recent runaway from a juvenile detention center in Golden. No family members had come to claim the body, and nothing the town cops had turned up had provided any new information or theories about what had happened.

Once Stanton and Jack heard all the facts the chief and his men had gathered, Stanton took Jack outside, and they both lit up their smokes. "Those wounds were all from the back or the side," Stanton said, "even the killing wound." The autopsy report confirmed as much. It noted the velocity of the arrows had been swift enough to send the shafts entirely through the soft tissue of the kid's thigh, calf, and arm. "But all from behind him or off to his side. Kind of like he'd been hunted. The blood trail they found was all over the place like the kid had been running. Wish I could have touched him."

They both went back inside after a while, and they talked some more to the chief. Stanton mentioned what he'd told Jack outside. The chief just shook his head and said, "No. That isn't possible."

Stanton tried to make his point by methodically setting out the scenario as he envisioned it, but the chief wasn't buying it.

Later that summer, some guy was arrested in Little Rock, Arkansas, after he and his buddy had raped and tortured a young girl of no more than twelve or thirteen. The girl died, and the scumbags were charged with first-degree murder. One of the men told the authorities down there it was his buddy who had actually tortured the girl. For a plea deal, he'd tell them what else his buddy had done up in Colorado a few months before.

"I remember when you and Stanton got the news on that one," Mike said after both of them had filled in the details of what they remembered of the case.

"Yes, I do. It was in the morning paper, and you set it down right on top of Stanton's desk. The headline read something like 'Idaho Springs murder victim was hunted to his death.' Seems the guy picked the kid up on the highway, hiked into the hills with him, and just told him to start running. Stanton read the story and looked at me. I stepped around his desk and read the story myself over his shoulder. I sat back down, and Stanton gave me a wink, and that was it. I don't believe we ever talked again about that one."

Mike lit another cigarette. "Not out of the realm of possibility with this one, Jack," he said, looking off into the nightfall. "You said one of the boys told you it was just a game at first."

"Yes, that's what he told me. And, no, it's not out of the realm of possibility." Jack glanced over to the pasture and saw the outline of Shy standing near the shed with his leg cocked. He then looked at Mike. "And I thought you didn't believe in the dead speaking."

"No, I still don't, Jack. Just think it's… coincidental is all."

Jack shook his head. "You staying over tomorrow?"

"No, I have to get back. Think I'll go into the office tomorrow afternoon and take a look at what my crew has come up with. I'll get that Skoal can into the lab, and then Monday I'll be ready to dig into this thing again. I hope they've identified those boys."

"They would have called if they had."

"Yeah," Mike said, "they would have."

Mike and Jack hugged each other again before they went to bed. Jack didn't know if they were both embarrassed to even suggest that they might want to sleep together. Both of them were beginning to sag a bit and turn gray. The picture of them in bed together struck Jack as a little silly. Hell, he hadn't shared a bed with anyone in more than eleven or twelve years. Oh, Mike still looked good. No question about that. But even the thought of kissing Mike struck Jack as well... Inappropriate would be the best word for it. For whatever reason, Jack always thought about what other cops, their colleagues, would think if they saw Mike and him entwined and sweating, doing the deed as they huffed themselves to exhaustion. Not a pretty picture.

As Jack lay in bed that night, he thought about the boys and the possibility that, yes, as the boy had told him, it had all just started out as a game. But he'd also said that he thought they—whoever *they* were—were his friends. Had the boys been lured into something that had gone terribly wrong? And who were *they*? Yeah, he thought, the story of his life. Who *were* they?

FIFTEEN

Mike left right after breakfast. Jack cleaned up the cabin, washed dishes, and changed sheets. Then he went out and took care of Shy's needs and, with a few cookies in hand, his wants. Thought about riding him but wanted to take care of something that had been on his mind for days. He went back into the parlor, found Tess's number in his cell, and dialed her on the landline. He heard static when she answered, so he knew she was up on her hill tending to her herd, and a conversation would be impossible. He managed to tell her who it was and asked her to call him when she got a better signal. He hung up and grabbed the notes he'd made on the boys and added everything that had occurred after his last entry, ending it with the conversation Mike and he had had last night.

He reread everything from start to finish. He was about to head outside and take Shy on that ride he'd promised himself he'd do when the phone rang. Tess was calling him back from the Depot Café in Oak Creek. He asked her what she'd think of coming down his way for a couple of days, and he'd pick her up if she needed him to. She said she and one of her sons were thinking about driving to Vail anyway, and she'd see him in a couple of days. He tried to pin her down on when she'd arrive, and she said she'd be there when she got there. He told her he'd keep his cell on him, and she could try that number, or if that didn't work, she could just wait for him at his cabin. He gave her clear directions and told her he was never gone very long. She said that'd be fine, and she'd see him soon.

Jack had known another Native, a Cheyenne when he worked patrol in downtown Denver. Shortly after he'd graduated from the Denver Police Academy, he'd been paired with a hardnosed old cop named Art O'Dell. O'Dell was a veteran of about fifteen years, and his passion was for the streets. By the time Jack became his partner, O'Dell had cruised the streets of downtown Denver more times he'd ever wanted to. O'dell had befriended a lot of street people who he ran into almost daily. One of them was a Vietnam vet, a Native by the name of Joe Jefferson. Jack got to know Joe, as well. When Joe wasn't drunk, he hustled for odd jobs, usually working for parking vendors or shop owners who never seemed to run out of things for Joe to do. Joe would sweep off the sidewalks in front of stores, monitor self-park lots to make sure people paid, run errands. That sort of thing. He also knew what a lot of the street people were up to, and he'd helped O'Dell and Jack out on quite a few petty thefts, assaults, and some robberies.

Joe and Jack would trade war stories every once in a while when O'Dell and Jack would walk through Civic Center Park, where a lot of the homeless spent their days. Some were there only to sell, buy, or steal drugs, others because they had nowhere else to go. Joe would sometimes sleep in the park and tag along with O'Dell and Jack as they'd make an early-morning walkthrough, rousing the folks and telling them to move on.

Joe had seen some heavy shit in 'Nam, as had Jack. Though they were both reluctant to talk about their war experiences with those who hadn't been there, they shared the camaraderie of fellow Marines. Joe was a bright guy and, like Tess, had what Jack came to believe was an innate mysticism about the world, life, death, and everything in between. Also, like Tess, time for Joe was not necessarily about minutes and hours, but rather something measured more by the sun and the moon, the seasons. The hours of the day were just artificial markers for which he had little value. Maybe, Jack thought, these were Native American traits that came naturally, unfettered by the white man's perception of life.

Before promoting into homicide, Jack lost track of Joe. When he started working with Stanton, he thought of Joe often once he'd taken on Stanton's own peculiar views. But, after talking to Tess that morning on the phone and understanding she obviously shared Joe's abstraction about time, he remembered one of the last times O'Dell and he had asked Joe for his assistance with a stabbing that had taken place in Civic Center Park. The victim wasn't dead when they found him but appeared as though he shortly would be. As always, nobody had seen or heard anything. Joe hadn't either, and Jack believed him.

Jack took Joe aside as O'Dell questioned some other folks. Joe told him the intentionally violent person's spirit oozes something that can be felt by others who are open to it. Later on, he'd think this was a presage of what he'd learn from Stanton. Joe told Jack he often experienced an uneasiness from such people. This almost palpable energy wafted off them even when they slept. That energy somehow lodged itself within the violent person's spirit. It was made stronger by the spirits of their victims that latched onto them. He said it was an even more palpable force if the victim had died from that violent person's hand. Jack remembered asking him how one became open to such a thing, how, as a police officer, he could learn to recognize it? Joe looked him in the eyes then and nodded. Joe told him he'd learn to recognize it soon enough. Joe had had a little to drink then, and, as Jack looked into his bloodshot eyes, he just smiled, knowing Joe was playing with him, as he sometimes did. But Joe had been right. After working with Stanton for a while, Jack *thought* Joe might have been right about this energy thing. At the point Stanton told Jack he believed a killer and his victim are forever after psychically connected, he *knew* Joe had been right.

A couple days later, Joe pointed out the hard case who had stabbed that guy in the park. The victim had died in the hospital the night of the stabbing. Jack asked Joe how he knew who it was, and Joe smiled and said he'd felt the disturbance in the guy's spirit.

After Jack finished talking with Tess, he knew he had to find Tyler and speak to him about those boys. He'd always, especially since he'd last talked to him, felt an unease coming off Tyler, and had never been able to determine why that was. He'd always just written it off as kind of a darkness the boy carried with him and left it at that. But now, well… He wanted to dig a little deeper into that. His gut hunches were pleading for it.

***

Jack tacked up Shy and rode him to the horse concession area where he saw Tyler out in the corral filling one of the water tubs and spreading flakes of alfalfa grass. He dismounted and tied Shy to a post and walked to the corral. Tyler saw him, waved, and brushed his hands together. He turned off the spigot and walked over to Jack.

"Been meanin' to stop by," Tyler said as he lifted his leg and rested his boot on the lowest fence post. "About time for another lesson?"

"Yes, it is." Jack noticed Tyler wasn't looking him in the eyes; he kept staring at the concession office where folks were lining up for their trail rides. "I wanted to talk to you, though, about the murders."

"Oh?" Tyler quickly glanced at Jack's face, then resumed his gaze elsewhere.

"Yeah. Want to pick your brain, just see if there's something we've both missed."

"Told you everything I know."

"Yes, but even the smallest detail... You might have seen something on that day or the day before that might be important. You're all over these hills every day, and—"

"Okay," Tyler said, lowering his foot to the ground. "But we've got a lot of business this morning, and it might have to wait 'til late this afternoon or maybe tonight."

"That's fine. Maybe we can do it while you give us a lesson."

"Sure," Tyler said as he began walking toward the office. "Gotta go, Jack."

Jack watched him walk away and, not for the first time, wished he was thirty years younger. We'd have a time, Tyler and me, Jack thought. He was a good-looking young man.

As Jack untied Shy's reins, it occurred to him he'd felt that unease again from Tyler, but not something evil, not something Joe would have said had come from the spirit of the dead.

***

Tyler stepped into the concession office, picked up the landline receiver, and dialed. He turned toward the wall and spoke almost in a whisper. Hanging up, he studied the whiteboard on the wall, where today's schedule was written with a red marker. He looked for Dakota and didn't see her. He went back outside and saw her helping to mount a group of six older men.

He stepped to her and put his hand on her shoulder. "Can you take my eleven o'clock for me?"

Dakota turned and smiled. "Not if they're kids. You know they won't let me take kids yet."

"I know." He shook his head. "It looks like it's just a mister and missus somebody."

"Okay, if you'll take my nine o'clock on Monday."

"I guess I could do that."

"Good. I think I might want to sleep in."

"Yeah. Okay," Tyler said. "Thanks." He walked back to the corral and topped off the water tubs, his mind racing with Jack's comments, and what Calvin would have to say when he saw him later.

***

It didn't take much to get Shy moving at a trot on the way back to the cabin. He'd been shaking his head, snorting, dancing around all the way to the lodge, and Jack had just nudged him a little on the way back, and they were off to the races. He was sorry he hadn't worked him in the pasture that morning. Tyler had taught him the first maxim of riding a young horse was to work out that horse's yah-yahs—

short gallops, kicking, rolling—before even thinking about riding them. Jack hadn't done that. In fact, he hadn't ridden him in a few days except for that slow walk up to the scene with Mike, and Shy was sure letting him know about that. When they got back to the cabin, Jack took Shy's tack off and worked him in the pasture for an hour. Better late than never.

After lunch, Jack went outside, grabbed his wheelbarrow and rake, and cleaned up the droppings in the pasture. When he was putting things away, he happened to look north of the cabin and saw Tyler riding Bear on the back trail that led to the Whisper River Ranch. He wondered why Tyler wasn't driving up there, and then he answered his own question or thought he had. Tyler was trying to get to the ranch without Jack seeing him.

Jack took a shower and then again sat down with his notes. He'd formed some theories and hoped Tess could help him work through them. He was just about to get busy and make up the beds when the landline rang. It was Mike calling from the CBI office.

Mike told him his crew had been checking missing persons reports from several Colorado jurisdictions that came through the NCIC system. They'd not come up with anything that might be related to the dead boys. He also said that he'd gotten the Skoal can into the lab, and it'd be another week or so for the DNA testing to be complete. He asked Jack about his day, and Jack told him he was going to talk to Tyler in more detail about the homicides. Mike cautioned him to be careful.

"You could send people running for cover, Jack," Mike said.

"What we've got, though, is pretty much of nothing," Jack said. "We both know that theories are great if they pan out. Only one way to test a theory."

"Yeah, I know. But, maybe you ought to wait until we at least check out that tobacco can. If we find a print, you'll have somewhere to start. DNA match would even be better."

When Mike said that it dawned on Jack, he'd somehow have to collect a DNA sample from Tyler. "Yes, it would. Haven't thought about how I'm going to do that. Maybe I'll just ply him with bourbon. Make a move on him and get a swab of something or pluck a few of his hairs out."

"Hah! That's a party I'd like to attend."

"Well, come on up. You'll even have clean sheets."

Mike told Jack his offer was tempting, and he was serious about that. They agreed that Mike would come up again before the summer was over, or if there were any more developments in the case. They said their good-byes, and Jack hung up the phone.

SIXTEEN

As he approached the ranch's common building, Tyler saw Calvin walking toward it. He reined Bear, dismounted, and tied the horse off to a porch post.

"You look harried and harassed," Calvin said, slapping Tyler on the shoulder. "What's up?"

Tyler took off his hat and wiped his brow with his shirtsleeve. "Jack wants to talk to me about the murders. I agreed to meet him at his place later."

Calvin stared at him for a moment, and then he reached into his chest pocket and pulled out a cigar. "That's how he said it? Specifically, he wants to talk about the murders?"

"Yeah. He was pretty specific."

Calvin looked around and nodded toward the front door. "Let's go up to the office."

Tyler followed Calvin upstairs, taking a seat in front of the desk. Calvin stepped to the window and looked outside.

"So, I guess he thinks you might have had something to do with it?" Calvin said without turning around.

"No. Hell, no. He just said he wanted to pick my brain to see if I could remember anything about that day."

"And do you?" Calvin turned around and looked directly at Tyler's eyes.

Tyler stared back. "You know as well as I do what I remember."

"Only thing I remember is all the hubbub going on when the law came up here because an old cop found some bodies up in the hills. That's all I remember, Tyler. Or, that's what I was told. Hell, I was in Denver when it all came down."

"Okay," Tyler said. "I know. And that's all I can tell him. I don't remember nothin'."

Calvin sat down and reached for a stick match. "Thing is—" He lit his cigar and sucked on it to get it glowing. "Cops have a way of digging until they find pay dirt."

"Well, he ain't gonna get no pay dirt from me."

"Uh-huh." Calvin huffed a cloud over Tyler's head. "You're going to outsmart an old cop, Tyler? He's probably chewed up and spit out more liars with better lies than you've got a thousand times over? That what you're going to do?"

"I... You gonna tell me what you got on your mind about this? You think I'm too stupid to just keep my fuckin' mouth shut?"

"I think—" Calvin paused, stood up again, and stepped to the front of the desk. "I think you need to disappear." He looked down at Tyler and leaned against the desk's edge.

Tyler looked up, studied Calvin's face for a moment, and smiled. "You're kidding. Right?"

"Not at all. You've become a liability, and I can't have liabilities. Ben needs to disappear, too."

Tyler started to stand, but Calvin raised his foot and lightly shoved it against Tyler's stomach. "I'm serious about this. I'll give you both five-hundred dollars, and you can clear out of here today. Head for Wyoming or Montana or some damned place that'll get you out of sight and mind."

When Calvin placed his foot back on the floor, Tyler eased up and walked to the door. "This ain't right, and you know it."

Calvin sat back down behind his desk. "I know that if you screw up, if you tell that sonofabitch, Jack, anything that might get his curiosity up, then we're all in for some serious business. You and Ben were accessories to murder, besides destroying evidence. How do you think you and Ben will handle prison, Tyler? Lots of ass rape going on in prisons, I hear."

"You'd be on the hot seat, too."

"Hah! No, not me. I was in Denver when it all went down."

"You fuckin' arranged the whole thing."

"Prove it. Only Ben can corroborate such a thing, and, well, Ben isn't the brightest bulb."

"You're one evil motherfucker."

Calvin slapped his hand against the desktop. "Either you get the hell out of here and out of Colorado on your own, or I'll find a way to do it for you."

"What's that supposed to mean?"

"You know what it means, Tyler."

Tyler matched Calvin's stare. Both men were silent for a moment, and then Tyler bowed his head. "Okay," he said, raising his head and shaking it. "Gotta get my horse outta here, too."

"Trailers for sale all over the place. Shouldn't be a problem. You tell Ben what I said. Tell him what I said about the alternative if you boys don't get packing."

Tyler turned and reached for the doorknob. "I think it's gonna take about a thousand for each of us," he said, looking at Calvin over his shoulder. "Maybe more, dependin' on what I can get a trailer for. Might take a while for us to find work, too."

"You do what you need to do. I just want you two out of here by tonight."

"We'll need cash."

"I've got it."

Tyler opened the door, gave Calvin one last look, and walked out of the office.

***

When Tyler didn't show up by seven that evening, Jack called Mike. They both agreed there wasn't a helluva lot either of them could do. Jack told him he might drive up to the ranch and see if he could find Tyler, but Mike again suggested he wait for the results of the lab work on the Skoal can.

"If the lab can't match any prints to the deceased," Jack said, "then I suspect the cavalry will be coming up here to have a little sit-down with Tyler to get his prints. If they don't find anything, then I'll have wasted a few days just sitting on my hands."

"Both true, if we tell the cavalry about our suspicions," Mike said. "And, I'll be leading the charge."

"I guess I just want to satisfy that feeling in my gut, Mike."

"Well, you do what you have to do. If they were involved, I suspect they're now alerted. If they don't clam up, they'll probably just vanish. If you go up there, you better take your weapon."

"Seldom leave home anymore without it, Mike."

Jack did grab his weapon and drove up to the ranch. He didn't know where Tyler lived, so he stopped at the main building, walked in, and saw a few folks hanging around the large dining table. They were all young people, the ones who worked at the lodge, mostly whom he'd seen at one time or another, and a few he'd never seen.

One young woman recognized him and said with a smile, "Hi, Mister Dolan."

Jack greeted them and asked his question. "I'm looking for Tyler Bray, the horse wrangler." A couple of the kids looked at one another, and then the young woman said Tyler and his roommate, Ben, had moved out late that afternoon.

Jack didn't think his surprise was evident to them as he digested what he'd just been told. "Do you know where they went?"

"Jack Dolan, what brings you here?" Jack heard Calvin's voice behind him, turned, and there he was with that ever-present cigar in his mouth, his smile spread across his face.

"Hello, Calvin. I was just asking about Tyler Bray."

Calvin put his hand on Jack's shoulder. "Let's go up to the office," he said, slipping his hand under Jack's arm and putting a little pressure on it.

Jack nodded and followed him up the stairs. He sat down in front of his desk, and Calvin offered him a drink.

"If you've got bourbon, sure," Jack said, noticing the stuffed heads on the wall.

"Sure do." Calvin opened a small credenza under those heads and pulled out a bottle and two glasses. "You need ice?"

"Not unless you've got it."

"I don't, but I can get some."

"No need for that. So, I hear Tyler has moved on."

Calvin poured about a finger in both glasses, handed Jack one, and took the other, then sat behind his desk. "Yeah, he did. He came to see me earlier, and he said he and his buddy, Ben, had decided to move on."

"You know where they're headed?"

"He didn't say, but the kind of work they do, I expect somewhere rural."

"Did he take his horse?"

"Yes, he did. Bought a trailer cheap from somebody around here, packed up his things, and off he went."

Jack took a sip of his bourbon as Calvin picked up a pen and began to tap it on his desktop. "Kind of sudden, wasn't it?"

"Oh, you know these types, Jack. They get a hair up their ass to move on, and they just do it—the cowboy way, if you know what I mean."

"Yeah." Jack nodded. "Go wherever the winds blow them."

"Exactly."

"Let me ask you something if you don't mind."

"Not at all."

"Did the Eagle County sheriffs talk to you about the murders of those two boys?"

Calvin stopped tapping his pen and downed his bourbon. "Two of them came over here the day you found the bodies. They talked to some of the folks that were around at that time. Or, so I was told."

"Were you... around for that?"

"No, no, I wasn't. As to being here when the murders happened... Let's see..." He stood up and walked over to the credenza. "I believe I'd gone into Denver a few days before those boys were killed." He poured himself some more bourbon, raised the bottle, and held it out toward Jack.

"I'm fine," Jack said. "So, if you had been around, would you have had anything to say about it? And, by the way, I don't think they've yet to figure out when those boys were murdered, just a broad time-frame."

Calvin walked back behind his desk and sat down. "One can assume, Jack, that the murders happened a day or two before you found the bodies. And, no, I wouldn't have had a thing to tell anybody."

"Nothing?"

"Nothing," Calvin said, staring directly at Jack with a smile. "The CBI come up with anything yet?"

"Not since we last talked, Calvin. Believe that was just yesterday."

"Oh yeah. Forgot about that."

Jack sipped a bit more of his drink, stood up, and put the glass on the desk. "Tyler's got one of my bits. If you hear from him, tell him I'd pay to have it shipped to me. Or, maybe he left it wherever he was staying. Or, better yet, if he's got a cell, you could give me his number, and I'll just give him a call."

"I just looked at his cabin a little while ago, and everything's gone. And, no, he didn't have a cell." Calvin stood up but made no effort to come from behind the desk.

"Okay." Jack nodded. "You mind if I take a look at his cabin?"

"Got it all locked up."

When Calvin didn't say anything else, Jack said, "Could you un-lock it?"

Calvin sat back down, picked up his pen, and started tapping again. "Nothing to see, Jack."

"Okay. Thanks for the drink." Jack set the glass on the desk, opened the door, and stepped out. As he walked down the stairs, he saw a couple of young people still at the dining table. Looked over his shoulder to see if Calvin had come out. Not seeing him, he stepped over to the table. Excusing himself, he asked the two young women if they knew where Tyler Bray's cabin was.

"Sure," they both said.

"Could you show it to me, or give me directions?"

They stood up and came from behind the table. "It's just a couple cabins down," one of them said. "C'mon, we'll show you."

Jack followed the girls outside, and they all walked west along a dirt road.

"Did Tyler tell anybody where he was going?" Jack asked.

"He and Ben were gone before we even got off work," one said.

"How'd you find out that they'd left for good?"

"I think somebody told us first thing when we got back here from work. Who told us that?"

"I think," the other girl said, "it was Dakota. Said something about the queers have flown the coop."

Jack stopped and watched the girls continue down the road. "The queers?" he said after them.

"Oh yeah," one girl said as they continued to walk. "Tyler and Ben

147

were an item. Everybody knew."

Jack caught up with them, and they stopped and pointed to a cabin about fifty yards away. "That's it," one of them said.

"Thank you," Jack said as the girls turned around and walked back the way they'd come.

***

As Calvin sat at his desk, thinking about how this thing was getting out of hand, his cell rang. He looked at the readout. Miguel. When the call ended, he laid the cell down and felt as though his blood had just drained from the body.

SEVENTEEN

Gertrude wasn't letting Mike off the hook for leaving her for two whole nights, and she hadn't stopped demanding attention since he'd retrieved her from his neighbor late in the morning. It hadn't helped that he'd gone into the office for a couple of hours, either. When he walked in the door shortly past six that evening, she was bawling from the couch. Tried to cuddle her for a bit, but she demanded to be let down and began to strut through the condo, giving voice to her discontent. He fed her and fixed himself a sandwich, and then both of them settled on the couch.

He reread the reports from his crew, but he wished he had more information. He knew he'd have to wait for the Eagle County coroner's findings for any hope the bodies could be identified. If they couldn't be identified by forensics, he'd have to ratchet up the efforts to look into the missing persons reports that came through the NCIC, even expanding the search to other states besides Colorado.

He stood up, walked into the kitchen area, pulled the bottle of Chardonnay from the refrigerator, and grabbed a jelly jar from the counter. He sat back down on the couch and poured his drink. Gertrude crawled into his lap.

"Sorry I left you, kiddo," he said, scratching the cat's head. "Got some bad business going on up in the hills." He sipped from the jar and immediately wanted a cigarette. But that would mean jostling Gertrude from her loll, where she was finally at ease, audibly purring.

Mike thought about his visit with Jack. Besides both of their predictable passions to do what they'd done best for so many years—investigate homicides—there'd been something else. At least for Mike, there had been. He was sorry he hadn't talked to Jack about this *something else* that had arisen almost immediately when Jack had met him at the base of the trail just off I-70.

He'd been anxious about the trip. It had stirred up old emotions he thought he'd left behind in a secret place he'd rarely visited over the last couple of decades or so. Jack had once been a gentle lover, albeit without any long-standing commitments from either of them. They'd both known it wouldn't work, and finally, Jack had broken it off. Mike had at the time agreed that, yes, it was dangerous what they were doing, and, yes, sooner or later, they'd be found out. Their careers would be lost, their dignity destroyed. Neither of them had seen much hope for themselves in the ever-evolving acceptance of gays and lesbians in America's police forces. Still, Mike had thought he and Jack could overcome whatever might happen to them.

Even the Denver Police Department had eventually come around. By that time, though, Mike was well into his forties, and Jack was fifty-something. As Mike had sped toward the Eisenhower Tunnel that Friday morning, he'd smiled with the image of Jack and he walking into the department one day holding hands, and announcing to their fellow officers they were gay, had been all their lives, and everybody could just get over it. The reaction might have been polite, but the silent shunnings would never have ceased. Jack and he would have been pariahs; two old cops who had fooled the others into believing they were just like them—hard-nosed woman chasers who simply preferred the single life. Cops would always accept their fellow officers' quirks. Mike doubted they would have been willing to accept two liars amongst them, especially with what that lie had been.

When Mike saw Jack step out of his SUV that morning, there had been something just so right about that. And when he'd finally gotten to Jack's cabin, met Jack's horse, and saw the contentment, no, the peace in Jack's eyes, well... Mike knew everything he'd been feeling lately about the job wasn't worth much more of his life. What Jack had was worth it. Hell, Jack was worth it, but that'd been what Mike hadn't talked about. Not that he was seeing himself living with Jack, riding horses, and basking in the great outdoors. Or was he?

Mike looked at Gertrude and saw she was fast asleep. Still wanting that cigarette, he started to ease his arm toward the coffee table to grab the pack when his landline rang. Gertrude opened her eyes and sprang up like a jack-in-the-box.

Mike reached for the receiver. "This is Mike."

"Sorry to be calling so late," Jack said.

"Hell, it's not late, Jack. I was just having that first sip of wine."

"Reading another book?"

"No. Been thinking about the boys, the case."

"That's what I'm calling about. Tyler and his roommate... well, I guess he was more than a roommate—name's Ben, and I guess they were lovers—"

"You're kidding me?"

"Not kidding. Seems everybody at the ranch knew they were. I

151

wouldn't have guessed it, but… Anyway, Tyler and Ben moved out. I talked to Calvin about it, and he said they just got a hair to move on."

"Did you talk to him before he left?"

"No, he never showed up. I saw him riding his horse on a back trail toward the ranch not long before he was to come and see me."

"Trying to sneak up there without being noticed?"

"I suspect so. When he didn't show this evening, I went up there and talked to Calvin. He said they'd cleaned out everything in their cabin, bought a horse trailer somewhere, and that was that. I asked Calvin if I could take a look at their cabin, and he told me it was all locked up, and there wasn't anything left there to see. He actually refused to let me see the place."

"Curiouser and curiouser."

"Yeah, but I found a couple girls who showed me where the cabin was, and it wasn't locked up—the door was actually hanging open."

"Wow." Mike lit a cigarette.

"I didn't have a flashlight on me, but the power was still on. They left some stuff there: utensils, glasses, clothes. I put a bunch of it in a sack I found on the floor and brought it back with me."

"Calvin see you do this?"

"Not that I know of. From what I could tell, he stayed in his office. At least the light was still on when I passed it."

"Good. We can have the lab look for DNA." Mike gently swatted Gertrude, who had jumped on his shoulder and was pawing at his hair.

"Gotta get it down there to you, though. I don't want to leave right now. Any way you know of that I can get it to you?"

"I'll call the Eagle County sheriff and see if they'll pick it up and bring it to Denver. Tomorrow's Monday, and I'll meet them at the office. Yeah, I can do this, Jack."

"Good deal. Just let me know, and I'll meet them at the I-70 turn-off."

"Will do. Get some sleep, Jack."

"Oh, I will. Feel like I've been through a wringer. One other thing, it'd be nice if we could put out a bulletin over NCIC with Tyler's and Ben's descriptions, the truck pulling a trailer. Can you do that, too?"

"Already decided to. I'll call as soon as I hang up. What are their last names?"

"Bray. B-R-A-Y. Blue Ford F250. Never had a reason to memorize the license plate, but believe it started with BP. Don't know what Ben's last name is."

"Never knew a cop who didn't consciously or subconsciously look at license plates."

"Yeah, well… I hope that's it."

"I'll get on it. Now get some sleep."

"Thanks, Mike."

"Good night, Jack."

Mike immediately dialed the main number for the CBI. He told the civilian who answered what he wanted and asked that he be notified when they found a match for the name, the vehicle, and when the bulletin had been issued. He emphasized it was time-critical, and then he hung up.

As he reached for the wine, Gertrude again nestled into his lap.

"Too many coincidences, baby," he said, stroking her head. He pictured Jack sitting before the fire, maybe with a glass of bourbon in his hand, probably thinking the same thing.

***

Jack hung up, brought his notes up to date, and reread everything from beginning to end. It occurred to him, not for the first time, that something about the Whisper River Ranch wasn't quite right. Or maybe it was just Calvin who'd become for him a mystery worth pursuing. It had been at the back of his mind when he was talking to Mike, but he hadn't mentioned it and didn't want to bother Mike again. He was curious about who actually owned the ranch and who Calvin Semple was—his history, his criminal record if he had one. If Jack had had a computer, he could have dug into those questions some time ago. But he'd promised himself when he moved to the cabin that he wouldn't do that. He'd had enough of computers the last several years he'd worked and didn't need that distraction.

Jack mixed up the embers in the fireplace, stepped out onto the porch, and looked for Shy in the pasture. He saw him out there, the moonlight seeming to have picked the horse to shine upon. Shy stood in the middle of the pasture, unmoving, probably sleeping. Jack was anxious for Tess to see him, to see how he'd developed into a fine horse, and he a passable rider. She would be happy about that.

When Jack went back inside, he looked at the sack of stuff he'd taken from Tyler's cabin. He stepped into the kitchen area, pulled two plastic baggies from the box, picked up the sack, put it on his coffee table, and opened it up. He put the baggies on like gloves, looked into the sack and pulled out a crumpled up, nasty-looking pair of underwear. Next came three filthy white socks, then a drinking glass, a shot glass, two forks, and a spoon. He pulled out a hand towel that was stiff with something and thought he knew what that something was. The last item was a three-inch-tall teddy bear dressed in a cowboy outfit, the word "Love" on one side of the vest and a heart on the other side. He studied the items for a moment and was sure a lab could get a good sample of DNA or hairs from most of them. He put everything back in the sack, took off the baggies, turned off the lights in the parlor, rechecked the fireplace, and then he went to bed.

***

Having slept most of Sunday, Harley Sweet woke up with a raging headache. He didn't regret the time he'd had in Vail, just that he'd spent too much time with the lovely ladies, the booze, and the nose candy one of them had insisted he try. He quickly showered and figured it would take about an hour to get to the Whisper River Ranch, where he'd have a conversation with Calvin Semple. He'd never met the man, but Miguel had told him to sit down with Semple and have a little talk about the situation that, in Miguel's words, "… was working its way to nothing good." Miguel hadn't told him to do anything other than just talk to Calvin. He'd also said to call him as soon as he was finished with the conversation. "You see what he has to say, tell me, and I'll let you know what we're going to do about it." Harley had understood what Miguel was telling him and perhaps preparing him for.

EIGHTEEN

Calvin Semple had watched Jack from his window with the two girls who'd taken Jack down the road toward the cabin. Had thought a moment about stopping Jack, telling him to get off the property, but knew immediately that was a bad idea. He couldn't afford any more attention, especially from the old cop.

He'd had his phone in his hand, ready to call Miguel Rosario and tell him about the latest developments, but he put the phone down for the same reasons he hadn't stopped Jack. As well as he'd covered his tracks for anything Jack could come up with, that wouldn't be possible with Miguel. And he sure didn't want to bring more scrutiny on himself from the one man who knew the entire story. If he told him what had just happened, he had no doubt Miguel would probably conclude he was as expendable as Denman and the old lawyer. When one of Denman's compadres had called to report what had happened to Denman and Schrock in Oak Creek, he began to wonder about his own mortality.

Calvin sat at his desk and tapped his pen on top of it. His third whiskey had done little to dull his senses. After considering his options for two hours, there was only one conclusion: he needed to get the hell out of there. The sooner, the better. He began packing his belongings and carrying them down to his truck.

***

Jack woke up, turned on his bedside lamp, and sat up. He hadn't really thought about it, but his subconscious had been yelling at him as he slept. If Tyler and his friend Ben had just packed up and left to avoid any more dealings with him or the law, Calvin wouldn't be far behind. He looked at his wall clock and saw it was just past eleven. If Calvin was going to bolt, how soon would he do it? Calvin hadn't ever impressed Jack as being a stupid man. When he'd spoken to him earlier, they'd both known that the screws were tightening, that both Calvin and Tyler were in his sights. Jack quickly dressed, grabbed his weapon, and was out the door in fifteen minutes. He thought about taking Shy along the same back trail Tyler had used, and hopefully, their approach would not be seen. They'd never ridden at night, though, and the prospect of doing that wasn't something he wanted to tackle right now. He decided he'd take the SUV instead, park it off to the side of the road maybe a hundred or so yards before he got to the complex, and just walk the rest of the way in.

When he walked to within fifty yards of the common building, the lighting on the porch revealed Calvin leaning on his truck, talking to somebody. The truck's bed was loaded with stuff, and Jack knew his hunch had been right—Calvin was getting out. Jack continued to watch the two talk and thought the other person looked like a kid, maybe in his early twenties. Maybe just one of Calvin's tenants, he thought. After a while, the kid stepped away from the truck, pulled what looked like a cell phone from his pocket, and studied it for a minute. The kid turned back to Calvin, said something, and they both went into the building, probably to use a landline if that was the kid's intent.

As Jack moved in closer, keeping behind the few pine trees that scattered the area, he looked up to Calvin's office and saw the kid standing by the window, a phone to his ear. Then Calvin came out the front door, lit up a cigar, and leaned against the front end of his truck.

When the kid came back outside, he and Calvin recommenced their conversation. At one point, Calvin kicked the dirt and raised his voice to where even Jack could hear it. "Goddamnit," he said, "I will not." Calvin walked back into the building, and the kid remained outside, once again trying to use his cell. He obviously wasn't getting a signal and looked in all directions as if in a quandary.

Jack had no idea what was going on, except Calvin was packed and ready to go. Who was the kid? What was Calvin *not* going to do? Jack then thought that if Calvin did leave, he couldn't stop him. He watched the kid for a few more minutes, then walked back to the SUV. The warning from his subconscious had been right. But what could he do about that? He didn't know.

Jack started the SUV and saw headlights coming down the road. His first thought was how could he explain his presence to Calvin, or if Calvin would even stop to inquire. But it wasn't Calvin. It was another truck, and as Jack was framed in the headlights, the truck slowed and stopped. It was the kid.

The kid hung his head out the window and gave Jack a wave.

"Howdy."

"Hello," Jack said. He got out of the SUV and walked toward him, trying to come up with an excuse for being where he was so late at night.

"I was wondering if you could tell me where I can find a telephone or a strong cell signal."

"Cells are iffy up here. I've got a landline you could use." Jack thought it almost providential he might discover who this kid was and what he and Calvin had been talking about.

"That would be great," he said, smiling.

"Okay, just follow me, and we'll head to my place."

He nodded and backed up a bit so Jack could turn the SUV around. Jack looked in the rearview, and was reminded of the few times he'd picked up someone from a bar and had used those same words: "Just follow me."

"I'm Harley," the kid said as they shook hands, a distinct countrified tinge to his voice. "Real convenient you bein' where you were just now."

"Ah, yeah," Jack said, still not coming up with a reason why he'd been where he was. "It's right here on the coffee table." Jack gathered his notes and stepped into the kitchen area.

"Thank you. Mind if I sit?"

"No, of course not." He was definitely a handsome kid with good manners.

Harley sat down and punched in a number. He turned his back to Jack as he waited for whomever he was calling to pick up. Jack feigned disinterest and began rinsing off the dishes he hadn't yet washed.

"He told me he won't do it," Harley said in a hushed voice. He listened for a second. "Yeah, the road up here is pretty deserted in places. ...Don't know if that'd work bein' dark and all, and him in the truck." After another pause, he nodded. "Yeah. Okay. I'll see what I can do." He hung up the phone, stood up, and turned. His serious expression quickly turned into a smile. "I sure appreciate this. Just had an emergency I needed to take care of."

"No problem," Jack said, stepping into the parlor. "You're new to the area then?"

"Oh, just passin' through. Have a friend up at the ranch there, and, well..." He stepped to the door. "I better get on the road. Thank you again."

Jack watched him from the door as he got back into his truck, turned around, and headed back the way he'd come. Jack couldn't see the intersection that would take him back to the ranch, or the other way that would eventually get him back to I-70. What he had seen, though, when Harley had sat down and leaned over, was the butt of a small semi-automatic weapon stuck in his waist.

***

After hanging up his phone, Calvin leaned his elbows on his desk, his hands holding his chin, and stared back at the glassy-eyed critters hanging on his wall. Miguel had called him after speaking with Harley, and he'd been adamant about taking care of the Tyler and Ben problem. Calvin didn't like adamant. And no one had ever talked to him the way Miguel had. Sure, on second thought, maybe he should have told Miguel he'd sent Tyler and Ben away. He knew, though, how Miguel wanted Tyler and Ben taken care of. Although he could have done that, he hadn't wanted to. But sending Harley to check up on him? No, he didn't like any part of it. He'd have to adjust his options. He reached under his desk and pulled his .45 from the little compartment he kept it in. He chambered a shell, opened his side drawer, and grabbed the four loaded magazines he always kept there. He stood up, walked to the door, and engaged the lock. He returned to his desk and sat back down. He didn't take lightly that Harley was prowling around in the dark. He knew what Harley did for Miguel, and he did it well.

NINETEEN

Jack didn't sleep well after the kid left and gave up on it at about five in the morning. He got up, dressed, fixed coffee, grabbed his notes, and carried them to the coffee table where he updated them again. Took his coffee out to the porch, where Shy saw him first thing and began to snort and act out as if scolding him for his breakfast. Jack walked over to the shed, tossed Shy some flakes of hay, filled a bucket a quarter full with the supplement he seemed to prefer, and held the bucket out to him.

As Jack was walking back to the cabin, he wondered again about that kid, Harley, and that weapon stuck in his pants. Sure, lots of folks up here carried. Some were quite brazen about it, their weapons kept in full view. But having witnessed the conversation between Harley and Calvin and the kid's conversation with someone else on the phone, Jack began to wonder if the kid's presence didn't have something to do with Tyler and his friend leaving. But what could it have been? And when would Calvin decide to leave as well?

Jack poured another cup of coffee, went back out onto the porch, and sat down. He felt like he'd been up all night, and actually had been except for the hour or so he'd drifted off. He was anxious for

Mike to call with any updates since they'd last spoke. His mind took him to another time, though, and he remembered Stanton. He had lost sleep quite a few times when they'd seen an urgency to pin down one suspect or another who they'd determined was about to bolt. He smiled, knowing he was doing a helluva lot of reminiscing lately, concluding it came with the creep into his senior years.

It'd been early on a Saturday morning years ago when Stanton and Jack had been awakened and dispatched to City Park in Denver. A young woman had been found under a tree, most likely strangled to death, her shirt laying by her side, her shorts and panties pulled down to her ankles. The person who had called it in less than an hour before said they'd seen a man running from the scene. Stanton and Jack found her lying on her stomach with her arms spread as if beseeching something. When Stanton turned her over, her eyes were open. He touched her, jerked his hand a bit, and looked at Jack.

"She didn't want to get on a bus. Going on a trip. His name is Jim or something similar."

Mike had been with them then, and they told him to finish the scene while they took off for the bus depot downtown. Once they got there, they looked around, saw the usual fare one sees at inner-city depots, including several desperate-looking folks biding their time before boarding whatever bus would take them wherever. They saw one young man just about to board a bus, ticket in his hand, his face newly scratched, and grass stains on his jeans. Stanton winked at Jack, and they both approached the young man. Stanton showed him his badge and told him he wanted to speak with him for a minute. The young man stepped away from the bus with them and started to shake. He bolted for the street, but Jack grabbed his shirt, pulled him back. Stanton stepped in and shoved the young man's arms behind his back.

"Your name Jim?" Stanton asked.

"No, it isn't."

Jack pulled the kid's wallet from his back pocket, looked at his driver's license, and told Stanton his name was Timothy, probably Tim for short. "Close enough," Stanton said. They took him into custody and learned he was about to embark on a bus to Reno. At headquarters an hour later, when out of the blue, Stanton had asked the kid why the girl hadn't wanted to get on the bus, the kid put his palms against the sides of this head and started talking. He told them the girl had changed her mind about going with him at the last minute, and they had gone into the park to discuss that. He'd only met her the night before, and she'd told him she wanted to get the hell out of Denver. He'd offered her a ticket to Reno, she'd accepted, and then she got cold feet. He said he'd gotten carried away when he thought a little loving would convince her to agree to come with him. She'd started screaming, and that had been that. Jack suspected the case would have become cold in a heartbeat, or at least as soon as that bus pulled out of the terminal.

Jack understood a cop learns a lot of lessons by just doing the job. Can't read that stuff in a manual, nor could anyone have fathomed such a thing because the dead had spoken of it... except for Stanton and Jack.

Jack finished his second cup of coffee, wishing the boy would have told him more on the day he'd found them off that trail. He again wondered if Tess could help him out once she got there. She'd told him she could read from the killing ground itself, or that is what he remembered her to have said. He hoped he was right about that.

As Jack rinsed out his cup, the phone rang. Mike told him they'd found Tyler's vehicle plate in the system, and the NCIC bulletin had been issued. Then Jack told him what had happened when he'd gone back up to the ranch last night, and about meeting the kid who needed to use his phone.

"So, Calvin is feeling some heat, too?"

"Apparently. He's even got his truck loaded. And he sure as hell didn't like what that kid told him. What I heard of the kid's conversation, though—if it was about what I think it was—it's pretty clear that somebody somewhere is calling the shots on this. Which reminds me, can you find out who owns that ranch?"

"What's the full name? Whisper something?"

"Whisper River Ranch."

"Okay. I'm at the office now, and I'll do a search. Got an email from the sheriff up there. He said the autopsy results will be available tomorrow. And that's about all that I've got going on."

"Good. You'll give me a call, then?"

"Oh, yeah. If you had a computer, Jack, I'd just send the whole thing up to you."

"No, I'm done with computers. They remind me of all the reasons I moved up here. And no possible missing persons' matches have come in?"

"Nothing on my desk yet. I expect that'll take a while, though."

"Okay."

"Your Indian coming up to see you?"

"Yeah, she's coming, but I don't know when. Tess is a free spirit in every sense of those words. She said she'd see me soon, though."

"Don't like the idea of that kid with a pistol stuck in his belt, Jack. He didn't know who you were, I take it."

"No way he could have unless Calvin told him. If he'd known, I doubt he would have stepped over my threshold. He was a looker, Mike."

"Seems you attract the lookers, Jack."

"Hah! Wish that were the case. Then again, maybe I don't. Getting too old for carousing."

Mike was quiet for a moment. "Well, I'll let you go. Be careful up there."

"Will do."

After talking to Mike, Jack thought he'd saddle Shy and take the back trail up to the ranch. He was curious if Calvin's truck was still there, or if the same wind that had blown Tyler away had also caught Calvin's sails. Of course, he was also curious about the kid, Harley. Had he gone back to the ranch after he'd left his place? What were his intentions?

***

Waking in his office chair, Calvin raised his head from the desktop. He tried to focus on anything except his raging headache. Didn't re-member drinking that much, but apparently, he had. He shook his head and immediately knew that was a mistake. He looked at the .45 within reach and the magazines next to it.

He'd known he wouldn't further irritate Miguel by doing what he'd decided to do. Not with Harley in the vicinity, who was surely watching to see if he'd defy Miguel's instructions to stick around. When he'd started drinking, he thought an alternate plan would shortly become evident. But it hadn't. Felt like a Peterbilt had run over him during the night. Clear thinking wasn't in his immediate future.

He slowly stood up, felt the stiffness in his neck, and thought a moment about just going to bed. There was a knock on his door. "Enter," he said, his throat raw. Remembering he'd locked the door after whoever was outside jiggled the doorknob, he stepped to the door and unlocked it.

It was Dakota Tate, the buxom girl who worked horses. She opened the door just a crack and stuck her head in. "Hi, Calvin. We're wondering if you're moving or something? Saw all the stuff in your truck."

Calvin cleared his throat. "No. Thought I'd clean up the place real good. Just storing some things in the truck so I can do that."

"Oh, good." She smiled. "We'd hate to see you go."

"Yeah, okay."

"See you," she said and closed the door.

Still not convinced he shouldn't just leave, Calvin went to his window and gazed down at his truck, the bed piled high and covered with a tarp. He studied the area and looked off to the stand of lodgepole pines where the ranch road curved out of sight. Harley had to be out there somewhere, watching and waiting. He stepped back from the window, his thirst working him to distraction. Grabbed a bottle of water from the liquor cabinet and downed it quickly. He absently reached for a cigar but thought sucking on the thing right now would turn his stomach. Maybe some toast, a little coffee, orange juice. He took his .45 from the desk and stuck it behind his belt at his spine. He pulled on his jean jacket and walked out of the office. His options still uncertain; he needed to settle his aching body before his brain would kick in.

***

Jack reined Shy behind a copse of aspens where he could clearly see the ranch's common building. Young folks were going into and leaving it, and Calvin's truck was still parked in front. He looked for Harley's pickup and didn't see it. Satisfying himself that Calvin had not left, and Harley probably had, he turned Shy and got him moving down the back trail toward home. As they were just about to come off the trail and head toward the cabin, he saw Harley's pickup parked in his drive. He was sitting on the hood. As Jack approached him, Harley slipped off the hood, waved, and stood there waiting.

"Back again," Jack said, stopping Shy near him.

"Beautiful horse," he said, patting Shy's neck. "Yeah, I need to use your phone again if you'll let me. Can't get a signal for my soul."

Jack nodded and dismounted. "Sure. Just let me get the horse taken care of, and we can go in."

When Jack stepped on the porch, he noticed the pine table had been shoved about a half-foot away from the window. He assumed Harley had done that. "Come on in," Jack said, unlocking the door and holding the screen door open for him.

"I sure appreciate this."

"No problem." Jack noticed Harley's hair was mussed, and he looked like he'd not slept in a while. He sat down on the couch and dialed a number. Jack didn't know why it hadn't occurred to him before but decided he'd *69 the phone after he left.

"He didn't leave," Jack heard Harley say as he stepped into the hallway. He didn't want him to think he was listening in, even though Harley had turned his back just as he'd done the day before. Jack stood just outside the bedroom, giving him a quick exit if Harley happened to turn toward him.

"Waited all night in my truck," Harley continued. "Checked the ranch this mornin', and his truck is still there. No sign of the other two you told me about." He waited a moment, stood up, and walked a few steps toward the window. "Yeah." He quickly turned, and Jack slipped into the bedroom, "It's a landline. Some guy I ran into." Another pause, and then, "Okay. Gotta get some sleep, though. I'll call you tonight."

Jack grabbed some folded sheets and walked out into the hallway.

"I'm done," Harley said. "You wouldn't happen to know a place where I could stay for a couple nights?"

"The Pinecone Lodge is just up the road." Jack set the sheets on the kitchen counter and went into the parlor. "Or, there's the ranch the other direction."

"No, I don't think the ranch... That lodge is east of here?"

"Yes, just up the road."

"Didn't even know that."

"Or, if all else fails, you could stay here. I've got an extra bedroom. I just don't know if the lodge will have any rooms this time of year." Jack did want to get to know this kid better to see what he was up to. And again, it occurred to him if he'd been thirty years younger, he'd have another reason for wanting to spend a little time with Harley.

"Wow. That would be great, but I don't want to put you out. I'll just head up to the lodge and see if I can get a room. Thank you so much."

Harley held out his hand, and as Jack shook it, he looked directly into Harley's eyes. *Dead eyes*, is what he thought. That didn't comport to the kid's otherwise youthful and somewhat innocent appearance.

"Okay," Jack said, following Harley out the door. Jack memorized Harley's license plate as he turned his truck around. Jack then looked at the window. He saw nothing to indicate entry had been attempted, but surmised Harley had figured breaking and entering would not be a smart thing to do. For whatever reason, he probably didn't want to risk bringing attention to himself. Jack shoved the table back where it'd been, went in the house, and dialed *69 on the phone.

"We're sorry," the woman's voice said, "your last incoming call cannot be determined and cannot be called automatically." *Incoming not outgoing*. Hell, Jack thought, he knew that. It wasn't full-blown dementia yet, but he was just slowly losing his marbles. Or that was the excuse he gave himself. He'd have to wait for his bill or see if he could get the number by just calling the phone company. He once again picked up his notes and added the latest events to them.

TWENTY

Miguel Rosario didn't like loose ends. He was not angry with Harley for not tying another one up, but furious at Calvin for causing this mess in the first place. Why Calvin would become involved in one of Denman's bright ideas was beyond him, but he had, and something needed to be done about that. For a moment, he remained sitting on his white leather sofa, staring at the phone as if a solution would be found there.

Miguel had been somewhat intrigued when the old lawyer, Otis Schrock, had called him last week on the Hyatt's house phone. Schrock told him Denman had visited with him the day before and related the whole story of what eventually ended up with the murder of two young men near the ranch. Denman had wanted the lawyer's advice on what he should do if anyone ever pointed the finger at him. But what had intrigued Miguel, and had led to Otis's demise, was that Otis had suggested in a roundabout way he needed to increase his fees to Miguel because, well, knowledge is power, and he'd never had to stretch his lawyer's oath this far with what Denman had told him. Miguel had asked Otis if he was threatening him, and Otis had said, "Of course not."

"Well, what are you telling me then?"

"Oh, you know me, Miguel. I have to start thinking about retirement. I'm getting old, and every penny counts."

Miguel had thought about the extent of Otis's knowledge of his enterprises and had made the decision right then and there that Otis had to go. "So," he'd said, "you're telling me that I need to buy you a nice condo in Florida. And if I don't, you're going to tell somebody about Denman's little visit and Denman's relationship to me? Is that what you're saying, Otis?"

"Oh, hell no, Miguel. As you know, we've shared a lot of secrets, but I've never had to deal with the more deadly aspects of your business. If I'm going to be put into that position, I think I'm going to have to ask for some additional remuneration. You know, to keep things all neat and tidy, all in the family, if you know what I mean."

Miguel had smiled. He hadn't thought the old guy had that kind of wiliness in him. "Okay, Otis. We can work something out."

"Good, I knew you'd see the logic of it."

"I'll give you a call later."

Miguel had hung up the Hyatt house phone and immediately called a friend in Vail who had once worked for him and asked him if he'd heard about the recent murders of two young men near the ranch. His friend had told him he'd heard the same thing, and the CBI was even involved in the investigation. When he got off the line with his friend, he dialed Calvin's number, furious Calvin had not told him what had happened.

"Yeah, Calvin," Miguel had said when Calvin had answered.

"Miguel. It's been a while."

"Can't wait for your explanation about this one, Calvin."

"What? What explanation?"

"Something happen up there I need to know about?"

There'd been silence on the line at first. "I guess you've heard about… Denman's deal?"

"You cocksucker, it was your deal, too. Why didn't you call me? What the fuck is going on out there?"

"I, ah…"

"You 'ah' what? Who else is involved in this?"

"Jesus Christ, Miguel, settle down. It was just a couple of faggots who rent from me. One works for the lodge, the other is a hunting guide. They weren't involved in the actual… *thing*, but just helped out. They're okay."

"No, they're not okay. Give me their names?"

"They're just—"

"Listen, you motherfucker, don't let them leave, and you take care of them. I'm sending Harley up there to get to the bottom of this."

"Yeah. Sure. But why Harley?"

"Don't you worry about that, and don't you leave either. Got it?"

"Sure. But—"

"No buts," Miguel had interrupted. "You leave, and I'll find you." And Miguel had slammed the receiver down.

Miguel had then texted Harley. He told him to call him at the *happy number* in fifteen minutes. *Happy number* was a euphemism for the Steamboat Hyatt house phone. Miguel would sit at the Hyatt and wait for Harley to make the call from the Depot Café in Oak Creek.

After Miguel had spoken with Harley, he called Otis Schrock back.

"Otis, Harley is gonna take care of Denman. I want you to put together fifteen grand in cash. You give that money to Harley when he comes to see you. Have it by tomorrow morning. Early. After that, you can come on up to Steamboat, and we'll talk about our new arrangement. Okay?"

"Yeah, I guess Denman has to go. He screwed up, Miguel. I see that. Hate to be involved in something like this, but, okay, I'll get the cash together. But what about Denman's friends? The ones who were in on the murders, too?"

"Denman give you names?"

"No. Just some of his leather friends. Of course, there's Calvin up at the ranch who put the thing together for them, and then there were the two boys, one a wrangler at the lodge, who helped with it all. Denman said Calvin got paid a bundle of money for setting this up."

"Don't worry about that. You just do what I've asked you to do."

"Sure will. Like I always do. Thanks, Miguel."

Thirty minutes later, Miguel had stepped into the Hyatt's bistro to have breakfast. He then drove to Holy Name Church, where he lit a candle in remembrance of his sainted mother. The next morning, Harley would have an excellent breakfast at the Flat Top Diner.

TWENTY-ONE

Jack stepped back into the cabin and dialed Mike's home number. When Mike's voice asked the caller to leave a message, he hung up the phone and walked into the bedroom, where he grabbed Mike's contact card from the dresser. He sat down and dialed the number. Mike answered after the first ring.

"Mike," Jack said, flipping the card in his fingers.

"Hey, Jack. I just finished looking at the state's website for the owner of the ranch. A company named Rambouillet Enterprises, LLC, owns the place. A guy by the name of Otis Schrock is the registered agent. He's a lawyer in, of all places, Oak Creek, Colorado. Isn't that where you bought your horse?"

"Sure is. Does it show the actual owner?"

"No. I'll have to do a little more digging for that."

"Well, good," Jack said, placing Mike's card on the coffee table. "Got a license number for you to look up if you would."

"Shoot."

Jack gave Mike the license number on Harley's truck. "It's a red Toyota pickup. Belongs to that kid who showed up last night.

Damned if he wasn't here again this morning. Name is Harley, something. He needed to use my phone one more time, and then he said he had to find somewhere to stay. I told him he could probably get a place up at the ranch, and he didn't like that idea at all. So, I told him about the lodge and also told him if they were out of rooms, he could stay here with me."

"Oh, the plot thickens. Didn't know you were into the young ones, Jack."

"Well, yes, the plot thickens, and I will admit I'm attracted to the kid. Purely platonic, though."

"Right!" Mike laughed.

"What I want to do is find out why he's up here, how he knows Calvin, and why he's carrying a weapon. Doesn't smell right, Mike. Besides, there's something about him... His eyes..."

"The eyes speak volumes. I'll grant you that."

"Yeah, they do." Jack saw Harley's truck come up the drive. "Listen, he's come back. I'll let you go."

"Be careful, Jack."

"I'm always careful."

Jack opened his door just as Harley was climbing out of his truck. "No luck?"

"Nah, they're all filled up. Said they take reservations three months in advance."

"Well, come on in and make yourself at home."

Harley stopped just before he stepped on the porch. "I really appreciate this, Jack. Don't know what I'd do if—"

"Don't worry about that."

"Okay. But I do have some things I gotta do. Noticed the lodge has a little restaurant, so I'm gonna eat somethin' and then I have to… You know, I just got some things I need to take care of."

"I'll fix you some lunch."

"No, that's okay. But I will come back tonight and…"

"Okay. That's fine. I lock up about ten."

"Okay. I'll be back by then."

"Good."

Harley smiled and returned to his truck. "Thanks again," he said as he climbed into the cab.

Jack waved and went into the cabin. He walked through the rooms and looked for anything that might give Harley a clue as to who he was or used to be. Took down a picture from the bedroom wall showing Stanton and him together, their weapons visible on their hips, toasting Stanton's last day on the job years ago. He put the picture in the closet. Coming back into the parlor, he looked at his notes and Mike's card on the coffee table. He picked those up, and took them into the bedroom, putting them in the closet with the picture. He then unsnapped his belt, pulled his holstered .38 from it, and set that, too, in the closet. Thinking a moment about that, he picked up the weapon and slid it under his mattress. When his phone rang, he walked back into the parlor and noticed the paper sack of items he'd taken from Tyler's and Ben's cabin.

"We have to stop meeting like this," Jack said when he heard Mike's voice.

"Jesus, Jack…" Mike sounded almost winded. "I just took a look at recent Colorado entries to the NCIC, and Otis Schrock—you remember? The registered agent for Rambouillet Enterprises that owns the ranch? He was killed Friday morning in Oak Creek. Shot with a small-caliber right between the eyes. Not only that, but there was also another murder up there right before Schrock's on the same day. Some guy by the name of John Denman. Denman's got a record here in Denver: assault, DWI, drugs, both using and selling, involved in some heavy-duty biker shit. He was only twenty-six, but he was a bad character, Jack. Routt County didn't call us in on this one."

"Jesus. One damned thing after another. Curious about the Oak Creek tie-in. Wonder if Tess knows about this?"

"I'm sure it's the talk of the town. She hasn't shown up yet, has she?"

"No," Jack said as he looked out the window. "I'll see if I can get her on the phone. Oh, the kid is going to stay with me, by the way. Forgot about Tess coming up here when I offered him a room. Really don't want him here when Tess arrives."

"Yeah, that would be awkward. She knows you were a cop?"

"Oh, sure. Like I told you, she knows a lot about me. I really don't want to spook the kid before I find out what's up with him. Did you run his license plate yet?"

"No, but I will in a few minutes."

"Okay." Jack stepped back from the window and sat down on the sofa. "Wish you were up here, Mike."

"Then you'd have a real dilemma—me, the kid, Tess, all vying for the same bedroom."

Jack's thought was that, no, Mike would sleep with him, and he smiled at the impossible scenario that presented. "I'll just have to wait and see what happens. Call me when you track down that license plate."

"Soon as I hang up. Watch your back."

Jack hung up, stood, and walked into the kitchen area where he thought a minute about fixing something to eat and decided against it. He wasn't hungry and knew why. Whenever a homicide investigation began to heat up with more loose ends than he could keep track of, he'd lose his appetite. Food became irrelevant, as it was now. He again noticed the sack with the items from Tyler's and Ben's cabin he'd put in the kitchen. He'd wanted to tell Mike it was ready to be picked up. But, hell, he couldn't leave the cabin now. He picked it up and took it into the bedroom, then stuffed it into the closet.

Jack walked across the parlor, out the front door, and headed for the shed where he grabbed Shy's rope harness and lunge line. As he opened the pasture's gate and remembered he needed to call Tess but figured he'd do that later. He needed to settle down, run things through his mind as he worked Shy in the round pen.

***

Harley backed into a thicket of scrub, hidden from the ranch road by a thick stand of lodgepole pines. He was exhausted from lack of sleep but would do what Miguel had told him to do: "Keep an eye on Calvin." He didn't know how he would do that, given that his eyes kept closing after he'd slumped down in the seat. He believed if he did sleep, he'd wake with any passing vehicle—the ranch road was only forty or so yards away. He thought about the prospect of a soft bed in the old guy's cabin tonight but knew if he'd told Miguel about that, Miguel would have nixed the idea. As his eyes closed once again, he wished push would come to shove with Calvin sooner rather than later. If Calvin were out of the picture, he could sleep undisturbed, regardless of Calvin's fate.

***

Calvin stepped outside the common building and considered unloading his truck. He should put his things back where he'd taken them from in his haste to just disappear while he still could. He couldn't now, not with Harley in the vicinity. He wished now he hadn't demanded Tyler and Ben leave. If they were still there, he could have redirected Harley's attention to them. It was what it was. As his two maintenance men entered the building for lunch, he told them to unload his truck when they were through eating and put his things just inside the door.

"Just set them off to the side out of the way," he said. If he could pacify Harley's curiosity about whether or not he was still going to leave by unloading his truck, that would give him some time to think about his options. As he began to turn and walk back into the building, a reflection of sunlight bounced off something in the distance, just off to the side of the road and within the thickly huddled stand of pine trees. He studied the area for a moment and saw the unnatural color of red behind the trees, and knew without a doubt Harley was watching and waiting.

TWENTY-TWO

After an hour, Jack unhooked the lunge line from Shy's harness, took the harness off, and tied Shy to a post where he brushed him down. When the sky momentarily darkened, he looked up. Saw that an afternoon shower was as probable as they usually were every day, and took the brush back to the shed. He set Shy loose and watched him amble to his water tub and take a drink. As he turned to go back in the cabin, he heard his landline ring and picked up his pace.

"This is Jack," he said, wishing he would've washed his hands before picking up the phone.

"That plate number you gave me is registered to some guy in Craig, Colorado, Jack."

"Not Harley, something?"

"Nope. The name is Herman Antonito. No criminal record, no nothing."

"Hmm… Another dead end, then?"

"I guess. Oh, and I think we might have gotten a hit on a couple likely missing persons. Restaurant up in Vail reported that two of their waiters haven't shown up for work in a few days, and they checked where they were living and didn't find anybody home. Said their vehicle was still parked at the trailer they lived in. The note on the report from the Eagle County sheriff says the restaurant manager stated it was very unusual for these guys to miss work or not to call in if they'd been scheduled. Names are Mark Harris and Brian Hill. Both are twenty-two, Harris is brown and brown, Hill is blond and blue. Average height, build."

"Location works." Jack grabbed a beer from the refrigerator and pulled the tab.

"Sounds like you're having a little refreshment."

"Yeah, I am. The sheriff in Vail is going to get any more information on these boys—friends, activities, that kind of stuff?"

"They will if I tell them we're interested."

"Might be a definite lead, especially once we get the autopsy report. You might ask them to find out if the manager knows what their sexual orientation is. Was."

"Okay. Any reason for that?"

"Just another hunch."

"Can't argue with that. You enjoy your beer. Think I'll call it a day and go home."

"Get some rest, Mike. Tomorrow morning will be here before you know it."

"Don't remind me."

***

Calvin sat at his desk, drinking his courage, mulling the idea that had come to him when he'd seen Harley's failed attempt to hide his truck amongst the trees. After his third shot, he stuck his .45 into his jeans, went downstairs, and walked through the kitchen. Went out the back door and stopped when he saw the entrance to the cellar. He looked behind him and saw a pile of slash that had been sitting there for years. He picked up an armful of it and tossed it in the small recess that led to the cellar door. After three more armfuls, he was satisfied that the door could no longer be seen. He walked the length of the building and then continued west behind the nearby cabins. Once he was sure he could not be seen from Harley's hiding place, he turned south across the open field bisected by the lazy stream that ran through it. He crossed the creek and continued until he reached an aspen grove, then he turned east toward the tall pines that flanked the ranch road.

As Calvin inched closer toward the back of Harley's pickup, he saw Harley's head leaning against the side window. Sleeping, he thought as he sat on his haunches and waited a moment. Seeing no movement, he crept closer. Could he do this? What choice did he have? He pulled the .45 from his waist, pulled the slide back, chambering a shell, the hammer cocked. He stood up, raised the weapon, and moved closer to the side window. Holding the .45 a foot from it, he raised his left hand and braced his hold on the weapon.

***

Intending to saddle Shy for a short ride to Piney Lake before dusk set in, then maybe past the lodge and up toward the place where he found the boys, Jack walked out of the cabin and stopped dead still when he heard it—a single shot, a thud-like pop that echoed across the landscape, its source not that far away. Simultaneously, he saw

Shy react to the sound with a quick jerk of his hindquarters, his back legs dancing a half-circle.

Jack waited a moment for another shot, not moving, staring toward where he believed the source of the gunshot had come. Ever since he'd returned from the hell of Vietnam, the sound of gunfire raised the hair on his neck. When another pop did not come, he walked to the shed, grabbed the saddle blanket and tack, and opened the gate to the pasture. He sat the items down and clucked for Shy to come. He responded, lowering his head and ambling toward him. Jack tied him off to a fencepost and returned to the shed for his saddle, deciding he'd ride toward where he'd heard the shot. He put on the orange nylon vest he sometimes wore when hunting season was in full swing.

***

Calvin froze when he saw the mess he'd made inside the cab. He reached for the handle and found the door was locked. He stepped back. *Gotta be kiddin' me! You locked the fuckin' door*! He stuffed the .45 back into his waist, looked at the ground surrounding him. He picked up a large rock, raised it with both hands, lifted it over his head, and threw it against the window, shattering it inward. He used the butt of his weapon to clear the safety glass from the door. Reaching over the windowsill, he pulled the inside door latch. He kept his body against the door, not wanting Harley to slide out when he opened it. The bullet had entered the top of Harley's head. Calvin reached his hand against Harley's shoulder and applied pressure as he opened the door. He shoved the body over, pressed the lock button, and then hurried to the passenger side. Opened that door, pushed the rock to the floor, and pulled the body farther over to that side of the cab. Slamming the passenger door, he hustled back to the driver's side, got behind the wheel, and started the truck.

***

When Jack reined Shy off the main road toward the Whisper River Ranch, where he was sure the gunshot had come from, he saw Harley's pickup in the distance turn onto the main road that would eventually end at the I-70 ramp. He still wondered what Harley was up to and gave a passing thought to the weapon Harley carried with him. Knew it was a small-caliber semi-automatic from the look of the butt, but the shot he had heard had come from a larger caliber firearm. He stopped Shy, scanned the thickset of pine and aspen trees directly in front of him, and then looked farther up the ranch road. He still couldn't see the compound of buildings from here. He turned back to the thick thatch of trees and watched for movement. There wasn't any.

"Ah, hell," he said. "Probably just some goddamned idiot firing at nothing in particular. C'mon, boy." He pulled the reins to the left and tapped Shy's stomach with his heels. "Let's go back the other way before the idiot shoots us. We'll head up to the lake."

***

Almost ten miles down the road, Calvin pulled to the shoulder where the canyon's drop-off was barely three feet to his right. He stopped the truck where the front tires were just inches from the edge. Leaving the motor running, he pulled the wheel to the right, left the truck in neutral, and stepped out of it. He looked north, then south, saw no one coming from either way, stepped to the truck's rear, placed his palms on the tailgate, and pushed.

As Calvin walked back toward the ranch, the acrid odor of gasoline and burning rubber wafted from the bottom of the canyon. He turned and looked at the plume of black smoke that rose above the tree line. He hadn't thought about the consequences of that, and now assumed he'd better get himself off the road and into the trees. Some sonofabitch was sure to get a hair up his ass and want to see what was going on. It would be just his luck that sonofabitch would be an Eagle County sheriff.

TWENTY-THREE

Dusk was full upon the land when Shy and Jack returned from their ride. Jack had kept Shy along the trail that bordered the lake, well past the path that led to the clearing where he'd found the boys. Since he'd lunged him earlier, he thought he'd just walk Shy without any climbing, and that's what he had done. After brushing Shy out, he went into the cabin and saw that the message light was blinking on the answering machine.

He washed his hands at the kitchen sink, then listened to Mike's message: "Give me a call at home."

Jack punched in Mike's home number, sat down on the sofa, and waited for the pickup.

"Hey, Jack," Mike said. "Only thing I've got right now is that those boys missing up in Vail were, as the restaurant manager put it, 'in a relationship,' which answers your question. Not much additional information on them, other than that they worked in a downtown Denver restaurant before being hired up in Vail. Both were probably originally from Indiana, though the manager wasn't sure about that."

"So no family information other than their relationship?"

"Nada."

"Okay. I guess we just wait and see on that one."

"Tess show up yet?"

"Not yet."

"Has the kid come back?"

"No. I saw him driving down the road, though. Maybe he had to go to Vail for something. I don't know. I expect he'll show up here in a little while."

"Well, tomorrow ought to be interesting. We'll get the coroner's report. I'll keep pushing for Eagle County to dig into the identity of those two missing boys. Now, tell me how your day was up there in paradise."

"Uneventful, Mike. Worked Shy, then rode him down to the lake. Thought it was going to rain, but it never did. Think I'll fix some dinner and wait for the mysterious Harley to show up. You going to settle in for the night?"

"Yeah. Gertrude is still letting me know she's been neglected. Guess I'll get some dinner too and maybe read a little. I'm actually bushed, so I might just go to bed in a little while."

"Okay then," Jack said, nodding. "Guess we'll talk tomorrow."

"I'm sure we will."

They said their good-byes, and Jack hung up the phone. He stood and looked out the front window, considering if he'd wait for Harley to show himself before he started fixing dinner, then thought better of it. He'd missed lunch and was hungry. He walked into the kitchen, opened the refrigerator, and pulled out a pound of hamburger and onion. He put the black iron frying pan on the stove, grabbed a knife, and began chopping the onion. Divided the lump of hamburger in two, just in case Harley hadn't eaten.

***

Staying off the road, Calvin slowly made his way due north through the forest as nightfall crept around him. The blackness enlarged the errant sounds of critters scurrying from his path, probably chipmunks, coyotes, deer, maybe even bears. He cursed his thoughtlessness in not planning better for the return trip to the ranch. He'd not anticipated the truck would explode in flames once it met the bottom of the canyon. Otherwise—and this is what he had expected—he'd simply thumb a ride back to the ranch road turnoff from anyone who happened to be driving down the main road. At this rate, he wouldn't get home until past midnight.

He'd not heard any sirens to his rear after he'd left the side of the canyon, which was a good sign the fire had burned itself out. The stream that meandered through the canyon had managed to douse the flames before anyone had sounded an alarm. Fire was something feared by all where the pine beetle feasted, and the detritus of generations of felled trees and dry slash layered the forest floor.

Worse yet was his yearning for a drink. He needed to calm down, figure out what his next move would be. He had to remain a step ahead of Miguel. Or maybe Jack Dolan should be his first concern? He didn't know. He needed to get back. He needed a drink. God, but he needed a drink.

***

Mike Day carried his jelly jar to the couch, sat down, and turned on the lamp. Gertrude lay on the coffee table, content for the moment as Mike opened the Hemingway to where he had placed his bookmark. He then reclosed the book and laid it upon the side table under the glow of the lamp. Didn't need or want Hemingway right now. What he needed right now was his own introspection of life, death, his future.

He lit a cigarette, thought about Jack's boys, their deaths, and the lonely place where Jack had found them. And, yes, he thought about Jack, too.

After Stanton had retired, Jack worked alone. At the same time, Mike, the new kid in homicide, was assigned to work with Miles Teague, a tired cop with a gut and a penchant for dreaming about his own retirement to the exclusion of his work responsibilities. Once Teague had left, Mike and Jack had been paired up by their lieutenant, a logical move given that Jack could mentor him, teach him the tricks he'd learned from the best of them—*Old Grim*. Besides that, the lieutenant had noticed the two had just seemed to be naturally paired as opposites. Mike was forever smiling, fidgety, talkative in spite of Jack's often quiet, even morose mien. So too, the two men had seemed to hit it off immediately after Mike had promoted into the division. The lieutenant wouldn't know, of course, that Mike and Jack would eventually share a bed, their love their impossible secret.

While eating dinner in a dive on Colfax Avenue not long after they'd been assigned as partners, Jack told Mike about what Stanton had taught him. The dead speak of their last moments, their final thoughts. Mike didn't believe him at first, but he realized Jack was not kidding, a fact that revealed a lot about Jack Dolan. Jack was a complex man with a streak of melancholy in him. Or maybe it was just that Jack's belief in all that mysticism, all that mumbo jumbo about the dead speaking, kept him in a state of sadness no matter what the occasion. Maybe understandably so.

Jack, too, so unlike his no-nonsense behavior in the office, was a gentle lover. Their sexual encounters were not so much remembered for the physical release they provided, but for the mental coupling. It had been a soulful thing that had always left Mike with the impression Jack, way down deep inside, begged for a deeper connection than simply the mere friction of the physical act itself. Mike sometimes wondered if Jack's lovemaking was the only way he knew to assuage the pain he'd shared with the dead when he touched them and listened to their mournful words. Or, too, maybe Jack had seen some heavy shit in 'Nam that still haunted him, that gave him an insight into the fragility of the body, the persistence of the spirit.

Mike smashed out his cigarette and finished off the Chardonnay in the jelly jar. At some point in Mike's reverie, Gertrude had snuggled into his lap. He absently stroked the cat, heard, and felt the soothing sensation of her purr. Leaned his head to the side and rested it on the couch's back. He closed his eyes and wished he was in the mountains, in a cabin where a fire crackled in the fireplace, where an arm caressed his shoulders.

***

Jack sat in the parlor until ten-thirty. Three times he'd gone outside, and once even walked to the road, looking west toward where he'd last seen Harley's truck. If the kid showed up later, he'd hear his approach on the pebbled drive outside the cabin. He stood up, scattered the glow of embers in the fireplace, set the screen tight against the firebox, and walked into the bedroom. Undressing to his underwear, he pulled his .38 from the holster he'd just unlatched from his belt, placed it on the side table, and crawled into bed.

Like a river always flowing, the images, sounds, aromas, and gut feelings about what had consumed him ever since finding the boys emerged one after the other. They rushed as if there was no end, with tributaries going every which way, into the darkness he could not see within. He rolled over, wondered what Mike was doing. If he'd yet to go to bed or was still reading about… whatever it was he read. Bestsellers? Love stories? Adventures?

Jack thought about the last book he'd read. It was a coming of age story about a kid who'd grown up in the Wyoming mountains where his daddy operated a dude ranch for wealthy clients. The kid had known the touch, the aroma, the feel of a horse under him since he was barely able to walk and had come to believe that within the eyes of horses, the face of God could be seen. If Jack remembered nothing else about that book, it was that particular image of the kid peering into the eyes of a horse and seeing what he had seen in Shy's eyes. The thought brought a moment of concern for Shy out there in the pasture, alone under the stars, and vulnerable to… well, whatever might be out there with an intent to harm him. Then he recalled looking into Harley's dead eyes, where he'd seen nothing but emptiness. The soul of a horse was a precious thing. A young man without a soul was something else altogether.

***

Finally emerging from the forest and into the copse of aspens where he could see the shadowy outlines of the ranch's structures, Calvin glanced at his watch. It was twenty minutes to midnight. He didn't know what hurt worse, his arms and hands which he'd scraped against the pine and spruce boughs and juniper bushes, or his legs which he'd knocked against unseen felled stumps and rocks that jutted up from ground over the entire route. His pants were ripped in places where errant, sharp dead limbs of trees had snagged them. Exhausted, he went into the common building, climbed the stairs to his office, and noticed that the red light on his landline was blinking.

He flicked on the light, grabbed the bottle of bourbon and a glass from the small cabinet along the wall, sat behind his desk, and propped his feet up. He leaned back in his chair, glass in hand, and drank the whiskey. He was as tired as he'd ever been. His body ached from the nearly ten-mile trek from the canyon. He thought a minute about soaking in a bathtub for a while, but he didn't have a bathtub. He was too tired for a shower. During his trudge, he'd thought about what his next move should be with Harley out of the picture. Now, the whiskey warming in his belly, not so much clearing his head as easing his pain, his body begged for sleep. He poured another shot and figured a little nap wouldn't hurt. Hell, if he was to make any kind of reasoned decision about his future, he had to rest for a while, get his head clear. He glanced at the annoying blink of his landline, downed the shot, and sat the glass on the desktop. He closed his eyes. Just a little nap, he thought. Just a little…

TWENTY-FOUR

Jack opened his eyes and rolled over as dawn barely lit the hallway to the bedroom, the early morning glow creeping from the large window in the parlor. He glanced at the clock on his side table—6:11. He sat up. His first thought was that Harley hadn't returned. He reached to the floor and pulled his socks from his shoes, put those on, then stood up and grabbed his pants from the chair he'd draped them over last night. He finished dressing by attaching the holster to his belt, then stuck the .38 into it. Feeling the early-morning chill, he put on his old cardigan, now beginning to unravel at the elbows.

As always, his first task in the morning was to open the front door, step out on the porch, and check to see if Shy was all right. He did that and saw the boy hanging out at the far end of the pasture, his head bent. Jack then went back into the cabin, made coffee, and carried the cup outside to sit in the pine chair. He looked east toward the Gore Range, where the sun had yet to peek over Mount Powell. Gray plumes of smoke from early-riser campers rose here and there. He thought he could almost smell the bacon frying over rock-lined fire pits.

He remembered the coroner's findings would be revealed today. Not that he wasn't fairly sure how the boys had died but was curious if his observation they had not been killed where he'd found them would be confirmed. Well, confirmed as far as any autopsy could go with such a thing: blood volume would tend to indicate if the boys had bled out before their hearts had stopped beating. The scene had not shown that much blood.

And where was Tess? He'd call her after a while and see if she could pin down her arrival time any better than she had. With so many dead ends, he was anxious for her to take a look at the clearing to see what she could see. And Harley? The mysterious Harley. What had happened to him? Whatever it was, he figured Harley could take care of himself just fine.

Jack walked into the cabin, rinsed out his coffee cup, and went out to the shed, where he separated out three flakes of hay from the bale and carried them to the pasture fence. He tossed them into the tub as Shy made his way across the pasture.

"Come on, buddy," he said, watching Shy shake his head as he neared the trough. As he leaned his arms on the pasture gate, he heard the rough sound of a diesel engine on the main road and then saw a big orange Dodge pickup pass in front of his property. His landline began to ring, and he ran back to the house.

"This is Jack."

"It's Tess. We're heading toward the lodge right now. Where you at?"

"Are you in an orange Dodge?"

"Yes."

"You just passed me. Come on back and take the first road to your right."

"Okay," Tess said, and the phone went dead.

Jack shook his head. *Leave it to Tess and her spirits to get a crystal clear signal up here.*

"This is my son, Saw," Tess said as she stepped around the front of the Dodge.

Jack turned to the thin young man stepping out of the driver's side, saw his dark complexion, his black hair tied in a long ponytail. Jack held his hand out to him.

"I'm Jack Dolan."

The young man shook his hand, smiled, and said, "Howdy."

"He don't talk much," Tess said.

"Well…" Jack turned to Tess. "Didn't think I'd be seeing you this morning."

"We figured we'd just take off early this morning. Saw is gonna go back to Vail for a while. There's your horse," she said as she turned and walked toward the pasture.

Jack turned back to Saw. "You want some coffee or something before you go?"

"Nah. I'll come back for her later." The young man got in the truck, backed down the drive, and turned onto the main road.

Jack followed Tess to the pasture. She had already opened the gate and was stroking Shy as he chewed hay. "Whaddaya think?" he asked.

"Looks good," she said, running her hand across the length of Shy's body and down his hip and stifle. "Bulked up some since I last saw him. You ride him much?"

"I try to every day."

"Good. A caged horse doesn't know its worth unless he's worked."

He nodded. He'd never looked at it that way but knew Tess was right. He'd often thought what life might have been for Shy if he'd simply left him up there on Tess's hill to run free. "I think he's happy," he said.

"Sure, he is." Tess looked at the cabin and the surrounding landscape. "Nice place, Jack."

"I like it… I love it. You want to come in and have some coffee?"

"Sure."

"What's your son got going on in Vail?" Jack asked as they walked toward the cabin.

"Got a girlfriend there, I think. As I said, he don't talk much."

"He a Bronco fan or something?"

"His orange truck?"

"Yeah."

"Nah, he just got a good deal on it. He don't like football. Thinks it's stupid."

"Okay," Jack said, smiling. He opened the screen door for Tess and followed her in. "This is the parlor and kitchen."

"And down here," Jack motioned toward the hallway, "are the bedrooms and bathroom."

"Yeah. Real nice place." Tess peeked down the hallway, then faced Jack. "Let's have that coffee. Got a feeling you want to talk to me about something."

"Yes, I do," he said as the landline began to ring. "Let me get that." Jack stepped into the parlor and picked up the receiver. "This is Jack." When there wasn't a response, he said, "Hello." He listened to dead air for a moment, and the call dropped off to a dial tone.

"Wrong number, I guess." He hung up the phone and went into the kitchen area to make coffee.

***

Miguel Rosario had expected Harley to call him last night. Now that he hadn't, he absently scrolled through his recent calls and pressed the number he knew Harley had called from yesterday. He almost asked for Harley, then realized his mistake. He'd spent so many years protecting himself, his identity, even to the extent of initiating the most important calls from house phones in hotels or other public places that this lapse in judgment was inexcusable. Sure, Harley had mentioned he was calling from *just some guy's* phone. Still, Miguel had long ago learned that *just some guy* could fuck things up royally in what might have seemed the most innocent of circumstances. He gritted his teeth and threw his cell across the room.

He'd tried to call Calvin last night, but there'd been no answer. Now, as he stood from the white leather couch, he turned toward his view of Storm Peak, still white-capped, and knew he couldn't just hang around his condo, trying to contact the two men who were at the center of his current dilemma. He thought about who else he could call and have them head down to the ranch to give Harley a hand. Why hadn't Harley followed his instructions and called him last night? It was not like Harley to ignore him. The kid was meticulous about following orders. He depended upon Harley. And who else was there? Miguel walked across the room to retrieve his cell, acknowledging he didn't have anyone else.

He could call any number of former and current contacts who would do anything he asked of them. But, most of them were crazy sonsofbitches, actual psychotics who'd be happy to help him out, but who, sure as shit, would fuck it up. Miguel didn't need any fuckups right now. The seriousness of the bind Calvin and Denman had put him in was like nothing he'd dealt with before.

He picked up his cell from the plush white carpet, checked to see if it still worked, and put it in his pants pocket. He walked into his bedroom and pulled a soft suitcase from his closet. He could be at the ranch in a little less than three hours. As he packed enough clothes for maybe two or three days and some toiletries, he thought he'd try to contact both Calvin and Harley one more time. But he'd do it from a safe phone, the one at the Hyatt. If he couldn't get either of them, he'd already be packed and could be on the road in forty-five minutes.

***

Mike Day had just entered his office when his landline rang. It was the Eagle County coroner who advised he had just emailed the autopsy findings on the boys to Mike's CBI account. A short conversation with the coroner revealed the obvious: the boys had been murdered. "Tortured before they died, and they'd been sodomized," the coroner said matter-of-factly as if he dealt with such a thing every day.

Firing up his computer, Mike almost picked up his phone again to call Jack to give him the news as soon as he read it for himself. He decided not to do that. Wanted to study the findings a moment before he shared them. He clicked on the .pdf file, *John Doe #1*, printed it, and then did the same with the other file, *John Doe #2*. He gathered the twenty sheets of paper, sat them before him on his desktop, hunched over, and began reading.

***

Calvin sensed that something had clamped tightly on his neck, the pain sharp and persistent. He opened his eyes to the uncomfortable glare of daylight. Shielded his eyes with his hand, reached for the cord, and pulled the curtains closed. He grabbed his neck.

"Goddamn," he moaned, massaging the knot he felt there. He tried to stand from his swivel chair and immediately eased back down. "Damn," he said, placing his palms against his face. He rubbed his eyes, felt the stubble down his face, and again saw the blinking red light on his landline. He pressed the play button on the phone, heard, "Calvin. Pickup." Miguel. "What the fuck is the situation up there? I need an update. You call me back. You fucking call me back!" Calvin pressed the stop button and stared at the phone as if waiting for something to leap from it. He shook his head, placed his palms on the desktop, and slowly stood up. He looked up at the ceiling, closed his eyes, and knew, just knew it wouldn't be long before the little bastard, Miguel himself, appeared in his doorway.

TWENTY-FIVE

Jack parked his SUV in the Pinecone Lodge's parking lot, and he and Tess climbed out. "It's just off the trail," he said, pointing east. "Up the mountain a bit."

"Okay." Tess followed him through the parking lot and onto the trail that skirted the lake. "You know anything about them? The dead ones?"

"No, not really. We've got some information on two boys that are missing from Vail, but other than that, nothing. We should have the autopsy report today. Doubt if the boys' IDs can be established from it, though."

"Nice up here. Real nice." Tess stopped a moment to take in the view, looking first at the lake and the rise of pine trees to the far side of it, then east to the looming, craggy-topped Mount Powell in the distance.

"Yeah." Jack stopped and turned to her. "It's a special place."

"There fish in that lake?"

"I guess there are. I don't fish. Fishing always seemed like a whole lot of doing nothing."

"I fish some on the Yampa. Big trout and pike. Fry 'em up in butter. Tastes like a slice of heaven."

Jack started moving again. "You believe in heaven, Tess?"

"I believe in the spirit," Tess said. "It remains."

Jack wanted Tess to go on, explaining what she had just said. He didn't ask her what had immediately come to his mind: Yes, but doesn't the spirit eventually go somewhere? When she said nothing more, he smiled. Tess wasn't one to waste words on such speculation. She knew what she knew.

After they had hiked about fifty yards, Jack stopped where the trail forked to the north with a gradual rise. "It's up there," he said.

Tess looked up the fork, moved in front of Jack, and studied the trail to the point where it was lost to the thick spread of pine trees that enveloped it in the darkness. She began walking up the fork.

Jack held back as Tess approached the clearing halfway up the first rise. When Tess got about thirty steps in front of him, he began to follow, kept his head down, and studied the path before him. Sensing he was almost there, he again stopped, looked up, and found Tess herself had stopped and was staring at the clearing. Watched her ease into it. He took the few steps to the entrance, stopped, and watched her.

Tess circled the perimeter of the place, staring at the middle of it where the boys had lain. And again, she circled it, never taking her eyes from where she had focused them. She then stopped, glanced at Jack, and nodded.

"One of them is here," she said.

Jack's entire body jerked slightly with Tess's words as he watched her step into the middle of the clearing.

"He mourns for the other one," Tess said, kneeling down and cupping her hands into the loose earth, just as Jack had seen her do in his dream. "He says they should not have done it." She raised her hands, letting the dirt filter through her fingers. "He says he thought it was just a game." She looked at Jack.

Jack nodded and went into the place. "Yeah, that's what he told me."

They both turned their heads toward the sound of something approaching. Suddenly, a doe leaped into the clearing with two fawns following. Tess froze as the mama deer led her children across the clearing and into the thick stand of pine trees bordering the other side. Just as suddenly, a ten-point buck appeared from where the doe and her babies had come, stopped with a grunt just feet from where Tess kneeled, shook its head, snorted, and wheezed. Tess slowly laid herself flat on the earth, her eyes to the ground as Jack reached for his weapon. The buck turned, stared at Jack for a moment, then turned again and appeared to fly into the thick forest wall.

Tess stood as Jack hurried toward her. "You okay?"

As Tess brushed herself off, she looked at him and smiled. "These blessings don't come that often."

"You mean because he didn't attack?"

Tess waved her hand at Jack. "No. Just that they were here."

Jack put his weapon back into the holster. "Well, bucks can be dangerous sometimes."

"Not this time," Tess said. "The one who speaks told me something else, Jack."

"Yes?"

"It didn't begin here. Higher up. Where they could see the stars."

***

Mike tried Jack's landline, then his cell. No answer on either. He left his office carrying the autopsy report, stopping at a desk where a young woman was studying a computer screen.

"Suz," he said, leaning down and placing the report on her desk, "those two kids who're missing up in Vail?"

"Yup, let's see," she said, flipping through a stack of hardcopy files on her desk. She opened up a file folder. "Brian Hill and Mark Harris."

"Anything about tattoos on both or either of them?"

"Well..." She briefly scanned the documents. "Nope. Nothing."

Mike laid the autopsy report on her desk, open to the page that contained two pictures of tattoos that had been found on the boys' bodies. "John Doe number one, and two. One just above the pubic area, the other on the left buttock. Not that their families would necessarily know about these, but maybe their friends would."

The young woman picked up the autopsy report and looked closely at the pictures. "Okay," she said matter-of-factly, "the buttock one is a duck with the words, 'Rhymes With...' below it, the other one is a..." She paused a moment and read the coroner's narrative, and then looked again at the picture. "Oh, it's one of those little devils with a pitchfork."

"Yeah. Would you add those to the profile of the missing boys only as a possible, not confirmed? Then contact those folks in Vail who called this one in. See if they know if those boys had tattoos."

"Sure. I'll get on it right now."

Mike nodded. "Thanks. I'll email the pics." He picked up the autopsy report and returned to his office. He placed the report on his desk and once again stepped out of his office. He really needed a cigarette. He needed to talk to Jack. Hell, he needed just to walk away from this goddamned job and get a life.

***

Tess stopped as she crested the first rise, studied the forest that still paralleled the path, looked to the other hillside. It topped out in a large, nearly treeless clearing. "Up there," she said, turning to Jack.

Jack looked up the hill. "A good place to see the stars."

"They would surround you at night," Tess said. "The wind, too." She turned back toward the upward path and began the ascent.

When they both reached the clearing, they stopped for a moment, both turning in a circle to view the landscape that spread out before them. The chill of a slight breeze flowing from the northwest gently brushed against their faces.

"You feel anything?" Jack asked.

Tess raised her head, looked at the sky, the puffs of purely white clouds in the distance, turned to Jack, and nodded. "Yeah, I feel something." She scanned the area, turned full circle, and walked several feet northward. She stopped, sat down on the ground, and placed her hands upon the earth.

Jack watched her silently, not wanting to disturb whatever she was sensing.

She stood up, looked at a stand of aspens to the north, and walked toward it. When she entered the clutch of trees, Jack followed. He found her again on her knees. "You've found something?"

Tess glanced over her shoulder and nodded. "Help me clear the slash," she said.

Jack stepped in closer, saw the pile of dead limbs, pine needles, and boughs piled three inches high. He knelt down and began uncovering whatever was beneath. "Clothing," he said as Tess tugged at what was clearly the leg of a pair of jeans. Once she had pulled the denim pants entirely away from the detritus, she sat back, placed the jeans across her lap, and drew her palms gently down the length of them. "Here's a T-shirt," Jack said, unfolding a ball of waded cotton.

"These are…" Tess began.

"Yes, they are," Jack said. "Tess, we need to just back away. We've got to get the forensics team up here. We can't disturb this further."

Tess folded the jeans, the material thick with dried blood, and laid them on the ground in front of her. "I know, Jack. I know…"

TWENTY-SIX

"I think we found the boys' clothes, Mike," Jack said into the landline, as he stood in the parlor. Tess sat on the sofa, her hands folded in her lap, her head slightly bowed. "Yeah, Tess and I. Up at the top, in a clearing. They were buried pretty deep." He listened for a moment and then said, "Okay. Tell them to go directly to the lodge. I'll meet them in the parking lot. ...We're okay. ...All right. See you then."

Jack hung up the phone. "Tess, you want something to drink?"

She raised her head and smiled at him. "You got a beer?"

"Sure thing." Jack got a beer from the kitchen and handed it to her. He went back to the kitchen and fixed himself a bourbon and soda.

"Those are the boys' clothes," Tess said as Jack sat down on the sofa.

"I know, Tess. But everything is probable until proven. At least to the cops, it is."

"Let's go out, Jack," Tess said, standing up. "I want to look at Shy and the mountains."

"Sure." He stood and followed Tess outside.

They sat at the pine table for a moment without speaking. Tess scanned the Gore Range to the east, then looked at Shy, who, having heard them come out, was standing with his head bent over the gate.

"One time," Tess said, "when I buried a horse I'd had for more than twenty years, I had my son dig a hole on top of the hill the horse and others seemed to like the most. That was where they seemed to be content and most at ease. My son brought the tractor up, and the digging was as easy as it could be. He then went down the hill, scooped the horse up in his bucket, and brought it back up the hill. As gently as he could, he put the horse in that hole and shoved the earth he'd just dug up on top of it."

"Ah, that's rough."

"Yeah, it was. But after that, the rest of the herd wouldn't come near that place. They'd stay off to one side of where we'd buried that horse. Wasn't until a year passed, that they slowly got comfortable again near that place."

"They could smell it?"

"Nah," Tess said. "The spirit was there. He'd been the stud, the top dog for so long. He'd sired a lot of the herd. Until the day he died of colic, he was still respected. He was a strong horse, Jack. It was as if the others thought that place was holy."

"What was his name?"

"Thunder. He was a squealer and a stomper from the minute he got his legs. I never rode him. Never wanted to. His spirit was just too... large. Your boys are that way, Jack. So young. So much spirit."

"I only got a response from one of them, though."

"Oh," Tess said, smiling, "the other one is there, too. When I touched the clothes, he was there. It wasn't the one who spoke to you."

Jack sipped his drink and noticed Tess hadn't touched hers. "The beer okay?"

Tess looked at the bottle. "Forgot I had it. Those boys were on my mind." She grabbed the bottle and tipped it to her lips, then set it back down. "They were happy, trusting boys."

"That's probably what got them into this mess. The Eagle County deputies should be on their way. We probably ought to head on over to the lodge."

"Gotta call my son," Tess said, pulling her cell from her pocket and standing up. "Don't know when he'll be coming back."

"You can use the landline." Jack watched her press her phone.

"Nah. Got a couple bars."

Of course. You've got bars. Jack stood up just as an Eagle County sheriff's cruiser crossed the road in front of his property. "There they are."

"You on your way?" Tess spoke into the cell. "Okay. If I'm not here, just wait."

***

"That looks like everything, Calvin," one of the two young men said as he took his ball cap off and pulled his forearm across his forehead. The other young man stood back and lit a cigarette.

"So, you moving somewhere?" the other young man asked.

Calvin handed a fifty to the first young man and walked around the bed of the truck, adjusting some items. "Yeah, I've got a little place just off I-70."

"You still gonna run the ranch?"

"Shit," Calvin said, unfolding a tarp he'd earlier tossed on the ground, "you couldn't get me away from here if you tried. Just found a place that suits me better is all. I'll be up here every day. Same as usual. Help me spread this over the bed."

Both young men took corners of the tarp and draped them over the load, and Calvin opened the truck's door and grabbed two bungee cords from the floor. "Let's tie it down," he said, and all three stretched the cords over the tarp.

"That looks okay," Calvin said, walking around the bed of the truck. He turned to the young men. "You can reach me on my cell if you need to. But I'll be here tomorrow. Anybody comes lookin' for me can come back tomorrow. Okay?"

"Yessir," both young men said in unison as they watched Calvin get in the cab, start the engine, and drive down the road.

Calvin couldn't see the oncoming cars as he navigated the narrow dirt road that would in about fifteen miles eventually end at the I-70 service road. In only the last hour, he'd decided his destination would be Montrose or maybe even as far as Ouray, both more than two hundred miles away. Places where he had, if not friends, acquaintances who would let him settle in with them for a few days while he figured out what he was going to do.

He maneuvered the Ford across the deeply rutted road, avoiding errant pine and spruce branches that would scrape the paint from the sides of the pickup, steering clear of rocks that would surely tear the undercarriage from the bottom of the truck. The thought occurred to him that he might come face on with Miguel making his way to the ranch.

"Wouldn't that be a bitch," he said, envisioning the wiry little guy sitting comfortably in his Lexus and doing his own maneuvering around the hazards of the road. Calvin slowed, leaned over, pulled his .45 from the glove box, and sat it on the console to his right. "Motherfucking sheepherding sonofabitch!" he spat out as he gave the Ford a little gas.

***

Mike Day and his forensics crew were once again rushing to DIA in the two Chevrolet Suburbans assigned to his unit. The flight to Vail would take at least forty-five minutes, maybe longer if they encountered bad weather, which they usually did when passing over the Continental Divide. Getting to the Pinecone Lodge would be another hour in vehicles provided by the Eagle County Sheriff. Just as they turned onto Peña Boulevard from I-70, Mike's phone rang.

"This is Mike." It was Suzanne, the technician who Mike had asked to update the NCIC description of the boys.

"We got a hit on your John Does one and two," Suz said.

"No shit?"

"Yeah, it was almost immediately after I added the descriptions of the tattoos found on the bodies. We got an inquiry from a cop in Fort Wayne, Indiana. He said a resident there, a worried mother, hasn't been able to contact her son. The kid had moved to Colorado several years ago with a friend. Seems the father passed away suddenly, and she's tried to call his place of residence and also his workplace to let him know. Said her son had a little tattoo of a devil with a pitchfork just below his navel. He'd showed it to her the last time she saw him."

"That's gotta be them."

"Yeah. The little devil one was Mark Harris. His friend was Brian Hall."

"You contact the Eagle County?"

"Not yet, but I will."

"We'll need a full description of the boys, Suz."

"Working on that right now, Mike."

"Thanks."

Mike cut the connection, grabbed two manila files from his briefcase, and pulled his pen from his shirt pocket. Below what he'd scrawled on the first file—*John Doe #1*—he wrote Mark Harris, then Brian Hall on the second folder. He put the folders back in his briefcase, then tried Jack's cell once again. Still, there was no answer. *Your boys have names now, Jack.* He glanced at the red-eyed, blue demon stallion reared up on his hind legs that greeted all who entered or left Denver International Airport. Thought the blue devil horse had given him a wink.

***

Miguel Rosario had only twice before made the trek to the Whisper River Ranch. Both times, he'd left his Lexus in Vail and driven up to the ranch with Calvin in Calvin's big-ass pickup. After having almost high-centered three times, Miguel damned himself for not renting a jeep or some vehicle that could navigate this nightmare road without fear of tearing the transmission out. As he looked out his side window, he saw the very steep drop into what appeared to be a bottomless canyon. Funny how he'd never noticed it before. Or, maybe he had and just hadn't said anything about it with Calvin sitting next to him. The last thing he needed to reveal to anyone was that he had a fear of heights. He eased to the right side of the road, closer to the hillside that went up and not down. When he saw the path he was taking would put a boulder right under the Lexus, he inched farther toward the left side of the road.

After taking a blind curve slowly, Calvin stopped his truck when he could see the road ahead. Yes, no doubt about it, he'd anticipated precisely what was happening. Miguel was on his way to the ranch. Right there in front of him. And the stupid sonofabitch was driving the Lexus and was on the wrong side of the road. Without thinking about it, just knowing it was what he had to do, Calvin shifted to his lowest gear and gave the Ford gas.

Miguel saw the truck and knew it was Calvin. Saw, too, that the pickup's bed was piled high with crap and covered with a tarp. He stopped his car, leaned over into the backseat for his bag, unzipped it, and had his hand on the Glock 29 he'd earlier thrown in there. Before he could turn his head back to his windshield, he felt the hard thump of Calvin's bumper, making contact with the right side of his car. On instinct, he pressed his gas pedal to the floor and turned his wheel to the right. He heard the screech of metal against metal, and just before he felt the weightlessness of falling, he saw the red cloud of dust the spinning wheels had aroused from below.

***

Tess and Jack watched as Eagle County sheriff's deputies followed protocol and taped off the perimeter of the stand of aspens where they'd found the clothing. Other deputies were scouring the area, some beginning their inspection fifty yards away and working their way inward.

"I guess we're going to do this again." The same deputy, who'd previously taken Jack's statement, approached him with his small notebook open and a pen in his hand.

"Guess we are," Jack said. "This is Tess Shinab. She actually located the clothing."

"You want to spell that last name," the deputy said.

Tess spelled her last name.

"First of all," the deputy said, "how'd you know to come all the way up here? I mean, it's quite a ways from the other scene."

"You won't believe it," Jack said.

"Uh-huh. Well, I guess you'll just have to try me."

After Tess and Jack had explained how they'd found the clothing, the deputy closed his notebook and put it in his pocket. "I think we're gonna have to record this. No one is going to believe me if I put that in my report."

"Fine," Jack said, giving Tess a wink. "We can do it at the lodge, or we can do it at my cabin. I've even got a tape recorder we can use."

The deputy nodded. "Let me see what the lieutenant wants to do. In the meantime, don't, um, leave town, or anything. I mean... There's no town, but... Hell, you know what I mean."

"We know what you mean," Jack said. "My cabin is just to the right of the lodge's access road, about two miles west. That's where we'll be." He gently pressed his hand against Tess's back, and they began to walk down the path.

TWENTY-SEVEN

"There's Saw," Tess said as Jack drove back to the cabin, both of them seeing the orange pickup parked in the drive. "Didn't spend much time with his girlfriend. If there is a girlfriend. Think he might go to Vail for some girl time without the strings if you know what I mean."

Jack laughed. "Yeah, I know what you mean, Tess. Can't blame him for that." He pulled the SUV to the side of Saw's truck. He and Tess got out, both noticing Saw was inside the pasture with Shy.

Tess returned Saw's wave and motioned for him to come in the cabin with her and Jack. When he shook his head, Tess smiled, and, as she followed Jack into the parlor, she said, "He's not the kind to make small talk with people he doesn't know. He'll be fine out there with your horse."

"Have a seat," Jack said. "You want another beer?"

Tess sat on the sofa. "No. Glass of water would be nice."

Jack walked into the kitchen, ran a glass of water, and poured himself another bourbon. "You think Saw wants a beer?" he asked as he sat next to Tess.

"Yeah, he'd prob'ly want one, but he don't need one. Too many times, one becomes ten."

Jack nodded. When his landline began to ring, he set his drink on the coffee table and picked up the receiver. "This is Jack." He listened as Mike explained he and his crew were a couple of hours away. "And Jack," Mike said, "the boys were originally from Fort Wayne, Indiana. Brian Hall and Mark Harris."

"How'd you track that down?"

"The autopsy revealed they'd both had tattoos. We added that information to the NCIC, and a Fort Wayne cop responded. Said one of the kids had shown the tattoo to his mother the last time she'd seen him. That was Mark Harris."

"And the tattoo?"

"Little devil with a pitchfork."

"Okay." Jack paused. "Okay. Thanks, Mike. We're, Tess and I, are waiting for a deputy to come and record our statements. ...Yeah, we told him how we found the clothes, but he's afraid if he doesn't get us on tape, there'll be a little skepticism about the story. ...Yeah, the spirits. ...That'll work. Just give me a call when you're on the ground and headed this way. ...Yeah, see you then."

"That's was my friend Mike," he said as he placed the receiver back on the phone. "He's with the CBI, Colorado Bureau of Investigation. He and his crew are coming up here to do the forensics. The boys have been identified. Mark Harris and Brian Hall."

Tess cradled her glass of water in her hands, looked at the rock-lined fireplace where the ashes within were black and gray. "Good to have names, I guess. Their mothers will want to know."

"The worst part of a cop's job." Jack sipped his drink. "Just thought of something I wanted to ask you about. There were a couple murders in Oak Creek a few days after I found the boys. A lawyer and somebody else."

He grabbed his notes from the coffee table, and before he could flip through them, Tess said, "Yeah, I know about those."

Jack laid his notes back down. "The lawyer was connected to the outfit that owns the ranch up the way. Rambouillet Enterprises—"

"That's a sheep," Tess said.

"Yeah, it is. It probably has nothing to do with the boys, but tell me what you know about the guys who were murdered."

"Otis Schrock was the lawyer. Been in Oak Creek for years. Old guy that knew everybody, but never seemed to work very hard. The other one was Denman. John Denman. Rode motorcycles. Dressed in black leather. He had a little house. A shack, really. He'd walk Main Street sometimes. Brushed up against me on the street one day, and I sensed a spirit."

"His spirit?"

"Nah, it wasn't his. When he passed me, I looked back at him. His spirit voice was sad and angry at the same time. Don't remember the words, but I remember feeling cold... the sadness of that spirit."

"Anybody talking in Oak Creek about the murders? Who might've done them? And why?"

"Everybody talks, Jack. I don't listen to all that stuff. Got better things to do with my time."

Jack took another sip of his drink. "Wonder where that deputy is? You sure Saw won't come in and at least sit down with us?"

"Lemme see," Tess said, placing her water on the coffee table and standing up. "Oh," she said, looking out the window, "he's sitting on the porch." She opened the screen door and stuck her head out.

217

"You wanna come in?"

Saw stood up. "There's smoke down toward the canyon." He nodded toward the south. "I'll be back."

Tess stepped out on the porch and looked at the plume of black smoke rising from where Saw had indicated. Saw turned his truck around and headed out of the drive toward the access road. Just as she was about to turn and come back in, an Eagle County sheriff's vehicle turned onto the drive.

"The sheriff is here," she told Jack as she walked back inside.

Jack stood. "Where's Saw going?"

"Toward the smoke. He fights fires sometimes."

"Fire! Jesus Christ, I've got to get Shy out of here." Jack shot off the sofa and ran to the porch, startling the deputy who was standing just below the steps. "Where's the fire?" he said, raising his voice.

"Down in the canyon," the deputy said, turning and pointing to the plume. "It's a car fire. Some jackass missed a curve. Fire rescue has already been notified."

Jack watched the plume for a moment. Sighing, he said, "Sorry. We do worry about fire up here. Come on in."

Jack pulled a side chair in front of the coffee table for the deputy, and Tess, and he sat back down on the sofa.

The deputy set his tape recorder on the table and, before turning it on, said, "Okay. Let's do this one more time."

***

When Calvin finally reached the I-70 service road, he pulled over, stepped out, and walked around to the right side of his truck. The damage wasn't that bad. His bumper was pushed in, and the front quarter panel was scraped. He watched as an Eagle County sheriff's cruiser came toward him at a high rate of speed and turned from the service road onto the access road to the canyon and the Pinecone Lodge beyond. Calvin got back in the truck and lit a cigar. He smiled, knowing that once fire rescue managed to get to the bottom of the canyon, they'd be surprised to find not one, but two burned-out vehicles and what was left of the drivers. He supposed it wouldn't be long before it would be discovered one of those drivers had a wee hole in the top of his head. Didn't matter. He'd be a long way away by the time that happened.

***

"He still doesn't believe it happened the way we said." Tess stood at the door and watched the deputy back up his cruiser and drive onto the access road.

"No, of course, he doesn't," Jack said. "You want that beer now?"

"Sure." Tess returned to the sofa and sat down.

"Mike should be here in a while." Jack grabbed a beer from the refrigerator and handed it to Tess, then sat as well. "Something about those murders in Oak Creek—given the lawyer's connection to the ranch—is bugging me. Don't know what it is, but my gut is telling me there's something there."

"I guess they're buried by now. Their spirit might be hard to…"

"Yeah, I suppose so. Probably doesn't have anything to do with the boys. Just a coincidence."

They both turned their heads toward the screen door when they heard the crackle of tires on the drive. "Bet that's Saw," Tess said. She stood up and looked out the window. "Yeah, he's back." She opened the screen door.

"Car went off the side of the road," Saw said.

"You get all the way to the fire?" Tess asked.

"Nah." Saw sat down on the porch step. "Just talked to a cop stopped up the road a bit. You ready to go?" He turned his head and looked up at Tess.

"Okay. You see your girlfriend?"

"Yeah. Spent some time with her."

"Okay," Tess said again and turned to Jack. "We're gonna head back. Guess we did what we needed to, huh?"

Jack stood up. "Thank you so much, Tess. It means a lot." He gave her a hug.

"You got my number," Tess said, handing Jack her beer. "Let me know."

"Yeah. Of course."

Jack watched Tess and Saw leave, set Tess's beer on the pine table on the porch, and walked to the pasture. He'd neglected Shy for too long today.

***

Two Eagle County sheriff's vehicles came up the access road. One continued going toward the Pinecone Lodge, and the other turned into Jack's drive and stopped. Mike got out of the passenger side, walked toward Jack, and waved. Jack opened the pasture gate, closed it, and met Mike halfway.

"You want to go up with us?"

"No," Jack said, wiping his hands on his jeans. "I'd probably just be in the way. Can you stop by before you leave?"

"Yeah, I'll do that. Brought the autopsy reports and the NCIC info on the boys." He handed Jack a manila envelope.

"Good deal. I'll take a look."

Mike walked back to the cruiser, stopped at the open door, and turned to Jack. "Mind if I stay over tonight?"

"Of course not."

Mike nodded. "I'll see you in a bit."

Jack stepped into the parlor, sat down on the sofa, and opened the envelope. He pulled out the NCIC bulletin first and studied the pictures of the boys' tattoos. Wondered if they had gotten them together, both psyched as they'd stepped into the tattoo parlor, both still anxious about how painful the inking would be. Wondered, too, what had led Mark Harris to show his mother the little devil below his navel? It had become the most important identifying mark on either of the bodies. Had he smiled and said, "Mom, you're gonna like this," lowering the front of his pants slightly? Jack wished he'd had the kind of mother who he could show something like that to, much less tell her he was gay.

Setting down the NCIC bulletin and picking up the autopsy reports, Jack hesitated before flipping over the cover page. DECEDENT was still noted as John Doe #1, with Mike's scrawl next to it, indicating Mark Harris. He scanned the report: Clothing, External Examination, X-rays, History, Pathological Diagnoses, Cause of Death, Gross Description of the organs, bones, extremities. He remembered Mike's comment: "Those boys were beaten to hell." Jack nodded. *Yeah, they were.* He then flipped through Brian Hall's report, noting as he had with Mark Harris's, that the anus had been lacerated. Swabs of both boys' rectums had been taken, but both had come up negative for semen.

"Either the sonsabitches wore condoms or..." he said. He finished his thought silently. *Or they stuck something else up there.* He flipped back through the Brian Hall autopsy and noted that blood volume was barely discernable. Both autopsies estimated death had occurred at least seventy-two hours before he'd found them. That would have been Sunday, now more than a week ago.

He laid the autopsy reports on the coffee table, stood up, and walked outside to the porch. He stood there a moment, then looked at Shy, who had a leg cocked, his body at ease with the world for the moment. He walked to the pasture fence and leaned his arms on the top rail. He bowed his head and shook it, his thoughts lost to the horror the boys must have gone through up on that hill where they could see the stars.

TWENTY-EIGHT

Twilight had already descended when Jack heard the sound of a vehicle coming up his drive. He'd been thinking about eating something but had forsaken that thought, pouring himself another drink instead. He set the glass on the coffee table, stood up, and walked to the door. When he opened it, he met Mike just about to step on the porch as the cruiser backed down the drive.

"Too late to get back to Denver tonight," Mike said. "You still got that extra bedroom?"

"Last time I checked I did." Jack opened the screen door and stood aside as Mike walked in. "Long day, huh?"

"The longest," Mike said, taking a seat on the sofa. He noticed the autopsy reports lying on the table. "You get a chance to look at those?"

"Yeah," Jack said, closing the door and walking into the kitchen. "Nothing really different from what we already knew. Blood volume was very low. You want scotch?"

"Sure. I want it. I need it. And, yeah, the boys were moved from somewhere else."

"You hear anything about the crash at the canyon?" Jack said as he fixed Mike a drink.

"Just bits and pieces. Fire rescue got down to the bottom, looking for victims. They're going to have to bring in some heavy equipment to get the vehicles out of there."

"Vehicles?"

"Yeah, they found two. Both burned to hell along with the drivers."

Jack walked into the parlor and handed Mike his drink, sat, and noticed Mike had set his cigarettes on the coffee table. "Mind if I have one of those?"

"'Course not." Mike reached into his pocket for his lighter and held it to the cigarette Jack had put in his mouth. "Okay, if I can have one, too? Can we smoke in here."

"Sure. We'll smoke up a storm."

"So, Mike said as he exhaled smoke. "We found all the clothes and almost nothing else. So far, no real evidence, though we haven't been able to pour over everything the deputies found in their search of the area. We'll take a look at everything in the lab."

"You saw those blood-soaked jeans?"

"Yeah. Lots of blood on the clothes. The beatings started before the clothes came off."

"Uh-huh," Jack said, sipping his drink.

They were both silent then, both with their own thoughts. "You okay, Jack?"

"Oh… Yeah, I'm okay. As okay as I can be, I guess. I was thinking about… Hell, no need to share it."

"Go on. Another case?"

"Yeah, another case. What the hell else do old homicide cops have except those memories of…"

"Go on."

Jack set his drink on the coffee table. "This has been at the back of my mind ever since I found the boys. Something kept nagging at me, and I finally remembered. It was before you came to homicide at the DPD. Stanton and I were working a case he'd gotten a gut feeling about. Missing young girl about eight or nine years old in North Denver. Anna Marie Canino. Old Italian family. The girl hadn't come home from school one day, and technically it was classified as a missing person. Hell, she'd been gone for less than twenty-four hours. But Stanton knew the family. He knew all those dagos over there, even knew the Smaldones. You know? The crime family? Anyway, he gets this gut feeling, and we head over to the family's house. We talk a bit with the mother and father, and then Stanton says, let's go outside where he starts walking around the house to the alley. He walks directly to an old garage behind the neighbor's house, kneels down beside the outside wall, and just stays there for a minute, touching the side of the building, the dirt below it. Pretty soon, this kid comes along. He's got his baseball mitt with him, and he's tossing his ball up in the air and catching it as he walks. Kid sees us and stops, then puts his mitt under his arm and opens the back gate to the neighbor's house. 'What's your name?' Stanton asks the kid. Kid says his name is Anthony and starts to go in the backyard. 'How come you left Anna Marie in there?' Stanton says. The kid freezes, drops his mitt and ball on the ground, and starts to bawl. Kid tells us that they were playing doctor, and Anna Marie didn't want to do what he wanted to do, and maybe he squeezed her neck a little too tight, and…"

"Jesus…"

"He'd buried that little girl under the floor in that old garage, Mike, then he'd gone off to play ball with his friends." Jack picked up his drink. "And I'm sitting here wondering what the sonsabitches did after they killed those boys. Did they go and have a drink and laugh awhile about those two faggots they'd fooled into playing their game? What'd they do, Mike? What'd they do?"

Mike scooted closer to Jack and put his arm around his shoulders. "May never know, Jack. You okay?"

Jack wiped his eyes and shook his head. He grasped Mike's hand. "And that's the goddamned hell of it. We might never know."

***

They shared a bed that night, both thankful for the feel of another man against their bodies.

Jack rose first, quietly dressed, and went into the kitchen. He made breakfast and had it ready when Mike finally stepped out of the bedroom.

"Smells good," Mike said, standing at the kitchen counter.

"Here's your coffee." Jack reached the cup over the counter. "The rest will be done here in a minute."

Mike looked at his watch. "Abe's going to pick me up in about forty-five minutes."

"They stayed over in Vail?"

"Yeah. Eagle County sheriff's get a discount at one of the hotels. The plane should be at the airport in a couple hours."

Jack placed two plates with scrambled eggs, toast, and bacon on the counter. "Just coffee, or you want some orange juice?"

"Coffee's fine."

"Okay," Jack said. He grabbed two sets of silverware and walked to the other side of the counter, where they both sat down.

"That story you told me last night? About that young girl?"

"Yeah."

"How'd Stanton know? I mean... He didn't touch her body or anything."

"Well, kind of dovetails with something Tess told me some time ago. She said her people, just like Wolf, speak to the dead and the dead speak back. Even after the dead have been buried."

"No shit. And Stanton..."

"Yeah, he said he'd heard that little girl. She'd said something like what one of the boys said: Just a game. She thought he was her friend."

TWENTY-NINE

Jack hadn't seen Mike since he and his crew had gathered up the clothing. Since that time, almost two weeks had passed with few updates. Mike continued to call about every other day. But, their conversations were more personal than anything about the boys. He did tell Jack that the Skoal can they found in the tent showed a thumb and forefinger print that didn't match either of the boys' and, for which, they got no hits from the NCIC. They both speculated about the bodies found at the bottom of the canyon—Harley Sweet and Miguel Rosario. Rosario's car had hit Harley's square on, and Harley's body had been nearly obliterated. Jack told Mike everything that had occurred with Harley, including what he'd seen of Harley's interaction with Calvin Semple at the ranch, and that Harley had carried a weapon.

Mike had the call Harley made at Jack's cabin traced, and they were both surprised to learn that it had gone to Rosario's cell in Steamboat Springs. The nagging thing about Rosario, though, was that his holdings, all under the parent firm, Rambouillet Enterprises, LLC, included the Whisper River Ranch. Calvin Semple was employed by Rambouillet Enterprises, LLC, the owner, one Miguel

Rosario. They already knew Otis Schrock was on file at the Colorado Secretary of State's office as the registered agent for Rambouillet. However, no other link from Schrock to Rosario could be made. When Otis Schrock was murdered, his office had been swept clean of all files, notes, and miscellaneous items. And the Denman kid who'd been killed the same day in Oak Creek as Schrock? He still could not be linked to the Schrock killing.

"Got a maze that goes nowhere," Mike had told Jack the last time they'd spoken. "But, we'll keep working on it."

"Helluva lot of coincidences, Mike. There's got to be something… It's been almost a month."

"I know, and I'll keep on it. Until I decide to retire."

"You make that decision yet?"

"Not set in stone, but I'm thinking about next spring."

"Well, if you need a place to chill out until then, or just somewhere to do some serious thinking about leaving the job, you know you can come up here."

"I do, Jack. And I thank you for that. You let me know if you think of anything else or hear of anything about the boys."

"I will. And you let me know."

"Of course. Stay well, Jack."

And that had been the last conversation Jack had with Mike. He wondered what would happen to the case if Mike decided to retire. Wondered if it would die, just fade away and become cold. He desperately hoped it wouldn't but knew how these things usually went. If some old dedicated cop or some ambitious kid didn't want to make a name for him or herself, the case would be laid aside, too complex to tie up all the loose ends.

***

Jack saddled Shy with the intent to ride him up to the ranch. He'd not seen Calvin since before Tess, and he had gone back up the hill and found the boys' clothes. Hell, he'd not seen him since he'd watched Calvin and Harley outside the common building, the night Harley had crossed his path.

When they reached the building, he noticed Calvin's truck wasn't there. Jack climbed off Shy, tied him to a porch post, and went inside. The same young woman he'd talked to weeks ago about Tyler's whereabouts sat at the long dining table by herself. When she saw him come in, she waved.

"Hello," Jack said, sitting down across from her. "Seems kind of quiet around here."

"Well, it is," she said as she nursed what looked like iced tea but was probably something more robust. "Since Calvin left, and then the owner of the place drove his car off the road, nobody seems to know what's going on anymore."

"Calvin left?"

"Yeah, the same day the guy drove into the canyon. Nearly two weeks ago."

"He take his things with him?"

"Cleaned out his office and his bedroom. Told Kevin he'd bought a place outside of Vail, and that he'd be back, but he never came back. Crock of shit, if you ask me."

Jack nodded, knowing the maze had just gotten more complicated. "So, he didn't leave a forwarding address or phone number?"

"Kevin has his cell number, but that hasn't worked since he left."

"Interesting."

"Tell me about it," the young woman said. "You're that guy that came looking for Tyler a while ago."

"Yeah. You haven't heard from him, have you?"

"No. He's long gone, too."

"Okay, then." Jack stood up. "What's going to happen to all of you who stay up here? With Calvin gone and..."

"That's what I'd like to know," she said as she tipped her glass to her lips and took a long drink. "They're even going to close the kitchen."

"Well, thanks for the info." Jack turned and walked back toward the entrance. When he got there, he stopped, turned to the young woman, and asked, "Mind if I go take a look upstairs?"

"Feel free."

He walked up to Calvin's office, opened the door, and saw it was indeed pretty bare. Only the furniture remained. He sat behind Calvin's desk and went through the drawers, but found nothing. He looked up at the wall and saw the intense stares from the animal heads hung there.

"If you could only talk," he said as he stood. When he went back downstairs, the young woman was gone, and the place was quiet, not even any sounds coming from the kitchen.

After Jack had brushed down Shy, he went into the cabin, called Mike, and told him what he'd found out. "He left the same day Rosario drove off the mountain."

"The same day we were all up there, as well as a slew of deputies.

How'd he manage to get out without anyone seeing him?"

"Suspect he left pretty early, or at least sometime before noon. I really should have kept a better eye on him."

"Ah, Jack... My head's swimming trying to connect all the dots. We'll track down his vehicle information and put out an NCIC alert that'll identify Semple as a POI."

"If you find his truck, you might want to take a look at it. Maybe some dents or scrapes, if you know what I mean. Anyway, just thought I'd let you know. Something to add to the file, I guess."

"You think he ran Rosario off the road? Why would he want to do that? No, better yet, why would Rosario be driving to the ranch on that particular day? Curiouser and curiouser, Jack. Listen, you take care."

"You too," Jack said, ending the call. He knew without even thinking about it that his hunches were right. But how could it all be put together? How could anything be proven at this point?

***

Late in the afternoon, Calvin Semple pulled into Glen's Premium Used Car lot in Montrose. He'd been on the road for over three hours, much of the time thinking about what he'd just decided to do.

"Welcome to Glen's. I'm Glen." A portly middle-aged man emerged from the office, wiping his hands on his tie that hung only to the top of his belly.

"Hi," Calvin said. "Got this pickup here I'd like to trade-in on..." He scanned the lot and saw three pickups lined up together. "I'll take a look at those." He began walking toward the pickup trucks.

"You got a helluva load there. You know, I didn't catch your name."

"Didn't throw it," Calvin said as he stopped at the first pickup with Glen trailing behind him. "Name's Calvin. And, I'll get all that stuff outta there before we make a deal."

"Well, good, Calvin. Now, this here is a two thousand and tenner with low mileage and nearly new tires. Tell you what. I'll take a look at your rig while you're checking out those beauties."

"Got a little damage on the right front. Nothing you can't buff out. And my truck is newer than what you've got here."

"Okay. Well, let me take a look-see, and I bet we'll have a deal goin' in no time."

After Calvin unloaded his belongings at Charlie Mason's small house on the west side of town—Charlie was an old friend who'd once worked for Calvin at the ranch—he drove back to the car lot where he took possession of a sun-dulled blue Dodge Ram that was four years older than what he'd had.

"I'll take those plates," Calvin said.

"Sure you will," Glen said. He opened his desk drawer and grabbed a screwdriver. "My help has gone home for the day, so I'll get those offa there myself."

"I'll do it." Calvin took the screwdriver, went outside, and took off the plates. He then made one last thorough inspection of the truck, inside and out, and handed the screwdriver back to Glen. "That Dodge quits on me, I'm coming back to see you."

"Oh…" Glen hesitated a moment. "I think I can say with 90 percent certainty you'll love your new truck."

"It's that 10 percent I'm worried about."

"Hah," Glen huffed out as Calvin turned from him, got in the Dodge, and left the lot.

THIRTY

Weeks turned into months. Soon after Jack noticed he'd never arranged to have the paper sack he'd stuffed with items from Tyler's and Ben's cabin picked up and transported to the CBI, he brought that up with Mike. They decided the items still might be useful, and he met an Eagle County deputy at the I-70 service road and handed the sack off to him for transport to Denver. If they were unable to link Tyler or Ben to the murders, all that time and resources to search for DNA on the items was probably a lost cause. Mike did tell him that he'd take a look at the items and see if any fingerprints might be lifted. He was especially interested in the stiff towel Jack had found for DNA testing.

If they could match the print on the Skoal can with something in that paper bag, they'd know Tyler had been in that tent. But still, they didn't know if the dead boys had ever been in that tent. By the first part of September, they knew a whole lot more about Miguel Rosario and his past. Seems the façade of a successful businessman was just that. They knew he'd gotten into trouble in his youth but didn't know what the CBI eventually pieced together. Rosario had been quietly setting himself up in the Craig area as a distributor of the vilest of drugs, heroin mostly. His respectable business career had apparently been made possible by all that dirty money. The CBI had also found some other instances where the old lawyer, Otis Schrock, was linked to Rosario, but nothing illegal. As for Tyler Bray, his boyfriend, Ben, and Calvin Semple, they remained lost to Jack and Mike as if the earth had swallowed them up.

Not long after three days of heavy rain in mid-September, some rock climbers set out to get to the bottom of the canyon from which the two vehicles and the bodies had been recovered. They dropped down only about twenty feet when they saw the side of the canyon was littered with camping items, a gray nylon tent included. Upon completing their climb, they were met by a park ranger curious about their activities, and they told her about what they'd found. The ranger, curious herself, did the same climb with two other rangers and gathered up the items that eventually ended up with the Eagle County Sheriff's Office. Two deputies who had been involved with the investigation of the boys' murders, cataloged the items and called the CBI about the find. The report eventually landed on Mike's desk, so he called Jack and said he'd be coming up the following Saturday to retrieve the items.

"Can you handle me for the weekend?"

"Sure," Jack said. "And, having experienced one winter up here already, I've started work on a stable for Shy. You can help me build the damn thing before it snows."

***

Jack was surprised to see Mike arrive in a new Jeep. He'd told Jack, no, he didn't need for him to meet him at the I-70 turnoff as before. He'd find his way up with no problem.

As Jack walked out of the front door, Mike stepped from his new vehicle with a smile on his face. "Whaddaya think?"

"Well…" Jack stood on the porch and noticed the temporary sticker on the back window. "Looks like a mountain conveyance for sure."

"My thought exactly," Mike said as he closed the door and walked to the porch. Jack thought he looked, oh, he guessed younger was the best word for it. Mike's smile was what he remembered from so many years before.

After they hugged, Mike turned toward the pasture and looked at the stable Jack was in the process of building for Shy. "You're making progress, I see."

"Yeah, I am. Digging the holes for the support posts was a bitch. But, yeah. C'mon, I'll show you. You get those items from the sheriff yet?"

"Yes, there in the back." He motioned toward his Jeep as they walked to the shed. "Two large evidence bags. I thought we'd go through them later."

"Sure. I want to do that. Look, Shy saw you coming." Shy was leaning his head over the fence, nodding it up and down, and Mike walked directly to him, reached out, and scratched his neck.

"Wow," Jack said, surprised he'd obviously lost some of his fear of horses.

"What?" he asked.

"Last time you were here, you avoided Shy if you could."

"Yeah." He smiled. "But last time I was here, I hadn't decided to do what I'm going to do."

"Retire?"

Mike nodded. "Exactly. Middle of May."

"Feels pretty good, huh?"

"Better than I ever dreamed, Jack. Also decided something else."

"What's that?"

"I'm going to get a place in the mountains. Got a broker looking for me as we speak."

"Good." Jack had always hoped Mike might move in. That they'd reconnect again. Not as intimately as they once had but surely enough to live together. "Let's take a look at my project."

They walked to the shed, and Mike saw what Jack had done, which wasn't that much. "You put those poles down far enough? You put cement down there, I hope."

Jack shook his head. "When was the last time you built a stable in the mountains?"

"Oh… Never. But I used to help Old Pop do his projects. He taught me a lot about this kind of thing, Jack."

"Okay," Jack said. "We've got two days, or most of two days to see what you learned."

"That'll work, and you won't be disappointed."

"You get breakfast before you came up the mountain?" Jack asked.

"No. And I've been thinking about one of your breakfasts all the way up here."

"C'mon then." Jack placed his hand on Mike's back. "Let's get something to eat."

They walked back to the cabin, where Jack pulled out his iron skillet and made scrambled eggs, hash browns, bacon, toast, and coffee. As they ate, Mike could barely take a bite without talking about his retirement and the pictures and information his broker had given him on available mountain properties. He was as animated as Jack had seen or heard him in a long time. Or at least since that day nearly two months ago when he'd again entered Jack's life. After breakfast, they went out front, pulled the evidence bags from the back of Mike's Jeep, and took a look. Everything they remembered had been in that tent wasn't there. The tent and the sleeping bags were, but little else. "I guess if they buried this stuff on the side of the canyon, they must have put the other items in last," Mike said.

"Yeah, the rest of it is long gone. Or maybe at the bottom of the canyon. Don't know if any of this will be helpful."

"Probably not." Mike started to repack the items in the evidence bags. "But... You know, if something ever comes up, we'll have all the evidence or potential evidence we could find."

"*If* something ever comes up," Jack said, knowing that was unlikely.

Mike hefted the bags back into the Jeep. "More than two months without a break, Jack."

"I know. I know," Jack said. "What say we put Old Pop's practical knowledge to work and put walls on that stable?"

"Let's do it," Mike said, closing the hatch.

***

It wasn't until late Sunday when they finally had time to relax. They'd gotten three walls of the stable up, as well as plywood on the roof. Through their labors, they rehashed what they knew of the boys' case. When they sat down on the sofa, drinks in their hands, with a fire going, Jack brought up what'd been on his mind ever since Mike had said he was looking for mountain property.

"That property search you're doing?"

"Yeah."

"I've been thinking... Well, I do have room up here, and... Well, since we're both on our own, so to speak..."

Mike turned a bit on the sofa and looked at Jack. "Jack, since I first walked up that hill the day you found the boys, I hoped you'd offer that to me. Hell," he said, pulling a cigarette out of his pack. "When I saw you that day and heard your story about moving up here, not a day, not an hour has passed that I haven't thought, damn, wouldn't it be great to just move in with Jack. You mind me smoking in here?"

"That's fine."

Mike held the pack out to Jack, and Jack took one. "Thing is," he lit Jack's smoke and then his own, "the more I thought about that, the more I thought about you and how you once told me it wouldn't work."

"No, no." Jack shook my head. "That was—"

"I know what you're going to say," he interrupted. "That was a thousand years ago, and we both knew it wouldn't work. We were on the job then, and it wasn't a time when two men could live together, especially two cops, and not be open to, uh, discovery. You know what I mean?"

"Of course I do."

"Well, I don't worry about that anymore. But I do worry about it working between us. Two old farts sitting around all day trading stories and lies and maybe trying to decide if we'll sleep together, or who'll clean the bathroom, or if you'll want a cat running around."

"Mike, I... Don't you think we could work those things out?" Jack laid his cigarette in the ashtray and took a sip of his drink.

"Maybe. Maybe not. If it's any indication of where my mind is right now, I've told my broker to look at properties less than twenty miles from here, from your place, this wonderful place."

"Your broker's probably got a whole lot of crap along the I-70 corridor, nothing like I've got here."

Mike nodded and took a sip of his drink. "Right. That's what she's coming up with. Mostly condos in the Vail or West Vail areas."

"At probably twice what I paid for this place."

"I don't know what you paid, but you're probably right."

When Mike didn't say anything for several minutes, Jack stood up, walked into the kitchen, and refreshed his drink. "You want some more?" he asked as he tried to make sense of what Mike had just told him.

"No, I'm fine."

When Jack sat back down, he smashed out the cigarette still burning in the ashtray and looked at Mike. "I guess it's only natural to be hesitant about such a thing. A life-changing decision, I guess. But just know that I offered, and we can leave it at that."

Mike reached over and squeezed his thigh. "Thank you," he said.

Just as the night before, they slept in separate beds. Monday morning rose with a chilling wind, and Jack headed for the parlor with the intent to make a fire. Before he turned from that hallway, he smelled the burning pine. Then he saw Mike kneeling before the fireplace.

"Read my mind," he said.

Mike stood and turned to him. "That's something cops learn fairly early. Reading the minds of both the innocent and guilty gets to be second nature."

"Yes, it does," Jack said. He walked into the kitchen area and started the coffee brewing.

After breakfast, they hugged in the parlor, and Mike got in his new Jeep and turned around in the drive. Jack watched Mike until he lost sight of him as he headed west on the access road.

***

The first snows came early, blanketing, it seemed, the entire world. It was mid-October, but since the local investigation of the boys' murders had slowed down, Jack had time in early September to begin the tasks he knew needed to be done before the first snows fell. Relying on what he'd learned the prior winter, he'd purchased two new blankets for Shy, stocked up on hay and other feed, and made sure the heater for Shy's water tank was still operating. After felling several dead trees on his property and cutting and splitting about half a cord, he'd seen the wisdom of buying an additional two cords from the caretaker of the Pinecone Lodge, a hardy, big-boned woman named Gladys, always in blue overalls. He'd hired her last winter to plow out his drive when needed.

He'd made four trips to Vail to stock up on food, water, candles, butane lanterns, batteries, alcohol, and everything else he figured Shy and he might need to last the winter. He'd stuffed the shelves of the larder to almost overflowing. Jack knew Eagle County would make no effort to keep the access road open, and his few neighbors would be on their own for the duration. They'd be cut off from the rest of the world, except for the occasional visit from the forest service ranger who, if possible, came up about once every two weeks on a snowmobile. He'd bring them their mail and do a general welfare check on the few people who lived there year-round. Just days before the snows came, he'd finished the enclosed stable Mike had helped him build, which he'd attached to the feed and tack shed.

It snowed for four days and nights. On the fourth night, Jack once again built a fire after taking care of Shy's needs. He poured himself a drink, sat on the sofa, and stared into the flames. He'd not eaten and was thinking about fixing something when the landline rang.

"This is Jack."

"It snowing up there?"

"For four days now. How are you, Mike?"

"I'm fine. Talking heads said we might see some of what you're getting up there before morning. Is it bad?"

"No, not that bad. It's pretty wet snow, though. Cold, too."

"Got a letter... Well, it wasn't addressed to me, but to the CBI. It was from both the boys' mothers, thanking us for finding their sons."

"Can't imagine what the mothers went through."

"Yeah," Mike said. "I wanted to write back and tell them who actually found the boys but thought I'd just leave it at that. I'm sure they don't need another reminder that their boys are gone."

"No, they don't need that."

There was silence on the line, then, "We're still looking into this, Jack. Nothing new, but we're still digging."

"I know you are, Mike. Hell, it'll stay with us both for a very long time. I suspect resources will begin to dwindle away, though. Can't spend time and money on dead ends for very long."

"I just wish something would pop up. There's got to be somebody out there who can tell us something."

Jack sighed. "Oh, they're out there. And, I doubt they're going to talk about this thing any time soon. Somebody will slip up someday. Tell a friend, or, hell, most likely one of them will end up in a jail cell someday and work a plea deal. That's usually the way it happens."

"I know. Just a second, Jack…"

Jack heard some rustling on the line.

"Sorry, Jack. Gertrude was climbing the drapes. Hate it when she does that."

"You and that cat."

"Yeah, well… She's the only thing I've got to come home to besides my books. Reading about wolves now. You have wolves up there?"

"Never seen any, though the locals say they're around. 'Course the locals tell a lot of lies. Why wolves?"

"Oh, you know. Trying to discern if there's anything to what you and Tess believe."

"For that, you're going to have to read about Native people too, Mike—the myths, the lore."

"That's the thing, Jack. I'm trying to understand if the myths and the lore actually, oh, translate into verifiable events. Not events, really… Hell, you know what I mean?"

"Sure. But if you don't believe what I've told you over the years about what Stanton taught me, and how Tess found the boys' clothes… If you don't believe those things, then you'll never wrap your brain around the wolf thing."

"Yup, you're probably right. Gotta give me credit, though."

"Oh, I give you credit for a lot of things. You find any good properties up here yet?"

"Not yet. Won't retire until May, so I've got a little time. Kind of want to have the new place paid off by that time, though."

"So, I'll see you in May?"

"Sure. We got a date."

"Helluva thing having to wait for six months for you to head back up here."

"It is, but you know what they say about absence and fondness."

"Yeah, I know what they say," Jack said, remembering the last night they'd shared a bed, and the last time he'd seen him. "Wish you were here right now."

"Yeah, me too. Listen, I'll let you go. You're probably tired and…"

"Miss you, Mike. Try my cell if you can't get through on the landline. Snow and trees have a habit of destroying outdated communications up here. Not that the goddamned cell is gonna work…"

"I'll do it. Bye, Jack."

"Good-bye."

As Jack hung up the phone, he stood, walked to the fireplace, and grabbed a poker. He shuffled the burning logs around and watched the embers rise. Realized he was more tired than he was hungry. Securing the metal mesh screen close to the fireplace, he thought a moment about checking on Shy. He decided not to, knowing Shy was fine, out of the elements and most likely too hot under the blanket he'd put on him earlier. Shy had grown his winter coat with a vengeance and probably didn't even need the blanket. Jack dumped what little remained in his glass into the kitchen sink and went to bed.

***

Mike took a sip of Chardonnay and lit another cigarette. He moved the copy of *Of Wolves and Men* from his lap and laid it next to him. As Gertrude roused herself from the back of the couch directly behind Mike's neck, Mike stood and walked across the living room to the windows that faced Cheesman Park. As he'd done almost every night for the past year, he studied the lighted windows of the apartment buildings within view. And again, he wondered what the people behind those windows were doing. How many were, like him, alone tonight. He glanced at Gertrude, sauntering across the carpet. *Well, not technically alone.* He then walked back to the couch, tapped his cigarette over the ashtray, and sat back down.

It had been a long time ago, he mused. More than twenty years ago, when he and Jack had decided to drive into the Front Range of the Colorado Rockies. It had been one of those rare Saturdays when neither of them was working nor on-call with the DPD dispatcher. Homicides had a way of occurring on Friday and Saturday nights. Neither remembered when they'd not been on the roster to work or required to stay close to the city to deal with the inevitability of another murder.

Mike had suggested they head up Highway 285 toward Bailey, which is where Old Pop used to take him when he was a child. Sometimes Old Pop would drive all the way over Kenosha Pass, and into the town of Fairplay. The town sat within the South Park basin, with the Mosquito Range of the Rockies to the west where 14,000-foot peaks rose to the sky. Jack had agreed, and when Mike had further suggested they stop somewhere and buy cheap fishing poles, Jack had shaken his head.

"Nope," he'd said. "Fishing is like watching baseball. If you're lucky, something will happen in your lifetime."

"Old Pop and I used to fish up there on the South Platte. It was fun."

"Nah. I'll bet you and Old Pop just enjoyed the time together. I bet you didn't catch very many fish."

"Sure, we did." Mike had smiled and added, "Well, sometimes we did. So, your father never took you fishing?"

"My father," Jack had begun, turning his head and looking out the side window of Mike's '72 Impala, "was indeed a fisherman. He was also an on-again-off-again drunk."

Mike had glanced at Jack, who was still looking out the side window. He'd never heard much about Jack's family, except for his wife and their very short marriage. "That must have been a bitch."

Jack had then looked at Mike, nodded, and looked out the windshield. "Yeah, it was. I guess he tried his best to be a father, but never really succeeded. He'd take me fishing, and I always refused to do it, opting to just explore the countryside. We never came up here, though. He preferred to head south, that area west of Colorado Springs."

"Your mother?"

"Hah," Jack had said, and it wasn't a laugh. "She's was... Italian."

Mike had waited for Jack to go on, and when he didn't, he said, "Okay. Must be where your... passions come from?"

"Oh, that and more." Jack had then lit a Lucky Strike. As he exhaled the first stream of smoke, he continued. "She was technically crazy. Clinically crazy, I guess, is the better word. She inherited from her mother a purely Italian devotion to the Catholic church—a belief in stigmata, the worth of suffering, guilt, all that shit." He'd paused and grabbed the pint of whiskey that sat between them, unscrewed the cap, and took a sip. "But, as crazy as she was, she seemed to, oh, know things before they happened."

"Ah," Mike had said. "Thus, your hunches about things."

"No, no. More than that. Her... voices, her visions—things no one else could see or hear—revealed things to her that usually proved true. She knew when people were going to die. She knew... Hell," he said, after taking another sip of whiskey. "When I was very young, playing out in the backyard, she came running from the house, knelt down in the grass, raised her arms to the sky, and just began to wail. An hour later, the phone call came. Her father, who had been fine just hours before, was dead. A massive stroke."

"Jesus."

"Yeah, and she also knew..." Jack had paused, took another sip from the bottle, and recapped it. "Look," he had said, pointing across the road to a row of small cabins set against the backdrop of a thickly forested mountain, "that's a motel. They've got vacancies."

Mike had looked and slowed the Impala. "You want to get a room?"

"Sure. I don't fish, so..."

And Mike had turned the Impala around at the next broad apron.

They had spent the rest of the day inside the cabin that offered a queen-sized bed, a fireplace, two chairs, a kitchenette, and a bathroom. No television, but there'd been a black rotary dial phone. They had used the bed to the exclusion of the other amenities, except for the bathroom. They'd showered before checking out when the shadows boded night.

Mike eased out of his reverie, becoming aware that Gertrude had at some point nestled into his lap, and he'd been stroking her for all of that time. He also thought about what Jack had told him about his family—his father, a drunk, and his crazy mother. Not for the first time, he wondered if maybe Jack's acceptation of unexplainable things, of his belief that the dead speak, was something that had come to Jack as an inevitability. Something from his Italian mother who perhaps heard and spoke to the spirits as well.

"No," he said, shaking his head. "Jack isn't crazy. Jack's just…" He wondered now just exactly what distinguished Jack from the rest of humanity, especially from the other men he had known intimately, albeit briefly during his life. "Hell, I don't know," he said, rousing Gertrude from her loll and standing. "I do know I love him," he said, thinking that he just might want to spend the rest of his life up in the hills under Jack's roof.

THIRTY-ONE

For the past ten months, Tyler Bray and Ben Jenkins had followed the amateur rodeo circuit as employees of Grimm's Rodeo Supplies and Setup Services, based in Amarillo, Texas. They had no real home and were on the road most months of the year, traveling with Grimm's caravan of three semis with four or five pickups following behind. Their stops had been small towns in New Mexico, Arizona, Oklahoma, and Texas. They stayed in inelegant motels for a week or so, then moved on to the next destination, where they'd set up the arenas or outdoor county fairs for the spectacle of a rodeo where young men would attempt to earn their spurs for the professional circuit. The only permanence in Tyler's life was Ben and Bear. They stabled the horse with a heavyset widow still living on her dead husband's forty acres. She had also rented out the upstairs bedroom to Tyler and Ben. The only permanence in Ben's life remained Tyler.

The day they left the Whisper River Ranch in Tyler's pickup, hauling Bear behind, they'd stopped at the I-70 service road at precisely the spot Calvin Semple would pull over when he made his departure. Tyler turned off the engine, slipped out of the cab, walked up the hill a bit, and sat on his haunches.

Ben soon did the same, and as they watched the traffic flow both east and west on I-70, Tyler said, "Which way?"

"Believe I want someplace warm for the winter, Ty."

"Been thinkin' the same thing. Grew up in North Texas. Nice enough place, I guess."

"Sounds good."

"One thing, though," Tyler said, standing. "We got to change the plates on the truck, and the trailer, too."

"Yeah, that'd be a good idea. How we gonna do that?"

"Well, let's drive into Vail. See if we can find a car parked off somewhere where nobody can see us, and just take the plates. We can find a horse trailer plate somewhere, too. Lots of them around."

"If we get caught, I—"

"Ain't gonna get caught, Ben," Tyler interrupted.

Ben nodded and stood up. "Okay. Let's do it."

After five hours on the road, they stopped at Raton, New Mexico, for a meal, gas, and water for Bear. After another three hours, they were in Amarillo, where Tyler bought a newspaper and scanned employment and rental ads. The old widow, Missus Clark, had welcomed them in as a mother reunited with errant children. After they had settled into the upstairs bedroom, after Bear was put in the pasture, fed, and watered, they stepped into Clyde Grimm's storefront office. Grimm had looked them over a bit from behind his desk and continued to chomp on the fat burrito he held in his beefy hand and told them, yes, he did need some help.

"Don't want no goddamned drunks or fuckin' nutcases, though," he said.

"Well, we ain't that," Tyler said.

"And I sure don't want no wannabe bull riders. Had more an enough of hirin' dipshits with an itch to ride a bull, who break their goddamned necks the first chance they get. You ain't in that category, are you?"

"Oh, hell no," Ben said.

And Grimm hired them on. Told them to pack lightly and be at the supply yard for loading first thing in the morning. "And first thing in the mornin' is five o'clock. Got it?" he added.

Tyler and Ben got it and were at the supply yard at four-thirty.

Not a day had passed, either when driving to the next destination or settling in for the night at one motel or another, that Tyler and Ben hadn't spoken of the boys they'd met in Vail and spent some time with in Avon. They both avoided as best they could speaking about their complicity in the boys' murders. Tyler thought about writing a letter to Jack Dolan, the old cop who'd found the bodies and sending it to him without a return address. He'd tell Jack everything that happened, why it happened, and who had participated. He didn't know all of the men who'd been there but knew Calvin and Denman had organized it.

"Oh, I don't know about that," Ben told Tyler each time Tyler had brought it up. "That'd only put us on the spot if anything... If they ever find us. And I bet they're lookin' for us."

"I feel like we gotta do somethin', Ben."

"You and me both. But, hell, what if they already figured it out? What if we're already off the hook?"

"Don't know about that. Got a feeling I won't ever be off the hook with this thing. I think you gotta be able to forget somethin' before you can truly be off the hook. Don't think that's gonna happen any time soon."

"I know what you mean, Ty."

And over the ten months, they'd done right by Mister Grimm. Although Grimm had them on the books as only part-time employees and paid the rest under the table, they knew they were doing better financially than they'd ever done. They were happy. Except for that nag, that daily nag about those two boys who they'd watched walk up the trail that night a year ago, when Ben had looked up at the sky and had said, "Them stars are real pretty tonight."

THIRTY-TWO

Jack's second winter in the cabin was much like the first, except he had the new stable for Shy, and that was a comfort for him. Whether or not Shy saw it as a comfort, Jack had his doubts. The boy seemed to prefer the pasture to the stable even during the coldest days, and he never appeared to mind the snow that accumulated on his back. After multiple times shoveling a path to the from the cabin, he took the Pinecone Lodge's caretaker, Gladys, up on her offer to sell him the oldest of the two ATVs she had. He could plow out that path rather than risk the heart attack she promised him he'd have. Gladys continued to plow his drive and the access road to the lodge with her Deere tractor, but Jack took care of the smaller stuff on his property. On days when the sun shined, and his drive and the access road to the lodge had been plowed, he put a halter on Shy and walked him a couple miles. Some days he'd even saddle him and ride those two miles, then turn around and do it again.

In early December, Mike called to tell Jack he'd finally gotten around to sifting through that sack of stuff Jack had gathered at Tyler's and Ben's cabin. Mike had given a glass and shot glass to the lab, and they'd found a couple fingerprints that matched what they'd taken off the Skoal can.

"So Tyler was in that tent," Jack said.

"Yes, he was. That doesn't tell us much, though, except that he was in that damned tent. Can't prove the boys were in there."

"No, we can't. But, I know, maybe you do too, that they were all in there at one point."

"Yeah, I believe that. But from what we saw in that tent, nothing happened there. No struggle, no violence, just a barely used campsite."

"Still nothing on the vehicles? Calvin's or Tyler's?"

"Nope. We're almost nine months into this thing, Jack, and... Well, it doesn't bode well for any resolution."

"Yeah, it's getting cold. Oh, it's been cold for a while. Are they pulling resources from the case?"

"Well, 'they' is the assistant director, and, yes, he's pulling resources. Other people are getting murdered, Jack."

"Funny how that never stops, huh?"

"Yeah." Mike sighed.

When Mike remained silent for a moment, Jack asked, "So, you put in your paperwork yet?"

"Can't do it until February."

"You're still going to get outta there? Right?"

"Oh yeah. Still looking at properties."

Jack didn't want to again bring up his offer for Mike to come and live with him. He didn't want to push it. Either Mike would or he wouldn't. "Okay. Well, I guess I'll take Shy for a little ride. Weather is pretty nice today, and we have to take advantage of that whenever we can."

"You be well, Jack."

"You too, Mike."

After they ended the call, Jack thought about Mike's voice, and how he'd sounded tired, maybe even depressed. The elation he'd seen months ago when Mike announced he'd definitely decided to retire was now gone. Or at least for today, it was.

Jack pulled on his parka and the felt cowboy hat he'd bought the last time he'd gone shopping and stepped out onto the porch. He stood there awhile in wonderment; the entire world had become white, the blue sky above the tops of the pine trees, the aspens only skeletons now, but dressed in pure white. He looked at the pasture where Shy had his head bent over the fence. As he walked toward him, he began nodding his head and nickered. He was ready to get moving.

***

In late January, on a morning when it seemed that spring might just be around the corner, Jack heard Gladys's Deere tractor coming up the drive. He looked out the window and saw her climb off the tractor and grab a large box that she'd strapped down behind the seat. When she walked toward his door, Jack put on his coat and stepped out.

"Brought you somethin'," she said, setting the box on the porch. "You don't want it, I can take it back." She opened the top of the box, and inside was a black-and-white puppy covered by a towel. "It's an Alaskan Malamute." She picked the puppy up, still wrapped in the towel, and held it out to Jack.

"Damn," Jack said, taking the little bundle and looking at the puppy's face. "Where in the hell did you get this?"

"Oh, the guy who lives about six miles south of the lodge showed up yesterday with two of these guys. Said his bitch had had them about seven weeks ago, and he wanted to know if I wanted one."

"How'd he get them to you?"

"Snowmobile."

"I'll be damned," Jack said, letting the puppy chew on his finger. "Who is this guy? I didn't even know anyone lived out there."

"And he doesn't want anybody to know, either. Closest thing to a hermit mountain man there is. Hell, he's got four Mals as it is. I'm gonna keep the other one. Whaddaya think? You want him?"

"Well, sure," Jack said. "I've been thinking about a dog, but..."

"Now, you got one. Got some kibble on the tractor for you."

Gladys walked back to the tractor as Jack held the puppy up, let the towel fall off him, and looked him over.

"He's got everything he's supposed to have," Gladys said, setting a bag of dog food on the porch. "If he gets an upset stomach, just boil up some hamburger. Give him some cottage cheese if you got any."

"What about shots and all that?"

"He'll be fine until you can get him to a vet. Hell, what'd dogs do before we started fawnin' all over them? Don't believe the guy has ever had his dogs vaccinated."

"Okay. Thanks, Gladys."

"No problem." She turned around and walked back to her tractor.

Jack hadn't had a dog since he was a kid, but after two weeks, he had taught him the bathroom was outside. And every time he'd take him out, it was a hell of a struggle to get him to come back in. He was a snow dog for sure. Jack introduced him to Shy, and every time after that when Jack opened the door, the dog made a beeline toward the stable or the pasture, wherever Shy happened to be at the time.

The day Jack got him, he'd called Mike at home that evening and told him what had happened.

"Excellent," Mike had said. "What'd you name him?"

Jack hadn't even thought about that but said, "I guess Marshall. Marsh for short."

"Of course that's his name," Mike had laughed.

They'd talked a bit about the case, but there wasn't anything new. Jack hadn't asked him about his retirement plans, as that seemed to have become an old record for both. It didn't need to be played over and over again.

***

Shy, Marsh, and Jack got through the winter just fine. Spring arrived with an abundance of mud, which Marsh and Jack both tracked it into the house. He'd never been much of a house cleaner but soon found if he didn't take care of the mess today, he'd have an even larger one tomorrow. But it was all worth it. New life was everywhere. The mule deer daily brought their spotted babies to the cabin, appearing to take pleasure in showing them off. Toward evening, the flash of gray foxes with their kits would cross his eye almost as phantoms, seldom pausing long enough for him to catch a good view of them. He'd decided he'd put up some bird feeders, and he hung them from an aspen limb about six feet in the air. He put up hummingbird feeders as well. Now he had a regular bird café off to the side of the cabin, with jays, nuthatches, hummingbirds, nutcrackers, woodpeckers by the hundreds, stopping by on the hour, every hour. He had yet to see a bear but knew they were out there. He suspected they stayed higher up on the ridges.

The glory of the spring, though, was colored as he knew it would be. As he marveled at what each new day brought, he also thought of the boys. Sometimes he felt them nearby, and in his head or in a whisper, he'd point out the sights and sounds of the springtime to them: *Look there at the elk, the calves so gangly with their long legs. And the chickadees upon the feeder. And there! You see that bobcat?*

Jack rose and retired each day with the boys on his mind.

THIRTY-THREE

Jack believed the proper name for this place was a glade and considered, too, it was more than that and required a name unique to itself. The interest in giving it a name had worked on him for some time, and he hadn't yet come up with any short litany of possibilities. Believed, for now, he'd continue to call it The Place as he'd lately been doing. A place of significance, he thought.

Shy was tied off amongst a swatch of grasses twenty yards from The Place because he still shied from it. He was happy, though, for the meal of sweet grasses. Marsh, now almost five months old, scampered about and sniffed the layer of pine needles and rocks with moss on their north sides. He investigated deer droppings, and the detritus of rotting grayed limbs and entire trees that lay upon the ground like warriors lost to a desperate battle. Jack sat cross-legged in the middle of The Place, glanced up, and saw the near oval of Colorado mountain blue sky framed by the tips of tall pine and spruce. Here and there, dying or dead lodgepole pine, some hued to gray, still stood and leaned one way or the other, witness that scavengers no larger than a flea could destroy whole forests. Such was life and death, Jack thought. As usual, he viewed it all with acceptance.

Somewhere along the line of the last sixty-plus years of his life, he'd given up trying to understand the whys and wherefores of things he could not change. Except for the whys and wherefores of the boys he'd found there a year ago. That, he believed, still mattered and required an understanding.

A place of significance.

Marsh ceased his inspection of The Place, stopped dead in his tracks, raised his head to sniff, and stared into the denseness of the forest beyond. Jack followed Marsh's line of sight and saw nothing unusual. He was almost certain no bears were nearby despite the Pinecone Lodge's former horse wrangler, Tyler, who reported almost a year ago he'd seen one on higher ground. Jack had smiled when he heard that. Tyler was sitting a family from New Jersey atop seventeen- and eighteen-year-old paint-colored horses that looked bored and lazy in the noontime heat.

"Yessir, I did see a lone grizzly," Tyler had said, pausing long enough to grab the can of Skoal in his rear pocket and pinch out a bit of what was inside, sticking it into his cheek. "But, nothin' at all to worry about," he had said, winking at Jack, "'cause they stay up high." The mama of the group had looked concerned, and the two tow-headed boys' eyes were wide as spring-bloomed crocuses. The daddy, just like Jack, had smiled, probably knowing the boys would be telling tall tales of Colorado grizzlies ten times over once they returned to the Garden State.

Jack didn't know why he remembered that story except that it was a good one. Tyler was now gone, but his whereabouts had been on Jack's mind since he'd left without a nod or a good-bye last July.

"Marsh," Jack said. "What do you see?"

Marsh glanced at him, sneezed, and returned his attention to the forest that surrounded The Place, his eyes, and snout directed toward whatever peculiarity he'd sensed. He then resumed his inspection of the ground layered in pine needles and curious scents.

Jack knew the odor of death still lingered there. Yet, he also knew time, and the elements had worked upon that odor to the point that even Marsh smelled it as an inarticulate hint of something not readily identifiable. Jack knew Shy's reluctance to enter The Place had again arisen because of his memory of it as a horrid place. Jack knew, too, that what had happened here had yet to see closure. That's was why he was there. That was why, whenever he could, he came again to The Place, sat down, watched, listened, and waited for an epiphany that would probably not come in his lifetime.

But the boys who once knew this place as the last place they would ever see in life still deserved his attention. His visits there were made with the hope he would eventually make sense of the questions one of the boys, so deadly quiet, had asked him when he bent down to touch their ruined heads. He somehow needed to make things right. Right as rain, he thought as he saw the predictable daily visitation of northeasterly bound cumulonimbus puffs darkening the oval of the sky at the tips of the tall trees above.

"C'mon, Marsh," he said, standing and brushing off the back of his pants and legs. "Let's go home." Marsh followed him from The Place. They paused when they stepped upon the rutted trail because Jack turned and looked back for a moment as if the hush and tenderness of the new rain spoke of things unsettled.

"C'mon," Jack said again, "Mike'll have lunch ready for us." Jack turned, untied Shy's lead rope from the Aspen branch, grabbed the reins from the horn, and led his horse and dog down the rutted path toward home.

This is what I believe

*I remember the first homicide I investigated as the lead detective.
I'd been paired with Jack Dolan for a couple of years, but one time
he was put on temporary assignment with the Fort Collins Police
Department. The chief up there had asked for help with a homicide
they couldn't solve, and our boss had sent Jack to help them out.
He'd left on a Friday night, and it was that same night when a young
man had been shot in the back of the head in Denver's Cheesman
Park. I was the senior man on call, and I responded.*

*Sure, I'd seen Jack and Stanton solve cases with ease, investiga-
tions that seemed almost magical. And later, I'd find out it was a sort
of magic. But I had been trained by academia, the majority of my
college education devoted to the science of investigative techniques,
and that's what I applied to that homicide in the park.*

*Long story short, with the help of the forensics expertise, the evi-
dence, the lab work, the logical probabilities, and all the long hours
I devoted to the investigation, I found the killer without Jack's and
Stanton's magic. He was convicted but found to be insane and was
sent to the state hospital in Pueblo. He was one of our own: A DPD
vice cop who'd become obsessed with a gay kid who wore black*

leather and had what the killer described as white eyes. One night while he was on what they called fag patrol in Cheesman Park, this cop thought he saw the object of his obsession receiving a blowjob in the bushes surrounding the park. He snuck up on him and, without seeing his face, shot the kid in the back of the head. It turned out not to be the object of his obsession, but just a kid with the same color hair and wearing a black leather jacket.

I've never met a cop who has worked in the vice bureau for a long time who wasn't half-crazy. This cop was completely crazy and said that White Eyes, as he called the victim, was unclean and wouldn't stay out of his bed at night, and spied on him when he took a shower or a crap in his bathroom. When I told him that his victim had brown eyes, he said that White Eyes could do that—change the color of his eyes.

The cop killed himself in that mental hospital by fashioning a noose with his bedsheet, not six months after he'd been taken there. When I heard the news, I thought justice had been done, and I was proud of myself for applying the skills that eventually brought justice to bear.

Michael Day

THIRTY-FOUR

Mike's days with Jack, Marsh, and Shy moved too quickly. Sometimes he wanted to stop time so he could and take a few moments to sort out the essential meaning of it all: of the pine-scented aroma of the air with no pollution; of the mountains, the Gore Range, stoic, unmovable, turning from black to blue, sometimes to silver as the day progressed; of the absence of sound, of hearing nothing when you paused and realized that's what you were hearing—nothing; of a sky so blue it defied description, and the clouds so white, so close, traveling on whispers of thermals from the northwest, pausing in their journey to wherever to give up what they carried—moisture so delicate and cleansing it could not help but renew the world, and all souls upon it; of the night sky spread with an enormity of wonder, of stars, galaxies, and perhaps other universes beyond; of Marsh's scampers, discovering this and that, running, running, running until his tongue hung wet, red, and long out of the side of his mouth; of Gertrude perched on the front windowsill, ignoring them all until it was time for them to sit on the sofa in the parlor, who abjured her devotion to cattiness only when she believed she could not be seen attempting to engage Marsh in play; of Shy whom he no longer feared, whose antics, his rolls, his nickers, his snorts, his farts, his yah-yahs were delightful, sending Mike back to his childhood where he could laugh at such things; of Jack, who could not escape The Place and the boys he'd found there.

Mike had yet to accept that the dead speak. Nor could he wrap his brain around the notion those who had died from intentional violence told the living about their last moments and who had murdered them. Perhaps that was because his career training was clinical, college courses that never delved into a cop's hunches or whispered revelations from the dead. Maybe, he sometimes thought, Jack was the better cop. Jack's belief in intangibles was the key.

Mike saw them from the porch. Jack was atop Shy, and Marsh followed behind. They were his family now, and he had made lunch for them. He'd tossed some flakes of grass hay into Shy's bin and refilled his water tank. He'd made sandwiches for Jack and him that he would place on the pine table on the porch when Jack finished unsaddling Shy, brushing him and turning him out into the pasture. Mike had a cookie in his pocket for Marsh.

Marsh hung around Jack and Shy for a moment, then ran to the porch and lapped water from the dish they kept there. When Mike came out of the cabin, Marsh turned to him, shoved his dripping snout into Mike's crotch, swishing his curved tail behind.

"Ouch," Mike said, wanting to bend over with the discomfort, but instead, he placed the dishes on the pine table. He then pulled the cookie from his pocket and held it over Marsh's head. "You know what to do," Mike said, and Marsh sat, his tail now washing the porch. "Good boy." Mike gave him the cookie and watched him dart off toward the pasture, where he lay down and took his time savoring it.

Jack stepped to the porch, took his cowboy hat off, wiped his brow with his arm, and then lay the hat off to the side of the table. "Can't believe how warm it is," he said as he sat in the pine chair.

"We'll need AC if this keeps up. You want a beer?"

"Sure. Beer is fine. And if you want AC, just wait an hour or two."

Mike went back inside, knowing that as afternoon approached, the clouds would gather above. Whether they brought rain or not, the day would provide another chill, the breeze from the northwest a portent of yet another frigid night ahead. He walked back out with two beers, set them on the table, and sat in the other chair.

"How was it up there?"

"Oh, the same," Jack said.

Jack had never asked Mike to accompany him on his visits to The Place. Only Shy and Marsh were welcome. Mike understood this. Shy and Marsh were not beholding to clinical analysis. They were as connected to Jack's intangibles as Jack was.

"It's tuna fish again," Mike said, apologizing.

"That's fine. I love your tuna fish salad." He sipped his beer and then lifted his sandwich from the plate. "What's her name used to make this for me. Not as good as yours, though."

"Elizabeth?"

"That may have been her name. Lived with her for a time. Even put a ring on her finger."

"You told me about that once."

"Yeah, well… You know, I've been thinking." He swallowed, then took another a sip. "You ought to have a horse."

"Yes, I should." Since Mike first moved in at the end of May, he'd thought the same thing but hadn't mentioned it. He was careful not to impose too much on Jack. Their renewed relationship was less than two months old, and it still seemed to be fragile.

"I bet Tess has another good horse we could take a look at. She's not that far, and we could go up there and be back the next day."

"Give her a call," Mike said as he held a piece of bread under the table for Marsh. Marsh stretched toward it, not standing from where he'd lain down at Jack's side.

"Believe I will," Jack said. "It's been so long since I talked to her."

"Not since you and she found the boys' clothes?"

"Oh, yeah, once since then. I think it was in March." Jack eased back a bit in the chair. "She wanted to know if anything had happened with the case. Of course, nothing had, and we just talked about horses and how we were dealing with the winter."

"They get bad ones in the Yampa Valley."

"They do, and I hope her son is helping with the herd."

Marsh suddenly rose to his feet and made a dash toward the pasture. Stopping just this side of the fence, he stuck his nose in the dirt and then leaped to his left, then his right.

"Probably a chipmunk," Jack said as he stood up and grabbed his plate. "You done?"

"I'll get the dishes," Mike said.

"You got them this morning. C'mon, Mike, this is called sharing the chores."

"Okay. I'll go muck the stable."

"Already done." Jack took Mike's plate along with his and walked into the cabin.

Mike absently patted his shirt pocket for cigarettes. They'd decided to try to quit smoking for a while or forever. Jack was doing well without them, and Mike was having a bit of a problem. He still wanted one, and the gum didn't help. The key was to keep moving, to keep doing something, anything that would take his mind off my craving. Yes, finally retiring had helped, but, damn, twenty times a day, he still patted his pocket. He stood up intending to find something to do when the landline rang. He walked into the cabin.

"Can you get that?" Jack said from the kitchen.

"Sure." Mike picked up the receiver, and it was Abe Gomez, who was probably sitting in Mike's old chair at the CBI. "Abe, how goes it?"

"Just keeps going and going and… Well, you know how it is down here. How are you and Jack getting along about now? You haven't shot each other yet, have you?"

"I suspect Jack might want to every now and then, but, no, we haven't."

Before Mike retired, he'd bought Abe dinner one night and told him what the deal was with Jack and him. He told Abe the whole story. Abe had become a good friend during Mike's time at the CBI. He had shared family stories with him, but Mike had never told him about Jack and his relationship. He'd wanted to for a long time because Abe seemed like the kind of man so comfortable with his own sexuality that it wouldn't have mattered about what Jack and he were up to. But Mike waited until almost his last day on the job to tell Abe. And when he did, Abe just kept slicing his steak and stuffing his mouth.

"Glad you've got someone in your life besides Gertrude, Mike," he'd said. "My only sister's son is gay, and that kid is smarter, tougher, and becoming more successful than my kids ever will. He's a public defender in Denver and got married last year in Taos."

Mike wasn't shocked by Abe's reaction because he wouldn't have told him about Jack and him if he hadn't thought Abe would take it exactly the way he had. When Mike began to express that he'd prefer it not be mentioned to anyone else, Abe stopped him before he'd gotten two words out of his mouth. "And," Abe had said, "it's nobody's business but yours and Jack's, and I'm humbled that you told me."

"Say," Abe continued, "thought you might like to know we got a hit on the NCIC bulletin we put out on one Calvin Semple. It's an old bulletin, but you know how cops' memories work. Anyway, it came from the sheriff down in Montrose County. Said they busted a guy by the name of Charles Mason, who they picked up as drunk and disorderly living in Montrose. They found burglary tools in his vehicle, got a warrant for his house down there, and found all sorts of stolen goods. They confronted the guy with all this evidence, and he started to talk. You know, trying to work out a deal for himself. He told the deputies about a friend of his who lived with him for about two months a year ago. It seems his friend had been involved in some bad business not far from Vail, some ranch out there. Said Semple got shitfaced one night and told him he'd run some guy's car off the road and killed him. Mason said Semple told him the guy had been his boss, and that he, Semple—and here's a quote—'...got that sheepherding sonofabitch before he got me.' Now, I'm thinking that sonofabitch he's talking about was Rosario. Whaddaya think?"

"Damn, Abe. This is a major break. It had to have been Rosario. They know where Semple is?"

"That's the problem. Mason said Semple just packed his stuff up one day, and he never saw him again."

Mike noticed Jack was now standing at his side. "It's Abe," he whispered, pointing to the receiver. "And Semple never discussed where he might be going?"

"Mason clammed up, Mike. They think he might know more, but I guess he's waiting to see what his information is worth down there in Montrose."

"Shit! You think the sheriff might make a deal with him?"

"He was going to talk to their district attorney after he got off the phone with me. I told him how important it was that we find Semple. He understood, Mike. He's going to give me a call tomorrow. Depending on what he says, we'll probably head down there."

"Okay, Abe. Thank you so much for letting me... us know. Please keep us informed."

"You got it, Mike. When are you and Jack going to want some visitors up there? I thought I'd bring my wife up?"

"Of course. Let me ask Jack." He put his palm over the receiver. "Abe wants to bring his wife up for a visit. You okay with that?"

"Sure." Jack nodded.

"Abe, we're here most of the time. Just give us a call."

"Good. Maybe in the next few weeks. Take care, Mike."

"You too, Abe."

When he hung up, Jack said, "What? What'd he say?"

Mike told Jack what Abe had related to him, and he could feel Jack's smile as well as see it.

"Goddamn," Jack said, and then he put his arms around Mike and gave him a hug.

They drove into Vail and sat down in one of the plushest and most expensive restaurants either one of them had ever eaten in.

As they began to dig into their entrées, Jack set his silverware down and took a sip of wine. "You know where we are, don't you?"

"No," Mike said. And then it hit him: they were eating in the restaurant where Mark Harris and Brian Hall had worked as waiters. "Yeah," Mike nodded, "I know where we are, Jack." The celebration of the news they'd gotten from Abe was not ruined but subdued. He assumed Jack's thoughts had again turned to The Place while he focused on their young and quite handsome waiter. Mike wanted to tell the kid to be careful with his life, to be smart with whom he befriended. He wanted to tell him life is precious and so short.

THIRTY-FIVE

Tyler Bray and Ben Harmon had four days off. They sat at Missus Clark's small dining table, where she had just set down plates of fried ham, eggs, toast, and potatoes. They'd not asked for this from their landlord, but ever since they'd moved in, this was what they'd gotten. She also enjoyed tending to Bear's needs when Tyler and Ben were on the road. She'd told them her own children had left the homeplace years ago. They never wrote or called, nor had they attend their daddy's funeral. "You boys are answered prayers," she told them and admitted that old women do get so lonely sometimes.

"Tyler, you need more orange juice over there," she said, rising slightly from her chair and reaching the carafe of fresh-squeezed over to him. "There's more where that come from," she added as she sat back down.

"Nice breakfast, Missus Clark," Ben said as he sliced the ham he'd forked onto his plate.

"Yes, ma'am, it is," Tyler said, dripping honey onto his toast.

"We should have said grace," Missus Clark said. "But, I guess since we're diggin' in, He'll give us a pass this time. You boys

Christians?"

"Yes, I am," Ben said.

"I was raised that way," Tyler said.

"Are you still?" Missus Clark glanced at Tyler as she picked up her coffee cup.

"Oh," Tyler noded. "Sure. Don't practice it much, but sure I am."

"What a friend we have in Jesus," Missus Clark said matter-of-fact-ly as she set her coffee cup back down and grabbed her fork.

"Ain't that the truth," Ben said, shoveling more eggs into his mouth.

"What do you boys have planned for today?"

Ben looked at Tyler. "I guess Tyler's wantin' to spend some time with Bear, and I'm... Well, I guess I haven't made any plans. Just nice bein' off work and all."

"You can help me do some repairs to that fence out there," Tyler said. "Bear's loafin' shed needs some work, too."

Ben nodded. "Okay."

"What work you do, I'll deduct it from your rent," Missus Clark said. "Only fair."

"No. No, ma'am. You're doin' enough for us as it is." Tyler drank his juice and refilled the glass from the carafe.

Missus Clark smiled and lay her silverware on her plate. "It's just a joy havin' you boys around."

After breakfast, Ben helped Missus Clark with the dishes, and when he went outside, he saw Tyler is in the pasture, working Bear with a lunge line and lariat. He had the horse worked up to a can-ter and lightly slapped the rope against his leg. Ben stood at the pasture's makeshift gate, then looked at the fence line that sagged in so many places he couldn't count them all. When Tyler unhooked the lunge line from Bear, Ben opened the rickety gate and walked across the beaten-down prairie grasses.

"He's lookin' good," Ben said, stopping next to Tyler, who was watching Bear nose the dry scrub.

"He's okay," Tyler said. "This place sure needs some work, though."

"Yeah, it does. That loafin' shed looks about ready to fall in on itself."

"That and her house, too," Tyler said, looking back at the two-story wooden structure, gray from neglect. "Dependin' on how long we stay, we can fix her up pretty good."

"You ain't thinkin' about leavin' already, are you?" Ben asked, staring at Tyler.

"No, not yet. S'pose the time will come, though. No tellin' when we'll have to move on, Ben. You know that."

"This thing ain't never gonna stop hangin' over our heads." Ben kicked the dry ground, and a small puff of dust rose and fell. "I been thinkin' that maybe if you did write that letter to Jack... You could tell him we didn't have nothin' to do with what happened."

"But we did have somethin' to do with it, Ben." Tyler walked toward the loafing shed, stopped, and turned around. "I'm gonna write that letter. Just gotta find the time to do it. And—" He pauses and pointed at their truck parked beside the house. "We gotta get rid a them plates."

Ben looked at the truck. "Yeah. Guess we gotta steal some Texas plates. Hear they kill people for doin' that down here."

"You didn't hear no such thing," Tyler said as he headed for the loafing shed.

"No, I didn't," Ben said under his breath. "But, I wouldn't doubt that's an option."

***

Calvin Semple had moved on to Ouray, Colorado, a small town sitting at the base of the San Juan Mountains in southwestern Colorado. He'd been here before and was still known to some of the locals as a guide to vacationers who showed up wanting the ultimate four-wheeler experience. Everybody wanted to see how their Jeeps and other four-wheel vehicles would fare against the rugged terrain above the town. He was also known to a few of the locals as a man who'd never learned many social graces, and as someone whose dark side was something to avoid. He was also known to the Ouray County Sheriff's Department. About a year ago, three of the deputies had taken note of an NCIC bulletin naming Calvin Semple as a person of interest in some bad business that had happened in Eagle County. And, as cops' minds worked, that information had settled like flypaper, riding engrams like red flags.

Calvin had arrived in the nighttime, knocked on the door of a dilapidated house with four Jeep vehicles parked in the driveway on a side street near the town center. Dick Noble, who operated a four-wheel rental outfit from his garage, had opened the door and smiled. There was his old compadre, Calvin Semple, standing there, and reaching a bottle of Uncle Jack out in greeting.

"How about a drink?" Calvin had said when the door opened.

278

They'd sat down in Dick's living room, where the component pieces of a transmission lay upon a plastic tarp in the middle of the floor. "Watch your step," Dick had said.

After they'd talked a bit, Calvin admitted to Dick he'd just gotten tired of babysitting dipshits near Vail and was looking for something else to do.

"Hell, you can work for me again," Dick had said. "You know the trails as good as anybody."

"Need a place to stay for a while, too."

"Right here. We got an extra bedroom. Got some engine parts in there, but the bed is clear."

"One other thing," Calvin had said as he lit a cigar. "I need to stay low profile."

"Christ, don't we all?"

"Really, Dick. There was some shit going on at my last job, and I got a feeling some assholes think I had something to do with it. The sheriff up here might... You understand?"

"Sure," Dick had said, tipping the bottle of whiskey over his glass. "What I really need right now is a mechanic. You can hang around the house, work on the cars, and... What exactly happened?"

"Just some bullshit, I didn't have anything to do with."

"Okay. Well, that's good enough for me. It's gettin' late, and I'm goin' to bed. You remember the bedroom is down the hall to your left, and the bathroom right next to it?"

"Yup." Calvin had nodded. "Got a shitload of stuff in my truck. Can I bring that in?"

"We'll have to clean out that bedroom tomorrow, and sure, you can move it in. I'll tell the old lady in the morning not to get her fat ass all in a knot about it."

Dick's wife *was* in a knot about this character who she remembered as being a jerk-and-a-half from years ago. She silently suffered all the crap now piled in the bedroom, which she'd always wanted to turn into her sewing and scrapbook room. God knew she and Dick were never going to have children. They'd tried and failed so many times that in the last five or so years, both had lost their desire to even think about it. Hell, unless Dick was drunk, he rarely touched her anymore.

For a week, DeEtta Noble had watched Calvin Semple come and go from the house to the garage and thought there was something off about him. He didn't talk much, and when he did, she was always left out of the conversation like she wasn't even there. She'd heard Dick and Calvin in the living room the night Calvin had arrived and had listened to this strange man say he needed to keep a low profile. She'd thought about that quite a lot. She'd thought, too, about getting this guy out of her house in any way she could and believed she'd talk to Mary Park about that. Mary was her best friend and was married to a deputy sheriff who might be curious about Calvin Semple.

THIRTY-SIX

Before Mike moved in with Jack, he sold all his furniture. He kept his books, though, and brought them with him when he moved. They were still in boxes in his bedroom. He'd not mentioned to Jack that if they shared a bedroom, the other bedroom could become a study for them. He could even set up his computer in there if they ever got satellite service. But as it stood then, Jack was adamant that computers were anathema to what he believed life should be about up there. Hell, Jack didn't even have a TV. And Mike supposed he understood Jack's feelings but still wondered about his reluctance to share a bed. They didn't talk about it, but Mike sometimes got the impression Jack was thinking about it. Not that Mike walked on eggs, but he did know at one point or another he'd have to raise the issue with Jack. If their relationship was going no further than sharing chores and meals, Mike didn't think that would be enough to sustain it. At least for him, it wouldn't. Mike loved Jack and believed Jack loved him. But he was beginning to think there was something in Jack that wouldn't allow him to love on a physical level. Mike did yearn for his touch.

Jack and Mike were mucking Shy's stable and cleaning up the shed when they heard the sound of an ATV coming up their drive. It was Gladys, the lodge's caretaker. She cut the ATV's engine and walked toward them, bending down a moment to greet Marsh, who had run out to her.

"Gentlemen," she said.

"How goes it, Gladys?" Jack said.

"Good. Looks like you're doin' some spring cleaning." She held her hand out to Mike.

"That we are," Mike said, shaking her hand. She stuck her hand out to Jack.

"Where you headed?" Jack asked.

Gladys shook her head. "Well, the owners of the lodge are workin' on leasing the ranch so their employees will have somewhere to stay over the season. They also want to update the main building and fix up those cabins on the ranch for paying customers. They want me to go up there and take a look around. Just see how much work has to be done."

"Who owns the place now that Rosario is out of the picture?" Mike asked.

"Yeah," Jack said, "there's got to be some probate issues."

"Hell if I know. I do know if they're really serious about this, I can't handle everything on my own. I'm trying to get the lodge ready for the season, and now they hit me with this."

"Well, if we can help, let us know," Jack said.

"Appreciate it. Just wanted to check in with you guys. And—" She bent down again and grabbed the stick Marsh has laid at her feet and threw it toward the pasture. "It appears your pup has worked out for you, Jack. You glad you took him?" She stood up, and they all watched Marsh scramble under the lowest rung of the pasture fence after the stick.

"Yes, he has. I'd like to thank the guy for giving him to me if he ever comes out of the forest."

"He likes his privacy, Jack. Especially when we get all those city folks up here. If I see him, I'll tell him, though. Listen, I got to get going."

"Thanks for stopping by," Jack said.

"Sure thing." Gladys climbed back on the ATV and fired it up.

Jack and Mike finished up their chore and walked to the cabin with Marsh tagging along as if some adventure was afoot. For Marsh, any damned thing was a new adventure. When Mike stepped into the kitchen area and opened the refrigerator, Marsh was right there, his nose nudging the condiments in the door rack. Mike saw Gertrude out of the corner of his eye leap onto the kitchen counter, as Jack came from the parlor and peeked into the refrigerator himself.

"What's for lunch?" he asked.

"What do you want?"

"Hadn't thought about it. Shall I clean up the barbecue?"

"Sure. Burgers?"

"Sounds good to me."

As they ate on the porch, Jack asked Mike if he was ever going to unpack his books. "I might even find something I want to read," he said.

"We need somewhere to put them, Jack. Otherwise, they'll just have to stay stacked on the floor."

"I know Old Pop taught you carpentry skills—witness the stable."

Mike smiled with that memory. "He did. By the time I went to college, I think we'd remodeled our old house twice, inside and out."

"Bookshelves shouldn't be a big deal. My dad never really taught me anything, except to fear him, which I did."

Ever since Mike had known Jack, Jack had spoken very little about his family. If he was willing to open that door, Mike wasn't going to let it go to waste. "What was he like, Jack?"

Jack wiped his mouth with a napkin and took a sip of his beer. "I can't remember a time that he ever touched me. You know, put his arm around me or held my hand. Never gave me a kiss that I recall. Still, to this day, I'm uneasy when I see a grown man give his boy child a kiss."

"You told me once he'd take you fishing."

"Oh, yeah, he did that. It was about the only thing we ever did as a family. If I told you about that, I probably told you I hated to fish. Still do." He grabbed his beer and scooted his chair back a bit. "Here's an example of one of our so-called fishing trips. I was probably thirteen. My dad had a big-ass Pontiac Chieftain, and I was in the backseat, and he and my mother were in the front seat. The plan was to go fishing and have a picnic up in the mountains. Can't remember where we went, but my father had promised he'd stop on the way back and let me and fire an old single-shot .22 rifle I'd found in the cellar." He paused for a moment and smiled. "It'd sure be nice to suck on one of your cigarettes about now."

"I've got an old pack we can open up," Mike said a bit too eagerly.

"Why not?"

Mike went into the cabin and grabbed one of three unopened packs from his closet. He got a couple stick matches from the hearth, an ashtray from the coffee table, and went back outside. "They're probably stale as hell."

"Doesn't matter," Jack said as he waited while Mike opened the pack. Mike tapped two out and handed Jack one. Jack slid the cigarette under his nose. "Smells good."

After Mike touched the flame to both the cigarettes, Jack took a drag and continued. "Like I told you, I refused to fish and instead climbed up a hill and back down. I waded downstream from where my father had tossed his line and fooled around a bit. Three or four times in less than an hour, I returned to the car and sat with my rifle in the backseat, brushing my hand against the smooth wooden stock. Opening and closing the bolt. I squeezed the trigger to hear the crisp click the firing pin made against the butt-end of the barrel. I really wanted to fire that weapon.

"I noticed, though, all through the morning that my father also returned to the car and had at least four times opened the trunk, leaned deeply into it, and fiddled with something inside. My mother was busy starting a fire in one of the rusted steel contraptions that dotted campsites up and down the shore of the creek."

Jack coughed with his second drag and tipped his beer to his lips. "When my mother called to me," he continued, "and told me to tell my dad lunch was ready, I walked to the creek where I'd last seen him standing, still flicking his line back and forth. I remember thinking he appeared unsteady on his feet. Well, I hollered at him, 'Dad, lunch is ready,' and he kind of stumbled as he turned toward me. He steadied himself and reeled in his line." Jack swallowed the last of his beer. "You want another one?" he asked as he began to stand up.

"Yeah, but I'll get them." Mike went and got another two beers and sat back down at the table.

"I don't know why I'm telling you this, Mike. It's not a pretty story, and..."

"We usually just talk about murders, Jack. I think I can handle this."

He nodded. "Okay. Well, I sat down at the pine picnic table where my mother had set a place for me, and we both watched as my father once again leaned into the open trunk of the car. He then slammed the trunk lid down and smiled—which was an event in itself, as it rarely happened. We both noticed the pinky of his left hand pointed up, a telltale erection that occurred each time that he got drunk.

"'How could you do this?' My mother was on her feet, her hands fisted, her arms stiff at her sides. 'How could you do this to us?'

"'Do what?' My father slurred his words and wobbled slightly with his next step.

"I wasn't surprised and didn't feel my gut collapse within me as it used to when this happened because by now, it was nothing new. The stiff pinky said it all. My father's multiple trips to the trunk of the Chieftain had provided the opportunity for him to sip more and more whiskey. My mother, too, was dipping into her own long-lived addiction to purposeful despondency, I guess is a good description. Her father had died of a whiskey-blackened liver—her own words—and her two brothers were already on their way to the same fate. Long before she'd married my father, she'd embraced a Carrie Nation persona when it came to alcohol. But she went further. She had a darkly mystical view of life that valued despair as an end in itself. I, even at thirteen, believed my mother's penchant for grief was a place she often preferred to be. It was an emotion she knew well and often bathed in."

Jack stopped for a moment, patted Marsh's head, and looked off into what Mike believed was the vividness of the memory he was telling him about.

"The picnic was uneaten," he began again. "The cooked hamburgers were tossed onto the ground, the condiments and pop thrown into the backseat. I listened to my mother rage through her sobbing as my father maneuvered the Chieftain around the curves, and up and down the hills of the mountain highway toward Denver. My mother spit out her favorite epithet, 'If I had a knife, I would bury it into your heart! I would shove it to the hilt!'

"Well, I stroked my rifle in the backseat and placed the end of the barrel inches from the back of my father's head. I opened the box of shells, pulled one out, opened the bolt, placed the shell inside, and closed the bolt. I snapped off the safety, then quickly snapped it back on. See, I understood if I were to kill my father, assuming the tiny bullet would actually pierce his skull, it was likely the Chieftain would sail off the side of the mountain and land a hundred yards in the riverbed below. My mother and I would be killed in the crash. I pulled the bolt back, snatched the shell out, and put it back in the box. I lowered the rifle and decided I would not kill my father that day, Mike. Not because I didn't want to; not for just the moment it'd taken me to flick the safety off; not just for that single moment when my mother began to whisper a *Hail Mary*. No, I didn't do it because I had absorbed some little wisdom from somewhere. I already knew that jumping into some things have inevitable consequences which, quite figuratively and literally, end up abysmally final."

"Damn," Mike said.

"Yeah. But if it could get worse, it did. Not a week after the failed picnic, I watched my father and two of his buddies hogtie my mother upon the parental bed. She'd fled to the bedroom upon seeing my father's compadres, knowing nothing good would come of the situation. Her ravings and eerie silences had turned on a dime to hyperactive meanderings about the house for at least four days prior. It was then my father was finally disposed to call upon his friends for assistance. The three of them carried my mother to the backseat of the Chieftain. They all got in the front seat, and my father pulled out of the driveway, leaving me on the porch with my cocker spaniel, Lady, beside me. I stood up after they'd turned the corner, let Lady precede me into the house, and then I walked into the backyard to the two trashcans that we kept there. During one of my mother's hyper periods, she undertook a frantic cleaning of my closet and carried to the trash three pairs of my shoes and two pairs of jeans. I lifted the lid, pulled my shoes and jeans from the garbage, and took them back into my bedroom." He smashed his cigarette out in the ashtray.

"She was... hospitalized?"

"More like locked up. Turns my stomach thinking about what they probably did to her. Damned cigarette made me dizzy, Mike." He took another sip of his beer. "Two weeks later," Jack said, "my father brought my mother home. She was meek, smiled unnaturally, and her eyes appeared as though she was somewhere else, seeing a world she didn't know. She asked if my father and I were hungry, and my father said yes, and she proceeded to cook dinner. After dinner, she went to bed, and I asked my father what was wrong with the cob corn. My father replied, 'Don't you say a goddamned thing to her about it. She boiled it for forty minutes because she's forgotten some things. You hear me?' He pointed his finger at my chest and poked me three times: 'Don't. Say. Anything.' And I didn't."

Mike looked at Jack, at his eyes, and knew this man had just revealed more about who he was than he'd ever hinted for all the years he'd known him. And Mike didn't know what to say to him as they both heard what was probably Gladys's ATV coming from the west. Jack stood up, stepped off the porch, and walked down the drive as Gladys turned into it. Mike followed behind, still trying to filter Jack's story, trying to sort out the meaning of it and what shadows had been left in Jack's heart and mind when he was a kid of only thirteen.

"Man, oh man," Gladys said after cutting the engine. She stayed seated and crossed her arms.

"That bad?" Jack asked.

"No, not really. The main building is in pretty good shape. The cabins need some work. But, I found an outside entrance to a cellar, Jack. It's behind the main building, and it was covered with brush. It's a rock cellar, and the door was secured with a lock and chain. Luckily the wood was rotted out, and I kicked in the door. Looked like they'd butchered critters down there. Blood dried to black all over the place—on the walls, covering a table, crusted on the dirt floor.

"Any animal bones, antlers, or hides?" Mike asked, the uncertainty of where the boys had actually been murdered crossing his mind.

"Not that I could see, but I didn't stay there long. Smells bad. Fuckin' eerie space down there."

Jack glanced at Mike, and Mike nodded. "Mike and I'll probably head over there. That okay with you?"

"Nobody up there, Jack. As far as I'm concerned, sure. Take a look. Thought about those boys who'd been murdered when I saw the place."

THIRTY-SEVEN

Jack put Marsh in the house, and then he and Mike climbed in Jack's SUV and drove over to the ranch. Jack parked in front of the two-story building, and they both got out.

"Seems odd not seeing a bunch of young people running around," Jack said as they both looked at the building and the deserted road that led down to the string of cabins beyond.

"So, Semple lived upstairs?" Mike asked.

"Yeah," Jack said, looking at a second-story window. "Let's take a look at that cellar." Mike followed him around the side of the building. They stopped next to the back entrance to the kitchen and saw the small door that sat below the building's floor level. Jack walked down the few rock steps to the door that hung open, the interior a dense black. "Forgot the flashlights," Jack said.

"I didn't." Mike pulled the two small LED flashlights from his pocket and handed Jack one. They sensed an almost overwhelming odor of dampness and rot, a moldy smell with something wild mixed in with it. They stopped just inside, shined their lights on the walls, the floor, and the single table in the room.

"This could be where it happened, Mike," Jack said as he took a couple steps into the interior.

"Yeah, and if it is, we'd better be careful. As far as we know, nobody has been down here in a while except Gladys. If there's evidence…"

Jack shined his flashlight on the ground from where they were standing over to the table. "It gets much darker near the table. See those darker areas?"

Mike shined his flashlight over the same area Jack had just covered. "Yeah. Blood could have pooled there. Do you know if they butchered game here? They did have a kitchen, didn't they?"

"Don't know if they did any butchering, but, yeah, they had a kitchen and a pretty big dining area. A lot of the lodge's employees lived here, and they did serve meals upstairs."

Mike looked at Jack's barely visible profile. "You're not getting any… feelings, are you?"

"Wish I was," Jack said. "Like Gladys said, it's certainly eerie in here. But, no, I'm not feeling anything. Believe we need to get your old crew up here."

"Read my mind, Jack. Might be nothing, but you never know."

"No, you never do," Jack said. He turned and shined his light one last time around the room. "Let's get out of here."

They climbed the few steps and stood outside, looking down at the entrance. "We ought to secure this in some way," Mike said.

"We'll get the plywood we didn't use on the stable. Just shove it into the doorframe."

When they got back to the cabin, they grabbed some sheets of plywood, a hammer, and nails from the shed, and put them in the back of the SUV. Parking at the same spot as before, they carried the items to the rear of the building.

They set the items on the ground. Jack sat on his haunches and looked into the cellar's blackness. "Maybe we ought to get Tess up here, too."

Mike stopped himself from saying that, no, the forensics team would find whatever was down there. "Yeah," he said. "Maybe we ought to."

***

Calvin Semple watched DeEtta Noble walk in front of the garage door and down the unpaved road toward the town center. He didn't like the woman, and he was sure she felt the same way about him. Today, though, she'd fixed her hair and wore something other than her constant stretch pants and sweatshirt. She was even carrying a purse. He thought it was about lunchtime and affirmed that by looking at the clock over the workbench. Dick had told him earlier that he was going to talk to the new owners of the Uncompahgre Star Motel. He wanted them to display his Jeep tour brochures, as well as get referrals from them. After that, he said he'd come by and take Calvin to lunch. Calvin had told him he didn't want to drive his vehicle around town because of the expired temporary sticker, and Dick had agreed to pick him up.

As Calvin pulled off his overalls, he heard Dick stop his vehicle at the base of the driveway. Dick tapped out a little beep from the horn, and Calvin stepped to the garage door and waved. He washed his hands in the kitchen, wiped them on one of DeEtta's clean towels, and walked through the garage to the street.

"You wanna lock up the place?" Calvin asked.

"Hell no." Dick shook his head.

Calvin climbed in the Cherokee, and Dick headed for the town center, to the only paved road in or out of Ouray—U.S. Highway 550. He pulled to the curb outside the Red Mountain Saloon. "They got some good steaks here."

As they got out of the Cherokee, Calvin looked up and down the road for the law, and then he looked inside the saloon. "Never raised any hell in this place," he said.

"It's new since you left, Cal. Some newcomers fixed up that old secondhand furniture store that used to be here."

"Oh, yeah. I remember," Calvin said as Dick held the door for him.

They sat at a table facing the street, the vista out the window that of the sparse noontime clumps of tourists searching for the perfect place to eat lunch.

"Not much going on this early in the season," Dick said as the waitress handed them menus.

"What'll you have, gentlemen? Anything to drink?"

They both ordered a beer and studied the menus.

During the meal, Dick proposed that Calvin should think about leading tours again. His seasonal mechanic would soon be back in Ouray and had promised to work for Dick at least through mid-August.

Calvin nodded and laid down his fork. "Don't want to do that, Dick. At least until I'm off the hook with that bullshit near Vail."

"When you s'pose that's going to happen?"

"I don't know." Calvin wiped his mouth with his napkin and looked out the window. "That's your wife over there, isn't it? Coming out of that restaurant?"

Dick looked. "Yeah. She took her girlfriend out to lunch. Spendin' my money on nonsense."

Calvin was just about to finish off his beer when he saw an Ouray County Sheriff's cruiser pull to the curb across the street. The deputy got out of the car and walked to the two women, then hugged Dick's wife's friend and shook DeEtta's hand.

"What's that all about?" Calvis said.

Dick again looked out the window. "Oh, that's Joe Park. His wife, Mary, is DeEtta's buddy."

Calvin wasn't hungry anymore. He again set down his silverware and grabbed his beer. "I remember him from when I was last here. He's been with the department for years. Right?"

"Yeah, he has. Nice enough guy, but a sonofabitch when it comes to enforcin' the law. Gets you on the little stuff."

As they drove back to Dick's house, Calvin considered if his decision to come to Ouray had been a mistake. The fact that he was known here did cross his mind when he left Montrose but figured he could keep himself virtually hidden by working out of Dick's garage. He would forego the chance he'd come face to face with some asshole cop by leading the four-wheel tours up into the hills as he'd previously done. Hell, he never knew when some deputy would hold everything up to check drivers' licenses and give their standard spiel about safety on the trails. Knowing that Telluride—a place he wasn't known—was just an hour south seemed, for now, to be his most likely destination. If he decided to leave.

Calvin got out of the Cherokee as Dick braked it in front of the house. "Gotta check on some parts," Dick said. "I'll be back in a while."

"Okay," Calvin said. As he walked to the garage, he saw Dick's wife and her girlfriend walking up the road. He figured he'd better make his decision sooner rather than later.

***

Mike showered when they got home from the ranch. Jack made a small dinner, just salad, and soup from a can and had it ready when Mike came out of his bedroom in clean clothes. Jack had already fed Marsh and Gertrude, and Mike and he ate sitting on stools at the kitchen counter. They discussed what they'd found, and after dinner, Mike called Abe at his home number and told him it would be a good idea for the CBI forensic team to come back up and gather what they could from the cellar. Abe said he'd talk to the assistant director and let Mike know. Abe also said it would probably be helpful if Jack or Mike called the Eagle County Sheriff and urged him to request the CBI investigate the new findings.

After Jack made a fire, they sat on the sofa. Gertrude was purring on Mike's lap, and Marsh lay at Jack's feet.

"I ought to shower, too," Jack said. "Just being near that cellar… Feel kind of dirty."

"Go ahead. I'll read some while you're in there."

Jack stood, and Marsh was on his feet as well. Both of them headed down the hallway. Jack shooed Marsh out of the bathroom and closed the door.

Mike picked up his book from the coffee table, opened it to the bookmark, but instead of reading, he thought about what Jack had told him at lunch. How many more stories did Jack have about his childhood? How many scars from that time in his life did he still carry? And how did it all relate to his tentativeness with Mike? How could he get on with the relationship he'd envisioned before he moved to the mountains? Jack was once a gentle and passionate lover. But now... Was it the boys? And if it was, why had this homicide affected Jack so profoundly? Mike had worked hundreds, maybe thousands of murders when he was with the DPD. Many were so gruesome that he'd had to turn his head away as Jack placed his hand upon a lump of something that used to be a living being. He wanted to make a life with Jack, and Jack was holding back for some reason Mike could not pin down. And he couldn't find the right words to begin the conversation about what was on his mind. He heard Jack turn off the shower. Marsh, who had been lying outside the bathroom door, got to his feet, and Mike reopened his book.

After a few minutes, Jack came into the parlor wearing his robe and slippers. "That feels good," he said as he walked into the kitchen, with Marsh his constant shadow. "How about a drink?"

"Sounds okay to me," Mike said, reclosing his book and setting it on the coffee table. Gertrude stirred in his lap.

"I hope the CBI can see sense in coming back up here," Jack said as he walked into the parlor with their drinks and sat on the sofa.

"Abe would be up here in a minute, but he's got the assistant director to deal with. Budgets were starting to tighten up before I left."

"Yeah. Always budget issues getting in the way of taking another look at an old case."

They sipped their drinks, and as Jack set his down on the coffee table, Marsh sat down in front of him and raised his front paws up to Jack's lap. "Oh, you good old dog," Jack said, scratching Marsh's neck and ears.

"Look at us," Mike said. "Just like a little family relaxing before bedtime."

"I guess that would describe us. The only one missing is Shy."

"And if there were a way to get him in here, that would complete the picture."

Jack looked at Mike and smiled. "You think you might stay a while then?"

"You don't think I'm going anywhere, do you?"

"Well..." Jack paused and took another sip of his drink. "I've been a little... oh... I guess I don't yet feel like we've, you've settled in here, Mike. I mean... Hell, I don't know what I mean." Marsh made a move as if he was going to leap up on the sofa, and Jack held him down. "No, you're way too big for that, Marsh. Lay now," he said, opening his hand over Marsh's head. Marsh laid down at his feet.

Mike wondered if this was the opening to the conversation he'd wanted to have with Jack for some time. "I," he said, trying to find the words. "This is a big change for me, Jack. I've never lived with anyone before, and..."

"Neither had I. Even when I was married, I didn't really live with her. Just occupied the same space under the same roof."

"I've been wondering... What you told me today about your childhood?"

"Yes."

"That's the first time you ever really opened up to me about your

297

past. That was a sad story, Jack."

Jack nodded. "One of many. He scooted closer to Mike and draped his arm across Mike's shoulders. "You're the first person I ever shared that with."

Jack's touch was the prize Mike hadn't thought he'd get tonight. Mike put his hand on Jack's thigh. "Sometimes talking about those… difficult experiences is cathartic. Sometimes—"

"Mike," Jack interrupted, "since I moved up here, I've tried to live in the present. And, no, some things you can never let go of as easily as you thought you could. But my childhood, and all those lifeless bodies I've knelt over… It never really goes away." He pulled his arm back and grabbed his drink from the table. Cradling his glass in his hands, he shook his head. "I guess it's going to take a while for me to actually achieve what I wanted to when I moved here. If I seem, oh, maybe distant is the right word, then I apologize. It's just gonna take a while, Mike." He set his drink back down, leaned into Mike, and kissed his lips. He pulled away a bit and looked into Mike's eyes. "Can you put up with me for a while longer?"

"Hey," Mike said, smiling. "I sold all my furniture. Where the hell else would I go?"

***

Annie Clark and Tyler cleared the supper dishes from the kitchen table, and Ben filled the sink with water. "You don't have to do that," Annie said. "I know you got better things to do."

"No, Missus Clark, I don't. I'm happy to help. Besides, Tyler wants to use the table for writin' a letter."

"Well, of course, you do." She lightly tapped Tyler's back as he grabbed a washrag to wipe off the table. "You got to keep family involved with your life. Ben, you should write to your family too."

"Don't have much family, but, yeah, I guess I could do that."

"You happen to have some paper I could use?" Tyler said.

"I sure do." Annie wiped off her hands with a towel and walked into the hallway between the kitchen and the parlor. She opened the side table drawer and pulled out a pack of writing paper and envelopes, both colored blue and showing bloomed sunflowers printed at the top. "You need a pen?"

"Yes, if you got one."

She returned to the kitchen with the paper and a pen inscribed with the words *Amarillo Seed and Feed* on it. She set them on the table, turned, and watched Ben at the sink as Tyler sat at the table.

"Thank you."

"I don't suppose you boys would like a little after-supper nip, would you?"

"Sure," Ben said, looking over his shoulder. "What you got in mind?"

"I've got some sherry and some bourbon."

"Bourbon," Tyler and Ben said in unison.

"Hah!" Annie laughed. "How'd I know that would be the answer?" She opened a cupboard, set three mismatched sherry glasses on the counter, and then she grabbed the half-full bottle of Old Crow bourbon and a nearly empty bottle of sherry from the shelf. She poured herself a half glass of sherry. "You boys can pour your own. Don't overdo now." As she walked across the kitchen, she added, "I'm gonna relax in the parlor."

Ben stepped over to where Annie had placed the whiskey and the glasses. "These are some small-ass glasses," he lowered his voice.

"Just do it halfway, Ben. Just like she did. We got more in the bedroom if we want it."

Ben poured the bourbon and set both glasses on the table. "Lemme finish these dishes."

Tyler took a sip, picked up the pen, and saw the flowers across the top of the stationery. He shook his head and began writing:

Dear Jack...

I wanted to write to you for a long time to let you know what happened that night to those two boys. Ben and me was pulled into the thing by Calvin Semple. We did what he told us to do because he held something over us and because we had nowhere else to live if he kicked us out. I'll start at the beginning because I think that's what you would want to know about. Ben and me met them boys in Vail at a bar. Their names was Mark and Brian. They was nice boys and didn't deserve what happened to them. And what happened was this. Calvin and one of his S&M friends got the idea it would be fun to hunt some human beings in the hills up above the lodge. Calvin told me and Ben to find two boys who'd agree to the game for $500, and that it was just a game and nobody would get hurt. We already knew Mark and Brian, and we thought they would agree, and they sure could use the money. Me and Ben set up a tent for them, and then we went into Vail and brought them down there, and we spent some time with them until it got dark. Calvin told us that around midnight we was to take the boys to the bottom of a trail and tell them to just go up that trail and be very quiet. We knew there was four *or five guys playing the game who'd paid a whole lot of money to do it, and they were up in the hills somewhere when we told Mark and Brian which way to go. Calvin told us to just go back to the tent and wait until somebody brought those boys back to us. We told the boys we'd stay at the bottom of the trail if they needed us, and we did for a time. But when nothing seemed to be going wrong, me and Ben did go back to the tent and we never saw those boys again. Me and Ben drank about a half bottle of vodka in the tent and we fell asleep. Calvin told us the next day that things got out of hand, and those boys were dead. He had me and Ben take that tent down and take everything in it to the canyon way up the road. We buried that stuff in the side of the canyon. Then he told us we had to leave because things were getting too hot. He was afraid I'd tell you what had happened. Me and Ben are so sorry for what happened and what happened never leaves us for a minute. The main guy Calvin dealt with in setting up the game was John Denman. I don't know who the others were, but were probably part of the motorcycle and leather crowd that sometimes came up to the ranch. Though I never seen it myself, some of the lodge employees said that Calvin kept a S&M dungeon in the cellar if that means anything at all. I don't know if that's true or not, but Ben told me that the cellar was for dressing out the kills the hunters made. I'm sorry that I can't tell you where me and Ben are. I know how lawyers can twist things around to where even the innocent are convicted. We're not so innocent, but we had no hand in killing those boys. I hope we can be forgiven someday, and I hope those boys rest in peace.*

Tyler Bray, Ben Harmon

"Okay," Tyler said as he scooted the piece of paper over to Ben.

"You read that over and then sign it if it looks okay to you."

Ben moved his index finger over each word as he read. He nodded. "Yeah, that's the way it happened."

Tyler scooted the letter back him, signed his name, and again shoved it over for Ben to do the same. After Ben signed it, Tyler folded it up and put it into the envelope. He licked the flap and sealed it.

"You don't know his address, though?"

"I'll send it to the lodge. That's where everybody picks up mail anyway. He'll get it."

As Annie walked into the kitchen, she said, "I think I'll turn in. You boys want just a little more?" She set her glass near the sink.

"Ah, no." Tyler glanced at Ben. "That was just enough."

"Good. We'll all get a good night's rest. See you in the mornin'."

"Night," Ben said. He stood up and grabbed his and Tyler's glasses, and carried them to the sink, where he rinsed them under the tap. "Gonna need a lot more whiskey for me to sleep good tonight," he said as he walked back to the table where Tyler was stuffing some chew into his cheek.

"Yeah," Tyler said as he stood up. "Let's go outside and check on Bear."

As they stepped off the back porch and walked toward the loafing shed, Ben looked up. "Real pretty night," he said.

Tyler spat and looked up, rubbing his hand against his cheek. "I don't think that letter is gonna take it all away, Ben. We still got to live with it."

"We do, Ty. Yes, we do."

***

From the garage, Calvin had listened to DeEtta Noble and Mary Park talk and laugh about one thing or another all afternoon. He kept looking for Dick to return, as it was getting late, and he wanted to have a conversation with Dick about the impossibility of him taking on tours when the season started up. Figured Dick's errand to get parts had probably turned into an afternoon of sitting on a barstool and shooting the shit with the locals. When he heard a car stop in front of the house, he looked out the garage door and saw an Ouray County Sheriff's cruiser parked near the driveway. Then DeEtta and Mary came out of the house, said their good-byes and Mary got in the cruiser. Calvin made his decision at that moment.

"What're you doin'?" Dick Noble said as he got out of his Chero-kee and saw Calvin's truck parked in his driveway, the bed already piled high with Calvin's belongings.

Calvin set the box he'd carried out the front door on the truck's open tailgate. "Movin' on, Dick."

"Why the hell for? You just got here."

"It's not working out like I thought it would."

"Hell, if it's about workin' tours instead of doin' the mechanics, we can work that out."

"Yeah, but you got the mechanic coming in, and DeEtta doesn't seem to like the situation."

"Fuck her." Dick stumbled slightly as he walked up the driveway.

"No, you can do that." Calvin turned and walked in the front door. Dick followed him in. DeEtta sat on the couch, smoking a cigarette.

"You have somethin' to do with this?" Dick said to DeEtta, his voice raised.

"Nope," she said, watching Calvin pass in front of her. "He just started cleanin' out his stuff."

Dick looked at her and shook his head. "Goddamnit." He walked down the hall to the spare bedroom. "Calvin, you don't have to do this." He stood in the doorway and watched Calvin grab a duffel bag from the floor and then scan the room.

"I got it all, Dick," Calvin said. He held his hand out. "I thank you for your hospitality."

Dick shook his hand. "Where you goin'?"

"Don't know yet. I'll know when I get there." He eased past Dick, walked down the hall, and didn't say anything to DeEtta as he walked out the front door.

Deputy Joe Park and his partner, Eric Domenico, watched the blue Dodge Ram pickup pull away from Dick Noble's house.

When Mary Park had called Joe from the restaurant, little did he know he'd hear that name again—Calvin Semple. When he later stopped in front of the Noble household to pick up his wife, he wanted to take a look around. Wanted to see if there was a vehicle there he didn't know and remind himself what the lay of that house was. He hadn't thought he'd get to see Calvin Semple in the flesh, looking out the garage door.

He'd restrained himself from getting out of the car and confronting the guy. They'd had run-ins before, and Calvin wasn't the most cooperative man he'd ever dealt with. Besides, he remembered that old NCIC bulletin from the CBI about Calvin being a person of interest in some nasty business in Eagle County.

When his wife got in the cruiser, she was giddy. "He's right there, Joe. You can get him right now." Joe had calmed her down, and as soon as they turned the corner, he pulled over and called Domenico on his cell.

As soon a Mary had climbed out of the cruiser at her and Joe's house, Domenico pulled up. They both got into Domenico's Chevy Blazer, took their hats off, and pulled on the two nondescript jackets Domenico had brought with him. They parked up the hill from the Noble house and sat there, watching Semple load his pickup. When Calvin got in the cab and started the engine, Joe keyed his handheld radio and alerted the uniformed deputy who was waiting in his cruiser near the town center for the call.

"He's heading out," Joe said. "Looks like he's turning toward you. Whichever way he goes on 550, you follow him, and we'll be behind you. I'll let you know when to stop him."

Calvin saw the cruiser pull in behind him, staying a couple car lengths behind. Don't panic, he thought as he fished in the nylon bag next to him on the seat and pulled out the .45. Shoved his legs against the steering wheel and pulled the weapon's slide back. He set it on the passenger seat and then noticed a gray SUV come from behind the cruiser, accelerate past the cruiser, and pull in in front of him. The cruiser's light bar began to flash. When the cruiser inched closer to him, the SUV's brake lights popped on and off in front of him.

"Fuck it," he said, knowing the predicament he was in. He could pull around the SUV and make a run for it, or he could simply stop, and... What? No, he'd come this far, and he would not be a part of what he knew would happen. He pressed the gas pedal to the floor, yanked the steering wheel to the left, and accelerated around the

SUV. He glanced in the rearview and saw the SUV had pulled over, and the cruiser was almost on his bumper. He stomped the gas pedal, saw the upcoming curve of the road, and then felt a violent shaking coming from the front end of the truck. He entered the curve, felt the hard crack of something in the steering column, then an immense grinding. The truck slewed right and hit the depression beyond the apron. The load in the bed flew off in every direction. The truck rolled over to the right, once, twice, then slammed up against the rocky hillside forty feet from the road. He was upside down, still strapped to his seat, and conscious. He looked to his right, and the .45 was there within his reach, having settled on the ceiling. He grabbed the weapon. Saw Glenn of Glenn's Premium Used Autos grinning at him: *I think I can say with 90 percent certainty you'll love your new truck*. Calvin Semple put the barrel of the .45 in his mouth and pulled the trigger.

THIRTY-EIGHT

Gertrude pawed at Mike's face. Mike had heard Jack get up a while ago, stopping in the bathroom, whispering to Marsh, and then he'd gone outside. Mike looked at the clock, and Gertrude leaped off the bed and sniffed at the bottom of the closed door. Mike had learned his first night here that Gertrude thought it her duty to pester Marsh during all hours of the night and through the earliest hours of the morning. Thus, the closed door. It was a little past six-thirty.

Mike still hadn't had the conversation he wanted to have with Jack. After Jack had asked him last night if he'd stick around a while longer, presumably until Jack could get used to their living situation, Mike just let it go with a smile. Living situation? The *loving* situation was what Mike was concerned about. He placed his feet on the floor, stood up, and dressed. Gertrude hopped on the bed, sat, and looked at him with a needful expression.

"Yes, young lady," Mike said, "I understand your needs, and they're about to be fulfilled." He opened the door, and she leaped off the bed and ran out of the bedroom.

Mike walked through the parlor and opened the front door. He cracked the door open, glanced at Gertrude hovering near her bowl, and then stepped out onto the porch. Jack was up at the shed, probably feeding Shy.

"You had your breakfast?" Mike hollered.

Jack turned and waved. "Not yet," he hollered back.

Mike walked back into the cabin, knowing he'd asked a stupid question. Of course, Jack hadn't had breakfast. The coffee was made, though, and Mike poured a cup. He fixed Gertrude's breakfast, filled her water bowl that Marsh consistently used as well as his own. He then set out the eggs, bacon, bread, set Jack's iron skillet on the stove, and turned on the gas. As Mike put a couple pats of butter in the skillet, it occurred to him that Jack used to make breakfast for him after they'd climbed out of that ridiculously small bed, in that ridiculously small apartment on Sherman Street in Denver.

Jack had moved into that apartment when he and Elizabeth separated and damned if he didn't stay there until he retired. Mike often tried to get him to consider a bigger place or at least a larger bed, but Jack would just smile and tell him he was fine where he was.

One time when they ate breakfast at the tiny table in Jack's apartment, Mike had asked him if he thought his approach to solving homicides, the mystical part of it, was taking too much of a toll on him. Something that was way beyond what the other murder cops found themselves experiencing.

"I've never thought about it, Mike," Jack had said as offhandedly as if they were talking about his tie choice as he dressed for work.

"Talking to the dead? Doesn't that get a little intense? I mean, we all feel something when we deal with dead bodies, but hearing them? Talking to them?"

"It is what it is." Jack had stopped eating and glanced out the window that faced Sherman Street. When he turned back, he asked

Mike, "You ever watch people? Just passersby, and wonder what is going on with them? If they've eaten today? If they know where the rent money is going to come from? Or if their kid has leukemia or something?"

"No, I guess I don't. Unless they're obviously stressed about something, I just usually ignore them."

"You don't wonder why they might be hanging their head, looking down at the sidewalk, instead of where they're headed?"

"No, not that, either. What's that got to do with your investigative prowess?"

"I guess what I'm saying, Mike, is that you and I are different. I don't know why, except maybe we've lived very different lives. Yeah, all this shit works on me, and sometimes I wish it didn't. I wish sometimes I could just walk into a murder scene, gather the evidence, and then walk out. But I can't. And even if Stanton hadn't told me what he had, I think eventually I would have heard those whispers from the dead anyway."

All Mike could do then was nod without saying a word. Soon after that, Jack told him it wouldn't work, and their personal time together all but ceased except for occasionally taking each other out to dinner or lunch. They did take one trip to Bailey and barely got out of the queen bed in the rental cabin nestled into a pine forest. It had been sublime. At least for Mike, it had. But that was the last of any physical intimacy between them. Mike had concluded Jack was too inside himself. He was too caught up in things Mike had never even thought about. Things that probably made it almost impossible for Jack to be able to relate to another person in a loving way. A person who, in spite of everything, did love him, and who wanted more. So much more.

"Smells good," Jack said as he walked in the front door with Marsh preceding him.

"Ought to be ready in just a few minutes."

"I'll wash up a little. Got horse all over me. Remind me I've got to call the sheriff this morning. Abe's right. If *they* request the CBI to come up again, it'll probably happen."

"Will do," Mike said, pulling the bread out of the toaster. He'd already lain the bacon on a paper towel and picked up the bowl of eggs to give them one last stir when the landline rang. Lowering the gas, he grabbed a hand towel and walked into the parlor. He wiped his hands and picked up the receiver. "This is Mike."

"Mike, it's Abe."

"You're starting early," Mike said, glancing at the clock.

"Got some news for you and Jack. Calvin Semple killed himself last night in Ouray."

"No."

"Yeah, the sheriff up there was going to take him into custody on that bulletin we put out after he took off. Long story short, he attempted to elude when they turned on their overheads and crashed his vehicle. Shot himself with a .45. Stuck the damned thing in his mouth and pulled the fuckin' trigger."

"Who's that?" Jack said, walking into the parlor.

"Just a sec, Abe." Mike held the receiver to his chest. "Calvin Semple killed himself up in Ouray. They were trying to stop him for that POI bulletin we put out way back when."

"No shit!"

Mike nodded and then put the receiver back to his ear. "Damn,

Abe. How'd they know he was there? In town?"

"Seems one of the deputy's wives got some information he was working for a guy up there and told the deputy. Thank God, the deputy remembered the name."

"I'll be damned." Mike looked at Jack and shook his head.

"Listen," Abe said, "you get a chance to call Eagle County yet? I'm going to run the cellar thing by the brass first thing this morning."

"No, but Jack's going to call them this morning."

"Okay. But make it as early as you can. Thought about this all last night, and I think we've got to go back up there."

"We think you do, too, Abe. I'll tell Jack."

"Okay. I gotta get goin', Mike. Give me a call later."

"I will. Thanks for letting us know."

"You bet."

Mike hung up and looked at Jack, who had pulled his notes from the side table near the window. "Helluva thing," Mike said.

Jack grabbed a pen from the side table drawer and wrote down what Mike told him Abe had said. "Our leads are all dead, Mike." He put the notes back in the drawer.

"Except for Tyler and Ben."

"Yeah, except for them. Goddamnit! I wanted so much to get my hands on Calvin again. He knew the story from beginning to end. I'd guarantee it."

"I know. Didn't seem to be the type to take his own life."

"Yeah, he was a tough sonofabitch."

Mike's mind immediately flashed images of Ernest Hemingway,

sticking that shotgun in his mouth in Idaho. "Yeah," he said. "He was."

***

It'd been three days since Jack called the Eagle County Sheriff's to see if they'd request the CBI's forensic team to come back up. The sheriff told Jack he'd be happy to do that. Mike talked to Abe twice since then, and Abe had heard nothing from his assistant director.

They'd just finished breakfast when Mike asked Jack if he'd fed Shy.

"Yes, I did. Why?"

"I just thought I ought to do it. You know, I've got to start some-time." Mike smiled and began moving the dirty dishes over to the sink.

"Okay. You can start tomorrow. You remember how I do it? Just a couple flakes, then—"

"I know. I know," Mike cut him off.

"Ought to start thinking about getting your own horse."

"I'll just stick with the cat for now."

"Okay. Can't be a cowboy without a horse," Jack said, standing.

"Yeah, well. Can't be a cowboy without cows."

"Good point, Mike," Jack said.

Jack and Mike worked Shy nearly every day since Mike had moved in. Jack rode him about every other day, and Mike was still reluctant to get on him. They'd not talked again about heading up to Tess's place and taking a look at what horses were available for sale. Mike saw how much work it was to keep a horse and hadn't yet decided if he was ready to do that. Jack had yet to call Tess and ask her about coming back to take a look at the cellar. Mike didn't know why he hadn't, and he hadn't asked him. Mike kept thinking there was a whole lot two people who are in love with one another should find it natural to talk about, but not them. He didn't know why that was.

Mike and Marsh went outside and walked over to see Shy, who was still chewing his breakfast. Marsh dashed off somewhere, and Mike called for him to come, seeing that he was exploring the back of the property near where Jack had told him there was a trail that led to the ranch. Marsh did come with something in his mouth. He ran past Mike and didn't stop until he reached the porch. When Mike stepped on the porch, Marsh dropped what looked like a gob of offal. He stood in front of the door and raised his paw as if to knock. Jack opened the door and let Marsh in.

"He brought us a gift," Mike said, kneeling down to take a better look at the mess. There was a metal edge of something nearly encased in a small rotten piece of wood and covered with thick mud. Jack stepped out on the porch as Mike worked the metal out. "It's a watch." Mike held it up by its black leather strap.

Jack leaned down, his hands on his knees. "Doesn't appear to be damaged. Let's take it inside and wash it off."

They both stood at the sink as Mike held the watch under warm water. "How do you think it got there?"

"Don't know," Jack said. "Not a lot of people know about that trail. It's seldom used. Tyler used it once…"

"Yeah, I remember." Mike dried the watch with a towel and was sure Jack was as curious as he was to know if there was an inscription on the back. There wasn't. "I bet it still works. No rust. Doesn't look like any moisture has gotten behind the lens."

Jack took the watch from Mike and studied its face. "Damn. It's a Rolex. Oyster Perpetual."

"Is that a good one?"

"Well, it's a Rolex. Don't know about that particular model. Maybe." He placed the watch on the towel. "Let's let it dry for a couple days. We'll see if we can get it going."

They both heard Gertrude voice a dangerously angry sound from the parlor. Mike looked over the kitchen counter and saw Marsh had her blocked into a corner, her hair up, his tail wagging.

"Marsh," Mike said a bit too sternly. "No! Come!" He saw Jack smiling. "What?"

Jack shook his head. "Nothing."

***

Tyler woke up to Ben's dick probing his ass. "Whoa," he said, turning over. "I ain't even awake yet, Ben."

"Don't have to be. You just roll back over, and I'll wake you up."

Tyler grabbed Ben's dick. "You eat your Wheaties already or somethin'?"

Ben kissed Tyler on the lips, leaned over a bit, and ran his hand up and down Tyler's ass. "Can't remember the last time I had it in you."

Tyler smiled and rolled back over. "Just lube it up before—"

They both froze when they heard a knock on the bedroom door and Missus Clark's question: "You boys up yet? Breakfast is almost ready."

Ben rested the top of his head on Tyler's shoulder and whispered, "Damn."

"We're just gettin' up now, Missus Clark. We'll be down short-ly," Tyler said.

"Don't want it gettin' cold," she said.

"My mother used to do that," Ben said. "Every time I'd start yankin', here comes a knock on the door. You s'pose mothers do that on purpose; that they know what you're up to?"

Tyler slid out of bed, stood naked, and stretched, his dick thick and pointing up ever so slightly. "Sure, they do. It's part a mother-in'. C'mon, let's get dressed and go down there."

"You owe me one," Ben said as he also stood naked, scratched his pubes, then stroked his dick a couple times. "Need the release, Ty. Need it bad."

"Yeah, well," Tyler said, pulling on his underwear. "We got to get to work. Mister Grimm is gonna tell us what our schedule is for the next month or two."

"You still owe me one," Ben said, crossing the room and tugging his own underwear off the back of a side chair next to the small chest of drawers. "I gotta pee, but I can't right now." He stuffed him-self into his underwear and grabbed his jeans. "Tell me somethin'. Why'd you wait so long to mail that letter to Jack?"

Tyler pulled on his shirt and snatched his socks from the tops of his boots. "Had to think about it for a while," he said, sitting on the bed and tugging on his socks. "Kept thinkin' if I should send it, and also if there was somethin' else that I needed to tell him."

"Well, he oughta be gettin' it any day now."

"I expect he will."

THIRTY-NINE

While living on the grid, Jim Smith gradually became aware that he was as innocuous as his name. As a matter of fact, most people seemed to dismiss him as quickly as they would an ant on a sidewalk, including the few women he'd worked his courage up to talk to. Not that he had much of a personality, but he did have one that most ignored or simply didn't acknowledge. He sometimes felt invisible. His dog always saw him, though. Well, dogs, considering he'd had one throughout his entire life. A menagerie of dogs was more like it, starting with the mutt his father had given to him when he was six years old and continuing up until the present day. It had been sixty years since he first saw the worth of a dog, and now he had four. He would have kept the two puppies, though, but his old boy, Jinx, wouldn't tolerate them, and Jim figured the one person he saw a few times a year, Gladys, might just give the puppies a good home. And Gladys had taken them both, as good an outcome to that dilemma as Jim could have hoped for.

Twelve years ago, Jim decided the indifference the world showed him, and his disdain for that indifference was reason enough for him to leave it behind. He'd fished and hunted in the White River National Forest for years, even spent weeks at a time camping in the Eagle's Nest Wildness up by the Gore Range. He'd decided to depart the increasingly disgusting enclave of Denver to live the rest of his life in a place he'd come to love. It didn't matter to him there were laws about folks homesteading on federal and state lands. He'd come to a point in his life where the laws on the books were irrelevant. People were irrelevant.

Selling his one-bedroom house in west Denver, he told his employer of twenty years—a company in Commerce City that made cardboard boxes—that they could shove it, cleaned out his bank account, and packed his few belongings in his '89 Chevy. He put his two Malamutes in the cab with him and headed for what had become his promised land. He built a two-room cabin six miles from Piney Lake, and through the years, lived off the earth, and his dogs did too. He loved his new life, but sometimes worried civilization was getting a little too close for his comfort. Over the years, he'd watched from afar the building and expansion of what some idiot had named the Pinecone Lodge and the revitalization of a ranch farther west called the Whisper River.

In the late spring and summer, Jim often hiked down his mountain. He watched from the cover of the forest the comings and goings of people intent on spending money to do what he did for free. Lots of fat-ass men and women with their chubby kids riding tired horses, packed in canoes, eating hot dogs and hamburgers, laughing and having a good time for a price. Sometimes he'd spend days hiking around the lodge and the lake and along the elk trails that skirted the ranch. He was always as quiet as he could be, his dogs even quieter, on these hikes. When he was about to step into view of some hunter or other hiker, his dogs would caution him with a whimper, or they just froze and stared toward where they sensed the danger to be. They did the same when critters were about: the large ones, like elk, mule deer, bears, bobcats, and the elusive but deadly lions. Jim had taught them to do this—the people no less dangerous than the critters. It had always worked to keep his presence hidden except once. And that was when he'd met Gladys, the winter caretaker of the lodge.

It'd been less than a year since Jim had made the forest his home, a time when Jinx was only four, and the female, Jane, was three, and both dogs were yet sufficiently trained to mirror Jim's cautions. It was springtime, the snow had mostly melted except for the thickest parts of the forest and the highest peaks. Jim and the dogs had made their way to the edge of the pine forest. They stopped for a moment to reconnoiter the activity at the lodge, which had just opened up for the season.

Suddenly the dogs tensed, and someone said, "Howdy," from Jim's left. It was the woman Jim would come to know as a friend who understood Jim's passions and didn't give a shit about Jim's way of life six miles into the wilderness. Her name was Gladys. Through the years, she had visited Jim's cabin many times, delivering odds and ends that Jim needed, and even giving Jim a snowmobile that had been idle for years. At first, Jim had refused it, but Gladys had convinced him being snowed in with appendicitis or some other affliction would come to no good end. Jim had understood the logic in that. Though he'd yet to use it much over the years, it had come in handy a time or two.

Now, as another spring arrived, Jim watched Jinx and Jane hobble on stiff legs in the small yard he'd fenced just a year ago. The fence wasn't so much to keep the dogs in but to keep the large critters out. Sarah and Sam, the youngest dogs, were by his side, and as they passed the yard, Jinx lets loose a single bark.

"I know, old man," Jim said, knowing the old boy could probably make it down the mountain, but not back up. "We'll be back in a while." He saw Jane had sat down, staring at him with a longing he understood. "C'mon," he said to the two younger dogs and walked to the path down the mountain he knew well. Wanted to find Gladys. Hoped he'd see her out and about. He'd had something on his mind for almost a year now and wanted to tell Gladys about it. He had almost told her when he'd brought the puppies down but decided against it when she asked him if he wanted to meet the man that might take one of the puppies. Jim begged off on that and just headed back to his cabin. But what he'd seen last summer still worked on him. It might have have been nothing, but then again...

***

Jack saddled Shy, and they were on their way to the lodge to pick up the mail. Jack told Mike that around mid-May was when the Forest Service handed the mail delivery responsibilities back to the USPS, and the lodge was where everyone picked up their mail. Allowing Marsh to tag along was something he would never do after the lodge opened for the season. There was little traffic on the road. Gertrude and Mike were cleaning today. Well, as Mike did chores, Gertrude watched from her usual perch on the table in front of the parlor window.

Mike had noticed when he first moved in that although Jack had a vacuum cleaner, he apparently never used it. Very little dust settled on things up there, but man and dog did tend to bring the outside inside. They didn't have a washer and dryer. The prospect of continuing to collect dirty clothes and bed linens for the once or twice a month visit to the laundromat in Vail was something they'd talked about. Jack told Mike to just get used to wearing the same clothes for two or three times longer than he did in Denver.

When Mike mentioned the sheets and other items ought to be washed weekly, Jack had smiled and said, "Not as far as I'm concerned." Jack then said that putting in a laundry room was something he wanted to do. Eventually. Mike didn't want to harp on these kinds of issues, and he didn't.

Finishing the indoor work, Mike made himself a scotch and water, took it outside, and sat at the table on the porch. Nothing much that he'd lately been worrying about—Jack's standoffishness, in particular—mattered right now. Mike smelled the air, saw the vast expanse of the mountain spring all around him. His reverie was broken when, not thirty yards in front of him, a hawk swooped down to the ground, latched onto a chipmunk, and carried it up, up, and away. Just like that, life became death. He looked to their access road and saw Jack and Shy just rounding the curve, with Marsh slightly behind. When Jack reined Shy onto their drive, Mike stood, held up his glass, and pointed to it. Jack gave him a thumbs-up, and Mike went into the cabin and make Jack a drink.

Jack tossed the mail on the pine table and sat. "Got a shitload of it." He took off his hat, laid it on the table, and pulled his red hankie from his back pocket. He wiped off his hands and lifted the glass to his mouth as he sorted through the envelopes.

"Jack Dolan care of the Pinecone Lodge," Mike read the address on a blue envelope with flowers across the top of it. "Looks like a letter from one of your sweethearts, Jack." As he shoved it over to him, the landline rang. Mike stood and went inside, leaving Jack to open the envelope.

"I hope you have good news," Mike said to Abe Gomez on the other end of the line.

"The Eagle County sheriff came through, Mike. The boss said we could come up and take a look, though it'll only be Carl Dunfree and me. And we've got to drive. He wouldn't authorize the plane."

"Excellent. When do you think you'll be up?"

"How's tomorrow for you?"

"Tomorrow's fine."

"Good. We'll leave pretty early, so I'd say before noon."

"Meet us at the cabin, and we'll take you over there."

"Sounds good. By the way, I got a call from a deputy in Ouray who helped sort through all the crap that was in Calvin Semple's truck. Said they found two duffel bags full of S&M shit—black hoods, whips, chains, even two pairs of leather pants, dildos, the whole megillah. This guy was a sick puppy, Mike."

"Jack said Semple had some biker types up to the ranch one time. Or, at least he actually saw them once. I wonder..."

"What?"

"You'll see when you get up here."

"Okay. See you tomorrow."

Mike hung up the phone and walked back outside. "That was Abe," he said, sitting back down. "They'll be up tomorrow morning."

Jack shoved a piece of blue paper over to him. "That's from Tyler."

Mike read the letter, then laid it back on the table. "Wow," he said. "Abe just told me he got a call from a deputy in Ouray. They went through the stuff Calvin had packed in his truck, and they found a bunch of S&M stuff."

Jack nodded and didn't say anything.

"They lured the boys up here, and then—"

"Yeah. Stripped off their clothes, then probably took them to the cellar, and..." Jack finished Mike's thought. He grabbed his hat, stood, and walked across the porch to the steps where he stopped. "I'm taking Shy out again." He stepped off the porch and walked toward the pasture. Uncharacteristically, Marsh didn't run ahead but stayed close to Jack's side, lifting his head, looking at Jack's face.

Mike watched them until they were lost from his sight. He knew where they were going. Knew Tyler's letter had worked as a switch on Jack, turning on whatever it was in him that was so dark and deep, so spiritual. He couldn't even begin to understand what Jack was feeling.

Mike went into the cabin, poured more scotch in his glass, and returned to the porch. He sat back down at the table and reread Tyler's letter. Putting it back into the envelope, he studied the flowered paper again. Of all the homicides Jack had seen, of all the dead bodies he'd touched, why had those two boys become so intensely present to Jack? And why, perhaps, more importantly, was Jack incapable of... What? Sharing with him? Letting him in on what he felt about the boys. Hell, why wouldn't Jack let Mike in on what he thought about the two of them dealing with this thing, this sadness they'd carried for almost a year? And why didn't they share a bed? Why didn't they talk as two people should about their feelings, one lover to another? Mike wondered if he would have to die himself before Jack saw the worth of placing his hand on Mike's head and hearing his whisper, *"Jack, I wanted so much more"*?

Mike placed the letter from Tyler on top of the mail. He grabbed the stack and his drink and went into the cabin. Placing the mail on the coffee table, he sat on the sofa and watched as Gertrude stretched on the table before the window, then leaped down and jumped up into his lap. He stroked her to a purr.

"Just you and me again," Mike said. "Just you and me."

FORTY

Jim Smith hunkered at the edge of the lodge's property, his presence hidden by a copse of pine trees, the deep shade of the trees casting him, Sarah, and Sam in black. He watched for movement around the structure, hoping it might be Gladys, but also knowing others were there, as the lodge was gearing up for the season. He was not afraid of people, but he long ago had lost any desire to deal with human beings. Except for Gladys, of course. Other people had never really had any interest in dealing with him, and he had no problem returning the favor. He heard a sound near the back of the lodge. He stood up and saw Gladys at the lakeshore turning over the landed canoes, obviously checking them for holes or wear in the fiberglass. One of Sarah's and Sam's pups was nosing around the edge of the water where Gladys worked. Jim put his fingers to his mouth and whistled, just one high-pitched sound he knew Gladys would recognize. Gladys looked toward where he was hidden. Jim stepped out of the shadows and waved. Gladys waved back and walked toward him, the pup running to where Jim and his dogs stood.

Gladys's dog was the first to reach them. Jim knelt and caressed the dog, who broke away from him and excitedly greeted his mother and father. The dog rolled on his back, and his parents sniffed him. Sam ran in a circle and assumed a play stance as his son got to his feet and began to talk, a voice peculiar to all Mals.

"What'd you name him?" Jim asked as Gladys finally reached them.

"Kodiak," she said, watching the three dogs scamper about.

"Good name. You give the other one to that guy?"

"Yeah. Jack named him Marsh."

Jim looked at her as if he was going to ask a question, but didn't.

"So," Gladys said, nodding toward the mountain, "how's it going up there?"

"Good as can be. Jinx and Jane are in that little yard I built. They're getting old. Didn't want to stress them by bringing them down. You about ready to open the place up?"

"Another couple of weeks."

Jim nodded. "Can you talk a bit?"

"Sure. I need a little break anyway. What's on your mind? You want to come down to the lodge? We can have a beer on the deck, and—"

"Oh, no. We can do it here." He glanced at the dogs who were running as a pack down the hill. "Sarah! Sam!" he shouted. "Come!" All three of the dogs immediately stopped, turned, and ran back up the hill. "Lay," he said, showing them his palm. All except Kodiak obeyed.

Gladys slapped her leg. "Kodiak." Kodiak laid down next to her.

"Let's sit," Jim said, easing down on the pine slash, and Gladys did the same.

"Last summer, I took Sarah and Sam to the base of Mount Powell. We were out for only two days, as I had to get back to Jinx and Jane at the cabin. We skirted the base of the mountain, then climbed up to the north ridge and headed west a little way. I set up camp that first night about a hundred yards west of that trail that tops out there. You know the one? You catch it down there on the other side of the lodge. Not sure what time it was exactly, but it was late, and the dogs perked up and stared east, toward the trail. It was real quiet, the moon was half-full, and I saw a couple flashes of light from where the dogs had pointed their attention. I got out of my sleeping bag, and we made our way about fifty yards closer to whatever was going on. I saw about six figures—you know, just shadows—of people moving around. Every couple of seconds, somebody would turn on a flashlight and turn it off. I swear I heard the sound of tape coming off a spool and some whispers. Couldn't tell what they were saying. Anyway, after a while, whoever it was started walking east, and they caught that back trail that opens up at the ranch. I didn't think much of it at the time, and me and the dogs just went back to our campsite. It was an hour or so before dawn that the dogs perked up again, and, sure enough, they were back. There was a little more light by then, and I saw there weren't six anymore, but just four of them. They were carrying something. Something heavy. Two of them had a bundle, and the other two carried one too. We followed them once they got to the ridge and watched them start down the trail. Sam was ahead of me and Sarah, and I don't know what happened to him, but he let out a squeal, and I called to him. When he came back, I looked for those figures on the trail, and they were gone."

"Was this about the time they found those bodies?" Gladys asked.

"I don't know when it was they found the bodies. You told me about it sometime after it'd happened. But, it was in July that I saw all this."

"Did you return the same way you came, Jim?"

"Yes, we did. I was gonna stay on the mountain another night but thought I'd better just get back home. I didn't know what those people were doing, and I guess I got a little spooked. The city people that come up here act like jackasses most of the time. Some of the hikers and campers do, too. Hunters usually don't like crowds, and if they're hauling something, you know what it is. But those bundles... I don't know what to think, Gladys."

"Well..." Gladys stood and brushed off the seat of her pants. Kodiak got up, too, and rushed over to where Sam and Sarah were still lying, trying to provoke them into play. "It could have been something to do with those murders, and maybe it wasn't. What I do think," she said as Jim also stood, "is that we need to tell Jack Dolan about this."

"The cop?"

"He's retired, Jim."

"Not sure I want to get myself involved with any kind of cop, retired or not."

"Tell you what... I'll tell Jack what you've told me. If he wants to talk to you, I'll come up to your place, and we'll set a day, time, and location for all of us to meet. He won't see your living situation, and you can tell him what you saw, which might be valuable information for him. That sound okay?"

"I don't know. One thing leads to another, Gladys. Next thing you know, they'll want me to come to court, serve me a subpoena."

"Like to see someone serve it, Jim. If anyone asks, I really don't know where you live."

Jim nodded. "Okay. We'll just see how it goes. I do feel better telling you about it, though. Gotta get back to the cabin. You take care, Gladys. Let's go," Jim said, and Sam and Sarah stood, sending Kodiak into an excited circle around them.

"One other thing, Jim. Sam and Sarah are brother and sister. Right?"

"They are." Jim smiled. "Know what's on your mind. Yeah, Kodiak and the other one—What was his name? Marsh?—were accidents. I've always tried to keep male and female separated during heat. Even with Jinx and Jane—who are not related—but I did let them do it once, and that's when Sam and Sarah arrived about six years ago. Jane had five pups, and three didn't make it. I watched Sam and Sarah real close, except for one time late in the spring when we had that big snow that caved in part of my roof. Sarah had four pups, and the two that lived I gave to you. They'll be fine. It's natural, Gladys. Wolves do it sometimes when they can't mix with other packs."

"Okay," Gladys said as Jim turned and walked away. "Thanks for telling me about what you saw," she called after Jim. He and his dogs were already stepping into the edge of the forest. "Kodie! Come!" she called to Kodiak, who stopped in his tracks, glanced at Gladys, and then turned to watch Jim and the dogs as they disappeared into the mountainside shadows.

***

Mike pulled himself out of his dark mood and decided he'd drive into Vail and give Jack some alone time. He wanted to see about getting satellite service, both TV and internet. He hadn't thought he'd miss not having it when he first moved in, but he had, and now felt totally cut off from the outside world. Besides, Jack would probably come back with his own mood, and Mike really didn't want to deal with that. Jack had been gone almost an hour, and Mike couldn't shake the feeling he wanted to be gone when Jack came back. He quickly wrote Jack a note and, as he shut the door behind him, he stuck it between the door and the frame where Jack would see it. Before getting into his Jeep, he looked back at the cabin, then turned toward the stable and pasture. Taking inventory, he thought. Or maybe it was just a last moment savoring a scene he'd come to love. It felt weird not locking the cabin's door, realizing he didn't even know if it had a lock.

As Mike drove west on the access road and was just about to turn left at the fork, a flatbed truck came down the hill and headed for the ranch. A load of lumber and wallboard was strapped down in the bed, and Mike's first thought was renovations were beginning. He then tensed with the thought whatever was in the cellar might already be compromised by workmen traipsing around there. He followed the truck and stopped next to it as it pulled alongside the main building. Six or seven men were already working, most with tool belts and one was holding a clipboard. Mike got out of his Jeep and approached the guy with the clipboard.

"Hello," he said.

The man smiled and yelled to the guy in the truck: "Put the sheet-rock under the porch, and you can just pile the lumber in front here." He looked at Mike. "Can I help you?"

"Didn't know all this was going on," Mike said.

"Yeah. We're getting it ready for the season. No major stuff yet, but they want it done yesterday. You live around here?"

"We're east of here a little way. You're not doing any foundation work, are you? Anything that would cause you to get in the cellar out back?"

"No. Hell, I peeked in there, and that's not a place I want to spend any time in. Felt my balls constrict to peanuts just opening up the door."

"You, too?" Mike said, smiling. "Listen, I'm just newly retired from the CBI, the Colorado Bureau of Investigation. That cellar might hold some evidence in a case I was working on before I left and is still ongoing. A CBI team is coming up here tomorrow to take a look at it."

"Christ! What happened there?"

"Oh, nothing to be concerned about." Mike didn't want to tell him any details if he could avoid it. "I just want to make sure that nobody goes in there until the CBI checks it out. You think you could tell your guys to just stay away from it?"

"No reason for anybody to go down there. Sure, I can do that. Somebody die down there?"

Yeah, I'm pretty sure somebody did. "No, nothing like that," Mike said. "It's just important that no one goes in there."

The man studied Mike's face for a moment and nodded. "Like I said, nobody has a need to go in there. And I *will* tell everybody."

"Thank you."

"No problem," he said.

As Mike got back in the Jeep, he noticed the clipboard man was still watching him, until one of the workmen distracted him. Losing his urge to drive to Vail, Mike went back home. If it was home. He was surprised that thought came to him. And it scared him a little.

***

Tyler and Ben headed east for Ada, Oklahoma, sitting in one of Grimm's smaller semis. The operators of the annual spring rodeo near Ada didn't lack for setup expertise. But the guy who ran it had called Grimm the day before in a slow panic. His voice laden with a syrupy Oklahoma drawl, he had told Grimm he'd miscalculated his needs for the event and wondered if Grimm would help him out. Grimm immediately told Ben and Tyler to load the truck and pack their bags.

Once they unloaded the extra pens at the rodeo site just a few miles from town, Tyler and Ben drove back to Ada and got a room in the Silver Spur Motel. It was clean and quiet, and Ben pulled the bottle of Wild Turkey from his bag, grabbed two glasses from the bathroom, and poured them each a generous shot. The whiskey drunk, they both lay down on the queen bed, nearly exhausted from the five-hour drive and the labor of unloading the metal pens and setting them up. They were soon asleep.

Annie Clark was walking back to the house from the loafing shed where she'd fed Bear, loved on him a bit, and filled his water tank. As she stepped on the porch, an Amarillo Police Department cruiser pulled off the road and entered her property. Looked at the driver and realized she knew him, had known him all his life. She retraced her steps off the porch and met him as he got out of the cruiser.

"Why, Richie Bend in the flesh."

"Hey, Annie," the officer said, closing his door. "How you doin' this fine day?"

"Just fine. I haven't seen you in... Well, I guess it's been a while."

The officer hugged Annie, stood back a bit, and looked at the old house. He saw the pickup with Colorado plates. "You got some company?"

"Oh, it's two boys who I'm rentin' out the upstairs to. They're workin' for Mister Grimm. He came and picked them up this mornin', and I believe they've gone to Oklahoma."

"Colorado boys?"

"Yes. They told me they used to work in the Colorado mountains, got tired a that, and come down this way to find work. They're good boys, Richie."

"I s'pose it ain't gonna stick if I tell you again they call me Dick now?"

"No, 'course it won't. You're Richie and always will be."

The officer smiled, walked over to the pickup, and looked in the window. "Those boys smoke marijuana?"

"Regular cigarettes sometimes. Why?"

"Marijuana is legal in Colorado. It ain't in Texas." He pulled a small notepad and pen from his chest pocket and wrote down the license number. "We got a policy to check out any vehicles with Colorado plates."

"Like I said, Richie, they're good boys. They pay their rent and help me out here. They're gonna scrape and paint this old house for me."

The officer took another look at the house. "It could use it for sure, Annie. You need anything from me? You okay on your meds and all that?"

"I'm just fine. I get my old Ford runnin' about once a week and go into town for my needs."

"Okay," he said. He walked back to his cruiser and opened the door. "Mama said to tell you, hello. You ought to go see her one of these days."

"Well, you tell her hi for me, too. And I will go see her. She doin' okay since your daddy passed?"

"She is. Just gets lonesome sometimes. Give me a call if you need anything."

"I will." She watched him pull back on the road and wondered if the boys did smoke that stuff. No, she thought, they don't. "And they're gonna paint my house," she said as she walked toward the porch.

***

Jack wasn't back yet. Mike grabbed the note from the door and tore it up. He stood in the parlor for a moment and thought about making an early supper, but decided he'd rather be outside, moving, doing something… What? Useful? He walked over to the shed, grabbed the shovel and rake, and stepped into the stable. There wasn't much to clean up, but the chore would keep him busy for a while, just mindless work that might calm him down a bit. His mind wandered, flashing images of Jack and him together in those dangerous days when they'd both felt the excitement of their trysts. They were lovers then, in every sense of the word. And they were happy in spite of the danger of being found out. He tried to remember what had happened to cause Jack to tell him they had to end the affair, that they couldn't continue as they'd been doing. He couldn't pin it down. Seemed like it had come out of nowhere. Oh, he knew as well as Jack did they were tempting the fates to strike them and hit hard. But, they were okay. They were careful. They even avoided the little drinking parties the other cops would put together at least once a week at the Log Cabin Tavern in North Denver. It was owned by a retired cop who would lock the doors and always have a couple women on hand, as well as all the booze they wanted.

When Jack and Mike didn't show up at some of those parties, their absences from the overindulgences caused more than a few gibes from their fellow cops. They'd wonder out loud if maybe Jack and Mike had spent the night together rather than with them.

"Who fucked who?" one or another would say. Then another would ask, "You eat that fudge after you cooked it?" It was, of course, all in fun. Jack and Mike would smile, throw some gibes back. Maybe that was it. While Mike could dismiss it all for what it was, maybe Jack couldn't.

Marsh was first to let his presence be known. He rushed into the stable and immediately back out. Mike saw Jack and Shy coming down their drive. He loaded what he'd raked up into the wheelbarrow, pushed it around to the back of the shed where he dumped it onto the pile they'd already started. He returned to the stable and put the shovel and rake back in the shed.

"I was going to get to that as soon as I got back," Jack said as he dismounted. He snapped a lead rope on Shy's bridle and then tied it off to a post.

"Nothing else to do. Were you at The Place?"

"Yes," he said, unwrapping the cinch.

Mike snatched the brush from the stable as Jack took Shy's saddle off, carrying it to the sawhorse in the shed. Mike pulled the saddle blanket off and handed it to Jack. "Thank you," Jack said.

As Mike brushed Shy's back, he said, "I saw a flatbed taking some building materials to the ranch a while ago."

"Really?"

"Yeah. I went up there and talked to the foreman about the cellar. Bunch of workmen up there, too. They offloaded some lumber and sheetrock."

"You told them to stay away from the cellar?"

"I did."

"Good."

Jack slipped Shy's bridle off and gently put the rope harness on him. "Didn't mean to be gone so long. Sorry."

"That's okay, Jack. It was something you had to do."

"I pray for the time it won't be necessary," Jack said, grabbing the other brush.

"When do you think that'll happen?"

Jack brushed Shy's neck and then leaned both his arms on Shy's back, looking at Mike. "I think we're getting closer to that time. I think we might have some closure with this thing pretty soon."

Mike looked at Jack's face and grabbed his hands. They stood there a moment, their arms atop Shy, their hands clasped. "I hope we do," Mike said, praying they could find some closure between them, and that his misgivings about them, just them, could be put to rest as well.

FORTY-ONE

After supper, Jack and Mike sat on the sofa. Marsh was in Jack's bedroom, the coolest place in the cabin, where he usually slinked off to whenever there were flames in the parlor fireplace. Gertrude lolled on the coffee table.

"I almost went to Vail today," Mike said. "I want to get satellite installed so we can have internet service, maybe TV as well."

"Ah, Mike…" Jack shook his head. "I really wanted to avoid all that. I haven't missed it a bit since I moved up here. Why don't you wait a while? You'll eventually get to where you don't feel you need it."

Mike had anticipated his response. At least they were having a conversation about something other than the boys. "Jack, I really think I need that outside contact. I want to watch a movie every once in a while. I want to stay in communication with the… The world, I guess, is what I'm missing."

"I left the world behind. Intentionally." Jack sipped his drink. "And by God," he sighed, "it caught up with me even here when I found those boys up on that hill."

Mike realized Jack was telling him that his world amounted to not much more than what he used to do every day, dealing with death by violence. The whispers of the dead probably the only truths he'd come to categorically believe.

"Was that all the world meant to you, Jack? Just the job? Just the—"

"Oh," Jack interrupted, adjusting himself so he could look directly at Mike. "It wasn't a job. It was a life, Mike. I got to the point where I knew I had to get away from it. I got tired of it. And I knew, oh man—" He shook his head. "I knew if I wasn't able to let it go, it would consume me. Eat me up like a fuckin' cancer. You had burnout, Mike. That's why you left. For me... Well, it was killing me."

"You never said... You never told me, Jack. Even when we started working on the boys' case, you were just the Jack I remembered. You were a cop again. It seemed like you were, ah, enthusiastic about getting back into... the game."

"The last hurrah and all that, huh?" Jack offered Mike a slight smile and then turned away from him.

"Maybe. If that's how you wanted to look at it."

"I looked at it," he said, a sternness in his voice, "as I looked at every other one, Mike. You still don't believe..." He paused a moment, his voice softening. "Call it a gift. Call it something Stanton taught me, though I know it's more than that. Call it something my mother gifted to me, which it probably was. I owed them because I heard them. All of them who were able to find some last scintilla of strength to tell me something, to share their sadness, to express their confusion about why they lay there, dead, so dead, so..." He stood and walked around the coffee table to the fireplace. He placed his hands on the mantel and leaned his head down.

Mike stood and walked to Jack. He placed his hand on Jack's back and gently rubbed it. "I didn't know, Jack. All I knew... I knew you were a good cop who had a different way of doing things than the rest of us. Well, you and Stanton had a different way. I didn't know how deeply it affected you. I'm sorry. I'm so sorry."

Jack raised his head and wiped his eyes with his fingers. He turned and wrapped his arms around Mike. "You don't have to be sorry, Mike. You don't have to do anything except be here. I want you here. I... need you."

After Jack went to bed, Mike checked the fireplace, put their glasses in the sink, and turned off the lights. He then walked to Jack's bedroom and looked in. In the nightlight's faint glow from the bathroom, he could see Jack in bed, on his side with his back facing the door. Marsh was curled up on the rug below the foot of the bed. As Mike turned to go to his bedroom, he heard Jack stir. Mike looked back in. Jack had opened the covers.

"Right here," Jack said, softly patting the mattress.

***

Tyler and Ben ate breakfast in the Prairie Kitchen, Ada, Oklahoma's longest-running downhome eatery where the locals loaded up on food like their mamas used to make. Or, in this case, like what the boys had come to expect from Annie Clark back in Amarillo. They would have most of the day to themselves. Still, they were obligated to be present for the rodeo and on hand if they were needed to replace or repair any of the equipment they'd set up yesterday.

"I ought to call Annie," Tyler said as they finished breakfast. He drank the rest of his orange juice and pulled his wallet from his rear pocket.

"That'd be a nice thing to do," Ben said. He leaned across the table closer to Tyler. "You see those cowboys over there? No, the other way."

Tyler looked at who were obviously cowboys, both fitting the image of young men he'd seen on TV bull-riding broadcasts in one place or another. Their faces were chiseled, their eyes bluer than blue, and their Wrangler jeans and colorful shirts exuded nothing but cowboy.

"Wow. Good lookin' men."

"Gonna enjoy that rodeo," Ben said as the waitress stepped to their table.

"You boys need anything else?"

"No, thank you." Tyler picked up his wallet and pulled out the credit card Grimm had given them before they'd left Amarillo. He glanced at the check the waitress handed him and gave it back to her along with the credit card.

"You oughta be in the rodeo, Ty. You could ride broncs for sure."

"And I could break my back it, Ben."

Ben nodded. "Yeah. And we don't have insurance."

"And we ain't as pretty as those boys, either."

They stopped back at the motel before driving the semi-tractor back to the rodeo site. Tyler sat on the bed and dialed Annie's number. He waited through four rings and was just about to hang up when she answered.

"Missus Clark, it's Tyler," he said. "…Yes, we did. Here safe and sound. …Well, good. …Thank you for that. Bear does like his oats. …What? Are we marijuana smokers? …No, no. We don't do that. …Well, there's nothin' to see in the truck. …Took our license number?"

Ben stepped out of the bathroom and stood in the middle of the room, listening to Tyler.

"Okay," Tyler said. "…Yeah, we'll prob'ly be back tomorrow sometime. …You're welcome." He hung up and looked at Ben. "Some cop came by and wrote down our license number."

"They're stolen plates."

"I know it, Ben. Jesus…"

"What're we gonna do?"

"Give me a minute to think." Tyler stood and walked to the door and then back again. "Goddamnit," he said, grabbing his keys from the nightstand. "C'mon. We gotta get to the rodeo. We got some time to think this through."

Ben watched Tyler open the door and walk into the parking lot. "Fuck," he said as he followed Tyler, shutting the door behind him.

***

Mike followed Jack out of the cabin as the black Suburban pulled into their drive. They waited as Abe Gomez stopped the vehicle. Gomez and Carl Dunfree got out.

"Gentlemen," Abe said as he walked to the front of the vehicle. "You remember, Carl?"

"Sure," Jack said, shaking Carl's hand.

"Carl, Abe," Mike said, shaking their hands. "Thanks for coming up."

"Thank you for the call, Mike."

They all turned their heads toward the access road when the sound of an ATV grew louder.

"That's Gladys," Jack said, and they watched the ATV turn onto the drive. "She's the lodge's caretaker."

"You stay here and talk, Jack," Mike said. He walked to where Gladys had stopped the ATV. "Good morning."

"Same to you. See you got company." She nodded toward the front of the Suburban.

"Yeah, it's the CBI. We're going to look at the cellar again. They brought up a forensics kit, and we need to collect whatever evidence might be in there. What brings you over here?"

"Jim Smith, the guy we got our pups from, came to see me yesterday. Told me about something he saw last summer. Might be nothing, but might have something to do with the murders."

"This is something all of us need to hear, Gladys. Can we head over to the lodge after we're done at the ranch? Will you be available?"

"Sure. I'll be around. If you don't see me, just ask. We've got a few staff working already."

"Excellent," Mike said. "I think it'll be about an hour or two."

"That works. See you then." Gladys reached for the ignition and paused. "Oh, by the way, Jack's and my dog are inbred."

"What?"

"Yeah. The parents are brother and sister. Nothing to worry about, though." She started the ATV and turned it around.

Mike didn't move for a moment as he watched Gladys turn onto the access road.

"Did she tell you what the guy saw?" Jack asked from the back-seat of the Suburban.

"No, just that he saw something. We can head over there after we're done with the cellar. Just take the fork to the right," Mike said.

As they approached the main building, they saw signs of an ongoing renovation. Workmen were carrying sheetrock from the porch to the inside of the structure.

"You ever find out what the status of the ranch is now?" Mike asked.

"Nothing definite," Abe said. "Rosario's sister apparently has his POA. Don't know if it's out of probate yet or not."

"Somebody has got to be calling the shots," Carl said.

"Just park over there, out of the way," Mike said. "The cellar is around back."

Abe parked the Suburban, and they all got out. The foreman who Mike talked to yesterday came out of the building and walked over to them. "You're back," he said. "I kept everyone away from the cellar."

"Thanks for doing that," Mike said. "Can I ask who hired you to do this work?"

"The owners of the Pinecone Lodge."

"So, you don't know who actually owns the ranch?"

"No." The foreman shook his head. "I heard the owner died a while ago, though."

"Yeah, we heard that too," Mike said, "We're going to be back there for a while. We won't get in your way."

"Take your time," the foreman said as Carl pulled two silver-colored suitcases from the back of the Suburban, and Abe hefted a battery-powered light bar. "I'd be interested to know what's in there, though."

"So would we," Mike said as he followed Jack, Abe, and Carl to the rear of the building.

"Smells like death," Abe said as he carried the light bar into the cellar.

Carl waited just outside the door as Jack and Mike helped Abe position the light bar. When Abe turned it on, he said, "Whoa..." The room was roughly twenty by thirty, with a sturdy table centering it. The walls were black with mold, and the dirt floor, especially around the table, was discolored in places, splotches, and larger areas darker than the outlying dirt.

"Look at the timbers above," Abe said.

They all looked up and saw large eyehooks in several places on the thick joists that supported the floor above. "Could be for lifting game," Carl said as he stopped under the threshold and spread a plastic tarp just to the side of the entrance.

"Or for something else," Jack said.

Carl stepped back outside, opened up one of the kits, and grabbed a box of latex gloves. He walked back inside and held the box out. "Grab your gloves, gentlemen. Let's get this show on the road."

FORTY-TWO

After they finished up at the cellar, Mike found the foreman again and asked him to try to keep people out of there. "Depending on what we find in the lab," he told him, "we might be coming back. You think that's possible?"

"I think so. We haven't yet had a need to get down there. The only thing I can think of is if some plumbing or electrical issues pop up."

"Okay. Can I give you my name and number? We're just east of here, and if you have to go down there, I'd appreciate a call."

"Sure." The foreman handed Mike his clipboard. Mike wrote down the information and gave it back to him.

"Thanks," Mike said.

"You sure nobody got killed down there?"

"We'll see." Mike left it at that and joined the others at the Suburban.

They later found Gladys at the lodge and sat down at a picnic table on the back deck that overlooked the lake. She told them what Jim Smith had told her.

They all traded a few glances with one another during the telling, and when Gladys was finished, Jack asked, "Can we speak to him directly?"

She smiled. "No, I don't think that's possible. I think that'd ruin the trust we've established with each other."

"He's not in trouble," Mike said.

"Oh, that's not it," she said. "I told Jack that Jim is the closest thing to a hermit there is, and, well… Tell you the truth, if this thing ever came down to delivering subpoenas or something, I probably wouldn't tell you where he is."

"Not much we could do with what he told you, Gladys," Carl said, "if this ever went to trial. It's just hearsay, and that wouldn't fly in court."

Gladys ran her hand down her cheek and looked at the lake for a moment. "Tell you what I'll do," she said, looking at back at them. "I'll hike up there and see if he's willing to talk to you. He won't want you up at his place, so I'd arrange a meeting place of his liking. I don't think he'll do it, but I'll try."

"Under the circumstances, that's all we can ask for," Mike said.

A young woman called from inside the lodge, "Gladys, we need you," and they all stood and shook hands. The men walked back to the Suburban.

Carl and Abe wanted to see the cabin. When Jack opened the door, Marsh dashed out and immediately ran toward the pasture, where he frantically nosed the ground and did his numbers. They all stood and watched until Marsh came running back. He greeted Abe and Carl and then lay down by his bowl. Gertrude was nowhere to be seen.

346

Mike took them on a tour of the cabin, ending up back in the parlor. It was already getting dark, and Abe wanted to head back to Denver.

"You mind if I wash my hands before we get out of here?" Abe said.

"No, of course not. There's some soap right there in the kitchen," Mike said.

"That's a good idea," Carl said. "After what we were digging around in… The wipes just don't seem to get it all off."

Jack and Mike stood in the parlor as Abe turned on the faucet. When Abe came out of the kitchen, he held the watch Jack had left drying on a towel next to the sink. "Is this yours?" he asked.

"No," Jack said. "Marsh came up with that. Found it on a back trail."

Abe studied the watch for a moment. "You know that kid's mother—Missus Harris? Her kid was the one with the little devil tattoo. She sent us a letter months ago asking if we had any of her son's belongings we could send to her. She was asking for several things, but one of them was a watch, an heirloom her father had given to the kid. She described it as an Oyster Perpetual. Thought that was an odd name for a watch. I wrote her back and told her, no, we hadn't found anything. Told her everything we had was evidence."

"Goddamn," Jack said, reaching for the watch. He placed it in his palm and sat down on the sofa. "It has to be his."

"Where exactly did you find it?" Carl asked.

"There's a back trail to the ranch behind our property," Mike said. "Marsh was digging around there and brought this up to us. It'd somehow gotten lodged in a piece of a branch or something, all of it covered with mud." He glanced at Jack, who had closed his hand over the watch and was staring at it. "Right, Jack?"

Jack looked at Mike. The expression on his face appeared as though he'd just realized he wasn't alone. "Um, yeah," he said. "That's where it came from."

Abe glanced at Carl. "I guess we've got something else to look at. That trail far from here?"

"It's at the edge of the tree line behind the cabin. I don't know, maybe fifty yards or so," Mike said. "It's too dark to go down there now."

"And we've got to get back to Denver," Carl said.

"Yeah, we do." Abe nodded. "Maybe we ought to take the watch, Jack. Hold on to it as evidence and..."

Jack stood. "We washed it, Abe. It's... We'll hang on to it for now. If it's needed or if we can eventually get it back to the boy's mother, we all know where it is."

"Okay," Abe said. "Kind of... eerie, finding it."

"Yes, it is," Jack said.

No one said anything for a moment. Carl finally broke the silence. "We do have to get back. As for coming back up to look at that trail... We'll have to get the okay again from the boss."

"That's reasonable," Mike said, again glancing at Jack, who was standing there, clenching the watch.

When Jack didn't say anything, Abe said, "Okay. Let's go. Thanks for helping out, and we'll be in touch."

Mike opened the door for Abe and Carl. Jack finally found his voice. "Thanks for coming up," he said, not moving, still standing near the sofa.

Mike walked them to their vehicle and turned back to the cabin when they pulled onto the access road. When he got back in the cabin, Jack was again sitting on the sofa, the watch still his hand.

"You okay?"

"Yeah. Yeah," Jack said. He stood and put the watch in his pocket. "I have to feed Marsh." He walked into the kitchen and grabbed Marsh's bowl. Marsh circled the counter and then vocalized at Jack, raising his head and shaking it.

"And I'll take care of Gertie," Mike said. "Sounds like he's scolding you for his late supper."

"I'm sure he is."

Gertrude emerged from wherever she'd been hiding when Mike opened her food can and dumped the contents into her bowl. Once he'd set her dish in her favorite spot, she slinked over to it with attitude. She wasn't happy.

"I'm not very hungry," Mike said.

"Nah," Jack said, rising up after setting Marsh's bowl on the floor. "Let's just have a drink. Lots of… processing going on for me right now."

"Sounds good."

Mike started a fire. The nights were still almost frigid, something Mike still hadn't gotten used to. He sat on the sofa. Jack came in with their drinks and sat next to him.

"Productive day, huh?" Jack said.

"Yeah, it was." Mike looked at Jack's profile. "You okay? Finding out about the watch was… I mean…"

"I know what you mean, Mike. And, no, I'm not going to go up to The Place to… to try to figure all this out. I am okay. But, damn, this thing just…"

Mike scooted over and put his arm around his shoulders. "Yeah, it just keeps going, and going."

After Mike came back from the kitchen where he refreshed their drinks, he sat on the sofa as Jack poked the fire. Jack reset the screen and sat back down.

"You remember," Jack said, grabbing his drink, "that case we worked, oh, I don't know, maybe twenty years ago? The one where the motel room was a mess, blood all over the place, but otherwise clean? Everything that you'd think would be in a motel room wasn't there? No clothes or toiletries. No luggage. The bed hadn't even been slept in?"

"Yes, I do," Mike said. "The victim was on the floor between the bed and the wall. Young woman, maybe twenty-five or -six."

"That's it. She'd checked in alone, and nobody had heard anything. Her jugular had been severed. We figured she'd been stabbed standing up, the blood shooting across to the walls. No rape. No trauma, other than the wound. When I touched her, the only thing I got was, 'The watch. He wanted it back.'"

"It was her father. He'd given her the watch on her last birthday. He found out she was... spending time with his business partner, a happily married man. He came into headquarters and confessed the very next day."

"He had her check into the motel," Jack said. "Told her he had a surprise for her. He was well known around town. Owned a bunch of furniture stores." Jack sipped his drink. "He just wanted that damned watch back."

"But he brought the knife with him, Jack. He wanted more than the watch."

"Yeah, but maybe not. He was well past sixty. Kind of frail. Did you believe him when he told us he brought the knife to protect himself?"

"From a woman that young? His own daughter? No, I didn't believe him," Mike said.

"The mother of that girl didn't want the watch. I've never understood that."

"Just a reminder of the tragedy, I guess."

"I guess," Jack said.

They both showered before bed. Mike assumed Jack wanted to sleep together again. He was sitting on the bed when Jack came into the bedroom from the bathroom. Jack smiled at Mike and then reached to the chair he'd draped his pants over. He pulled the watch from the pocket, studied it again, and then put it in the side table drawer. "Let's hit the hay," he said as he pulled the covers over both of them.

"The mother needs that watch back, Mike. That's where it belongs."

"I agree, Jack," Mike said as he turned off the lamp, hearing Marsh tiptoe into the room and lie down at the foot of the bed.

***

It was almost midnight before Tyler and Ben reloaded the semi-trailer. The rodeo itself had been as festive as they always were, the locals whooping it up until the awards were handed out, and the lights were turned off. Tyler and Ben watched it all, their thoughts not on the festivities, but on what they'd learned from Annie. Both of them had hung around the staging area, their shirt pockets showing hang-tags reading STAFF. They wondered what the hell they would do af-ter they loaded the equipment back into the truck and were ready to head back to Amarillo. When they did back up the semi to the trailer, attaching the cables and airlines, they climbed in the cab with Ben behind the wheel.

"I guess we got two options," Ben said, grabbing the wheel with both hands. "We can just go back and see what happens, or we can go back, leave the truck in Grimm's yard, and hop on a bus to some-where."

"You actually think I'd leave Bear with Annie? What about the stuff we've got in her house?"

"Just clothes. And Bear... She'd do right by him, Tyler. I don't think—"

"No, you don't think, Ben. Look, I ain't leavin' Bear. And I don't think we can just keep runnin'. We been runnin' too long."

"I know." Ben hung his head and shook it. "What option you thinkin' about?"

"We get goin' right now and we'll be back by five or so. You let me off at Annie's, and I'll get the horse trailer hooked up to the truck, get Bear in there, and get our stuff from the house. You take the semi to Grimm's, and I'll pick you up. If he's there, ask for our pay. We'll go from there."

"Where we goin' from there? And what if the cops took our truck?"

"We'll figure that out when we get there." Tyler waited a moment for Ben to start the engine. When he didn't, Tyler reached over and switched on the ignition himself. "C'mon, Ben. Time is wastin'."

FORTY-THREE

Daylight was almost upon them as Ben pulled to the side of the road just before Annie Clark's drive. Their pickup was still parked next to the house.

"Okay," Tyler said as he opened the door. "You know the plan. I'll be there in about half an hour, maybe a little more."

"What are you gonna tell Missus Clark?"

"That we're takin' Bear to a horse show or somethin'."

"She'll see you get our stuff from upstairs."

"Jesus, Ben. I'll tell her we're stayin' there a couple days. I don't know. You just remember to try and get our money from Grimm."

"You want me to give him his credit card back?"

Tyler pulled his wallet from his back pocket but didn't open it. "No. If he ain't there, we might need this. We'll call him on the road and tell him to apply our pay to the card charges."

"He ain't gonna like that."

"Listen, Ben. We're in a situation here where we can't be thinkin' of all the stuff that might go wrong. We just gotta go. Now!" Tyler climbed down off the semi and walked toward the house.

Annie opened her front door and stepped onto the porch. "You're back," she said, wiping her hands on a towel. "Just in time for breakfast."

"Hi, Missus Clark," Tyler said, stopping at the porch steps. "We are back, but we're leavin' again."

"Oh, no. You gotta have some breakfast. You got another job already?"

"Well, no. But, we wanted to take Bear down to, ah... There's a horse show near Lubbock, and... We gotta get movin' if we want to get down there in time. Might stay a couple days, and I wanted to pack some things."

"Ben takin' the semi back?"

"Yes, he is. I gotta get the horse trailer hooked up." Tyler turned and walked toward the side of the house.

"Richie came back and took the plates off your truck," Annie said as she stepped off the porch and followed Tyler. "Said they was stolen plates, and he wanted me to give him a call soon as you boys got back."

Tyler stopped and looked at the truck. "Damn," he said. "Who's Richie?"

"He's that police officer I told you about when you called. He also took the plate off the horse trailer."

Tyler shook his head and stared at Annie. "You gonna call him?"

Annie looked at Tyler for a moment, then smiled. "You come in and have a cup of coffee. We'll talk about this." She turned and walked back to the porch.

"That truck of yours in workin' order?" Tyler said.

"Yes, most of the time."

"I need to go get Ben."

Annie nodded. "Keys are in the ashtray. You're comin' back? Right?"

"Love my horse too much not to."

***

Deciding they'd walk the back trail where Marsh had found the watch, Jack took care of Shy's needs, and Mike joined him and Marsh at the stable.

"Where should we start?" Mike said.

Jack took off his gloves, brushed hay off his shirt, and looked north of the cabin. "Down there where Marsh picked it up. We can follow it to the ranch, and then backtrack to where it almost intersects the trail to The Place."

"Sounds good."

Mike waited for Jack to finish up, and then they headed north, avoiding the deeper patches of mud that still spotted the area and would probably still be there next month.

"From what that guy told Gladys," Jack said, "I think it's pretty clear what happened."

They hadn't talked about this last night as they sat before the fire, and that surprised Mike. Maybe Jack had been too caught up with the news about the watch. But, now that he'd mentioned it, Mike knew it was something they'd both concluded.

"Yeah. They were taken to the cellar alive. Then…"

"Dumped at The Place," Jack finished Mike's thought. "We'll see what the cellar evidence reveals, but—" He paused a moment as they both stepped over a fallen pine. "The scenario works."

"I'd say The Place wasn't exactly where they'd planned to put the bodies, but the guy spooked them, and they just quickly… dropped them."

Jack stopped, bent down, and sifted through an accumulation of slash just off to the side of the trail. "You know," he said as he stood and brushed his hands on his pants, "there are apparently three other people out there besides Denman who know exactly what happened up here. I honestly don't think Tyler and Ben were involved, other than what Tyler wrote about."

"I agree about Tyler and Ben. But those others, whoever they were? Like we've discussed before, chances are they won't be forthcoming unless they happen to find themselves up on charges for something else. Maybe not even then. Fat chance their consciences will kick in."

"They have no conscience, Mike."

"No. No, they don't."

They heard a power saw in the distance. "Got an early start this morning," Jack said, looking toward the ranch, where he could see the main building in the distance.

"The crew is probably staying up here."

"I suspect they are. Driving in from Vail every day would be a bitch. Let's keep going." Jack continued to walk the trail as Mike followed behind. Marsh preceded them, periodically stopping to sniff something to the side of the trail.

"By the way," Mike said, "I don't think I told you that Gladys said Marsh is inbred. His mother and father are sister and brother."

"The hermit told her that?"

"Yeah. I guess it doesn't matter, but we probably ought to get him fixed pretty soon."

They both stopped when Marsh leaped to the side of the trail, picked something up, and vigorously shook his head.

"What's he got?" Mike said, stepping to Jack's side.

"Marsh," Jack called.

Marsh turned, got back on the trail, the rabbit in his mouth still struggling to get free. As he approached them, Jack knelt. "Come," he said, motioning with his hands. "Let it go, buddy." Marsh let it go, and as the rabbit raced back into the scrub, Marsh immediately ran after it.

"Nature will prevail, Jack," Mike said as Jack stood and shook his head.

"I know. Life and death. The way of the world. Marsh!" he called again. "You see him?"

"Yeah, he's… Here he comes."

Marsh appeared from the scrub, his mouth and forelegs bloody.

"At least he didn't eat it," Mike said.

"No," Jack said, walking again toward where the trail opened up at the ranch. "It was just a game. Just a fucking game."

***

Annie poured coffee from her percolator, blackened on the bottom, but nevertheless still functional. Tyler and Ben sat at the kitchen table, both looking as weary as two young men could be.

"I put the milk in the china creamer," Annie said. She returned the percolator to the stove and sat at the table. "So, you boys had a good trip to Oklahoma?"

"It was okay, I guess," Ben said, spooning sugar into his cup.

"Nothin' special," Tyler said. "Did you call that cop?"

"No, I didn't." Annie sipped coffee, then she wiped her mouth with the lace-edged hankie she kept stuffed up the end of her blouse sleeve. "I thought we'd just talk about things. Just the three of us."

Ben looked at Tyler, then at Annie. "What you want to talk about?"

"First off, I guess I'm curious why you had to steal plates for your truck and horse trailer?"

Tyler squirmed a bit in his chair and looked at the ceiling for a moment. "We," he began, then stopped and looked at Annie. "We had some trouble at the place we come from."

"From Colorado?"

"Yes. We worked in the mountains. I think I told you I was a horse wrangler at a tourist kind of place up there, and Ben was a guide for hunters and fishermen."

"Yes, you mentioned that. You know, I told Richie, the policeman, that you are good boys. I think I can tell, and I believe that. But—" She reached both her hands out and placed them palms down on the table. "But there's a reason good boys would steal license plates. That's what I want to hear about, that's what's important."

"We worked for some son-of-a… a man," Ben said, "who made us do somethin' we ain't proud of and regret a whole lot."

"Ben," Tyler said.

Ben looked at Tyler's hard stare and shook his head. "We got to tell her, Ty."

The two men held their stare for a moment, and then Tyler shook his head, sighed, and turned to Annie, and asked, "Can you keep this to yourself, Missus Clark? We don't need some cop hearin' this story, and… Can you do that, Missus Clark?"

Annie hesitated before answering. "I expect Richie will be workin' tomorrow or the next day. No need to get him involved right now. If I didn't think I could trust you boys, I would have called him already."

"Maybe we'll be gone tomorrow or the next day," Tyler said.

"Yes." Annie smiled. "you might be."

Tyler nodded. "Okay. Here's what happened. The first thing you got to know is that Ben and me are… gay." He paused and waited for a reaction, and when none came, he continued. "Calvin, the guy we worked for, knew what we are and…"

And so the story was told again. First in a letter to Jack, and then as they sat with an old woman whose sense of the world, other than what she'd seen on TV, had never gone beyond the flat scrub of the Texas plain where she'd lived her entire life. She'd been to Dallas twice and Oklahoma City once, and had returned to her home thankful for the peace it provided. She had raised four children in the house, three boys and one girl who escaped to the world beyond the first chance they'd gotten. They'd never looked back, nor cared enough for their mother to see if she was alive or dead. She had watched her husband work himself to death, trying to tame land that had had another idea. Life could not help but be all tied up in compassion and melancholia. She watched the boys as they told their story. When Tyler's voice broke, and he began to sob, and Ben stood and embraced Tyler, crying too, she knew her hunch was right: these were good boys whose sense of their world was not dissimilar to her own.

FORTY-FOUR

As Jack and Mike had suspected, the samples they'd collected at the cellar were found to be contaminated. It'd been almost two weeks since they'd gathered them, and Abe had called twice with the bad news. Animal hair, dirt and dust, mold, moisture, and rodent feces all contributed to the contamination. However, Abe said there were still a few samples that might reveal something important. Jack and Mike were are not optimistic. Jack had told Mike despite what the lab had found or not found, they both knew what had happened. "In our guts," he said, "we know."

They asked Gladys to talk to the hermit, Jim, to see if he'd be willing to speak to them, to tell them in his own words what he'd seen that night. Gladys came by a few days later and said Jim refused to do that. That too was what Jack and Mike suspected would happen.

They'd discovered nothing of interest on the back trail, almost four miles from end to end. One morning they decided to continue down the intersecting trail until they came to The Place. They stood outside it for a minute, and Jack asked Mike if he wanted to go in. They did go in, staying to the outer perimeter. Without saying anything, Jack took Mike's hand in his, and they watched Marsh inspect the area where the boys had lain, and then Marsh padded over to them and sat at Jack's side. When clouds gathered overhead, darkening the space even more than it naturally was, they walked out. They followed the trail to the lodge, and down the access road to home.

Jack and Mike sat at the pine table on the porch. As they sipped beer, the day began to fade, the inevitable breeze from the northwest carrying the expected daily cooldown. Shy walked the pasture, his head down, stopping only when he found a suitable spot to pull up grasses. Marsh lay at Jack's feet. Mike looked at the window, and there was Gertrude, her eyes closed.

"We'll head to Vail tomorrow," Jack said, "and see what they can do as far as getting us satellite up here."

Mike had left the subject alone since he'd first mentioned it. "Really?" He asked.

"Sure." Jack smiled at Mike. "Unless you're not going to hang around for much longer."

"Oh, I'm hanging around. I sold—"

"All your furniture. I know, Mike. Maybe we could even find some dirty movies on the net. Get us inspired to, well…"

"I don't need a movie to inspire me, Jack. I just need you to… Relax, is, I guess, the right word."

"The thought of two older men doing it. I mean that image… All that white hair, muscle tone gone to hell. When are you going to start running again, by the way?"

"I've been thinking about it. Probably as soon as I can walk up to the lodge without losing my breath. This elevation is a bitch."

"Yeah. It took me a while to get used to it." Jack grabbed his bottle and sipped.

"We ought to do it together."

"Okay. Whenever you say."

Marsh sat up and got to his feet. He walked off the porch and stood in the drive.

"He heard a car coming, I think," Mike said, looking toward the access road.

They saw an old Ford pickup round the curve, its engine sounding like it was on its last legs, its tailpipe huffing. When the truck pulled into their drive, Jack stood as Marsh ran to it.

"I'll be goddamned," Jack said.

"What?"

"It's Tyler and Ben."

***

Tyler and Ben sat on the sofa, and Jack and Mike sat on two side chairs pulled up to the coffee table. Mike had brought out beers, while Marsh sniffed the boys up one side and down the other. Gertrude was hiding, probably in the bedroom. They traded updates on their lives since they'd last seen each other, and then Jack asked *the* question after an uncomfortable silence between them.

"Why'd you do what you did? You led those boys to their deaths."

"I wrote it all down, Jack. It was all there in the letter I sent you."

Jack shook his head. "No, the reason was not in that letter. There was something else that made you do it."

Tyler hung his head, and Ben spoke. "We're queer, Jack. Calvin knew that, and we were afraid it would get out. Hell, if that was common knowledge, you think any hunter or fisherman would want me to take them out for an overnight in the forest? Or let Tyler take little boys on horsey rides?"

Mike just felt sad when Ben said that. For all the evidence attitudes were changing, underneath the fancy dressing, he knew biases were still there, burning as brightly as they always had.

"We would have lost our jobs," Tyler said. "We'd have to move."

Jack didn't say anything for a moment. He then nodded and said, "Yeah. Okay." He glanced at Mike. "In another time and place, Mike and I were in the same situation. Well, more me than Mike. We're queer, too, Ben. I don't know how I would have reacted to a similar situation. No, that's not true, is it Mike?"

Mike looked at Jack and smiled.

"Mike and I loved each other," Jack said, "in a place and time where it would have taken a whole lot of courage to reveal that to the world. I think Mike was willing to let the world see us for who we were, but I wasn't. I was a coward back then. Mike was—" He glanced at Mike and nodded. "Yeah, Mike was much stronger than I was in those days."

"You and Mike?" Tyler said.

"Wow," Ben said.

"Yeah, me and Mike," Jack said. "We're trying to capture some of what we left behind so many years ago."

"Wow," Ben again said.

"But two boys were not murdered because of what we did," Jack said.

"We didn't know," Tyler said. "If we would have known what

would happen…"

"But we didn't," Ben said. "This thing has ate at us for all this time. We're sorry, and we don't know what we can do to… How are we supposed to make this right?"

"You could go talk to the sheriff," Jack said. "Tell them what happened. You won't be free of this until you own up to it."

"They'd arrest us," Tyler said.

"Probably would," Jack said.

"We gotta get Missus Clark's truck back to her," Ben said. "And Bear is still out there. Nah, hell, we can't…"

"We could take care of Bear," Mike said. "For as long as…" He stopped himself, knowing the probable sentence for accessory to murder was no walk in the park. "…until you could take care of him yourself."

"We'll think on it," Tyler said.

There was another lengthy silence.

"Have you been on the road all day?" Mike said.

"Ten hours," Ben said. "Missus Clark's old truck is… old."

"You can stay here," Mike said. "We've got a second bedroom. The bed is small but comfortable."

"Yeah. Stay with us," Jack said. "Stay a couple days if you want."

Tyler and Ben traded glances. "Yeah, we'd appreciate that," Tyler said.

Mike stood and walked into the kitchen, where he set his bottle on the counter. "I'll put some clean sheets on the bed."

"You want another beer?" Jack said.

"I'm fine," Ben said.

"Me, too," Tyler said. "I'm just tired."

Jack stood and gathered up the empty bottles. "Okay," he said, walking into the kitchen. "Go ahead and bring in whatever you need. Watch the door, though. We've got a cat around here some-where who'll get out."

Tyler and Ben stood, both stretching with sighs.

"I'll help Mike get that bed made," Jack said, walking into the bedroom.

"So, whaddya think?" Jack said, stepping into the bedroom.

"It's sad, Jack."

"Yeah, I suppose it is." Jack grabbed the end of the bottom sheet and stretched it over the foot of the bed.

"I don't get the feeling they'll turn themselves in."

"No, they won't. Maybe later after they've thought about it some more."

"Maybe. You think we're obligated to…"

"I'm retired, Mike."

Mike smiled. He'd heard what he hoped to hear. "So am I, Jack. So am I."

Author

George Seaton lives and writes in Pine, Colorado, a mountain community an hour from Denver. He shares his life with his husband, David, and their Malamute, Kuma.